The Last Remains

Also by Elly Griffiths

Elly Griffiths

The Last Remains

A DR RUTH GALLOWAY MYSTERY

QUERCUS

First published in Great Britain in 2023 by

QUERCUS

Quercus Editions Ltd
Carmelite House
50 Victoria Embankment
London EC4Y 0DZ

An Hachette UK company

A CIP catalogue record for this book is available
from the British Library

HB ISBN 978 1 52940 971 0
TPB ISBN 978 1 52940 973 4

Lines from 'Charms for Grime's Graves' by Michael Rosen
are reproduced by permission of the author.

10 9 8 7 6 5 4 3 2 1

Typeset by CC Book Production
Printed and bound in Great Britain by Clays Ltd, Elcograf S.p.A.

Papers used by Quercus are from well-managed forests and other responsible sources.

For Andy, Alex and Juliet.

Come skill and the cunning needed;
Lay out the lie of the land;
Secret stories, beneath the feet
Locked up in layers, in levels below.

Did dried stripes of grass, straddling the slope
Summon and point people to this place?
Did Old Grimm make mounds and hollows
Out of the earth? Or urns for the dead?

Unlock the store of stories here.

Michael Rosen, 'Charms for Grime's Graves'

Nothing in this world is hidden forever.

Wilkie Collins, *No Name*

PROLOGUE

Sunday 24 March 2002

The bonfire is burning brightly now, its heart molten gold.

'I'm a fire starter,' says Cathbad.

'Everything's so dry,' says Emad, 'that's why. It hasn't rained all week.'

'Boring.' Emily throws leaves at him.

'We should give thanks to the gods,' says Leo. 'We should pray to Grim, the hooded one.'

'Leo,' says Amber, who is sitting huddled in her blanket, 'it's nearly Easter. It's Palm Sunday, for goodness' sake. Have some respect.'

'Easter was a pagan festival first,' says Leo. 'People have celebrated equinoxes and solstices since prehistoric times.' But he smiles at Amber and, when the wine is handed round in plastic cups, his hand touches hers.

'Grim's Gaben.' Leo gives the toast.

'Grim's Gaben,' chorus the students. Only Mark mutters, 'Grime's Graves,' rather defiantly. Cathbad is busy with the fire, using a long stick as a poker, allowing oxygen to feed the flames.

The barbecue is slower to ignite. It's late by the time the vegetarian burgers are cooked. Crisps are circulated. Mark's dog, Odin, comes to sit in the circle, tongue hanging out.

'Don't feed him,' says Mark. 'He's on a diet.'

'We shouldn't be eating crisps,' says Thomas. 'It should be venison or haunches of lamb.'

'I thought you were a vegetarian,' says Amber.

'I'm talking about the aesthetics of the thing.'

But when Cathbad takes the baked potatoes from the embers, they are found to be raw on the inside and generally inferior to the offerings from the Great God Walker. Leo opens another bottle of wine. Darkness falls over the strange pockmarked fields. The nearby pine forest murmurs. The campers move closer together. Thomas gets out his guitar and sings Beatles songs. All you need is love. Odin crawls towards Emily and starts eating her discarded burger bun.

Cathbad was right, thinks Emily, there is magic in a communal fire. Sitting with her friends in this sacred landscape, drinking warm wine and listening to Thomas trying to remember the words of 'Eleanor Rigby', she thinks she has never been happier in her life.

Then a hooded figure emerges from the trees.

CHAPTER 1

Friday 11 June 2021

The unassuming shop in a King's Lynn backstreet has lived many lives. Once, beyond most people's living memory, it was a bakery. The oven still remains and has, in successive iterations, been a focal point and dining nook and was also, for many decades, boarded up completely. The building has been a café, a greengrocer's and an 'Emporium of Wonder' (a junk shop), and is now well on its way to becoming a café again. A sign outside says 'The Red Lady Tea Rooms, opening August 2021', and another informs interested passers-by that Edward Spens and Co are in charge of the renovation.

Gary Bright is enjoying his work. This is the part he likes, knocking things down. The rest – the rewiring, the replastering, the endless conversations with architects and owners – can be dull at best and frustrating at worst. But swinging your sledgehammer at a brick wall never gets old. Gary swings. The old wall trembles at first and then, as Gary lunges again, it caves inwards. Through the dust,

Gary sees a black void. This is odd, because he had expected to see a chimney breast. The plans had shown that there was a fireplace in this semi-basement and the café owners wanted it opened up again. 'It will give the place some character,' says Elise Monkton, the terrifyingly enthusiastic new manager. 'There's probably a Victorian surround or some lovely tiles . . .' But, as Gary moves forwards, all he can see is darkness. Cold air comes from the recently exposed space and suddenly, ridiculously, Gary feels afraid. Get a grip, he tells himself. This isn't an episode of *Most Haunted*. You're a builder and you've got a job to do. Looking through the gap, he sees something white, almost glowing. Is it chalk? Gary leans into the void and sees that what he is looking at is a complete human skeleton, laid out like a Hallowe'en prop.

Someone screams. It's a few seconds before Gary realises that it's him.

Dr Ruth Galloway is having a difficult day. Teaching is over and final papers are being marked. The students have had a tough year, mostly in lockdown, communicating with their tutors only via Zoom. But they have produced good work and Ruth is proud of them. This should be a time when she is getting ready for graduation ceremonies, planning for the next term and lobbying the university for more money and resources. Instead, graduations have been cancelled again and Ruth is waiting for a committee to decide if her department will even exist next year.

'Any news?' David Brown appears at her door with minimal knocking.

'No,' says Ruth. 'The executive board have only just started their meeting.'

'They should have invited you.'

'Board members only,' says Ruth. 'It's awful. Like being sentenced to death in your absence, without being able to plead your case.'

It's a melodramatic analogy, she knows, but it's how she feels. Her job is who she is. Dr Ruth Galloway, Head of Archaeology at the University of North Norfolk. And now the university, in its wisdom, thinks that the department is 'unprofitable' and the board are considering closing it altogether.

'It's madness,' says David, pacing around Ruth's office which would, in ordinary circumstances, drive her mad. 'I mean, you're a renowned archaeologist. You've got an international reputation. You've been on TV.'

It sounds very racy, thinks Ruth, but she knows what David is trying to say. She *is* a fairly well-known archaeologist. She has consulted on Roman bones in Italy and appeared on television there. She has written three well-reviewed books and was also part of a rather lurid TV series called *Women Who Kill*, alongside her ex-partner Frank Barker, an American historian. It is largely due to Ruth that UNN has a good name for archaeology. But Covid has hit them hard. Most of their postgraduate students come from abroad and this income stream has disappeared overnight. Student numbers are also falling, the number of firm-offer holders for 2022 considerably down on 2021. When the board announced 'major cost-cutting measures', Ruth knew that she would be in the firing line.

'They've said they'll keep staff on,' says Ruth. 'Move us to history or geography.'

'That's an insult,' says David. 'I won't stay here to be insulted. I'll go back to Sweden.'

David used to work at Uppsala University and presumably they would have him back. Will Ruth stay and be insulted? She looks out of the window towards the artificial lake, at its best in the sunshine. Two students are playing frisbee, their laughter echoing around the low-lying buildings of the campus. Ruth rubs her eyes. Either her window is dirtier than usual or she is near to tears.

She's relieved when the phone rings though she does wonder who could be contacting her on the landline.

'Dr Ruth Galloway?'

The upper-class voice is vaguely familiar. A board member? A journalist from one of the posher papers?

'Yes.'

'This is Edward Spens. I run a building firm. You might remember me . . .'

'Yes, I do.' Ruth's memories are almost entirely unpleasant. First there was the body under the door of an ex-children's home. Then there was the Second World War plane with the pilot still inside. In Ruth's experience, calls from Edward Spens are never good news. ·

'Well . . .' The embarrassed laugh suggests that Edward is remembering the same events. 'It's ironic really but I think we've found another body.'

*

Ruth is happy to escape from the university for a few hours. She resists David's attempts to join her and drives the short distance to King's Lynn. She parks at the station and walks through the narrow streets, following the directions given to her by Edward Spens. This is one of the oldest parts of town, the houses Victorian or older. But it's not far from the shopping centre and the museum where the henge timbers are kept. Ruth might pop in and visit them later. Although her druid friend Cathbad thinks that the wooden posts should have been left in the sand, a prey to time and tide, Ruth approves of the way they have been displayed in the museum. She really must ring Cathbad. He's still not fully recovered after nearly dying from Covid last year. A Victorian skeleton would definitely cheer him up.

The terraced house, now covered in scaffolding, stirs some memories for Ruth. Did she visit it once with Cathbad, when it was an antique shop or something similar? Cathbad loves truffling through old photographs and random pieces of pottery.

There's a newly painted sign above the door. The Red Lady Tea Rooms. This, too, sparks a memory and a feeling of slight unease. The Red Mount Chapel, a strange hexagonal building in the middle of a park, a path on the way to Walsingham. The site of another death. Ruth shakes her head to clear these thoughts and pushes open the door.

'Ah, Ruth.' Edward Spens is obviously expecting her. He looks older than when she last saw him, with a suggestion of thinning hair, but he's still a tall commanding figure as he strides across the newly sanded floorboards. White teeth flash in a tanned face. Where has Spens acquired such a tan? Lockdown only ended in March and travel restrictions are still in place. Plus, the grin emphasises the fact that Spens isn't wearing a mask. Ruth is wearing hers, complying with Covid rules about meetings indoors. Besides, it's always a good idea to wear a mask when visiting a building site. The Red Lady Tea Rooms looks like just the sort of place where asbestos runs wild.

Edward steps forward as if to shake hands then makes a pantomime of remembering social distancing and bows in an ironical namaste.

'Hallo, Edward,' says Ruth. She assumes they are on first-name terms although she would really rather he addressed her as Dr Galloway.

'How have you been in the crazy new world of ours?' says Edward, managing to relegate Covid-19 to an amusing one-liner.

'I'm coping,' says Ruth. 'Now where's this skeleton?'

'Typical Ruth,' laughs Edward. 'Forget the social niceties, where are the bones?'

There are many replies Ruth could make to this: he doesn't know her well enough to say what is 'typical Ruth'; she is working and not at a cocktail party and human bones are no laughing matter. But she just waits until Edward leads the way down a flight of picturesquely uneven stairs.

The downstairs room is a semi-basement, low-ceilinged and lit only by a sash window that looks out onto a wall. Edward presses a switch, hanging precariously from a cluster of wires, and artfully arranged spotlights illuminate the space. The floor is covered in sheeting and three walls have been stripped back to their original brickwork. But Ruth's eyes are drawn to the fourth wall which has an uneven hole in the centre. She steps closer, avoiding the builder's equipment which seems strewn everywhere. Archaeologists would be much neater, she thinks.

The cavity shows a boarded-up chimney breast. Next to this is a gap about half a metre deep, running the length of the room. In this space lies a fully articulated human skeleton.

'Gave old Gary a shock, I can tell you,' says Edward. 'He's gone straight home. What do you think? Is it Victorian? These houses were built in the 1860s.'

'No,' says Ruth, straightening up, 'it's modern.'

'How can you tell?' says Edward, sounding impressed and sceptical in equal measure. 'I thought you had to do carbon-whatsit testing.'

'Carbon-14 testing can help establish the age of bones,' says Ruth, 'though it can be skewed by natural phenomena like solar flares and can be out by as much as a hundred years. But I can see a metal plate on the distal fibula. This means that the person had fairly recent surgery on their ankle. I'm afraid we have to call the police.'

Before Ruth herself can consider the implications of this, her phone buzzes. David Brown.

They're closing us down. Found out on f-ing twitter.

CHAPTER 2

Ruth drives back to the university in a state of barely contained rage. The brief thought comes into her head that this is how Nelson always feels when he's behind the wheel. But she files Nelson away for another day. She left the Red Lady Tea Rooms as soon as DC Tony Zhang arrived. Tony, as ever, looked like he could hardly contain his excitement at the thought of a new case.

'We'll check the missing persons' files,' he told Ruth and Edward. 'Can you say how old the skeleton is, Dr Galloway?'

Ruth was grateful for the respectful form of address although she actually wouldn't have minded Tony calling her Ruth. He even babysat Kate last year.

'I can't be sure yet,' she said. 'But the metal in the foot looks fairly new. Inserted in the last twenty years, I'd say.'

'Is it a complete skeleton?'

'Yes, fully articulated, completely defleshed.'

'I'll inform the coroner,' said Tony, sounding thrilled. 'Can you excavate?'

'You don't really need me if it's recent,' said Ruth, 'but

given this is a historical site I'll apply for a Home Office licence. I need to get back to my students now.'

'But the boss is on his way,' said Tony. 'I'm sure he'd want to see you.'

'Tell Nelson to send me an email,' said Ruth. She allows herself a slight smile at the thought of Nelson's face when he gets this message. Nelson is now living apart from his wife, Michelle, and Ruth knows that people are assuming that it's only a matter of time before he moves in with her, Ruth. But it's more complicated than that. Ruth and Nelson have a child together, but Ruth doesn't want Kate to think that they are now one big happy family, if that's not the case. Nelson also has three children with Michelle, two grown-up daughters and a young son. He wants to have what he calls a 'proper chat' about it but Ruth thinks it's too soon. Which is partly why she's now driving like a fury through King's Lynn's myriad roundabouts.

Only partly, though. Right now, Ruth's main concern is her department and her livelihood. David sent her a screenshot of the announcement because Ruth does not have a Twitter account.

In the face of challenging economic pressures and declining interest in the subject, UNN regretfully announces the closure of its archaeology department.

We need to fight back, David texted. *I'm starting a twitter account.* Ruth sighs as she approaches the familiar sign for the Natural Sciences building. She fears and distrusts social media, but David is probably right. Perhaps they'll have their own hashtag. It's all very depressing.

As Ruth predicted, DCI Harry Nelson is not delighted to be greeted with the news that Dr Galloway has just left, nor is he mollified by the email suggestion. He paces the basement room several times, muttering.

'Long time, no see,' says Edward Spens, which doesn't help the situation.

'Every time I see you, Mr Spens,' says Nelson, 'there's another bloody dead body. Anyone else would get suspicious. Maybe I should be suspicious?'

Edward Spens laughs although there's no sign that this is a joke.

'Dr Galloway says the body is relatively recent,' says Tony Zhang. 'There's a metal pin in the ankle. She's going to apply for a licence to excavate.'

'We need to search the missing persons' files,' says Nelson, 'and the title deeds to the shop. Who had it before you?'

'It was an antique shop,' says Spens. 'The Emporium of Wonder. Owner went bust because of lockdown. I got it very cheaply.' He grins like this is a good thing. Which it obviously is for him.

'Bit of a new departure for you, isn't it?' says Nelson, who has come to a stop by the hole in the wall. 'I thought you were all about building huge estates of hideous modern houses.'

'Executive homes,' corrects Spens, but without rancour. 'This is for the wife really. Kids are growing up, she fancies getting into the catering business. I've bought two premises, one in King's Lynn and one in Holt. They'll both have managers but Marion will oversee things.'

Nelson has only met Marion Spens once, but he can imagine her being one of nature's overseers.

'I'll need the name of the previous owner,' he says.

'Sharon Gleeson,' says Edward promptly. 'I've got her details here.' He takes out an iPhone that looks as big as a laptop. Nelson remembers a time when they all assumed that phones would get smaller and smaller but now the latest ones barely fit in your pocket. His private phone is several years old and has a cracked screen. He has a more up-to-date version for work but he's not about to tell Spens the number.

'Give the details to my sergeant,' he says. 'I need to seal the site. It's a crime scene now, until further notice. Tony, you wait here until the SOCO team arrives. I'm going to talk to Dr Galloway.'

They all know that he doesn't mean via email.

Nelson arrives at the university intending to have a serious talk with Ruth, starting with the dead body and ending up with why the hell won't she move in with him. But he finds her office full of people, all of them looking very glum, even for academics.

'Oh, hallo, Nelson,' says Ruth. 'You've caught us at a bad time. The university's closing us down.'

'Closing you down?' says Nelson. 'What do you mean?'

It's David Brown who answers. He's not one of Nelson's

favourite people (it's not a long list) but Nelson can understand why he's feeling aggrieved. Nelson feels the same whenever his boss, Superintendent Jo Archer, mentions retirement.

'It's a disgrace,' says David Brown. 'They're closing one of the most prestigious departments in the university.'

'Who's closing you?' says Nelson. 'I thought you lot had jobs for life.'

'The academic board,' says Ruth. 'Some of us have tenure – which I imagine is what you mean by "jobs for life" – but that just means that they have to offer us posts elsewhere. They're closing us down because, apparently, we're too expensive.'

'It's political,' says an intense-looking young woman. 'This government doesn't understand anything that isn't about profit and loss. Anything that isn't *useful*, in their terms. They don't understand learning for its own sake.'

Well, neither does Nelson, exactly, but over the years he has definitely come to appreciate Ruth's knowledge and expertise.

'But you're famous,' he says to Ruth. 'You've been on TV.'

'That's what I keep telling her,' says David. 'She's the most high-profile lecturer at UNN. She's the jewel in the university's crown.'

Steady on, Nelson wants to tell him. He's not keen on the proprietorial note in Brown's voice when he talks about Ruth.

'And you're a police consultant,' Nelson says to Ruth. 'That's useful, if you like.'

Ruth gives him a reluctant smile. 'Gee, thanks, Nelson. But the problem is, not enough people want to study archaeology. As Fiona says,' she nods at the intense-looking young woman, 'it's all about money and an archaeology degree doesn't exactly lead to a high-earning career. When archaeologists advise on new builds, they're usually the lowest paid person on site.'

'That reminds me,' says Nelson. 'I want to talk to you about a building site.'

'OK,' says Ruth. She turns to her team. 'Let's leave it for today. We've got the weekend to prepare our fight back.'

'We can't afford to take that long,' says David. 'I'll start the Twitter campaign tonight. We won't let them kill archaeology.'

Isn't archaeology already dead? thinks Nelson. But he doesn't say this aloud. He doesn't want to break the suddenly more optimistic mood.

When the last of the team has left, Nelson sits down opposite Ruth. This is a different office – far bigger and grander – but it reminds him of the first time he met Ruth, when he came to the university to ask for her opinion on some buried bones. He feels a fresh surge of respect for her. David Brown is right. It would be a disgrace if all this specialist knowledge were lost to the world.

'Tough day?' he says.

'I've had better. Sorry to leave the site but I really needed to get back here.'

'That's OK. Tony says you're going to apply for a licence to excavate.'

'Yes. I'll do it later. It's an awful thing, isn't it? A bricked-up skeleton. Like something from a horror story.'

'It's certainly a suspicious death in my book.'

'I'd better go,' says Ruth. 'I need to pick Kate up from Cathbad's.'

'I'll come with you,' says Nelson. 'I'd love to see Katie. And we can have a chat.'

He can tell by Ruth's face that this is what she has been dreading.

CHAPTER 3

Kate is now at secondary school, a large comprehensive just outside King's Lynn. The logistics have proved complicated because Ruth's cottage on the edge of the Saltmarsh isn't on any public transport route. Ruth drives Kate to school in the morning but she finishes at three thirty, two hours before Ruth, and considers herself too old for a childminder. In the end, it was Cathbad who came up with a solution. Kate would take the bus to Wells and spend a few hours with Cathbad and his family until Ruth came to collect her. Typically, Cathbad refused to be paid ('money poisons everything') which leaves Ruth in the uncomfortable position of being grateful all the time. But the arrangement has worked well so far. Kate loves spending time with Cathbad's children, Michael and Miranda. Michael, who is due to join her at the school later this year, hangs on her every word about Form 7EJ. Miranda, three years younger, is in awe of this new Kate with her blue blazer and tartan skirt (rolled over at the waist to shorten it). Cathbad dispenses healthy snacks and sometimes even helps Kate with her science homework.

Ruth spent many sleepless nights worrying about the transition from tiny, cosy primary school to Lynn High, with its endless corridors and baffling one-way systems. The previous summer had been blighted by these fears. Covid was still rife, although cases fell in July and August, and Ruth couldn't face a holiday. Shona and Phil departed for Rome and sent hundreds of envy-making pictures in which it seemed that they had the Italian capital all to themselves. Ruth visited her father in London, the first time she'd seen him since the pandemic started, but she and Kate sat in the garden and didn't risk going into the house. Still, home wasn't a bad place to be. The weather was miraculously sunny, and Ruth and Kate spent a lot of time on the beach or taking Cathbad's dog, Thing, for long walks. The only drawback was the hundreds of visitors who flooded to Norfolk, baulked of foreign travel, scattering litter and crowding out all the cafés. Nelson had been in Blackpool, visiting his mother, and Ruth was grateful for the breathing space. It was only at night that the dread returned. How would Kate cope without her best friend Tasha, destined for a private school in Holt? How would Covid affect Kate's schooling? Would she have to wear a mask all the time? What if Ruth got sick? What if Kate got sick? And, a familiar favourite for the early hours, what was going to happen with Nelson?

But, in the event, Kate has settled in well at Lynn High. She has made friends and seems to be enjoying the new environment. Ruth often wonders where Kate gets her sociability. Ruth has a small circle of close friends but still finds large gatherings difficult. Nelson frequently says that he has no time for friendships, although he's close to his family and colleagues. But Kate has an enviable ability to like and be liked. Ruth also approves of Kate's new best friend, a tall, slightly eccentric girl called Isla who plays the saxophone. Isla lives in Wells too so she and her sax can accompany Kate on the bus.

Ruth has found things rather more difficult. She remembers, last November, crying when, driving to work, she heard on the radio that a drugs company, Pfizer, had developed a vaccine against Covid, believed to be ninety per cent effective. But it was hard to stay cheerful through the second and third lockdowns, especially during the bitter months of January and February 2021, when cases surged and it seemed that Covid would be here for ever. Even though Ruth has now had two doses of the miracle vaccine, she still doesn't feel as invincible as she had hoped. The country is opening up but there's a dark cloud called 'the Delta variant' on the horizon. When will it end? thinks Ruth, parking outside Cathbad and Judy's cottage. Surely it's time for some good news?

Nelson's Mercedes has been behind Ruth's Renault for the whole journey, making her feel stressed at junctions, but he has had to park in the next street. Ruth waits for him, hoping that there won't be time for the dreaded heart-to-heart.

Cathbad opens the door before they have time to knock. This could be his famous sixth sense or it could be just because Thing, the bull terrier, is barking excitedly.

'My two favourite people,' he says. 'I am blessed.'

Cathbad smiles seraphically, but Ruth still can't get used to seeing him looking so thin and frail. Cathbad frequently thanks the gods – and the NHS – for his recovery from Covid but he's still lacking in energy and, shockingly, sometimes uses a stick to walk. There's no sign of it today, though, and when Cathbad hugs Ruth, she's relieved to find him feeling more substantial.

'No need to hug me,' says Nelson. 'Covid has its uses.'

Ruth and Kate are officially in a 'bubble' with Cathbad's family, which means they can socialise. Ruth and Nelson are not in a bubble, although they have done a lot more than hug.

Kate is in the garden with Michael and Miranda. She waves at her parents but doesn't come over. It's no longer such a novelty to see her mother and father together and, besides, she's busy showing her friends a new TikTok dance. Judy, Cathbad's partner and a DI on Nelson's team, is still at work.

Cathbad makes tea and Ruth fills him in on the day's developments. He is satisfyingly outraged.

'Philistines! There's no appreciation for beauty or knowledge. You must fight this, Ruthie.'

'We are going to appeal,' says Ruth, rather wearily. She feels that she has been fighting things – Covid, the university, her own feelings – for too long. She has even given up telling Cathbad not to call her Ruthie.

'David Brown said that Ruth was the jewel in the university's crown,' says Nelson.

'So she is,' says Cathbad, putting a plate of flapjacks on

the table. 'Their light in the darkness, to use a less royalist and colonialist image.'

'I don't know,' says Ruth. 'Maybe it's a sign that my time at UNN is up.'

The words come from nowhere but, as soon as they are out in the world, Ruth has a vision of her future: a new house, a new job, different horizons. Is Nelson in the picture? She's not sure.

She realises that Cathbad is watching her closely.

'When you've finished your tea,' he says, 'why don't you and Nelson take Thing for a walk on the beach?'

Thing races across the sand. Cathbad used to take him for two longs walks a day but, since Covid, hasn't felt strong enough for more than a stroll to the park. This was why Ruth and Kate took over dog-walking last summer, but Ruth had hoped that Cathbad would be back to striding along the beach by now. Thing's exuberance shows that this isn't the case.

The tide is going out and the wet sand glitters in the early evening light. Everything is golden and blue. In the distance, the beach huts are outlined against the pine trees like a postcard from a different age. Surely, thinks Ruth, even Nelson must love Norfolk at times like this?

But Nelson says, kicking a piece of seaweed, 'Cathbad still looks bloody awful. I would have thought he'd be completely better by now. It's been more than a year. And he's always been so fit.'

'He nearly died,' said Ruth. 'It takes a long time to recover from that. And a lot of people suffer from Long Covid. The symptoms can go on for months, even years. I've been reading about it.' She doesn't add that she'd been reading about it because she, too, is worried about Cathbad.

'He has ringing in his ears, apparently,' says Nelson. 'Tinnitus. He told Judy that he thought it was the universe trying to send him a message. Nutcase.'

'Never discount Cathbad's sixth sense,' says Ruth. 'It's saved you a few times.'

Nelson grunts and kicks a stone into the sea. Ruth knows that he doesn't like to think about the many times that Cathbad has turned up just when he was needed: guiding Nelson across the treacherous marshes, appearing through the mist at the helm of a boat, materialising in Italy after an earthquake. Cathbad even claims to have visited the dream realm in order to rescue Nelson. According to Cathbad, Nelson performed the same service for him when he lay in a coma last year.

'I think he's getting better, though,' says Ruth. 'He's doing yoga again and he's less breathless. The brain fog's improving too. We were doing the crossword together the other day and he was much quicker than me, especially with the anagrams . . .' She stops, aware that she's babbling.

'Ruth,' says Nelson. 'What are we going to do?'

Ruth turns away, pretending to look for Thing, who spoils the charade by turning up, panting, at her feet.

Nelson puts his hand on her arm. 'Ruth?'

'What are we going to do about what?' says Ruth, pushing her hair out of her eyes.

Nelson sighs. 'What are we going to do about us? Are we going to continue the charade of me sneaking over to your godforsaken house after dark or are we going to come out in the open as a couple? Are you going to move in with me?'

How many times over the years, thinks Ruth, has she longed for Nelson to say something like this? All those times she watched him go back to Michelle, all those weekends, birthdays and holidays when it was just her and Kate. When Michelle told Nelson, at the end of the first lockdown, that she wanted a separation and followed this up by moving to Blackpool with their youngest child, Ruth's first reaction had been admiration. Finally, Michelle had done something to break the deadlock. Ruth and Nelson were free to be together. And, as much as possible during successive lockdowns, they have managed this. But now the future looms – as wide as the sea and equally full of dangers.

'I just don't want to rush things,' begins Ruth.

'Rush things?' says Nelson. 'We've got a twelve-year-old child, for God's sake.'

This is true but, for all of Kate's life, Ruth has also been a single mother.

'Look, Ruth,' Nelson's voice softens, 'if your department does close, there's no reason even to stay here. I could make Jo's day and go for early retirement. We could go anywhere in the country. Anywhere in the world.'

Ruth looks out to sea, blaming the sand for her stinging eyes. This is what she has always wanted to hear. Why, then, is she suddenly scared?

'It's difficult at the moment,' she says, 'what with all the uncertainty at work. I mean, I don't even know if I'll have a job next week.'

This isn't quite true and Ruth knows that Nelson knows it. But he says, mildly for him, 'I just want to talk. That's all.'

'We will,' says Ruth. 'Soon.'

'Never thought I'd hear an academic avoiding the chance to talk,' says Nelson, but he smiles as he says it and the walk back to Cathbad's isn't as awkward as it could have been.

CHAPTER 4

Back at Cathbad's cottage, Kate is getting ready to go home. Michael is helping her pile books into the sports bag that is the only socially acceptable school accessory. Kate also has her PE kit and a paper bag full of flapjacks.

'Something for the journey,' says Cathbad.

'Thank you,' says Ruth. 'You're so kind.' And he is. It just feels that she's always thanking him these days.

'When's Judy back?' she asks.

'I think she'll be late tonight,' says Cathbad. 'Some new development at work.'

'That's right.' Nelson looks up from his phone. 'I need to be getting back to the station. Builders have found a skeleton in an old house in King's Lynn. Well, a shop really. Used to be a junk shop. The emporium of something or other. You probably know it, Cathbad. Sounds right up your street.'

Ruth isn't looking at Cathbad because she's trying to gather up the rest of Kate's things. It's her daughter's face that first tells her that something is wrong. Kate's mouth is open in an O of shock. Then Michael shouts, 'Dad!' and Cathbad falls at her feet.

It's Nelson who moves fastest. He rolls Cathbad onto his back where he lies, looking, with his long white hair, uncomfortably like a graven image. Nelson lowers his head to listen to Cathbad's heart. 'It's OK,' he says aloud, 'he's just fainted.'

'Nelson?' says Cathbad faintly.

'Just stay lying down for a few more minutes,' says Nelson. 'Bloody typical. Anything to get attention.'

Thing is trying to lick Cathbad's face. Michael pulls him back. Ruth puts her arm round the boy, who is shaking.

Nelson helps Cathbad to his feet. 'Let's go into the kitchen. Michael, son, could you put the kettle on? Hot sweet tea is what he needs. That's what my mum would say, any road.'

The mention of Nelson's mother (not her biggest fan) unnerves Ruth but Kate goes to put on the kettle and get out the teapot. It's typical of Cathbad that he uses loose leaves and not tea bags. In a few minutes Cathbad is sitting at the table, with Michael on one side and Thing on the other, and a mug of tea and a flapjack in front of him.

'Low blood sugar,' says Nelson knowledgably.

'Where have you been hiding your inner Florence Nightingale all these years?' says Cathbad.

'Shut up and drink your tea,' says Nelson.

Miranda comes in. She is now dressed as the Little Mermaid.

'What's happening?' she says, in an accusatory voice.

'Nothing, sweetheart,' says Cathbad. 'I just tripped over, that's all.'

'Stay with him,' says Nelson in an undertone to Ruth. 'I need to get back to work.'

Judy, obviously alerted by Nelson, is back in half an hour. Ruth is pleased to see her, partly because she has been wondering whether she should prepare a meal and worrying that it won't be up to Cathbad's culinary standards. Judy has, very sensibly, brought pizzas with her. Ruth and Kate eat with the family. Cathbad seems his old self but, once or twice, Ruth catches Judy looking at him anxiously. At least it's Saturday tomorrow which means that Ruth won't have to feel guilty about Kate going to the house after school or think of alternative arrangements.

'See you on Monday,' says Cathbad, when Ruth and Kate get up to leave.

'Are you sure you'll be all right?' says Ruth.

'Of course,' says Cathbad. 'I can feel my inner strength returning.'

'All the same,' says Judy, 'it might be worth visiting Dr Patel.'

'I don't want to bother Rita,' says Cathbad. 'I'll do some healing yoga tomorrow.'

It's still light when Ruth reaches home. The sky over the sea is azure blue with a paler line on the horizon. But it's dark enough to activate the security light which casts an unearthly glow over the long grass of the marshes and the hollyhocks in Ruth's garden. The cottage has looked very different since Zoe, Ruth's half-sister, moved next door. Not only is the garden full of flowers, their colours changing subtly with the seasons, but there are window boxes and urns overflowing with begonias and impatiens. Ruth approaches the front door, feeling soothed. How can Nelson say that her house is godforsaken? Ruth doesn't believe in God but, if she did, it would be a deity of the marshes, an elemental creature of sea and sky.

Zoe's light is on, which always makes Ruth feel comforted. She doesn't talk to Zoe every day but she knows she's there and she appreciates this fairly new presence in her life. Zoe's Maine Coon cat, Derek, watches from her window. The house on the other side has a paved forecourt instead of a front garden and this is now occupied by a huge jeep. The weekenders must be in residence. Presumably they've been unable to have their usual exotic summer holiday because of Covid and have decided to grace Norfolk with their presence. Nevertheless, it's surprisingly cosy to have all three houses occupied.

Flint, Ruth's cat, is sitting on the sofa. He meows loudly but doesn't get up because he is punishing them for being late home. Kate goes to pat him but Ruth stays at the door, looking out over the darkening marshland.

How can she bear to leave it?

CHAPTER 5

Saturday 12 June

Ruth has applied for an emergency coroner's licence to exca-
vate the bones and this comes through on Saturday morning.
The coroner has ruled that the bones are 'forensic' which
means they might form part of a court case. Ruth contacts
Ted Cross from the field archaeology team and heads in to
King's Lynn. She also leaves a message for Nelson.

Kate will be on her own in the cottage all morning. Ruth
is not too worried. Zoe says she'll pop in at lunchtime and
the weekenders are already crashing about with kayaks
and surfboards when Ruth leaves at nine a.m. Kate is quite
content to be left with Flint, her phone and, ostensibly, her
homework, but she does want to go to the cinema with Isla
in the afternoon. Ruth promises that she will take her and
prays that she'll be home in time.

Ruth is not surprised to find Nelson waiting for her at
the Red Lady Tea Rooms. Ted is there too and the two men
are talking intently. Approaching, Ruth hears the words

'given him enough chances' and 'sudden death'. What *can* they be talking about? Then she catches 'Southgate' and realises that it's the European Football Cup, which has just started. Does Irish Ted support England? she wonders. Ruth is allergic to football. Another consideration about moving in with Nelson, who even has a tattoo as a testament to his love for his favourite team, Blackpool.

Nelson looks at his watch. Another irritating habit. Ruth isn't late, in fact she is ten minutes early.

'Hallo, Nelson, hallo, Ted.' Ruth has parked at the station and is carrying her excavation kit: trowel, brush, measuring tape, line level, storage bags, charts (so-called skeleton sheets), pen and pencils. She remembers the first time she met Nelson, crossing the marshes to investigate buried bones, and how embarrassed she'd been by this motley collection of tools. Now she's rather proud of them. Ted, obviously expecting heavier work, is carrying a pickaxe and a hammer.

There's police tape over the front door and a uniformed officer standing guard. Nelson tells him that he can 'bugger off for a coffee' and leads the way into the house.

The shop feels claustrophobic, smelling of plaster and something even less pleasant. In the basement, the walls are still bare brick and the void exposed by the builder looks dark and ominous. Ruth peers through the gap. The skeleton is lying between the new wall and the old one, as if someone created the space for just this purpose. Ted strides over and swings his axe meditatively. He looks like Thorin from *The Hobbit*.

'Better get this knocked down, Ruth.'

'Yes,' says Ruth, 'but carefully. The bones are right behind the wall. '

In a few minutes the wall has been destroyed and brick dust fills the air. Ruth is glad that she's wearing her mask. She shines her torch onto the bones, which are lying in the newly exposed space by the chimney breast.

'They're articulated,' she says. 'Someone placed the body here with some care. I think the cadaver might have been wrapped up – there seem to be traces of fabric – which explains why the bones have remained in such good condition. They wouldn't have been able to move as they decomposed.'

'Do you think the body putrefied here?' says Ted.

'I don't think so,' says Ruth. 'A brick wall wouldn't mask the smell, for one thing, and the leakage would be quite voluminous.'

'The soup,' agrees Ted.

Nelson makes an inarticulate noise in the background.

'You hear about bodies being mummified sometimes,' he says.

'That only happens naturally in very dry conditions,' says Ruth. 'Deserts, say. Or when the gastrointestinal tract is removed. Putrefaction is driven by bacterial enzymes. It looks to me as if this body has skeletonised elsewhere, then been moved to this cavity.'

'Was it buried before then?'

'I don't think so. And you'd expect scavenging animals to have removed some of the bones if it had been left in the open. A lot depends on the presence of flies and maggots too.'

Ruth takes a picture of the skeleton next to her measure. It's not very tall, which adds to her conviction that they are looking at the remains of a woman. When they start removing the bones, placing each one carefully in a paper bag and marking it on the chart, she becomes more convinced. The skull is heart-shaped with small mastoid bones and a straight forehead. When she mentions this to Nelson, he asks what male foreheads are like.

'They slope more,' says Ruth. 'And there's a larger nuchal crest at the back of the head.'

'You make us sound like Neanderthals.'

'All humans outside Africa have some Neanderthal DNA,' says Ruth.

'And I've got more than most, right?'

'I've never said that.'

'I'm pretty sure you have. So, we're looking at a woman?'

We're looking at what was once a woman, thinks Ruth. She will never get used to the fact that these bones, now marked 'femur, tibia, fibula', etc, were once a human being who walked and talked. Did she walk into this house, Ruth wonders, and never leave it? Is that why the rooms seem so sad and oppressive?

'I think so,' she says. 'The pelvic bones look female too. There's a wide, shallow sciatic notch. There's something else about the skull too. See that indentation?'

Nelson leans forward. 'Yes. Could it be cause of death? Blunt force injury?'

'Possibly, but could also have been caused by a fall or even occurred post-mortem when the body was moved.'

'Someone certainly moved this body,' says Nelson. 'Any thoughts on her age?'

'Adult. All the teeth have erupted and the epiphyses – growing ends – of the bones are all fused. Beyond that, it's hard to tell.'

'So, we're looking at an adult female. Is that all you can tell me?'

Ruth sighs. Nelson should know by now that she's not able to tell a person's date of birth by looking at their bones. 'A woman who once broke her left ankle and had a plate fitted,' she says.

'What about DNA?'

'We might be able to get DNA from the bones but it's often difficult when the skeleton is articulated,' says Ruth. She is sure she's told him this before. 'Putrefaction destroys DNA. Some bodily fluids will have leaked onto the fabric wrapped around the corpse, maybe even onto the concrete below. It would be easier if the body had been buried in the earth. Then we could take soil samples and we might get DNA from the residue. I'll get Ted to break up the concrete, just in case.'

'I thought you could get DNA from anything these days.'

'There is a little bone that's very useful for extracting DNA,' says Ruth. 'The petrous portion of the temporal bone. We always look there.'

'I always look down the back of the sofa,' says Nelson. 'But you know best. I'll phone Tanya with the good news.' Ruth is sure that DS Tanya Fuller will get on with the task of identifying the dead woman with her usual energy and efficiency. Tanya is in charge because Judy wants to stay home with Cathbad. Ruth texted that morning to ask how he was and wasn't completely reassured by the jaunty thumbs up she received in return. For a start, she has never known Cathbad to use emojis.

Nelson stomps upstairs and Ruth and Ted get back to logging and bagging the bones. Ted hums as he works. Ruth wonders if she can tell him to stop.

'So what do you reckon?' he says. 'Someone murdered her and then built the wall in front. Are we looking for a killer builder?'

Ruth thinks of Edward Spens. She doesn't like him much but she can't imagine him bricking up a skeleton. He'd get someone else to do it for him.

'There's a crack on the skull that could be blunt force trauma,' says Ruth. 'But it could have happened when and if the bones were moved.'

'She could have been poisoned,' says Ted. 'It's often poison in Agatha Christie.'

'I think poison's quite tricky in real life,' says Ruth. 'I read somewhere that Christie used to work in a pharmacy. Maybe that's where she got her specialist knowledge.'

'That metal plate on the ankle looks quite new,' says Ted. 'That should help identification. Surely someone would remember a young woman going into a shop and never coming out again?'

'You'd be surprised,' says Ruth.

*

Cathbad is walking on the sands. He knows that Judy has taken the day off to look after him and he's grateful but, just now, he wants to be alone. Well, alone with his dog, which amounts to the same thing. He tries to empty his mind, to be aware of the sea and the cry of the seagulls, of his own breath rising and falling in his chest, but his thoughts remain earthbound. He thinks of a sign, two children holding hands. The perfect chocolate box image, except that they are both bright green. He thinks of a bonfire, of youthful voices laughing, and the laughs turning to screams. He thinks of holes underground, of tunnels leading to other tunnels, a rabbit warren for humans.

Breathe in for four, out for eight. He remembers telling Ruth this when she began to suffer from panic attacks. But it's easier to advise other people. Ruth seems calmer now but not as happy as Cathbad hoped she'd be. There's a stubborn force binding Ruth and Nelson. The question is, should Cathbad help them to break it?

Cathbad picks up a piece of driftwood and throws it for Thing. He's not an efficient retriever – like Nelson's Bruno – and often gets distracted. Now he's discovered a jellyfish marooned in the sand. It's a disconcertingly bright blue, like something from a science fiction film. Cathbad thinks of the green children again. In for four, out for eight.

'Leave it, boy.' The tide is coming in so Cathbad decides to leave the creature where it is. Soon it will be returned to its element, as we all will in the end. He thinks of the henge, the wooden timbers rising from the sea. 'They belong here,' he'd said to Erik, 'part of the cycle of nature, part of the sea and the tide.' But Erik had taken them away, talking of scientific research and the pursuit of knowledge. It was the first betrayal. And now Erik is dead and the henge is reconstructed in Lynn Museum. Cathbad should go to see them. Before it's too late.

That's the thing. It's easy to talk about time and tide and the cycle of nature. It's more difficult when you're the one facing the long journey into the unknown. Cathbad has visited the portals of the underworld before and has been able to come back. This time it will be different. That morning, when Judy forced him to have a lie-in, Cathbad had found a quotation in one of his poetry books. Tennyson. From *Ulysses*.

> *Death closes all: but something ere the end*
> *Some work of noble note, may yet be done.*

Cathbad walks on, his dog beside him.

'OK,' says Tanya. 'Let's get to work.'

Her only audience is DC Tony Zhang, who is already at work, but Tanya never misses a chance to sound like DCI Jane Tennison.

'Nelson says Ruth's pretty sure the remains are female,' says Tanya, 'and relatively young. We should be looking for any woman, aged between eighteen and, say, thirty-five, who went missing in the last twenty years.'

'Ruth said something similar yesterday,' says Tony. 'I've been looking at all the misper files since 2000 but I haven't found anyone that fits. I've contacted the neighbouring forces too.'

'Dave Clough will probably come charging in saying he's solved the case,' says Tanya. Clough, once on Nelson's team, is now a DI in Cambridgeshire. Tanya likes him – they all do – but that's no reason to let a former colleague steal a march on you.

'What about the metal pin in her ankle?' says Tony. 'Shall I ring round the hospitals?'

'I was just going to suggest that,' says Tanya. 'The pin itself might help us age the body. I don't know if these things go in and out of fashion.'

'My brother's a doctor,' says Tony. 'I could ask him.'

Tony often talks about his family, so Tanya knows about Mike, *the clever one*. 'Good idea,' she says, going back to her laptop. Tony's a good cop but she doesn't want to get caught up in the outer branches of the Zhang family tree.

Ruth is finished with the bones by midday. They are then sent to the lab to be cleaned and will eventually go to the coroner's office. Nelson would have liked to have had lunch with her in King's Lynn but Irish Ted is still hanging around, so they all end up going to the pub. Then Ruth says she has to get back because Kate wants to go to the cinema with a schoolfriend. There are many things Nelson wants to say but he can't say them in front of Ted, so he mutters something about Covid and social distancing.

When Nelson gets back to the station he is met by Tanya and Tony, radiating smugness and excitement according to temperament. Apparently, Tony has been in touch with his brother, a junior doctor on an orthopaedic ward, and he says that metal pins – like the one on their skeleton's ankle – are rarely used now.

'It's all absorbable implants now,' he tells Nelson. 'There's less chance of post-operative infection and—'

'Spare me the *Holby City* stuff,' says Nelson, 'and give me the basics.'

'Stainless steel pins, like the one on our skeleton,' says Tanya, 'were only used between 2000 and 2005. Mike, Tony's brother, sent us an article about it.'

'That's great,' says Nelson. 'Narrows it down a lot. Ruth thinks the surgery was done when the deceased was an adult. We need to ring round hospitals and private clinics.'

'I'm on it,' says Tony.

'Have you checked the mispers?'

'Yes,' says Tony, 'but there's no one that really fits. I've sent a message about the surgery to neighbouring forces. I mean, Lynn's a busy place. Lots of people pass through.'

'If they've got any sense, they keep going,' says Nelson, although he has lived twenty, mostly happy, years in King's Lynn. 'We need to look at the building where the bones were discovered too. Have you checked the land registry?'

'Intel are on it now,' says Tony. 'It's one of the oldest buildings in King's Lynn. I looked on a history site and they said it was a bakery in the 1600s or thereabouts. But the building is older than that, probably about the same age as the Exorcist's House. You know, by St Nicholas's Church.'

Nelson remembers having this building pointed out to

him, early in his acquaintance with the town. It's a strange little building attached to the wall of the graveyard, where abandoned tombstones form a grisly picket fence. From the outside, it looks like a picturesque cottage until you note the crucifix on the roof. And the fact that it's as creepy as hell.

'We're not looking for some bloody sixteenth-century ghost,' he says, 'we're looking for a woman who was alive in the year 2000.'

'It was an antique shop until 2020,' says Tony. 'I think I remember going there once, looking for a present for my mum. She's very difficult to buy for because . . .' He stops, probably because he's seen Nelson's face.

'Prior to that,' he continues, rather hastily, 'it was empty for a while but before then it was a greengrocer and before that a café called the Green Child. Maybe some sort of green connection there?'

'Let's leave the guesswork out of it,' says Nelson. 'Just find out who owned the place between 2000 and 2005.'

Tanya and Tony go back to their screens. Nelson retreats to his office and thinks about King's Lynn. It's a strange place, an uneasy blend of ancient buildings, like the Exorcist's House and the Tuesday Market Place where – according to Cathbad – a witch's heart is embedded in one of the surrounding houses, and hideous modern estates and shopping centres. The quay is undeniably attractive, smooth water and gliding swans passing between brick-front houses. Nelson remembers having lunch with Ruth, not long after they first met, in one of the waterfront pubs. She'd told him that the place had once been by the sea. 'Lynn means tidal pool,' she'd told him. And it was an important port once. But now the town feels a bit like it has been forgotten, left out of history, like its hero Captain Vancouver, who apparently discovered Canada, although Nelson has a shrewd suspicion that it was there already.

Nelson remembers the first time he saw the suburb where he now lives. He'd started the job but was living in police accommodation. Michelle had come down for the weekend and found a house for them. 'It's a new build,' she said, 'no one's ever lived there before. Four bedrooms, one en-suite. And it's in a *cul-de-sac*.' She'd said this like it was the most wonderful thing in the world but all it meant was that no one ever passed by, you were trapped with your smug middle-class neighbours for ever. And now Michelle has escaped back to Blackpool and Nelson is trapped on his own. He told Ruth that he'd go anywhere in the world but, really, Nelson yearns for the north and home.

He's brought back to reality by the buzz of his phone. Clough.

'Hi, Cloughie.'

'Hi, boss.' Technically, Clough no longer reports to Nelson but old habits die hard. Nelson suppresses a smile. He knows his prodigy well and he can tell by his voice that Clough has news for him.

'I think I've found your missing girl,' says Clough.

CHAPTER 6

'A Cambridge student called Emily Pickering,' says Clough. 'She went missing in 2002. Her parents gave a very full description. Including the fact that she had surgery on her ankle two years earlier.'

'Where do they live?' says Nelson.

'Lincoln.'

Nelson considers. Lincoln is over an hour's drive from King's Lynn but Nelson doesn't consider that far. However, visiting bereaved families is a specialist job. Normally he would delegate it to Judy but he doesn't want to disturb her weekend. He could send Tanya but sensitivity is not really her thing and Tony is too junior.

As if reading his mind, Clough says, 'Can you send Judy? She's done all the family liaison training.'

'She's at home. Cathbad's not too well.'

'Is he still suffering from Covid?' says Clough. 'I got it at Easter and it was nothing. Just a mild cold.'

'We all know you're superhuman, Cloughie,' says Nelson. 'Not to mention vaccinated.'

'Shall we go to Lincoln?' says Clough.

'Seeing you and me on the doorstep might finish them off altogether.'

'I'm good with families,' says Clough, sounding hurt.

'OK,' says Nelson, deciding. He wants to move the case forward and, besides, does not fancy an afternoon alone in the cul-de-sac. Even his dog, Bruno, is with a dog walker. 'Ring them first, Cloughie, and prepare them, since you're so good with people. I'll meet you there.'

Gordon and Naomi Pickering live in the old part of Lincoln, near the cathedral and the castle. Nelson has to navigate a labyrinthine one-way system and drive through gateways more suited to horses than his Mercedes. So he's not really in the mood to appreciate the beauty of the ancient city. The cathedral bell is striking four when he parks in front of the solid Victorian house. Clough's flashy jeep is already outside.

'What took you so long?' says Clough.

'Bloody Norfolk drivers,' says Nelson.

'This is Lincolnshire,' says Clough.

'Same difference.'

Clough smooths down his pink polo shirt. Nelson averts his eyes from it. In his opinion, Clough has been dressing more and more inappropriately since he left Nelson's aegis. He blames Cassandra, Clough's actress wife.

'Did you ring the family?' he says.

'Yes. I explained that we've found remains that might be Emily's.'

'How did they take it?'

'Calm,' says Clough. 'Resigned.'

'There's often an element of relief when remains are found,' says Nelson, 'but we have to tread carefully.'

It's not often a DCI and a DI make house calls together but Gordon Pickering, a retired GP, seems reassured by their seniority.

'We only had a DS before,' he said. 'He never really seemed that interested.'

'It must have been a terrible ordeal for you,' says Nelson. They are sitting in a comfortable room filled with books and family pictures. A brown Labrador pants at their feet.

Naomi Pickering, a bird-like woman in mud-stained dungarees, says, 'It was a nightmare. It's all been a nightmare. It's the not knowing . . .'

Gordon makes a patting gesture without making contact. Clough says, 'Can you tell us about Emily?'

Naomi reaches for a framed photograph on the mantelpiece. It shows a pretty curly-haired girl in what look like graduation robes.

'This is Emily at her matriculation,' says Naomi. Then, seeing the blank looks, 'You matriculate at the beginning of your Cambridge career. It means joining the roll. Emily was reading archaeology at St Jude's College. She never got to graduate.'

Several things about this statement make Nelson uneasy. Archaeology is one. And Ruth once taught at St Jude's College. Also, Emily reminds him of someone.

'Do you have other children?' asks Nelson, making sure

to use the present tense. Naomi produces another picture of a fresh-faced graduate. 'Sophie. She's two years younger. She's a doctor now.'

Emily was twenty when she vanished in 2002. She would be nearly forty now, Sophie in her late thirties. But, here in this room, they are both eternally young.

'When did you last see Emily?' asks Clough. He's doing the sensitive thing quite well, thinks Nelson, leaning forward, engaged and unthreatening. Nelson realises his own arms are crossed and uncrosses them.

'She was coming home for the Easter holidays,' says Naomi, 'but she was doing a field trip first. We thought she'd just been delayed but, when it got to Good Friday and she hadn't turned up, we contacted the college. Emily had left the field trip on the Monday and no one had seen her since.'

'Where was the field trip?' asks Nelson.

'Grime's Graves,' says Naomi.

'Where's that?' says Nelson.

'It's in Thetford,' says Naomi. 'There are all these old mines there. From Stone Age times.'

This, together with the sinister name, makes Nelson feel very twitchy. Then Gordon says, as if he has been holding it in, 'It was all his fault. Emily's professor. Ballard. I've always thought he had something to do with it.'

'Gordon . . .' Naomi makes a shushing gesture. 'You can't say things like that. Remember . . .'

'I don't mind how many times he sues me for defamation,' says Gordon. 'I still think he was involved. Him and that so-called druid. What was his name? Cathbad.'

Clough and Nelson stare at each other. Sensing a change in the atmosphere, the dog starts to bark.

Nelson and Clough drive to the nearest open space, a recreation ground where a bad-tempered game of Saturday football is in progress. They park and get out of their cars.

They lean against Clough's jeep and, for the first time in years, Nelson wishes he still smoked.

'Do you think it's our Cathbad?' says Clough.

Gordon Pickering told them that Emily was part of an 'elite archaeology group'. 'They used to do all sorts of weird things: go to stone circles to watch the sun come up, eat Stone Age food, spend the night in bloody caves underground.' The group had been led by Professor Leo Ballard but another member had been a druid called Cathbad.

'It certainly sounds like our Cathbad,' says Nelson. 'He would have been living in Norfolk at the time and working at a university. Remember, he was a lab assistant at UNN.'

'It's hard to imagine Cathbad doing a real job.'

'He's had a few of them. He used to be a postman.' And found time to deliver a few poison pen letters to the police, Nelson remembers.

'Are you going to ask him about Emily?'

'I'm going to drive over to his place now,' says Nelson. Although he doesn't say this to Clough, he can't forget that, when the body in the wall was mentioned, Cathbad had fallen in a dead faint at his feet.

Nelson is in luck. Cathbad is on his own.

'Judy and the kids have taken Thing for a walk. I'm just making a cake.'

Cathbad is the only person still making cakes, thinks Nelson. He remembers, during the first lockdown, when all anyone could talk about was making banana bread. Even Ruth had bought the ingredients before letting the bananas blacken and the flour collect weevils. But Cathbad has a mixing bowl all ready. He's wearing an apron that says Wonder Woman.

'How are you feeling?' says Nelson, sitting at the table.

'Fine,' says Cathbad. 'Friday was just a blip. I went for a long walk on the beach this morning.'

And he does look well, humming as he moves around the kitchen. But is it Nelson's imagination or is there something watchful beneath Cathbad's apparent serenity?

'I wanted to ask you something,' says Nelson.

'Ask away.' Cathbad is cracking an egg. He keeps chickens; Nelson can see them in the garden, roosting on the roof of the shed and pecking their way through the flower beds. Maybe this is why the yolk is so orange, almost fluorescent.

'Does the name Emily Pickering mean anything to you?' says Nelson, watching as Cathbad folds the egg into the mixture.

The spoon pauses.

'Emily Pickering?'

'Yes,' says Nelson patiently.

Cathbad gives him one of his direct stares. 'Once I knew Emily Pickering very well indeed.'

'How come?'

'We were part of the same archaeology group.'

'Led by Leo Ballard?'

'That's right. It was Leo and a group of his students. Emily was one of them. We were all close for a while. Then, one day, Emily just disappeared. Oh my God . . . Was it her body you found? In the wall of the café?'

'We think so,' says Nelson. 'I'm sorry. It must be a shock if she was a friend of yours.'

Cathbad has gone very white. Is he about to faint again?

'How do you know the remains are Emily's?' he asks.

'I can't tell you any more,' says Nelson. 'It looks as if this might be a murder investigation.'

'Murder?'

'Take some deep breaths,' says Nelson.

'I'm OK,' says Cathbad. 'But . . . it's so horrible . . . Have you told her parents?'

'Cloughie and I have just been to see them. But, tell me, Cathbad, how did you know it was a café? I described it as a shop before.'

'It was a café when I knew Emily. The Green Child Café. Funnily enough, I was thinking about it only this morning.'

'The Green Child? What sort of a name is that?'

'It's an interesting legend. I've got a book about it somewhere.' Cathbad looks across the room to a bookcase squashed between the door and a sofa. Who has a bookcase in their kitchen? Or a sofa?

'Don't worry about that now,' says Nelson. 'Do you remember who owned this café?'

'Yes, it was a man called Peter Webster. A really inter-esting person. Very interested in spirituality.'

'Really?' Nelson's detective senses are immediately on alert.

Cathbad laughs, looking more like himself. 'That's not necessarily a sign that he was a madman, Nelson.'

'Was?'

'He died about ten years ago. Cancer. I went to the funeral. A humanist service and a green burial.'

'What does that mean?' says Nelson. He thinks he's had enough of green things for the day.

'The body is returned to the earth. A wicker coffin. A woodland site. No headstone. Wood is life, stone is death. It's what I want for myself. Remember that.'

'Why should I remember it?' says Nelson. 'You'll outlive me. Now, what can you tell me about Emily? You must have known her quite well.'

'Poor Emily,' says Cathbad. 'She really was a lovely girl.'

He's about to say more when the door opens and dog and children burst into the room. Judy brings up the rear.

'We had a race home,' she says. 'I came last. Hallo, Nelson. What are you doing here?'

But Nelson is looking at his best detective with new eyes. Flushed from exercise and with her hair loose, she looks years younger.

She looks like Emily Pickering.

CHAPTER 7

Sunday 13 June

Sundays are different, thinks Cathbad. Back home in Ireland it was a day dominated by the Church: the bells ringing, women still wearing mantillas, all the shops shut. Cathbad's mother, Bridget, went to mass every Sunday even though she was considered by most people – including herself – to be a witch. Bridget Malone was also a single mother, something that was still considered shocking in a small Irish town in the 1960s. But Bridget had glided through it, supported by her mother, Fionnuala, who hadn't turned a hair when she learnt that her daughter was pregnant and refusing to say who the father was. The two women brought Cathbad up between them although, of course, he was Michael Malone in those days. Bridget continued to go to mass and to take communion. The priest, Father Seamus, hadn't turned many of his remaining hairs either, had continued to treat the unconventional family with respect. When Bridget died of breast cancer at the age of thirty-six, when Cathbad was sixteen, she had been given a full requiem mass complete with weeping nuns and the choir singing '*Panis Angelicus*'.

'Let's go to church,' says Cathbad over scrambled eggs. The hens are almost laying too much these days. Both children have demanded cereal instead.

'Church?' says Judy. 'Why?'

'It's Sunday. It's what people do.'

'We don't.' Judy, like Cathbad, was brought up as a Catholic. Her father, Pat, a bookie, is also of Irish heritage. Cathbad gets on well with his quasi father-in-law although he suspects that Judy's mother, Christine, preferred her first husband, Darren. Well, only husband, if you're being pedantic about it.

It seems that Darren is on Judy's mind too.

'I'm beyond the pale as far as the Catholic Church goes,' she says. 'Being divorced and everything. Where does that phrase come from? Is it to do with Ireland?'

If Judy wants to talk etymology, so be it.

'I think it literally means "outside the fence",' says Cathbad. 'A pale can mean a stake. As in Dracula and impaling. But you're thinking of the Pale of Dublin, a part of Ireland that was under English control in the Middle Ages. Anything outside that was considered wild and lawless. Beyond the pale.'

'And your wild and lawless idea today is to go to church?'

Cathbad grins. 'Why not? I really should give thanks for my recovery last year.'

'I thought you lit a candle in the Slipper Chapel at Walsingham.'

'One candle is never enough.'

'That sounds like a *Two Ronnies* joke. I don't even know where the nearest church is.'

'Our Lady Star of the Sea. It's a short walk away.'

'If it's called Our Lady, I'm assuming it's Catholic?'

'Of course,' says Cathbad. Somehow, he'd never thought of attending any other sort of service.

'I'd like to say a prayer for Emily too,' he says, after a moment's silence.

Judy loses her quizzical look. Cathbad knows that she wants to ask more about Emily but she's aware that it's a sensitive subject. Cathbad assumes that she won't be part of the investigation because of his own involvement in the case. After all these years, he's still a bit vague about police procedure.

'OK,' says Judy. 'It'll be something different anyway. We're going to church,' she tells Michael and Miranda.

'Will there be sweets?' says Miranda. 'We went once before and there were sweets.'

'That was Easter,' says Michael. 'There are only sweets at Easter.'

Cathbad tries to remember when the children had attended a church at Easter. There was one occasion, after the murders in Walsingham, but Miranda had been a baby then. Maybe Judy's parents took them one year.

'We'll get ice creams after mass,' says Judy.

Cathbad notes that she's still a Catholic at heart. It was one of the first things he learnt when he moved to England. Only RCs talk about 'mass'.

*

Ruth and Kate are also eating ice creams. They are having a day out in Lincoln with Zoe. It's where Zoe was brought up and Ruth had once expressed a desire to see the castle. So they are now in the old part of the town, with the cathedral on one side and the castle on the other. In front of them is a beautiful bookshop, Lindum Books, all crooked beams and bay windows, like something from a fairy tale. Ruth feels as if she has found her spiritual home. Well, one of them anyway.

It's good to get away from death and bones for a while. And from Nelson. He'd wanted to spend Sunday with them. When Ruth told him that she was going to Lincoln with Zoe, Nelson had said 'Lincoln?' rather sharply. 'Why not?' asked Ruth. 'What's wrong with Lincoln?' Nelson hadn't answered. Ruth thinks that he's still rather ambivalent about Zoe.

They finish their ice creams and walk through the gateway into the castle grounds. 'It's fascinating,' says Zoe. 'You can walk around the walls and look in the towers. There was a prison here in Victorian times too. It's very spooky.'

It seems that Ruth is not that far away from death and bones after all. She thinks of the girl whose body she excavated yesterday. There's something very medieval about being bricked up behind a wall, a barbaric punishment usually reserved for erring women, nuns who broke their vows, women who deceived their husbands. Didn't George I have his wife's lover bricked up?

Zoe is thrilled to have the chance to be their guide. 'I used to come here with my mum and dad when I was young,' she says, as they climb the steps to the ramparts. 'The guidebooks go on about the Magna Carta but that's really very dull. Just a piece of parchment. I loved the story about Lady Nicola de la Haye. She was the constable here and she defended the castle when it was besieged by Richard I's men. She held out for over a month.'

'Was she on King John's side then?' asks Ruth. She knows that her view of John as a fool and possible child-murderer has been influenced by that less-than-accurate historian Shakespeare.

'Yes, she was. And she defended the castle from the French later on.'

'Was that when they wanted to put Louis on the throne?' says Ruth. 'He's always left out of the history books, but I think he was actually proclaimed King of England.'

'That was the barons,' says Zoe. 'John always had trouble with the barons. But Nicola held Lincoln Castle for King John. She must have been quite a woman. She lived here until she died in her seventies. My mum almost named me Nicola because of her.'

But in the end Zoe's adoptive parents had kept the name that her birth mother – Ruth's mother – had given her. Dawn. Zoe herself changed it later.

'Was your mum keen on history?' asks Ruth. She knows that Zoe loved her adoptive parents, who both died some years ago, but she rarely talks about them.

'Yes, she was,' says Zoe. 'I think, in a different time, she might have gone to university but she left school at sixteen and went to secretarial college. She loved historical romances – Georgette Heyer and Jean Plaidy – and she loved people like Nicola. Strong women.'

'I remember going to Eltham Palace with my mum, *our* mother,' says Ruth. 'It's all Art Deco inside now – really beautiful but a bit strange. There's not much left of the Tudor part. But I could never get over the fact that Henry VIII had grown up there, almost next door to me. I think that's what first got me interested in the past. That and Georgette Heyer.'

'Did Jean – our mum – like history too?'

'She would never have said so,' says Ruth. 'She didn't want me to study archaeology. She wanted me to do something useful like accountancy. But I suppose she must have had some interest because she was the one who took us to Eltham Palace. Not Dad.'

Ruth would like her father to meet Zoe but so far he has resisted doing so. She resolves to bring the matter up again on her next visit to see him in London. Zoe has such a wistful look on her face when she talks about their mother Jean. Ruth thinks that seeing the house in Eltham would bring her closer to the birth mother she never met. Maybe they could visit the Art Deco palace too.

Kate has run further along the wall and now comes back to hurry them along. Ruth walks behind, enjoying listening to Kate talking to her aunt. Zoe's stories seem to owe quite a lot to her imagination but Ruth is happy to let her own thoughts drift. She welcomes spending the day in the early Middle Ages. It stops her thinking too much about her own middle age and whether she wants to spend it with Nelson.

It's the more modern part of the castle that shakes her. The Victorian prison was run according to the separate system, something that Ruth first encountered during a dig at Norwich Castle. That was when they uncovered the bones of a Victorian murderess called Mother Hook, a case that had led to the TV programme *Women Who Kill* and Ruth's association with Frank. Ruth can hear his mellow American voice now. 'The separate system was a way of keeping prisoners completely isolated . . . They had to wear masks at all times . . . The idea was to stop criminals consorting with other criminals . . . but, of course, there was a major drawback.' 'What was that?' Ruth remembers asking. 'They went mad,' Frank told her.

Zoe's tour takes them into the prison chapel which has recreated the seats, like horse stalls, that prevented inmates from seeing anything other than the (presumably hellfire) preacher. The museum has added the grisly finishing touch of a coffin on a trestle table. Ruth thinks of last year, during the fiercest lockdown, the hospital patients dying alone, their loved ones forbidden from visiting them. She doesn't think she has ever been in a sadder room.

'I don't like this bit,' says Kate. 'Can we go and see the Magna thing?'

'OK,' says Zoe. 'I think it's in one of the vaults.'

'Is there a café?' asks Ruth.

'Candles,' breathes Miranda. She is transfixed by the lights in front of the Lady Altar. 'We can't blow them out,' Cathbad tells her. He hadn't expected such prime seats at Our Lady

Star of the Sea. They had arrived just as mass was starting and a kindly steward motioned them into a front row on the right. There's clearly an attempt at social distancing, with every other pew left empty. Most of the congregation are masked, as are Cathbad and Judy. A statue of the Virgin Mary stares down at them: white robe, blue cloak, one plaster foot firmly pressed on the snake of evil.

Cathbad is finding the whole experience quite hallucinogenic: the hand-held cross, the incense, the green vestments of the priest. He is getting high on his own memories. He was briefly an altar boy and it had been his job to swing the thurible, the metal censer that contains the perfumed smoke. 'Gently now,' Father Seamus would say, 'we don't want to asphyxiate the good folk in the congregation.'

'What's that smell?' hisses Michael.

'Prayer,' replies Cathbad. Judy gives him a look.

Cathbad doesn't recognise the entry hymn. It's something jolly about coming to the table of the Lord. The choir sounds sparse – maybe they are socially distanced too – accompanied only by a guitar. Cathbad remembers organ music and words so dreary that they used to send a thrill of despair running through him. 'Soul of My Saviour', that was one of them. 'Deep in thy wounds, Lord, hide and shelter me.' There is something almost heroically morbid about wanting to wallow in someone's blood and gore. It's hard to imagine a guitar accompaniment.

The responses have changed too. The answer to 'The Lord be with you' is now 'And with your spirit', not 'And also with you'. Cathbad thinks it's probably a literal translation from the Latin and one which rather misses the point of the exchange. Both of his children look at him reproachfully when he gets the words wrong. He knows they are all humouring him by this trip. Since he nearly died from Covid, his children have been very kind to him, and he finds that he misses the cheerful callousness of pre-sickness days.

Scripture readings and then the gospel. Cathbad finds himself tracing the sign of the cross on his forehead, lips and chest as he was taught at school. Turning, he catches Judy doing the same. She smiles, rather sheepishly. Suddenly Cathbad loves her so much that he feels as if his heart is about to burst, like the painting to the left of the altar which shows Jesus pointing reproachfully to this organ, which is glowing through his robes. Sacred Heart of Jesus. Pray for me.

At communion, Cathbad gets up to join the line moving, without order but without any sense of urgency, towards the altar. 'Are you taking communion?' whispers Judy. She probably remembers the teaching that you can't take communion unless you've been to confession beforehand. Aren't you meant to fast too?

'I'm just going up for a blessing,' says Cathbad. 'Anyone else want to come?' His family shake their heads.

Cathbad crosses his arms across his chest. 'God bless you, my son,' says the priest, in a voice that is both mechanical and comforting. Cathbad finds himself swaying at the altar rails before his arm is taken by an elderly lady who guides him back to his pew. 'Are you all right?' says Judy. 'I'm fine.' Cathbad tries to give her a reassuring smile and the choir starts a mournful dirge that can only be 'Soul of My Saviour'.

CHAPTER 8

Monday 14 June

'Emily Pickering was a second-year archaeology student at St Jude's College, Cambridge. On Saturday twenty-third of March 2002 she went on a weekend field trip to Grime's Graves, a prehistoric flint mine near Thetford in Norfolk. On Monday twenty-fifth, she left Thetford, supposedly to visit her parents in Lincoln. She was seen on CCTV at Ely station, heading towards the town centre, at midday on the twenty-fifth. She was never seen again.'

Nelson looks around the room. Dramatic pauses are not in his nature, but he realises that he has inadvertently created one. There's complete silence apart from the operatic sound of Super Jo's voice, rising and falling somewhere in the distance.

'Emily's parents, Gordon and Naomi, suspected her tutor, Leo Ballard. They said that he had an unhealthy relationship with Emily and with all his students. Leo was questioned by the police but had an alibi for the twenty-fifth – he was with friends in Cambridge all day – and subsequent investigations failed to find anything against him. Eventually Ballard sued Gordon Pickering for defamation of character. The other people on the field trip were also questioned. Four students and a junior lecturer. Plus Michael Malone, aka Cathbad.'

All eyes turn to Judy, who is standing at the back of the room, but she says nothing. Cathbad's not a suspect but he is a potential witness and, because of this, Nelson can't put Judy in charge of the case. He's decided to lead it himself, with Tanya as his deputy. Jo won't like it, but Nelson doesn't think she'll interfere. But it's not the thought of crossing swords with Jo that is troubling Nelson – he quite enjoys sparring with his boss – it's something else entirely. Is it Ruth? It usually is. Or is it something more sinister, something to do with Cathbad and the place with the nasty name? He pushes these thoughts aside and continues with the briefing.

'Emily's remains were found behind a wall in a house in Red Mount Street, King's Lynn. In 2002 the property was a café called the Green Child. It was owned by a man called Peter Webster who has since died. His wife is still alive, but she has dementia and is in a care home. The couple had two daughters, Gaia and Freya. We're still looking for Gaia but Freya hasn't changed her name so she was easy. She lives in London. She's thirty-nine, the age Emily would be now.'

Nelson surveys the team. Tanya, looking keen. Tony, looking excited. The other people in the room are mostly civilians: data analysts, forensics experts and community support officers. DNA results are not through yet, but dental records have identified the skull as being that of Emily Pickering. The metal ankle plate has been traced to a batch used at a private Cambridge clinic in 2001. This is now a murder enquiry.

'We need to talk to Emily's parents again,' says Nelson. 'Also to Leo Ballard and anyone who was there that weekend at Grime's Graves. And we should follow up on the Ely link. It's on the way to Lincoln from Thetford but why did Emily go there without telling anyone? And we need to investigate the Green Child café. Did Emily know the place? King's Lynn is quite a way from Lincoln and from Cambridge. Tony, you can go and see Freya Webster. See if she, or any of her family, knew Emily. I'm going to lead this one. Tanya's the deputy SIO. Judy, you'll have to take a back seat this time. Any questions?'

Tanya's hand is up immediately. 'Did Ruth have any thoughts on cause of death?'

'There was an injury to the skull but she couldn't tell if it was the cause of death. The pathology team might find out more.'

'So it could be natural causes?' says someone.

'Nothing very natural about bricking up a girl's body behind a wall,' says Nelson. 'It's a suspicious death at the very least. Someone deliberately concealed Emily's body, causing her parents untold distress. I'd say that person has some explaining to do, even if they didn't kill her. Tanya, a word in my office.'

He wishes that Tanya didn't look quite so pleased.

*

Ruth comes into work on Monday to the baffling news that #saveunnarch is trending.

'It's my Twitter campaign,' says David, who appears before Ruth has finished her coffee. 'My SaveUNNArch account has three thousand followers already. They're going to run something in the *EDP*. They might want to interview you. Next step is to get the nationals involved. And the Council for British Archaeology.'

David rubs his hands together. Ruth can see that he's energised by the fight whereas she has to have meetings with management, unions and junior staff, all of whom are talking like the closure is a foregone conclusion.

'I'm starting a petition,' says David. 'They can't ignore us.'

'Over forty thousand people signed the petition to save the archaeology department at Sheffield,' says Ruth. 'And they still got closed down.'

She remembers how shocked she had been by the decision. Sheffield's archaeology department was world famous but the university had closed it all the same, despite opposition from the Council for British Archaeology and a sternly worded letter from Ruth herself.

'We need to call an emergency general meeting,' says David. 'We can't let this happen behind closed doors.'

'Yes,' says Ruth, catching fire from his enthusiasm. 'Let's call a meeting. Get the UCU involved. We won't go down without a fight.' She's even prepared to have her photo on the front page of the *Eastern Daily Press*.

'Contact any influential people you know,' says David. 'I've been in touch with ex-colleagues at Uppsala. Do you know anyone high profile at Cambridge? You taught there, didn't you? And what about that TV series you did? *Women Who Kill.*'

Strange that she was thinking about this programme, and about Frank, only yesterday. Frank Barker had been the show's presenter and, for a while, Ruth's boyfriend. Ruth and Frank even lived together, briefly, but their relationship never really emerged from the brooding shadow of Nelson. Frank asked Ruth to marry him and, when she said no, returned to America. Ruth would really rather not ring him for a quote. She manages to get rid of David by pretending that she's interviewing a potential PhD student but, almost as soon as the door slams behind him, it's opened again and a whimsical voice says, 'Knock knock.'

'Shona,' says Ruth. 'Come in.'

Shona teaches in the English department and she and Ruth have been friends for almost twenty years. They've been through a lot together, including a rather traumatic holiday in Italy six years ago. Their relationship has even survived Shona moving in with Ruth's ex-boss Phil. Shona is always talking about disappearing on a sabbatical with Phil and their son, Louis, but she still seems to be at the university, floating around organising ceilidhs and all-night poetry readings. Now she envelops Ruth in a hug. 'I'm so, so sorry. We were away at the weekend or I would have come round. Phil and I are heartbroken for you.'

'Thank you,' says Ruth. 'But it's not over yet. We're organising an emergency meeting.'

'I'll be there,' says Shona, her tone still implying that her role will be that of chief mourner.

'David's started a Twitter account,' says Ruth. 'SaveUNN-Arch is trending.' If she says this often enough, she might start understanding it.

'David's a dynamo, isn't he?' says Shona. 'Phil says he wishes he'd been in the department when he was in charge.'

Ruth remembers that Shona has always been rather a fan of David. Still, she doesn't like the implication that he's the driving force behind the department. And Phil's remark is just plain irritating. 'David's certainly putting a lot of energy into the campaign,' she says.

'Oh, Ruth,' says Shona, with a little laugh. 'He's doing that for you.'

'What do you mean?'

'David's always been sweet on you. Phil and I were just talking about it the other day.'

'We need to tread very carefully on this case,' Nelson tells Tanya. 'Emily's parents have already been through hell. We don't want to stir things up with Ballard either. Especially since he's shown that he's not averse to going to court.'

'There was no evidence against Ballard last time, was there?' says Tanya, sitting on the edge of her chair and taking notes.

'He had an alibi for the day Emily disappeared,' says Nelson, 'but it seems a bit of a shoddy investigation to me. No real forensics of any kind. It was never treated as a murder enquiry, just a missing person. Of course, we didn't know about the link to the café then. The previous owner must be one of the main suspects this time round. But Ballard is still important. See if you can strike up a rapport when you interview him today.'

'I'll try,' says Tanya, sounding doubtful. 'I'm not sure I'll have much in common with a Cambridge academic.'

'I'm going to see if Ruth can give us any inside information,' says Nelson. 'She taught at St Jude's. She must know Ballard. I'll ask her about this Grime's Graves place too.'

'Does Ruth know about Emily?' says Tanya. 'That the remains are hers, I mean?'

'No,' says Nelson. 'I was waiting until we heard about the dental records.' He'd wanted to drive over to Ruth's place yesterday, but she'd said that she was spending the day with Zoe. In Lincoln, of all places. He doesn't like the way this case is edging nearer and nearer to Ruth. Nelson and Bruno had spent the day brooding.

'Maybe Ruth's been to a May Ball with him,' says Tanya brightly.

'I don't think May Balls are quite Ruth's thing,' says Nelson. He has no idea what they entail but the words conjure up images of posh people in bow ties, punts on the river, arrests for drunk and disorderly behaviour.

'Well, we certainly didn't have them at Loughborough,' says Tanya.

Nelson calls just when Ruth is thinking about lunch.

'Hi, Nelson.'

'Ruth.' Nelson rarely has time for the niceties. 'We've got a positive identification on the bones found in the café.'

'Oh. That's quick.' The police investigation, grisly though it is, feels like a welcome relief after a day of talking about closures, demonstrations and emergency meetings. Ruth is conscious of sitting up straighter.

'A twenty-year-old student called Emily Pickering. She was identified by dental records. She was from Lincoln but studying at Cambridge.'

'Lincoln? I was there yesterday.' It suddenly seems ominous that she was thinking about bricked-up bodies and Victorian prisons.

'I know,' says Nelson. 'You were having fun with Zoe.'

'Which college was Emily at?' asks Ruth, ignoring this.

'St Jude's. Studying archaeology.'

This is definitely beyond a coincidence. An omen, Cathbad might say. The case no longer seems like light relief. Ruth thinks of the courts and archways of St Jude's, of her panelled office filled with portraits of long-dead scholars. It was a beautiful place but, despite everything, she's not sorry to be back amongst the plate glass and breeze blocks of UNN.

'Emily studied with a man called Leo Ballard,' says Nelson. 'Do you know him?'

'I know of him,' says Ruth. 'He's a very well-known archaeologist. He's retired now but I once met him at a college dinner.'

'Not at a May Ball then?'

What's Nelson getting at? 'I've never been to a May Ball in my life, Nelson.'

'Ballard used to take students to a place called Grime's Graves. Have you heard of it?'

'Yes,' says Ruth. 'It a Neolithic flint-mining complex. Really fascinating. I did a dig there about eighteen years ago.' It's partly where Flint got his name.

'We think Emily went there just before she died. On some sort of field trip.'

'With Leo Ballard?'

'Yes. What's he like?'

'I didn't speak to him for long but I got the impression that he was a very charismatic teacher.'

'Charismatic?' Nelson says the word like he distrusts it. Ruth doesn't altogether blame him. She once had a charismatic tutor, Professor Erik Andersen, and that association eventually proved to be a deadly one.

'He had this way of staring at you,' says Ruth. 'Like he really wanted to hear what you had to say.'

'Emily's parents suspected him of being involved in her murder,' says Nelson. 'He eventually sued them. Not a very classy move.'

'No,' says Ruth. She tries to remember Leo Ballard, a rather emaciated figure in his college gown, with wild curly hair like a dandelion clock. He'd seemed urbane and charming, slightly amused, not like a man with murder on his conscience.

'He was interviewed at the time,' says Nelson, 'and we're

interviewing him again tomorrow. I just wondered whether you had any inside information. I don't suppose you could get in contact with him again, out of the blue?'

'Funnily enough,' says Ruth. 'I can think of an excuse.'

CHAPTER 9

Tanya finds Cambridge annoying. Loughborough University might not be far away geographically but, in Tanya's opinion, it's light years away in terms of wearing normal clothes and not having silly names for things. And the bikes! Tanya is a keen cyclist but she wears a helmet and obeys traffic rules. Several times during the drive through the city DC Bradley Linwood has to take evasive action when some long-haired millennial swerves in front of them, balancing a latte in one hand. According to Tanya's calculations, term is almost over (they're even called something different in Cambridge), but there still seem to be plenty of students around. And the tourists are almost worse. People still aren't going abroad and it seems to Tanya that every retired couple is in Cambridge that morning, taking selfies of themselves in front of the colleges.

'Out of the way, Grandpa,' she mutters, as an elderly man steps in front of the car to get a better view of the Mathematical Bridge.

'Stay at home and save lives,' says Bradley. They are on

the same wavelength, which is why Tanya requested him as her partner.

Leo Ballard lives in Madingley, on the outskirts of Cambridge. It's a relief to be out of the town centre but it's an oddly desolate spot, a long straight road with three houses on one side and a military cemetery on the other. A large building glimmers in the distance but Tanya doesn't know if it's a stately home or another bloody college.

Leo Ballard is tall and thin with a mop of grey hair. He's dressed like a tramp in a crusty-looking jumper and threadbare cords but he greets them in the confident upper-class tones of a baron welcoming serfs to his fireside. He ushers them into his study, a room so full of books that it actually makes Tanya feel sick. There are bookcases on every wall, titles in no apparent order, spines vertical and horizontal, some upside down. There are books on the desk, table and sofa and in a tottering tower by the door.

'It's a bit of a mess, I'm afraid,' says Leo, not sounding even slightly apologetic. 'I don't let my wife or the cleaner tidy in here.'

Let my wife. Tanya doesn't like the word 'wife', despite having one and being one herself, but it's a long time since she's heard such a sexist sentence. It has clearly never occurred to Professor Ballard to clean up himself instead of issuing orders. He's now smiling, showing a wide gap between his front teeth. Tanya thinks Leo must be at least sixty, maybe even seventy, but he obviously still thinks he's charming.

She moves a small mound of books and sits on the sofa.

Bradley perches on the other end. Leo swivels his desk chair to face them.

'So . . .' he says. Tanya is willing to bet that he routinely starts his tutorials this way.

'So,' echoes Tanya. 'As I said on the phone, we want to talk to you about Emily Pickering, a student on your course who disappeared in 2002.'

'I'm assuming you have some new information,' says Leo.

'We have discovered the remains of a young woman who has been formally identified as Emily,' says Tanya. She watches Leo closely. He meets her eye but one leg is trembling violently. She can almost hear the coins rattling in his pocket. Leo is more nervous than he looks. Also, who has loose change these days? Everything is contactless since Covid.

'You've found her?' he says at last.

'We've found her remains.' She deliberately doesn't say where.

'I hope that will be some comfort to her parents.'

'I understand you sued them in 2008.'

'I was very sympathetic to them. I *am* very sympathetic to them. But there comes a point where you have to defend your good name. There were some very damaging allegations.'

'They accused you of killing Emily?'

'They didn't know what they were saying. They were grief-stricken.'

But you still dragged them through the courts, thinks Tanya.

'We've reopened the case,' she says, 'and so we're talking to everyone who saw Emily before she disappeared. I understand that she attended a field trip, led by you, on the weekend before.'

'Yes. I made a statement at the time.'

'I've read it,' says Tanya. 'I'd like you to go over that weekend again, if you don't mind.'

'It was twenty years ago.'

'You might have remembered some extra detail in that time.'

Leo sighs and looks at the ceiling. 'I took Emily and three other students on a field trip to Grime's Graves. We had a chance to explore a deeper shaft – not the one currently open to the public. It was a great opportunity.'

'How did you choose the four participants? There must have been lots of other archaeology students.'

'They were my personal tutees. It's a particularity of Cambridge. One-to-one tutorials. It's a very special relationship.'

Bradley makes a sound that's halfway between a cough and a laugh. Tanya says hastily, 'I have the names of the students here. Emily Pickering, Amber Fletcher-Ellis, Thomas Westbourne, Emad Hussein. Who else was on the trip?'

'A junior lecturer, Mark Oldbury. And a man called Cathbad. That wasn't his real name. It was Michael something. He was a lab assistant at one of the new universities, but he'd studied archaeology. Interesting chap.'

Bradley and Tanya exchange glances.

'Have you kept in contact with any of these people?' asks Tanya.

'I kept in touch with Mark for a while. He's teaching at one of those northern universities now.'

One of those northern universities. One of the new universities. Academic snobbery is alive and well in the Ballard household, thinks Tanya.

'So,' she says briskly, 'what happened on that field trip in 2002?'

'We had a good few days digging. Some very interesting finds. Flint flakes, part of a wooden shovel, an antler that was probably used as a pick. We went down into the mine shaft. We slept in tents on site. On Sunday night, we had a barbecue and someone – I think it was Thomas – played the guitar. It was magical. Then, on Monday, we went our separate ways. I understood that Emily was going home to her parents for Easter, which was the next weekend. I drove her to the station, then I went to meet friends in Cambridge. I spent the whole day with them. I remember Emily waving goodbye to me. That was the last time I saw her.'

Tanya can't remember if the detail about the lift to the station was in the original statement. Now, they would take Ballard's car apart but she's not sure how forensics worked in the early noughties.

'How did Emily seem that day?'

'Exactly as she always seemed. Cheerful, friendly, interested. She really was a lovely girl. I can see her sitting in this room, just where you are . . .'

'She came *here*?'

'Yes.' Leo sounds surprised. 'It's quite usual for tutors to see students in their homes.'

Another reason to go to Loughborough, thinks Tanya. At least teaching happens in actual classrooms, not in book-lined lairs.

'So, Emily didn't seem worried on that last day?'

'No.'

'She was seen in Ely at midday on the twenty-fifth. Do you know why she was there?'

'I've no idea. Ely's on the way to Lincoln. Perhaps she just fancied a visit. It's a beautiful place.'

'Did you ever go to a café in King's Lynn called the Green Child?'

'I don't think so. I'm not a fan of King's Lynn . . .' He stops. 'Is that where she was found? In the café?'

'I'm not at liberty to say,' says Tanya. 'Thank you, Professor Ballard. We'll be in touch.'

On the way out, Bradley surprises Tanya by asking Leo how Grime's Graves got its name.

'Good question,' says Leo, favouring Bradley with his gap-toothed grin. 'It's thought to be after the Anglo-Saxon god Grim, one of the names of Woden, or Odin, sometimes called the hooded or masked one. In old Norse "grimr" means "masked". It survives in some English place names like Grimsby. Grim's Gaben means the masked one's quarries. The name eventually became Grime's Graves. Of course, the shafts had all been filled in by Anglo-Saxon times, but the area has a rather strange, uncanny appearance. It's interesting that they knew there were mines down there.'

Interesting is not the word Tanya would have used.

*

Tony enjoys his trip to London. It feels rather strange to be travelling on a train in the middle of the day. The carriage is empty apart from two teenage boys sharing a can of lager. Neither of them has a mask on and Tony wonders how long it will be before they are also sharing Covid. The journey feels surprisingly fast, the flat countryside rushing past like an advertisement for rail travel. As they pass Cambridge Tony wonders how Tanya is getting on with the mysterious Professor Ballard. He thinks that she would be a match for any creepily charismatic lecturer. Pity she wasn't in *The Secret History* (Tony's favourite book) really.

The outskirts of King's Cross, grey and rain-swept, fill him with unexpected happiness, as does the view of Arsenal's Emirates Stadium, adorned with giant posters of the players' backs. Tony has never dared to admit to Nelson that he supports the north London team. Freya Webster lives in Walthamstow, but she works in a bookshop on Charing Cross Road, which is where Tony is meeting her. Then he is going to Clapham to see his parents, having promised Nelson that he'll catch the first train back to King's Lynn in the morning. All this puts a spring in his step as he emerges from Leicester Square Tube station, breathing in the heady mix of Chinese food and exhaust fumes. When Tony was at school, people – pupils and teachers – routinely assumed that his parents worked in a restaurant or a take-away. Tony's brother Mike hated it. 'It's a racist stereotype,' he'd say. 'Can't you see that?' Tony could see it, but he also remembers wishing his parents had done something so interesting. After all, everyone loves Chinese food. Instead, his father was a tax accountant and his mother stayed at home with the children. Until Tony's little sister Lily died and she retrained as a nurse. But nothing was the same after Lily died.

Charing Cross Road is full of bookshops, from the luxurious Foyles to musty establishments that look like they have strayed from the pages of Dickens. Freya works in a place called Between the Lines, which falls somewhere between the two. The bay window displays the latest titles, leaning heavily on crime, but inside there are armchairs and piles of second-hand books, their covers soft with age.

'It's impossible to see anything in here,' says Freya. 'But Madge, the owner, likes ambient lighting.'

'It's very cosy,' says Tony, falling over a small table.

'We specialise in cosy crime,' says Freya. 'Perhaps that's why. Let's go upstairs. It's quieter there and we'll actually be able to see each other.'

As they climb the steep staircase, Tony asks about the phrase 'cosy crime'. He's heard it before but has never been sure what it means. Surely, it's an oxymoron?

'It is really,' says Freya. 'It means crime without too much gore and bloodshed. Often there's humour and lovable characters. Set in an old people's home or farmers' market. That sort of thing.'

'I hate to break it to the writers,' says Tony, 'but murder usually means bloodshed.' As he says this, he thinks of the bones behind the wall. There was no blood there but he's pretty sure that a murder had occurred. He wonders whether Freya is conjuring the same image.

Upstairs is certainly lighter, partly because there's a large sash window looking out over the street. This area seems reserved for children's books. Tony and Freya sit on bean-bags next to a cardboard cut-out of the Gruffalo.

Tony tells Freya about the discovery of Emily's body. She's heard some of it before but gasps when Tony describes the skeleton lying beside the boarded-up chimney breast.

'I remember that fireplace so well,' she says. 'We had an electric fire there, but it looked like the real thing.'

'Tell me about the café in your parents' day,' says Tony.

'It was called the Green Child,' says Freya. 'Do you know that legend?'

'No,' says Tony. Despite going to the University of East Anglia, he's rather ignorant about Norfolk legends. But, then again, there are so many of them.

'I think it was in the twelfth century. Two children, a boy and a girl, suddenly appeared in a village called Woolpit, in Suffolk. They spoke a strange language and they were bright green. They said they'd come from an underground land. They were herding their father's cows – also green, apparently – when they heard a bell ring and found them-selves in Woolpit.'

'Gosh,' says Tony. 'What happened to them?'

'I think the boy died but the girl grew up and got mar-ried.'

'Was she still green?'

'I'm not sure. Maybe the green wore off. My dad loved that story. That's why he gave the café that name.'

'Do you remember Emily Pickering coming to the café?'

'Yes,' says Freya and her face suddenly becomes quite different, softer but also more wary. 'She used to come for the Folklore Fridays. It was a pet project of Dad's. People would come to the café and talk about Norfolk myths and legends, read short stories and poems. Sometimes there'd be a singer. Dad loved all that stuff. Black Shuck, the Lantern Men, the Fairy Cow, the Southwood Pond.'

'Sounds fascinating,' says Tony. Did Freya really say 'fairy cow'?

'Dad thought so,' says Freya, pleating the cotton of the beanbag. 'Some of the stories are quite horrible, though. There's a church in East Somerton where a witch was buried alive. Her wooden leg grew into an oak tree that eventually destroyed the church. According to the legend, if you walk round the tree three times saying her name, the witch will appear.'

'There's a lot of that, isn't there?' says Tony. 'Saying someone's name three times and them appearing. Like in the film *Candyman*.'

'Yes,' says Freya. 'If you say "Bloody Mary" three times at St George's in Yarmouth, Mary Tudor's face appears in the window.'

'You remember the stories very well,' says Tony.

'Dad used to tell them to us at bedtime,' says Freya.

Tony's police senses are on full alert now. But, then again, Tony's mother used to tell her children Chinese ghost stories and they all thought it was a great treat. But something in Freya's tone implies this wasn't the case with her.

'Tell me about Emily,' he says.

'She hardly ever missed a Folklore Friday,' says Freya. 'She used to come with a friend of hers from university. Thomas, I think his name was.'

'Did you know Emily well?' asks Tony. 'Were you friends?' They were the same age, after all.

Freya's face changes again. Her voice sounds younger. You can hear the hurt in it. 'Emily wouldn't be friends with me. She was clever. She was at university. I'd left school at sixteen and was working in the café. A waitress, that's what I was to Emily. She talked about archaeology and history, all the books she'd read. Dad thought she was marvellous.'

'She sounds annoying,' says Tony. Meaning it.

'Oh no,' says Freya, with another shift in tone. 'She wasn't. She was lovely. Everyone liked her.'

'Did your dad like her?' Tony is aware that he is now treading on dangerous ground, the treacherous marshes of Norfolk folklore, in fact.

'He liked her,' says Freya. 'But there was nothing odd in that. He liked everyone.'

'Did Emily's lecturer, Leo Ballard, ever come to the café?' asks Tony.

'No,' says Freya. 'But Emily and Thomas talked about him all the time. Especially Emily. Leo this. Leo that. I got quite sick of the name, to be honest.'

'We know that Emily travelled to Ely on Monday twenty-fifth of March, the day she disappeared,' says Tony. 'She was seen walking up from the station towards the high street and caught on camera looking in a bookshop window. Do you have any idea why she would be in Ely?'

'No. Unless ... I think she might have been at school there,' says Freya. 'I think she mentioned it once.'

Tony makes a note. It occurs to him that Freya remembers a lot about Emily.

'Could Emily have been on her way to King's Lynn that day?' he asks. 'On her way to the café?' It would have been a rather roundabout route but still possible.

'No,' says Freya. 'She couldn't have.'

Tony is surprised at her certainty. 'Why?'

'The café was closed on Mondays,' says Freya.

Tony wonders whether this was known at the time of Emily's disappearance but no one seems to have thought to check with the café, despite it being one of her favourite haunts. He asks, trying to be tactful, when the wall was built in the downstairs room.

'I think it was in 2002,' says Freya, 'because that was the year I left home. Met a boy and moved to Norwich with him. Didn't last, of course.'

'In 2002?' That was the year Emily disappeared. 'Do you know when?'

'I think it was at Christmas because the café was closed then. Dad did most of the work himself. He loved DIY.'

Emily went missing in March. The wall was built in December, nine months later. Where was her body before it was hidden behind the wall? Or was she even alive until then? All Tony knows is, if DIY-loving Peter Webster were alive, he'd be helping the police with their enquiries. Does Freya know that her answers are condemning her father? Does she care? Tony asks if Freya has any pictures of the

Green Child café and, rather to his surprise, she produces a photograph from the child-sized table nearby.

'Just one. We didn't have camera phones then. I think Dad took this. He was keen on photography.'

Tony leans forward to look at the picture, then, remembering social distancing, leans back. Freya pushes the image towards him. It shows three people sitting at a table. A curly-haired girl is looking straight into the camera, a blond boy is looking at her and a man, instantly recognisable as a younger Cathbad, is laughing. A girl with her hair braided around her head is standing behind Cathbad, almost out of shot. In the background is a chimney breast in which an electric fire has been fitted. There is something chilling about seeing Emily in the very place where her body was to be concealed.

'Is that you?' says Tony, pointing to the figure in the background. She's standing, he notes, like a waitress about to take an order. *That's what I was to Emily.*

'Yes,' says Freya. 'God knows why I used to have my hair like that.'

'Did you know this man?' He points at Cathbad.

'Cathbad? Yes. He often came to the café, especially for the Friday sessions. He was good friends with Dad.'

'Did he know Emily too?'

'Yes. He was another one who was nuts about her.'

This is another line of enquiry altogether and a potentially embarrassing one. Tony likes and respects Judy, who has taught him a lot. It won't be easy raising the subject of Cathbad's feelings for murdered Emily. Tony hopes that he won't be the one to do it. He asks if he can have a copy of the photograph and Freya says there's a photocopier downstairs.

'I found the picture in an old album,' she says. 'I haven't looked at it for years.'

Somehow Tony doesn't believe her.

CHAPTER 10

Ruth is rather surprised when her email is answered immediately.

Dear Ruth

This government's attitude to the arts is positively barbaric. At this rate there will be no archaeology departments left and, if we can't understand our past, how can we understand the future? I will certainly write a strong letter to your chancellor and sign petitions et al.

I definitely recall meeting you at St Jude's. I seem to remember that you had a conversation with my wife, Alice, about childcare. How interesting that you participated in the dig at Grim's Gaben in 2006. I'm afraid that my association with the place was at an end by then. It would be good to meet one day – perhaps in Cambridge? – and discuss tempora and mores.

With all good wishes

Leo

Ruth reads this twice. She nods approvingly at the first sentences but winces inwardly at 'et al'. She wishes that she'd had a more intellectual conversation with Mrs Ballard – also an academic, she thinks – but she had been preoccupied with Kate changing schools after the move to Cambridge. She notes the archaic 'Grim's Gaben' and the frankly ridiculous '*o tempora, o mores*' reference. And why was Ballard's 'association' with the flint mines at an end by 2006? Ruth forwards the email to Nelson, smiling inwardly at the thought of his reaction.

Sure enough, in a few minutes, Nelson is on the phone.

'Pretentious idiot. What's all that about tempura and moors?'

'It's a Latin phrase. "*O tempora, o mores!*" Means something like "Oh the times, oh the customs!". I don't know who said it. I didn't do Latin at school.'

'Still bloody pretentious.'

'Agreed.'

'Tanya interviewed Ballard this morning. She thought there was something definitely off about him.'

'I can't imagine that they'd get on.'

'Tanya's very sharp.'

'I think so too. Do you think Ballard might have had something to do with Emily's disappearance?'

'He's definitely a person of interest. After all, he was one of the last people who saw her alive.'

'I think I will meet him in Cambridge.'

'Well, if you do, be careful. You know he was a friend of Cathbad's?'

'I didn't know that,' says Ruth.

'Cathbad was even on the field trip, the one before Emily died.'

'So, he knew her too?'

'Seems so.'

Ruth wonders why this information makes her feel quite so anxious. She can hear the echo of her own feelings in Nelson's voice.

He says, 'I'm driving over there now to have a word with him.'

'What do you mean, have a word with him? Is he . . .' Ruth hesitates, hardly able to form the words. 'Is he a *suspect*?'

'He's a witness,' says Nelson. 'We're talking to everyone who was with Emily that weekend. That's all.'

But, somehow, Ruth isn't reassured.

'This is a bit unusual, isn't it?' says Cathbad. 'The DCI making house calls.'

'Doctors make house calls,' says Nelson. 'This is just a chat.'

'I don't think they do any more,' says Cathbad. 'Even lovely Dr Patel. Well, it had better be quick. I'm picking up the kids in a bit.'

It's only two o'clock. Either schools are finishing earlier these days – which wouldn't surprise Nelson – or Cathbad is not keen on a chat with his old friend. They are in the kitchen, with tea and flapjacks, but somehow the atmosphere isn't as peaceful as usual. Even Thing seems to be finding it hard to settle, wandering around, sighing and looking out of the window.

'I wanted to talk about Emily Pickering,' says Nelson.

'Yes, I rather thought you did.'

'The bones in the café have been formally identified as her last remains. We'll make a statement tomorrow.'

'My heart goes out to her parents,' says Cathbad. 'I hope this will bring them some closure.'

'Did you ever meet them?'

'No, but Emily often talked about them.'

'You were on a field trip with Emily the weekend before she disappeared.'

'Yes.'

'Come on, Cathbad. Help me out a bit. Who was there? What happened? I know the parents suspected Leo Ballard. Tell me about him.'

Cathbad sighs and looks into his teacup as if expecting to see the future there. His recent weight loss makes him look older and Nelson notices that the leather bracelets he wears on his wrists are hanging loose.

'Leo was – is – a brilliant man but he was like Erik. He mesmerised his students. He made them see new patterns, new constellations. He broke their worlds up and put them together again. That's dangerous. All his students, but Emily and Tom in particular, were dazzled by him. We had an incredible few days at Grime's Graves. You must go there. It's a fascinating place. Leo had all sorts of theories about it.'

'What sort of theories?' Nelson prompts because Cathbad is staring at the tea leaves again.

'Theories about ritual and sacrifice. I mean, he was a serious academic. He knew all about the Neolithic – well, as much as anyone can know without being there. That's why I love prehistory. It's all storytelling really. But Leo sometimes went a bit far. There are stories and there are mysteries. I sometimes think he confused the two. We had a good weekend at Grime's Graves, though. Some rather significant finds. On the last night, we had a feast. A party. We were all sitting around the campfire when suddenly this figure leapt into the light. It was cloaked, wearing a mask. Now, Grime's Graves is named after the god Grim, the masked one, a very sinister incarnation of Odin. You can imagine how shocked everyone was.'

'Who was it? The person in the mask?' Nelson is pretty sure that Leo didn't tell this story to Tanya.

'That's just it. We were all there. The four students, Mark, Leo's assistant, and me. There was no one it could have been. Everyone was screaming, rushing about. Mark's dog barking. In the chaos, the figure disappeared.'

'And the next day Emily disappeared.'

'We all thought she was going home to her parents for Easter. The day of the bonfire was actually Palm Sunday, which should have been a good omen. Her parents raised the alarm later in the week. The police took it seriously. They interviewed all of us.'

'What did you think had happened to her?'

Cathbad looks into his cup again and then raises his eyes to meet Nelson's. His irises are very pale blue. Nelson has noticed before how this makes his stare particularly disconcerting.

'At first, I thought – hoped – that she'd run away. I knew things were difficult at home. As I say, Emily often talked about her parents. But, as time went on, I did start to fear the worst.'

'Did you know the café where the body was found? It was called the Green Child then.'

'Yes. I went there quite a lot. The owner, Peter, was an interesting man. Very drawn to the druidical religion.'

'Did you meet Emily there?'

'Sometimes. Peter used to hold these Folklore Fridays. They were soirées really.'

'They were what?' Whatever they are, Nelson doesn't like the sound of them.

'Gatherings. Social events. We'd meet at the café to talk about local myths and legends. Sometimes there would be a folk singer.'

'Jesus wept.'

'They were very special evenings.'

Nelson looks directly at his friend.

'Cathbad, you fainted dead away when I said a body had been found at the café. I think there's something you're not telling me.'

The pale blue gaze doesn't falter.

'It brought it all back. The café, Peter, Freya, Emily. She was such a lovely girl, Nelson. I think I might have been a bit in love with her.'

'She was years younger than you. She must be Maddie's age.' Maddie is Cathbad's grown-up daughter.

'Not quite. I was thirty-six in 2002. Emily was twenty.'

Cathbad often claims not to count the years on the temporal plane but Nelson notices that his mental arithmetic works when it has to.

'Was Leo Ballard in love with her too?'

'I think so. Tom definitely was.'

'Thomas Westbourne? One of the other students?'

'That's right. It was all very highly charged.'

'So highly charged that a girl was killed.'

'Yes.'

'Cathbad,' Nelson leans forward. 'You might be a nutcase, but you've got good instincts. Who do you think killed her?'

Cathbad looks out of the window. Two of the hens are on the roof of the shed. Thing barks at them and then looks enquiringly at his master. Cathbad pats the dog. 'It's OK, boy.' Then he turns back to Nelson. 'I think it was someone who loved her,' he says at last.

'You've just told me everyone was in love with her.'

'Exactly.'

For someone supposedly on an elevated spiritual plane, Cathbad can be very annoying.

Tony's mother tells him that he's lost weight, his father that he's looking more like his grandfather every day. Neither of these things are true but Tony accepts that they are his parents' way of showing affection. The house on Clapham Common is the same, neat and comfortable, with Tony and Mike's graduation pictures beaming from the wall. There are no photos of Lily on display, which always makes Tony feel sad. His mother has her picture on her bedside table and Tony often used to sneak in to look at it, Lily in a pink dress holding her favourite toy rabbit. It was taken when she was five, the year she died from meningitis. Tony took a photograph of the framed portrait before he went away to university. He used to worry that he would forget what Lily looked like but now he knows that her image is branded on his heart for ever.

'I've made your favourite supper,' says Min, Tony's mother.

'I bet your mum's a great cook,' is one of the less offensive things people say to Tony. But, in truth, Min has never been keen on the labour-intensive dishes of her native Guangdong province. She was quick to embrace convenience foods, especially when she was training to be a nurse. Hao, Tony's dad, was a better cook and, at weekends, would produce slow-boiled soup and shahe noodles. Tony is interested to learn what his mother considers his favourite dish.

'Kung pao chicken,' says Min, in answer to his enquiry. 'That was always your favourite.'

Tony thinks it was actually Mike's but he's very happy to sit down to a home-cooked meal. He's not a great chef either and mostly exists on Deliveroo.

Min asks about his flat. She doesn't like Tony living alone and often suggests that he gets a flatmate.

'It's a one-bedroom flat,' Tony explains, not for the first time. 'But, it's fine. I've got friends. I play in a five-a-side football team.' It was Clough who introduced him to the team of current and ex-police officers. Tony's an indifferent player but he always turns up for practice, which makes him Man of the Match most weeks.

'You were always good at sport,' says Min.

That was Mike too but Tony isn't going to argue. His Chinese name is Chongan, which means second brother. Says it all really.

Both parents ask about his work. They hadn't wanted Tony to join the police. He'd studied economics at university, which seemed the perfect foundation for becoming an accountant, like his father. They hadn't pushed the matter, though – they aren't that kind of parents – and always try to show an interest.

'I'm working on a strange case at the moment,' says Tony. 'A skeleton found bricked up in a wall.'

'That happened to your uncle Wang Lei,' says Min.

'Really?' Unlike his brother, Tony loves stories about the extended family. Wang Lei seems to have done most things but, even so, this one is a surprise.

'Yes, he found a mummified cat in his garden wall.'

'That's not the same thing at all,' protests Hao.

'Yes, it is!' says Min. 'Wang Lei contacted the previous owner, an old man who'd had to move into a home. He said he mummified the cat because he loved it and wanted it with him always.'

'He couldn't have taken a photo?'

Tony allows his parents' bickering – the soundtrack to his childhood – to wash over him. He is thinking: did someone love Emily so much that they wanted her with them always?

CHAPTER 11

Tuesday 15 June

'We know several things that we didn't know yesterday,' says Nelson. 'We know that Leo Ballard drove Emily to the station on Monday twenty-fifth of March 2002. We know that a mysterious masked figure appeared during the last night of the Grime's Graves dig. We know that Emily used to frequent the Green Child café and go to some weird get-togethers there . . .'

'Folklore Fridays,' says Tony helpfully. 'Apparently Peter Webster, the owner, was very keen on that sort of thing.' Tony, who had travelled up on the early train, is looking as bright-eyed and bushy-tailed as ever. The visit to his parents has obviously done him good. Nelson is always slightly envious of people who still have both parents. Nelson's father died when he was fifteen.

'Surely Peter Webster must be our main suspect?' says Tanya.

'I think so too,' says Nelson. 'According to Tony here, he built the downstairs wall in December 2002.'

'He did the work himself, too,' says Tony. 'I asked and Freya said that her father was keen on DIY. She also said her father adored Emily. I couldn't work out if she realised how creepy it sounded. He took this picture.'

Tony produces the photocopy with a flourish. The team crowd round, all distancing forgotten.

Emily Pickering stares out from the grainy photocopy. Judy goes closer. Does she see the resemblance that's so obvious to Nelson? Emily, with her springy hair and wide-apart eyes, looks like a younger Judy. She looks, in fact, very like the young DC that Nelson first met in 2007. Is this why Judy is looking so intently at the snapshot? Or is she looking at Cathbad? He hasn't changed much, although his beard and shoulder-length hair are still black in the photograph. He looks happy and rather piratical, but this could be because he is wearing a hoop earring in one ear. Are Cathbad's ears still pierced? Nelson can't remember, which shows what a lousy witness he'd make.

'Is that Freya?' Tanya points at the figure standing in the background.

'Yes,' says Tony. 'She was waitressing at the café. She left home in 2002 to move in with a boyfriend. It didn't work out. She married someone else and they had two children but she's divorced now.'

Tony always gets the personal stuff, thinks Nelson. It's one area where his relentless sociability pays off.

'Do you think Freya suspected that her dad might have had something to do with Emily's disappearance?' asks Nelson.

'I don't know,' says Tony. 'She talked quite openly about the Folklore Fridays and all that. I think she really admired Emily and felt quite hurt that she didn't notice her more. She said that Emily thought of her as a waitress. Freya got a degree later and said that she hoped Emily would be proud of her.'

'Might be worth talking to Freya again,' says Nelson. 'You seem to have built up a rapport with her, Tony. We need to trace the other daughter too. Didn't Freya have an address for her?'

'She said not,' said Tony. 'Claimed they weren't in contact.'

'That's interesting in itself,' says Nelson. He can't imagine losing contact with his sisters, infuriating though they often are. 'What was the sister's name?'

'Gaia,' says Tony. 'I looked it up and it means "Goddess of the Earth". Freya said that her father was very interested in earth magic.'

'That doesn't automatically make him a murderer,' says Judy.

'No, but he owned the house where the body was found,' says Nelson. 'He built the wall that hid it. If Peter Webster wasn't dead, we'd be questioning him under caution now.'

'What about a séance?' says Tony brightly.

Nelson ignores this. 'What about Webster's wife?' he says. 'What did Freya say about her mum?'

"Freya said that she doesn't really recognise anyone any more. I didn't get the impression that she visited the home much. Freya said that her mum didn't have much to do with the café anyway. She was busy with her own work. I think she was a secretary.'

'I still think Leo Ballard might have had something to do with it,' says Tanya. 'I thought he was very creepy. And Emily's parents suspected him at the time.'

'I can see why,' says Nelson, 'but it's hard to see how Leo could have concealed Emily's body at the café. As far as we know, he never went there and didn't know Peter Webster. It was Peter Webster who built the wall. We don't know exactly when Emily's body was hidden there or where it was in the intervening nine months. Ruth doesn't think that it was buried, or left in the open. She also thinks her bones were wrapped in a blanket or rug. Forensics might get something from that.'

'Why were Emily's parents so convinced that Leo was involved?' asks Judy.

'They said he was obsessed with Emily and behaved oddly during the investigation. I've looked back at the transcripts and Leo does come across as a bit of a . . . a bit odd, quoting Latin and talking about mythology. But he had a solid alibi for the day Emily disappeared. He was with friends all day. And he always swore there was nothing inappropriate in his relationship with Emily. It was normal for a tutor to be close to his students, he said.'

'He said something similar to us,' says Tanya. 'I thought it sounded very dodgy.'

'Let's keep close to Ballard. Is he married?'

'Yes,' says Tanya. 'And he was very sexist about his wife.'

'Talk to her,' says Nelson. 'If Ballard is a male chauvinist pig, she might be willing to dish the dirt.'

'Probably under his thumb,' says Tanya. 'I can see Ballard as a gaslighter.'

Nelson knows what this means. He attended an online course about coercive control earlier that year. It was at his own request, something which might have surprised Tanya.

'Go and see her all the same. And we need to talk to Emily's parents again. The family liaison officer was with them today. It's an emotional time for them. But I think we need to take a closer look at them too. Cathbad said that he thought things were difficult for Emily at home. The original investigation didn't uncover anything untoward but maybe they didn't ask the right questions. After all, we only have her parents' word for it that Emily didn't return home that Monday.'

'You really think they could have killed their own child?' Sometimes Tony sounds too naive to be a police officer.

'It happens,' says Nelson. 'As we all know. We still don't know why Emily was in Ely that day either.'

'Freya said she went to school there,' says Tony. 'I looked it up and there's an independent school there called King's. It looks very posh from the photos.'

'Follow it up,' says Nelson. 'But we need to tread carefully. Superintendent Archer made a statement this morning confirming that the bones are Emily's. There'll be a lot of press interest in the case.'

Nelson watched the press conference from the safety of

his desk. Leah, who'd found the link for him, watched it too and said she thought Super Jo had had her roots done specially. Nelson couldn't comment on that – he always used to be in trouble for failing to notice when Michelle had been to the hairdresser – but he thought Jo had done a good job of handling questions. The police were reopening the case, following several lines of enquiry, please respect the parents' privacy, etc. They won't, of course.

'We need to check everything,' he says now. 'We should look at any forensic exhibits too. Forensics has come on a lot since 2002. I don't suppose Leo Ballard still has the same car, for example?'

'I wouldn't think so,' says Tanya. 'There was a car in his drive. It looked newish.'

'What make was it?' asks Judy.

'I don't know. I'm not like you. I don't read *What Car?* magazine.'

'It was an electric Kia EV6,' says Bradley Linwood.

'Well, he certainly didn't have that in 2002,' says Nelson. 'But we could try to trace his original car if it hasn't gone for scrap. And we need to talk to anyone who saw Emily that weekend.' He glances at Judy. She must know that this includes Cathbad. But Judy's face is blank. Nelson has always admired the way she can keep her emotions in check but he wishes he knew what she was thinking.

He goes on. 'We need to talk to the other students – particularly Thomas Westbourne – and the assistant lecturer, Mark Oldbury. There might be other contacts too. We should work closely with Cambridgeshire CID.'

'We'll have Dave Clough in here every day,' says Tanya. 'Eating chips and telling us what to do.'

'He's a reformed character,' says Nelson. 'He tells me that he's practically vegan these days.'

Though Cloughie had insisted on stopping at a burger van just outside Lincoln.

Ruth is surprised to see that the lecture hall is full for the emergency general meeting. She's also surprised to learn that she's chairing the meeting.

'Just give an update and then take questions,' says David. He has put a table and three chairs on the dais, one for him, one for Ruth and one for the branch officer of the University and College Union, Becky Smallwood.

'We should have a ballot on industrial action,' says Becky. 'This isn't any way to run a university.'

Ruth agrees whilst disloyally wondering if anyone will notice if university lecturers go on strike in the summer. She looks out over the raked seats. Shona and Phil are sitting together at the front, which is rather disconcerting. But Ruth also spots a lot of her students as well as all the staff members of the archaeology and history departments. At the very last minute the university vice-chancellor, Colin Bland, slides into the room and stands by the back wall. Ruth squares her shoulders and takes hold of the microphone.

'Thank you for coming,' she says. 'You may have heard that last Friday the executive board made the decision to close the archaeology department at UNN.'

'Shame,' shouts someone.

'I think it is a shame,' says Ruth, looking in the direction of the speaker. 'It's a shame that this decision was taken in private with no members of the department present. It's a shame that it was announced on Twitter. It's a shame that the board took the unilateral decision to close down a department rated amongst the top in the world for archaeology.'

This is stretching it a bit but UNN is number thirty-six in the QS world rankings for archaeology. Cambridge is number one. Ruth is surprised at the warm applause that greets her words. Getting into her stride, she continues, 'I first came to Norfolk to participate in the excavation of the Bronze Age henge on the Saltmarsh. It's an area that is uniquely rich in history and archaeology. UNN Archaeology has been involved in some of the highest profile research in recent years, from the causeway across to the marshes to the Second World War bodies at Sea's End and the recent medieval grave in Tombland.' She pauses. All these discoveries have also been linked to modern deaths and more recent trauma but now is not the time to go into that. 'The decision to close the department will not only harm the academic reputation of the university, it will harm the global study of archaeology.'

David stands up. 'Dr Galloway can hardly say this herself, but she is a leading figure in British archaeology. She has published three books, appeared on television, and is an advisor to the police. She left a highly prestigious position at Cambridge University to lead the department here. The university will make itself look ridiculous if it sidelines its most prominent academic.'

More applause and shouts of 'Good old Ruth'. Colin Bland raises his hand.

'Let's hear from the vice-chancellor,' says Ruth.

Colin is Australian and Ruth suspects him of overdoing the accent because it makes him sound charming.

'No one is a bigger admirer of Dr Galloway than me,' he says. 'But these are tough times. Covid has hit us for six. And archaeology student numbers are down. It's a trend we've seen across all British universities. I hope that Dr Galloway will continue her research and post-graduate teaching.'

'Where will the archaeologists of the future come from?' asks Ruth. 'We need to run undergraduate courses in order to have post-graduates in the future.'

Colin seems disinclined to answer this. Becky Smallwood stands up. 'The UCU is going to fight. We will not accept this forced closure or the compulsory redundancies. We will ballot our members on immediate industrial action.'

'You can help,' David tells the audience. 'Write to the vice-chancellor, write to your MP. Sign our petition. Details on Twitter. Hashtag SaveUNNArch.'

Ruth asks for questions and several people ask about timing. The existing students are reassured that their courses will be completed. Eileen Gribbon, one of Ruth's second years, asks if there will still be a third-year field trip.

'There will,' says Ruth, firmly. Luckily, there are plenty of sites in Norfolk.

'You're the best, Dr Galloway,' says Eileen, with tears in her eyes.

Ruth feels buoyed up by the support but, deep down, she can't escape a sinking feeling that her department is doomed.

CHAPTER 12

Back in her office, Ruth finds another email from Leo Ballard.

> I'm unwilling to let the native hue of resolution be sicklied o'er with the pale cast of thought. Why not meet tomorrow, at Grime's Graves? I've been persona non grata at the site for some time now but the current custodian is well disposed. Do you fancy a stroll amongst the dead? Ring me if so.

There's a mobile phone number underneath.

Is Leo Ballard trying to sound as sinister as possible? thinks Ruth. *A stroll amongst the dead.* And what does the first sentence even mean? She thinks it's a mangled Shakespeare quote but is unwilling to give Ballard the satisfaction of googling it or asking Shona. On the other hand, she doesn't have any teaching on Wednesdays and she would like to see Grime's Graves again. She's also interested to know why Ballard, once such an expert on the flint mines, has been unwelcome at the site for the past twenty years.

She can't face phoning, so she sends an email suggesting

that they meet at the Exhibition Building at nine thirty. After the emotion of the department meeting, she fancies a morning away from the university. David has sent several messages suggesting 'a council of war'. Ruth knows that she should meet with her colleagues but she can't help suspecting that David, for one, is rather enjoying being in battle mode. Ruth is just steeling herself to call him when her internal phone rings. It's Prisha, her PA.

'Sorry, Ruth, but Anglia TV are outside. They want to interview you.'

There's nothing Ruth wants less than to appear on the local news, but she knows it's her duty to put the department's case. She switches her phone onto selfie mode and winces at her reflection. Her hair, newly washed that morning, now looks greasy because she has run her hands through it so many times. Her nose is pink, and she seems to have acquired new shadows under her eyes. Oh well, it's what she says that matters. She's wearing her work clothes, black trousers and a loose white shirt, but, in a desk drawer, she finds a red scarf. She drapes that round her neck and hopes for the best.

The first person she sees is Shona, who is deep in conversation with David. In the light of Shona's comments about David, this makes Ruth feel even more nervous.

'Is that what you're wearing?' is Shona's first, surely rhetorical, question.

'You look great,' says David.

Shona comes over and rearranges the scarf, flicking one end over her shoulder in a way that reminds Ruth of illustrations of *The Little Prince*.

'Remember to smile.'

The interviewer explains that, because of Covid, they are using a special extendable microphone. A furry object appears under Ruth's nose.

'Dr Galloway. What's your reaction to the proposed closure of the archaeology department?'

'I'm shocked,' says Ruth. 'The executive board didn't consult us, and we only learnt about the decision via social media.' She wonders if she sounds completely out of touch, like a judge asking, 'What, pray, is a tweet?' She soldiers on. 'The archaeology department at UNN is one of the best in the country. We're going to fight this short-sighted and ignorant decision.' She pauses. 'Short-sighted' is good, 'ignorant' less so. She doesn't want to sound like an intellectual snob. Like Leo Ballard. Et al.

'Why is archaeology important in this day and age?' asks the reporter.

'Archaeology is the study of ordinary people,' says Ruth. 'Everyday people,' she corrects herself. 'It's not about kings and queens. It's about real people living their lives. Farming, baking, mining. When we examine artefacts – see a fingerprint preserved on a Bronze Age tool or a dog's pawprint on a Roman tile – we are linked to their lives. Norfolk has the oldest human footprints outside Africa. They were found in Happisburgh. Eight hundred thousand years old. Almost a million years old. It's archaeologists who have helped us to understand them.'

When she finishes a cheer goes up in the background and

a banner appears from the upper windows of the Natural Science block.

SAVE UNN ARCH. DR RUTH ROCKS.

Ruth hopes the camera doesn't catch her wiping her eyes.

When she arrives at Cathbad's house, Kate and Michael are watching her on television. Ruth averts her eyes from the giant figure on the screen, red nose matching red scarf.

When the interview is finished, the camera pans to the banner hanging from the windows. Kate and Michael both cheer.

'That's wonderful,' says Cathbad. 'Shows the strength of feeling amongst the students. They're a good bunch at UNN.'

'I know,' says Ruth. 'I've been really touched by their support. The meeting was packed today. But I can't stop thinking about Sheffield. They put up a hell of a fight and were still closed down.'

'Did someone do your make-up before you went on TV?' asks Kate.

'No,' says Ruth. 'I wasn't wearing make-up.'

'I thought not,' says Kate.

'You were great,' says Cathbad. 'Passionate but also calm and articulate.'

'Thank you,' says Ruth. Perhaps it's part of the sixth sense but often Cathbad says exactly what you want to hear. While Kate is collecting her belongings, Ruth tells Cathbad about the trip to Grime's Graves.

'Be careful,' says Cathbad.

'Of what? Falling down a shaft?'

'That too, but I meant be careful of Leo. If he wants to see you, it's because he wants something from you.'

'Nelson suggested that I contact him.'

'Well, Nelson wants something from you too.'

Ruth doesn't encourage this train of thought. 'What's Leo like?' she asks. 'You must have known him quite well, twenty years ago.'

'He's charismatic,' says Cathbad. 'I told Nelson that he was like Erik but, where Erik was a teller of tales, Leo finds out what you want and then offers it to you.'

'That sounds very sinister.' Ruth wonders what Leo thinks she wants. To be accepted by Cambridge academia? To save her department? To discover the truth about Emily Pickering?

'It can seem very benign,' says Cathbad. 'All those years ago, I was quite lost. I was living in a commune, missing Erik and the camaraderie of the henge protests.' He grins, perhaps thinking of the fact that he and Ruth had been on opposite sides about the henge. Ruth, part of the excavation team, had been instrumental in removing the timbers.

'Leo was kind to me,' says Cathbad. 'He knew I wanted a friend. He knew Mark wanted a father.'

'What did Emily want?'

'I was never sure,' says Cathbad, rather sadly.

When Ruth and Kate get home, Zoe is in the front garden, tying hollyhocks to a stake. Flint and Derek, Zoe's cat, watch from their separate doorsteps. Kate greets her aunt casually and goes into the house. Ruth sits on the step beside Flint, who allows her to stroke him.

'I saw you on telly,' says Zoe. 'You didn't tell me you were going to be on.'

'I didn't know,' says Ruth. 'I didn't even have time to put on any make-up.'

'You looked great,' says Zoe. 'And were so articulate.'

'Really?' says Ruth. 'I didn't say half the things I meant to.'

'You were terrific,' says Zoe. 'I can't believe they're closing your department. You didn't say anything about it on Sunday.'

Zoe sounds slightly hurt. Ruth says, 'We were having such a nice day. I suppose I didn't want to think about it.' Which is mostly true.

'How can they do that, though? Just close down an entire subject?'

'It's happening a lot,' says Ruth. 'This government seems biased against archaeology. They've scrapped the A level and now they're closing university departments. Boris Johnson claims to be a classicist but he seems pretty anti-history, if you ask me.'

'Maybe he doesn't want his own skeletons dug up,' says Zoe. 'What will you do?'

'We'll fight it,' says Ruth, 'but I'm not feeling that confident.'

'You could get a job anywhere,' says Zoe. 'Not that I want you to move. Not after I've taken all this trouble to track you down.' She smiles but Ruth knows there is truth in her words. Zoe had originally rented the cottage because she knew it was next door to her half-sister, although Ruth had been unaware of the relationship at the time. It's been a long journey, in every sense.

'I don't want to move,' says Ruth. And, right then, in the golden evening, breathing in the scent of the garden and the sharper tang of the sea, she means it.

'By the way,' says Zoe. 'Someone came looking for you today. A young woman.'

Ridiculously, Ruth thinks of Emily Pickering.

'Did she leave a name?'

'No. I asked her but she said not to worry, she'd come back.'

Ruth thinks of this intermittently as she cooks supper, oversees homework and marks papers, but no one approaches the houses on the edge of the marshland.

CHAPTER 13

Wednesday 16 June

'Welcome to Grime's Graves,' says the National Trust sign, next to a less welcoming notice saying that it is closed to visitors. Ruth, driving through the gates, can see nothing but a long road, with trees on either side. She remembers the site being a huge field, although it's surrounded by Thetford Forest. But, suddenly, the sky opens up and she's driving through a wide space of sun-bleached grass. It reminds her of the ghost fields, the abandoned airbases scattered throughout Norfolk, now mostly converted into farms but retaining some of the vastness and menace of their original use.

There's a small hut in the middle of the field, with two cars parked outside. Ruth has seen plenty of aerial photos of Grime's Graves, the eerie lunar landscape pockmarked with craters, like the surface of a golf ball. At ground level it's hard to see the undulations but Ruth knows they are there. Over four hundred of them, she seems to remember.

Each depression marks a mine shaft, long since filled in. Ruth thinks of the wood between the worlds in *The Magician's Nephew*, a book she once read to Kate. Each pool in the wood led to a different world but there were so many and they were all the same. It was possible to get lost in the in-between place for ever. Ruth had found the concept terrifying at the time. Kate had found it funny.

Two men are sitting at a picnic table outside the building which seems less like an exhibition centre and more like the shed Phil has recently installed in his garden 'for his writing'. Ruth recognises Leo Ballard by his wild grey hair. He waves as she approaches.

'Well met!'

Oh God, is she going to have to talk in cod Shakespearean all morning?

'Hallo,' says Ruth, when she is close enough not to shout.

'This is Jamie Stirland,' says Leo. 'He's the custodian here. He's going to take us down.'

Take us down? Ruth had imagined a peaceful chat in the open air (complying with social distancing rules), perhaps accompanied by a coffee from a Gaggia machine that had suddenly materialised in the middle of the field. But it seems that Leo plans a descent into the mine itself. Ruth looks doubtfully down at her shoes. She never wears heels but her flat loafers, perfect for teaching, are not ideal for clambering down ladders. She wonders if she has some trainers in the car. She hasn't been to the gym since pre-lockdown but, equally, she hasn't tidied her car either.

The trainers are there. Ruth puts them on and pulls an old jumper over her white shirt. Thus attired, she follows Leo and Jamie towards the place where a small kiosk sits embedded in one of the lunar depressions, looking like a rocket about to be propelled into the atmosphere.

'Don't worry,' says Jamie. 'It's very safe. There's a metal staircase and everything.'

'There's a deeper shaft over towards the woods,' says Leo. 'That's just a ladder.'

'We can't take visitors down there,' says Jamie. 'You need a safety harness for one thing. Here, you'd better wear this.' He hands Ruth a hard hat. 'It's seven metres down.'

'Thirty feet in old money,' explains Leo, who seems like the sort of person who mourns the passing of imperial measures.

Ruth is not a fan of enclosed, underground spaces. When she visited Grime's Graves before, it was to participate in a dig exploring the surrounding area. Although some of the volunteers had gone down into the mines, Ruth had not felt tempted to join them. But she feels reluctant to back out now. After all, it must be safe. The sign outside says 'not suitable for children under five'. That means Kate could make the trip. Kate *would* make the trip.

Ruth looks at her phone. There's no signal but maybe she can use the torch. She's relieved when Jamie presses a switch inside the kiosk and light fills the underground chamber. Jamie prepares to descend. 'Go down backwards,' he tells Ruth. 'That's what I always say when we have school parties here. You go backwards into the past.'

Ruth approves of introducing children to pre-history. She's just not so sure about descending below the earth with two men she hardly knows. But she turns and feels with her trainer-clad foot for the first rung. Whatever Jamie says, it's more of a ladder than a staircase.

The metal steps take several twists. When Ruth finally reaches the bottom, she finds herself in a circular space with cave-like openings all around.

'The galleries,' says Jamie. 'They're tunnels that go further into the rock. The miners would have crawled along, maybe in the dark, feeling for the flint.'

The galleries are closed off behind grilles. Never, thinks Ruth, am I ever going to explore them. She looks up. Leo is still descending, his feet clanging on the metal steps. The chalk walls seem incredibly high, studded with jet-like stones. Ruth comforts herself with something that she learnt during a previous underground excursion. The Channel Tunnel was rerouted to go through chalky soil because chalk is so incredibly strong. These walls have stood for over four thousand years. They are not going to collapse now.

'There are three layers of flint,' says Jamie. 'Top, wall and floor. The Neolithic miners dug the shafts, using only antler picks and animal bones, like scapula. They excavated the flint and broke it into smaller nodules which were hauled to the surface in wicker baskets. We've found the rope marks. Then they filled in the shaft with rubble. It was all very efficient.'

Leo has joined them. He's slightly out of breath. Ruth

doesn't know how old he is, but he must surely be over seventy. That's not old these days but Leo doesn't look at the peak of fitness.

'We found a fingerprint on one of the antlers,' says Jamie. 'The miners probably put clay on their hands to help their grip. The clay preserved the print.'

As she said during the emergency meeting, Ruth is always moved by things like this. To think that a Neolithic miner touched something over four thousand years ago and the mark remained.

Leo is wiping his brow with a handkerchief. He seems uninterested in the fingerprints of the past. 'What about the ritual element?' he says. 'I've always thought that descending into the mines might have been an initiation ceremony. Maybe they took young girls down here, into the womb of the earth, when they reached puberty.'

Jamie shoots him a look. Leo said that the custodian was 'well disposed' towards him but Ruth isn't so sure. She finds Leo's words pretty creepy herself. As for Nelson, he would probably have arrested the man long before he reached the word 'puberty'.

'There's some evidence of ritual,' says Jamie. 'There are hearths on some of the shaft floors which may have had a ceremonial purpose. We found the skeleton of a dog but maybe he just fell into a shaft. There are rabbit and fox bones too. But, as I say, primarily this was a sophisticated mining operation.'

'Maybe women even came down here to give birth,' says Leo.

'My wife is nearly nine months pregnant,' says Jamie. 'I can't imagine any woman going underground to have a baby.'

'I thought you'd found a fertility figure in one of the shafts,' says Leo, sounding disappointed. 'Also chalk phalluses. The mines could be seen as vaginas and the phalluses a symbol of penetration.' He grins at Ruth, yellow teeth glowing in the darkness.

'You said the mines were wombs a minute ago,' says Ruth. 'I hate to break it to you, but they're not the same thing.'

'Anyway, the Venus figure is thought to be a fake,' says Jamie. 'It's unlike any Palaeolithic or Neolithic carving that I've seen. It's smiling, for one thing.'

'Maybe she had something to smile about,' says Leo.

'Would they have had light down here?' says Ruth, rather hastily. 'You mentioned them feeling for the flint.'

'We've never found lamps or tallow in the mines,' says Jamie. 'One theory is that they would have had a mound of chalk here at the bottom. The sunlight would shine down the shaft and reflect on the white stone.'

'What if they were here in the night?' says Leo. Ruth is certain that he's imagining midnight rituals, probably involving nubile virgins.

'That's unlikely,' says Jamie. 'Shall we go up?'

Ruth agrees immediately. She's the first to climb the ladder, this time going forwards into the present. When she gets to the surface, she steps out of the kiosk and breathes deeply. The air feels wonderfully sweet, smelling of grass and dew.

'Fancy a coffee?' says Jamie. 'There's a machine in the exhibition centre.'

Now you're talking, thinks Ruth.

Sitting at the picnic table, drinking the surprisingly good coffee, Ruth feels her archaeologist's sense returning. She asks about the excavations.

'A clergyman called Canon William Greenwell was the first to explore one of the shafts,' says Jamie. 'That was in around 1850. About twenty-eight of the mines have been excavated since then.'

'I seem to remember that there are over four hundred of them,' says Ruth.

'We think there are at least four hundred and thirty-three,' says Jamie. 'They were numbered in 1915 but there may well be more. The surrounding land is owned by the Ministry of Defence so we can't dig there.'

Ruth hadn't been so far wrong when she thought of the ghost fields.

'What about the Anglo-Saxons?' says Leo. 'They were the ones who gave the place its name, after all. Grim's Gaben.'

Ruth remembers that Leo had used the archaic name in his email.

'Or Grim's Graven,' says Jamie. 'The Anglo-Saxon kings of East Anglia saw Grim, or Odin or Woden, as their direct ancestor. They definitely saw this place as special. There's Grimshoe Mound at the eastern end of the site. It was probably a meeting place of some sort.'

'I've had some interesting meetings there myself,' says Leo.

Ruth wonders what he means. Leo has a way of making the most ordinary remarks sound somehow unsavoury. She wants to know more about Grimshoe. She knows that 'hoe' or 'howe' means a low hill or a burial mound. Her dig had excavated nearby but she seems to remember that they found only some indifferent pottery and evidence of a Bronze Age midden.

Leo seems reluctant to abandon the god Grim. 'The Anglo-Saxons made sacrifices to Odin, or Grim, before wars,' he said. 'It's easy to imagine that happening on Grim's Hoe here. It's always a good thing to appease the gods. Isn't that what your friend Cathbad would say, Ruth?'

Ruth is jolted. She didn't realise that Leo knew about her connection to Cathbad. She manages to reply, fairly coolly, 'Cathbad is very interested in belief systems. Are you still in touch with him?'

'Sadly no,' says Leo, sipping his cappuccino rather noisily. 'We were brothers once, united in our spiritual and emotional journey.'

'You mentioned the dig here twenty years ago,' says Ruth. 'Cathbad took part in that, didn't he?'

Jamie, perhaps embarrassed by the sudden intensity of the conversation, mutters an apology and moves away, pretending to tidy the leaflet display outside the cabin.

'Yes,' says Leo. 'That was an unforgettable weekend.'

Ruth waits.

'I understand that you performed the excavation of Emily's remains,' says Leo.

It sounds very cold put like that, thinks Ruth, and 'performed' is surely the wrong verb. But she agrees that she was the lead archaeologist involved.

'Emily was a remarkable girl,' says Leo. 'She had a very good mind but she was also intuitive, almost magically so. I've never had a pupil like her and I've taught many, many students.'

'It must have been a great shock when she went missing,' says Ruth.

'Well, at first I just assumed that she'd gone off with a friend or a boyfriend,' says Leo. 'It was only as the weeks went by that I started to fear the worst.'

'Did Emily have a boyfriend?'

'I think she was romantically involved with Thomas Westbourne, another student on the course,' says Leo. 'But it wasn't serious. Boy–girl stuff. There was Cathbad too.'

'What do you mean?'

Leo now looks like he's enjoying himself. 'Cathbad definitely had a fling with Emily. I thought you and Cathbad were such friends. Hasn't he told you about his dark past when he was the jolly postman seducing women on his daily rounds?'

Ruth looks at Leo stonily. She hates to hear him talking about Cathbad in this way but, even so, there's a tiny bit of his narrative that rings true. Cathbad *was* once a postman and Ruth has noticed before that he's very susceptible to pretty women. But Emily must have been at least fifteen years younger than Cathbad. A similar age to his daughter. No, she doesn't believe it. Instead she asks about the other students on the course, Amber and Emad.

To her surprise – and consternation – Leo laughs aloud.

'My spies were right! You are a detective, Ruth. Did DCI Nelson send you here to cross-examine me?'

Ruth is too taken aback to reply. Still smiling, Leo says, 'I've got nothing to hide. Tell DCI Nelson that. And DS Fuller too. She was an interesting woman, I thought. But, since you have come all this way, and descended into the womb of the earth, I will say this. Look to the sister.'

'Whose sister?'

'I'll leave you to work that one out yourself,' says Leo. 'Sisters are doing it for themselves.' He laughs again, enjoying the joke.

CHAPTER 14

'Emily was always clever,' says Naomi Pickering. 'Both the girls were. We didn't push them, but they were just good at things. Not just schoolwork but sport – Emily played hockey for the county – and music. Both of them did grade eight on the piano.'

Tanya smiles politely. She doesn't believe about the not pushing for one second. After all, who paid for all those piano lessons?

'Where did they go to school?' she asks.

'King's Ely,' says Naomi. 'Sophie loved it there. She even asked to board as a senior. But Emily didn't like it so much so we moved her to the Minster in Lincoln. We always listened to the girls and did what was best for them.'

This is said rather defensively. Tanya is willing to bet that the Minster is also a private school. She thinks it's interesting that achievement is still so important to Emily's parents. But it's good. Until Tanya asked a random question about A-level results, Gordon and Naomi had been reserved, almost defensive. But now Naomi, at least, is almost expansive, getting out a team photograph to show Tanya.

'I played county hockey,' Tanya can't help saying. 'The standard is very high. Did Emily play at university?'

Naomi's face clouds. 'She played a bit in the first year but then she got injured. Broke a bone in her ankle. She had to have a metal pin put in. After that, she gave up. Only thought about studying. And those archaeology trips. Suddenly nothing mattered except archaeology.'

'We didn't want Emily to do archaeology,' says Gordon. 'She had science A-levels. She could have studied medicine.'

Like Sophie, thinks Tanya. And you.

'Tell us about Emily at Cambridge,' says Tanya. 'Was she happy there?'

'She changed,' says Gordon. 'She changed as soon as she met him.'

'She was happy,' Naomi interrupts. Rather hastily, thinks Tanya. 'She loved the college and she loved the work. It was just that . . . her world seemed to be becoming smaller when it should have been getting bigger. At school, she had lots of friends. At St Jude's, she only really saw the other members of her tutorial group – Tom, Amber and Emad. And Ballard, of course.'

'She was always talking about Ballard,' says Gordon. 'She had tutorials at his house, used to babysit his children. It wasn't a healthy student–teacher relationship. I said that in court, and I'll say it again. It was as if he hypnotised them all with his talk of gods and ghosts and underground kingdoms.'

Tanya can just imagine this. She'd like to tell Gordon Pickering that she agrees with his assessment, but instead she says, 'What about Emily's relationship with her fellow students? We've heard she might have been romantically involved with Thomas Westbourne.'

'She liked him,' says Naomi. 'But I don't think they were boyfriend and girlfriend. The four of them did everything together, as far as I could see. Tom, Amber, Emad and Emily.'

'Amber married Tom,' says Gordon. 'Did you know that?'

'I didn't,' says Tanya. She looks down at her phone. Another cryptic message from the boss. *Ask about the sister.*

She waits until Naomi has finished telling her about the time Emily scored the winning goal in a needle match against Suffolk.

'What about Emily's sister, Sophie?' she says. 'Did they get on well?'

'Very well,' says Gordon. At the same time, Naomi says, 'Well, they argued like all sisters.'

Tanya waits.

'Sophie's two years younger than Emily,' says Naomi. 'I think she felt in her shadow for a long time. It's different now, of course.'

'Sophie's a registrar at Edinburgh Royal Infirmary,' says her father.

'Where did she go to university?'

'Leeds,' says Gordon. 'It's excellent for medicine.'

And a long way from you, thinks Tanya. As is Edinburgh.

'Did she visit Emily at St Jude's?' asks Tanya. 'Did she meet Leo Ballard?'

'She visited once,' says Naomi, looking rather wary. 'Emily took her to a party. I don't think Ballard was there.'

Neither of them ever uses his Christian name.

'Sophie's married now,' says Naomi. 'Her husband Stephen's a doctor too. They've got a baby girl.'

'What's her name?' says Tanya. She doesn't think she spotted any baby pictures in the crowded room.

'Emily,' says Naomi.

Ruth arrives back at the university to the news that the vice-chancellor is looking for her.

'I said you were at a meeting,' says Prisha.

'Thank you,' says Ruth. 'I'm not going to ring Colin. He can come and find me if he wants to talk.'

'You've got white stuff on your trousers,' says Prisha, as Ruth turns to go.

'Have I?' Ruth tries to twist round. 'It's chalk dust. How annoying. I thought I'd got it all off.'

'I've got a clothes brush somewhere.' Prisha opens a drawer.

'You're amazing,' says Ruth. 'Thank you.'

In her office, she brushes her trousers, rather ineffectually. She should really take them off but there's no lock on the door and she doesn't want the vice-chancellor to come in and find her half naked. Somehow that wouldn't say 'serious irreplaceable professional'.

She has only just started reading and deleting emails, when there's a perfunctory knock on the door.

'G'day.'

Oh God, it's Colin Bland being all Australian.

'I just wanted a word, Ruth.'

'Of course. Take a seat.' Ruth isn't going to stand up. Besides, her trousers are covered in chalk.

'It's a bad business about your department.'

'You're telling me.'

'The university really values the work you do, Ruth, but student numbers are down.'

'They're down in lots of other departments too. Computer science, for one. I don't see them facing the axe.'

'There are lots of other factors.'

'Tell me three of them.'

Colin sighs but doesn't answer. Instead he says, 'I've got a proposition for you, Ruth.'

It sounds very improper. Or maybe that's just the accent again.

'How do you fancy becoming Dean of Humanities?' asks Colin.

Alice Ballard works at a charity shop in Ely. 'Something to stop me from going mad when I retired,' she said over the phone. Tanya arranges to meet her in her lunch break, grateful for the chance to explore Ely, a place that has begun to assume mythic proportions in the investigation. Tanya leaves her car at the station and deliberately follows the route taken by Emily as revealed on CCTV. She wonders why they didn't do a reconstruction at the time, perhaps using Emily's sister, Sophie. What did the boss mean by 'ask about the sister'? It's annoyingly cryptic but she's learnt to trust Nelson's hunches. Tanya has a sister and a brother. Joe is a teacher and Cathy does something nebulous in marketing. Joe's biggest secret is that he was actually christened Boris; his name, like Tanya's, inspired by their mother's Russian ancestry. Tanya gets on perfectly well with her siblings but she doesn't think that they impact her life in any way.

But she enjoys the walk. Emily's route takes her along a footpath with fields on one side and the cathedral looming on the horizon. 'The ship of the fens' it is sometimes called and Tanya can almost imagine it surrounded by water, in the days when Ely was an island before the fenland was drained. She passes a children's playground, a couple of dog walkers, an elderly man sitting on a bench and reading the *Telegraph*. The place could not be more innocuous if it tried.

Tanya goes through a gateway and passes in front of the great church. It really is incredibly impressive, a huge tower with stained-glass windows and battlements rising up to the sky. Tanya doesn't know much about its history and hasn't liked to ask in case the answer turned out to be boring. The bell is tolling midday as she passes.

Tanya turns into the high street. Topping's bookshop is immediately visible, painted a tasteful blue with a black-board outside advertising author events. Why would anyone pay to listen to an author talking about their books? thinks Tanya. People really are weird. The rest of the street looks slightly less prosperous, though, and there are several charity shops. A woman is standing outside one called Little

Lives. She's tall with grey hair in a shiny bob, neatly dressed in a white blouse and blue linen trousers.

'Alice?'

'Yes. Sergeant Fuller, I presume?'

'Do call me Tanya.' The boss told her to keep things informal. Besides, it's Detective Sergeant.

'Shall we walk in the cathedral grounds? We'll have more privacy and I like to get fresh air in my lunch break.'

'How often do you work in the shop?'

'Two or three days a week. As I said on the phone, it's something to keep me busy. Retirement's not easy.'

Isn't it? Tanya would have thought it was the definition of easy. Mind you, the boss seems hell-bent on putting it off for as long as possible.

They walk through another archway and the cathedral, the mother ship, is in front of them once more. Alice squints up at the towers. 'We've got peregrine falcons nesting here. It's very exciting.' Tanya notices several people with binoculars trained on the roof. As with author talks, it's a whole other world. Tanya and Petra go running in their spare time, they swim or play tennis. They don't sit around staring at birds. 'It takes all sorts,' Tanya's mother used to say but Tanya knows that her own nature is less tolerant.

'As you know,' says Tanya, 'we're reinvestigating the case of Emily Pickering. It's now a murder enquiry.'

'Yes,' says Alice. 'I heard that you'd found her remains. It's very sad.'

They walk round to the back of the cathedral. There's a

sort of additional church on the side with arched windows at each end so you can see all the way through to the sky. Alice tells her it's called the Lady Chapel and is devoted to the Virgin Mary.

'It's the largest lady chapel attached to any cathedral in Britain.'

Tanya has seen, on a previous case, where devotion to the Virgin Mary can get you. But there's no doubt that the cathedral is impressive. If you like that sort of thing.

They sit on a bench and Tanya gets down to business. 'Did you ever meet Emily?' she asks Alice.

'Yes,' says Alice. 'She used to babysit our boys.' Emily's parents said this too and Tanya had wondered about it at the time. Leo Ballard must have been at least in his fifties when he taught Emily. Rather old to have children who needed babysitting.

'Nicholas and Matthew would have been around six and eight then. They're twenty-five and twenty-seven now. Both with lives of their own.' She pauses, pushing back her hair with one hand. 'We had a daughter, Saskia, but she died. Cot death. Or Sudden Infant Death Syndrome as it's known now. She was six weeks old.'

'I'm so sorry,' says Tanya. Her most recent appraisal might have suggested that she was lacking in empathy but she has no problem feeling sympathy for the woman sitting next to her. The name of the charity, Little Lives, suddenly makes sense too.

'It was awful,' says Alice calmly. 'Leo and I . . . I think we went almost mad for a while. But then we had Nick and

Matt and life carried on. I was so grateful to get pregnant again. I was forty-three when Matthew was born.'

That makes her around sixty-eight now, thinks Tanya. She asks if Alice has any memories of Emily.

'It sounds awful now,' says Alice, 'but I don't especially remember her. She was just another of Leo's students. They all merged into one after a while. Clever, polite, a bit intense. The sort of girl who'd have been head girl at school.'

Tanya has often regretted that her school didn't have a head girl. She would have had the badge, if so. 'You were a lecturer too, weren't you?' she says.

'Yes. I taught English literature. I still do a bit of private coaching.'

'Did you have tutorials at the house too?'

Is it Tanya's imagination or does Alice stiffen slightly? 'No, I saw my students in my college rooms.'

'Is it unusual to have students coming to your house, babysitting your children?'

'No,' says Alice. 'Not especially. Students are generally short of cash.'

'I have to ask you, what was your husband's relationship with Emily Pickering?'

'She was his student. That's all. Leo took a great interest in his students. As any good teacher does.'

'Emily's parents thought he took an unnatural interest.'

Alice turns to look Tanya full in the face. She has very blue eyes, undimmed by age. 'I feel very sorry for Emily's parents. They lost a child. I know what that feels like. Believe me, my heart breaks for them. But Leo had nothing to do with Emily's death. His relationship with her was purely pastoral and educational. And I don't want you using any cod psychology and thinking that Emily was a replacement for his dead daughter. He was her teacher. That was that.'

It wasn't what Tanya was thinking. But it's definitely an idea worth considering.

Nelson sits in his office thinking about sisters. His two older daughters, Laura and Rebecca, have always got on well, often forming an alliance with their mother against him, the only male in the household until George came along – and Bruno, of course. They are both fond of Katie too, although her existence was initially a great shock. What will their relationship be like as Katie gets older? Nelson has two older sisters, Grainne and Maeve. He wouldn't say he was close to them, exactly, but they are blood relations and that counts for something. He wonders what Ruth really thinks about her newly discovered sister, Zoe. They seem delighted with each other now but will it last? For himself, Nelson finds Zoe's presence rather intrusive.

His phone buzzes. Nelson knows it will be Ruth. He hasn't heard from her since her trip down the mines, apart from the rather cryptic message saying that Leo Ballard had told her to 'look to the sister'. Nelson passed this on to Tanya, despite not having a clue what it means.

'Ruth. Back on dry land?'

'I wasn't under water, Nelson.'

'You know what I mean. How was it?'

'Very interesting. I actually went down into one of the shafts.'

'Was that safe?'

'Totally. I wore a helmet and it was all very organised. There's even electric light down there. It was a bit spooky, though.'

'Did Ballard come down into the mine with you?'

'Yes. That's partly what made it spooky. You know he said that thing about "look to the sister"? Well, he said something else too.'

'What?'

'He said that Cathbad had an affair with Emily.'

'Did he?' says Nelson.

'You don't sound surprised.'

Nelson considers this. 'I don't think I am. When I spoke to Cathbad on Monday it was clear he was hiding something. And he even said he was in love with Emily.'

'But she was so much younger than him.'

'He was thirty-six, she was twenty. It's not impossible.'

'It's not very ethical either.'

'Not very wise,' says Nelson, 'but I wouldn't say unethical. He wasn't her teacher. Ballard was. He wasn't married. Ballard was.'

'Ballard certainly said some very creepy things today. All about women being taken down into the mines as an initiation ceremony. Even giving birth down there.'

'I'm going to have a word with Ballard myself.'

'And Cathbad?'

'I'll pop in to see him tonight.'

There's a pause as if they're both waiting. Then Nelson says, 'I could come over to yours afterwards?'

'OK then,' says Ruth. But it doesn't sound like a concession. It sounds as if she's smiling.

Nelson is smiling too but he consciously rearranges his face into a frown when there's a knock on the door.

'Come in.'

It's young Tony. He's holding out his mobile phone. 'Sorry, boss,' he says. 'I've been pinged.'

For a moment, Nelson doesn't understand. *Pinged.* Is that something young people do? But then Tony says, 'Must have been on the train or the Tube. I've got to isolate for ten days.'

He's talking about the NHS app, which tracks your movements and tells you when you've been in contact with someone who has tested positive for Covid. A great idea, in theory, but in practice half the workforce seems to be off sick at the moment. Well, not sick, thinks Nelson resentfully, just lazing about at home.

'That's bloody inconvenient,' he says. 'We're short-staffed as it is.'

'I know. I'm sorry.'

'Well, if you have to isolate, you have to isolate. You can go through all the material on Emily Pickering. All the evidence from the first enquiry. Let us know if we're missing anything.'

'OK, boss.'

Tanya will have to go to London and interview Tom Westbourne. Then she'll probably get 'pinged' too. Not for the

first time, Nelson curses Covid-19 and the horse of the apoca-
lypse it rode in on. He hardly notices that his own phone
is buzzing.

It's not the NHS app but something more surprising. His
old friend Sandy Macleod, now retired from Blackpool CID.

'I've got a proposition for you, Harry.'

CHAPTER 15

'A proposition?' says Nelson. 'I'm married.'

As soon as he says this he wonders if he *is* married any more and the thought gives him a sudden stab of pain.

'Aye,' says Sandy, who likes to adorn his Lancastrian accent with vestiges of childhood Scots. 'I saw your missus in town the other day.'

Did Sandy wonder why Michelle was in Blackpool without Nelson? There's no clue in his voice but then Sandy has always specialised in Deadpan Copper.

'What's your proposition?' says Nelson.

'Top brass got in touch with me because they're looking for a retired murder detective. I'm not looking to do any work. It would interfere with my golf. So, I thought of you.'

'I'm not retired.'

'I heard a rumour that you were thinking of it.'

Does Jo's spy network reach all the way to Blackpool?

'You're one step ahead of me then.'

'That wouldn't surprise me. This job, though, it's an inter-esting one. They're after someone to head up the cold-case investigation team. What about it? Aren't you missing the bright lights of the Golden Mile?'

He is, of course.

'Cold cases?' says Nelson. 'I'm working on one now.'

'Good luck,' says Sandy. 'Shall I mention your name to the super just in case?'

'Why not?' says Nelson.

'Your little lad was with Michelle. He's growing up fast.'

'He is,' says Nelson. As he says goodbye, he wonders how much his old friend knows. Or guesses.

Nelson calls a rather depleted team meeting with Tanya and Bradley. He explains that Tony is isolating.

'Why doesn't he just delete the app?' asks Bradley.

Nelson secretly agrees but he knows he should be encouraging responsible Covid-prevention.

'I've told Tony to go through everything on the original case,' he says. 'He might spot something the previous team missed. I'll ask for some extra manpower – person power, sorry, Tanya – but, until then, we'll just have to cope. We can do one-person interviews, recording them on body cams. Tanya, you go to London to interview Tom Westbourne. Better drive to cut down the risk of getting Covid on the train.'

'Did you know that Tom was married to Amber Fletcher-Ellis?' says Tanya.

'I didn't,' says Nelson. 'That is a turn-up for the books. Still, it means we can kill two birds with one stone. Emad Hussein is in London too. Bradley, you go to Manchester and interview Mark Oldbury. And we need to talk to Ballard again. Ruth saw him today and he was acting very strangely. He told her to "look to the sister".'

'So that's what that was about,' says Tanya. 'I asked about Sophie Pickering. Apparently, she visited Emily at Cambridge once.'

'The mum said she was in Emily's shadow,' volunteers Bradley.

'Ballard was probably just trying to muddy the waters,' says Nelson. 'But I still think he might know something.'

'I thought he was a creep,' says Tanya.

'According to Ruth, he thought you were "interesting",' says Nelson. 'What did you make of the wife?'

'I quite liked her,' says Tanya. 'But she seemed very defensive about Ballard. Insisted that there was nothing odd about his relationship with Emily. She said Emily was like all the others, but she only seemed to mention female students. Oh, and the Ballards had a daughter who died.'

'That's really sad,' says Bradley.

'She died at six weeks old. Sudden Infant Death Syndrome. They went on to have two sons who are grown up now. Alice said that we mustn't assume that Emily was a replacement for their dead daughter.'

'Well, if we weren't thinking that,' says Nelson, 'we are now.'

'Exactly.'

'I think I should go and see Ballard,' says Nelson. 'My guess is he won't find me nearly so fascinating.'

'Do you know when we'll get the forensics on the remains?' asks Tanya.

'Any day now,' says Nelson. 'I'm hoping there'll be something that will tell us where the body was kept between March and the wall being built in December.'

'She could have been alive all that time,' says Bradley.

It's a thought. Nelson mustn't underestimate Tanya's new sidekick.

Nelson nearly makes a clean getaway but, just as he is descending the stairs, a siren call echoes after him: 'Can I have a quick word?'

Nelson retraces his steps to find Super Jo bouncing gently on her exercise ball. It makes Nelson feel slightly sick, for all sorts of reasons. He fixes his gaze on a point above his boss's oscillating head. Her office seems to be full of watercolour prints and bunches of flowers. Their scent makes Nelson want to sneeze.

'How are you doing with the Emily Pickering case?'

'OK,' says Nelson. 'I could do with more staff, though. Judy can't be involved and young Tony's isolating.'

'He hasn't got Covid, has he?'

'No, he's been pinged by the app.' Nelson can hardly believe that these words have just come out of his mouth or that Jo nods sagely, as if they make perfect sense.

'Why can't Judy be involved?'

'Cathbad knew the girl. He was interviewed by the original investigation.'

Nelson doesn't repeat what he's just learnt from Ruth. Jo knows Cathbad, of course. At Cloughie's wedding he told her that she was an 'old soul' and she's been repeating it ever since.

'I'll see what I can do,' says Jo. 'Maybe Dave Clough has someone he can spare. After all, she lived in Cambridge. It's his case too.'

'I'll ask him.'

'I just wondered,' says Jo, 'if you'd thought any more about the Big R?'

'The big what?' He knows exactly what she means but he's going to make her say it aloud.

'Retirement.' Jo smiles at him while wobbling gently from side to side. 'I thought you might want to go back to Blackpool, to be nearer George . . .'

Has she been talking to Sandy? Nelson wouldn't put it past her. He thinks of Michelle walking along the beach with George. That wasn't where Sandy had seen them but it's where Nelson's imagination places them, with the Central Pier in the background and the tower casting long shadows on the wet sand.

'There are lots of consultancy options out there now,' says Jo. 'Some forces are even advertising for retired coppers to become civilian SIOs.'

The word 'civilian' still feels like an insult.

'I'm not interested,' says Nelson. 'I'm just interested in solving this case.'

This time, Cathbad looks resigned rather than nervous. 'Fancy a walk on the beach?' says Nelson. 'We can take that idiot dog of yours. I've got Bruno in the car.'

Nelson collected Bruno from the dog walker after work. He knows this is because he's hoping (planning? expecting?) to spend the night at Ruth's.

'That sounds idyllic,' says Cathbad. 'I'll just tell Judy.'

From inside the house Nelson can hear the piano playing and Judy saying something that ends on a laugh. What would she say if she knew why Nelson is calling? Perhaps she already suspects? Thing barks. Presumably he understands the word 'walk'. Bruno is the same.

In a few minutes, the two men, accompanied by their dogs, are walking the path between the dunes to the beach. Are the animals appropriate to their owners? wonders Nelson. Bruno is a German shepherd, from a litter of police dogs. He's protective and vigilant, pointed ears always on the alert for danger. On the other hand, he's much better-looking than Nelson. Thing is an English bull terrier, with a jolly grinning face and a piratical patch over one eye. Like Cathbad, he stands out from the crowd but Nelson thinks that he has a simpler nature than his master. Cathbad, Nelson knows, is a complicated creature.

'So what's this about, Nelson?' says Cathbad, as they walk towards the beach huts. The tide is coming in and the sand is shrinking as the sea approaches. Closing off all avenues of escape, like a good police enquiry.

'It's about Emily Pickering,' says Nelson. He throws a grimy tennis ball that he found in the car and both dogs chase after it.

'What about her?' says Cathbad.

'Were you having an affair with her?'

'Depends what you mean by affair?'

'Oh, for God's sake, Cathbad!' Nelson's voice is so loud that two seagulls take off in fright and Bruno looks round anxiously, allowing Thing to steal the ball. 'Were you sleeping with her? Yes or no.'

'I slept with her once,' says Cathbad. 'Does that constitute an affair?'

'Did you tell this to the original police enquiry?'

'They didn't ask.'

'It seems to me that they didn't ask much. But why didn't you tell me? You knew it was relevant to the enquiry. You're married to a police officer, for crying out loud.'

'We're not married,' says Cathbad. For a moment he sounds odd, unlike himself. It reminds Nelson of the first time they met, when Cathbad was a suspect in a murder investigation. Then, Cathbad had seemed devious and cunning. In the intervening years, Nelson has got used to his inability to answer a question directly but, just now, it seemed perilously close to obstructing the police with their enquiries.

Cathbad seems to know what Nelson is thinking. He takes a deep breath and throws the ball that Thing has retrieved. He has a good overarm. Nelson wonders if Cathbad has ever played cricket.

'I slept with Emily once,' he says. 'It was after one of the Folklore Fridays. We had a great session on the Sheringham Mermaid including a debate on how mermaids have sex. We'd probably drunk too much of Peter's home-made cider . . .'

He pauses. Nelson cuts in, using his interrogation voice. 'Did you go back to your place? Hers?'

'We couldn't go back to my place,' says Cathbad. 'I was living in a commune. There was no privacy. Emily was still living in halls.'

'So what did you do?'

'We went back to the café,' says Cathbad. 'Freya gave us the key.'

No wonder Cathbad reacted so violently to the mention of the café, thinks Nelson. It wasn't just a place where he went to have cosy chats about mermaids. He also notes that, not only did Freya Webster have a key, she was prepared to lend it out.

'It sounds sordid,' says Cathbad, rather defiantly. 'But it wasn't.'

'I'll take your word for it,' says Nelson. 'Does Judy know?'

'I'm going to tell her,' says Cathbad. 'I need to set my affairs in order.'

'Do you think Leo Ballard knew about you and Emily?'

'Maybe. Like I say, he was good at working out what people wanted. He must have known that I wanted Emily. You know, Nelson, I can see her now, walking towards me . . .'

Nelson looks across the bay, half-expecting to see a young woman striding over the sand. But there's only the two dogs, play-fighting over a piece of seaweed.

'There's not much time left,' says Cathbad.

Nelson doesn't know if he's referring to the tide or something else entirely.

*

'Does Judy know?' says Ruth.

'He says he's going to tell her,' says Nelson.

'I'm sure she'll be all right about it,' says Ruth. 'I mean, it was a long time ago and it was only once.'

Nelson doesn't reply and Ruth wonders if he's thinking about another 'only once' that changed both their lives.

They are sitting in the garden, Nelson with a beer and Ruth with a glass of red wine. Kate is upstairs in her room. Bruno is lying panting on the grass. Flint is watching from the lower branches of the apple tree, looking like the Cheshire Cat. It's domestic bliss, of a sort. There's even a casserole in the oven. Lancashire hotpot. Ruth took the recipe from a packet of stock cubes. She hopes Nelson will appreciate the northern connection.

Nelson takes a swig of his beer. He seems to want to change the subject.

'I had an offer today.'

'An offer you couldn't refuse?' says Ruth.

'I never thought I'd hear Dr Ruth Galloway quoting *The Godfather*,' says Nelson.

'Is it *The Godfather*?' says Ruth. 'That's the one with Marlon Brando, isn't it?'

'Don't let Cloughie hear you say that. He loves those films. There are three of them. Brando's only in the first one. Cloughie can quote whole chunks of it.'

'I can imagine,' says Ruth. 'What was the offer?'

'Sandy Macleod from Blackpool. Remember him? He said they're looking for a retired murder detective to head up the cold-case team.'

Ruth shivers. She remembers, all right. For a second, the evening birds are drowned by the noise of a funfair. Lights flash and the screams from the roller coaster turn into something sharper and more sinister. She shakes her head and the soundscape recedes.

'Are you all right?' says Nelson. 'You've gone white. Mind you, the thought of Sandy would do that to anyone.'

'I'm fine,' says Ruth, although her voice sounds strange in her own ears, as if it's coming from a long way away. 'Well, were you tempted by Sandy's offer? I thought you never wanted to retire.'

'I don't,' says Nelson. 'But I'm going to have to one day. It would be good to have something to do. I'm not going to spend all day playing golf like Sandy.'

'And do you see yourself going back to Blackpool?'

Nelson pauses before replying. In fact, it seems that the whole world is silent. Even the birds have stopped singing. Ruth thinks of Kate upstairs in her room. When Ruth was young, she played Radio One loudly until her parents told her to turn it down. But Kate has her headphones on which means that Ruth can't enter her musical world, even unwillingly. The thought makes her sad.

'Maybe,' says Nelson at last. 'But I'd want you and Katie to come with me.'

Before Ruth can answer – to say what? That she never wants to leave Norfolk? That she had a tempting offer of her own today? – Zoe appears on the other side of the fence. Bruno barks, just once, like a butler announcing a guest.

Nelson makes an impatient noise, but Ruth is glad of the interruption.

'Hi, Ruth. Hi, Nelson. Ruth, I just wanted to tell you, the girl came back today.'

'What girl?'

'The girl who came looking for you the other day. Young woman, I should say.'

'You didn't tell me this, Ruth,' says Nelson.

'Why should I?'

'Someone treks all the way out to this godforsaken place to see you. Twice. It's got to be important. She's hardly selling Avon.'

That ages you, thinks Ruth. She doesn't think anyone has sold Avon toiletries door-to-door for years. She can't imagine Michelle buying any of the products. Maybe Nelson's mum was a fan.

'She seemed nice,' says Zoe. 'Young. Maybe early twenties. Again, I asked if I could take a message but she said no.'

'Description?' barks Nelson. He sounds like he's taking a witness statement. Ruth would tell him to mind his own business, but Zoe says, amiably enough, 'Tall, slim, long dark hair in a ponytail. What my mother would have called "well-spoken".'

'She doesn't sound too sinister, does she, Nelson?' says Ruth.

But she wonders why the innocuous description makes her feel very slightly scared.

CHAPTER 16

Thursday 17 June

The university still seems determined to look its best. A light breeze ruffles the ornamental lake as Ruth drives past on her way to the Natural Sciences building. The trees look bright green against the pale blue sky and there is still some blossom blowing over the grass. Ruth has the last of her PhD vivas today. The students always get very stressed about vivas, and it is nerve-wracking having to defend your work to a panel of experts, but, for Ruth, it's almost always a celebratory occasion. She loves hearing students talk so passionately and knowledgably about their research and it's great to tell them afterwards that they've passed. 'Congratulations, Dr Whatever.' In all her years of teaching, Ruth has only failed one PhD student.

This is what she'll miss, she thinks, as she strides along the corridor to her office. She'll miss teaching students, watching them grow in confidence, make connections, organise data, read the landscape. If she becomes dean, she'll lose this day-to-day contact. It'll be all administration, fundraising and meetings. All the same, she wonders why she didn't tell Nelson that she too had received a job offer. After Zoe had retreated into her own house, Ruth called Kate down and the three of them ate the rather boring hotpot and watched *The Last Kingdom* (Ruth's temporary obsession). Then Kate had gone to bed and, much later, Ruth and Nelson followed and had very unboring sex. It's all very complicated. And very simple.

In her office, Ruth has a cup of strong coffee. If she leaves UNN, she's definitely taking her espresso machine with her. She's scrolling through her emails while she waits for the other panel members to arrive, David Brown and the external examiner, Jeanne Hanisko. Jeanne teaches at Cambridge and Ruth is hoping to get a moment to talk to her about Leo Ballard.

'We've got more than two thousand signatures on the petition,' says David, coming in with a self-important flurry of papers and laptop. 'And nearly five thousand followers on Twitter.'

Before Ruth can answer (she imagines Twitter followers as a long line of desperate people, like an airport queue), Prisha puts her head round the door to say that Professor Hanisko is downstairs. She also offers to make David a drink, which Ruth thinks is taking hospitality too far. Ruth turns back to her laptop to avoid watching David fold himself into his chair as if he's a giant having tea with a hobbit.

There's one new email.

Test results on Red Mount Street bones.

*

Tanya makes good time on her journey to London. Unlike Nelson, she does not believe in exceeding the speed limit but, as she drives a hybrid, there's a certain satisfaction in cruising along at sixty without wasting any battery power. She's listening to Alanis Morissette, a distinctly private pleasure because Petra does not share her taste for emotional mezzo-contralto voices.

'You, you, you oughta know . . .' sings Tanya, as she turns onto the London Road. Tom and Amber Westbourne live in Highbury, a highly desirable area by the looks of it. Tanya and Petra finally moved into their dream home in February, but Tanya is still addicted to the property sites. A four-bedroom house in Canonbury Park costs well over two million pounds.

Tom and Amber's place looks like it's worth every penny of that. It's in a brick terrace, all hanging baskets and sash windows. Amber, who opens the door, is smart-casual in jeans and a stripy top. Tanya, who has only seen pictures of Amber at twenty, wouldn't have recognised her. The lank, shoulder-length brown hair is now a chic crop with bronze and gold streaks. As Amber ascends the stairs in front of her, Tanya guesses that the woman weighs two stone less than she did in 2002.

Tom and Amber have taken the morning off work. They mention this as if to show how helpful they are but also to make Tanya feel slightly guilty. She doesn't, though. The couple are both lawyers. Tom is a barrister, Amber a solicitor specialising in family law.

Tom, too, bears little resemblance to the gawky student

with glasses and messy hair. Now his blond quiff looks sus-
piciously gelled and he's either wearing contacts or has had
laser treatment.

'I left Cambridge after ... what happened,' says Tom.
'Read history at Edinburgh. Amber and I met again doing
the law conversion course in London.'

'Did you keep on with archaeology at St Jude's?' Tanya
asks Amber.

'Yes,' she says, somewhat defiantly. 'It was hard ... after
Emily ... but it was my passion. There's no money in it,
though.'

She smiles as if this is a joke but Tanya, looking around
the room, thinks that money is very important to Amber
Westbourne (née Fletcher-Ellis). She wonders what it must
have been like to continue the same course, presumably still
taught by Leo Ballard, with Emily missing, presumed dead.

'Can you tell me what you remember of the day Emily
disappeared?' she says. 'I know you must have been through
it countless times before but sometimes buried memories
do surface, years after the event.' This is a pet theory of
Judy's. Tanya is never sure about it but her words seem to
reassure the couple.

'It was Monday morning,' says Tom. 'We took down the
tents and put them in Mark's camper van. Leo drove Emily
to the station. Emad and I went in the van with Mark. He
drove us back to Cambridge. Neither of us went home for
Easter.'

'I left early,' says Amber. 'My parents live in Durham so I
had a long way to go. Leo took me to the station.'

Leo was apparently happy to be a taxi service that day, thinks Tanya. But only for the women students. She thinks of Alice Ballard saying, 'They all merge into one after a while.'

'What about Cathbad?' she asks. It still seems odd to think that he was there that day. She doesn't know Judy's partner that well but he's part of the scenery at Lynn station. It had been terrifying last year when he got ill.

'He didn't stay the night,' says Tom. 'I think he was a postman and needed to get up early.'

'How did Emily seem that morning?' asks Tanya.

'I didn't really talk to her,' says Tom. 'We were all busy packing up – well, Emad and I were – making sure the fire was out, that sort of thing. I last saw Emily sitting in Leo's car. I waved and she waved back.'

'Weren't you in a relationship with Emily?' says Tanya.

Tom answers without embarrassment. Tanya supposes he's used to answering this question. And Tom and Amber have been married fifteen years and have two children, their pictures scattered artfully around the room. Presumably any awkwardness and jealousy is long gone.

'We were in an on-off sexual relationship,' says Tom. 'It wasn't that serious. We were friends. We were all friends.'

'Tell me about the sleeping arrangements at the camp,' says Tanya.

Tom and Amber exchange a look. 'Emad and I shared one tent,' says Tom. 'Emily and Amber another. Leo had his own tent and Mark slept in the van. He had his dog with him. Leo insisted that men and women had separate quarters.'

'He said we had to remain pure,' says Amber, her voice flat. 'It was one of his things.'

'Sacred rituals,' says Tom breezily. 'You know.'

Tanya doesn't know but she very much wants to find out.

'It's like only virgins can find unicorns?' says Amber, her voice rising like a teenager's. 'Not that we were all virgins but Leo thought we had to remain pure to commune with the spirits at Grime's Graves. We went down into one of the mines. It was like an initiation ceremony, Leo said.'

'In what way?' asks Tanya.

'Well, we had to fast beforehand,' says Tom, once again sounding as if he wants to get this part of the story over with as quickly as possible. 'No wonder we were all so hungry at the barbecue.'

'It was frightening,' says Amber. 'You had to go down a rickety ladder. I bet it's all health and safety at Grime's Graves now but it certainly wasn't then. There was no light. We had a candle each and, one by one, we had to blow them out. Then we were in complete darkness. Leo said it was the only way to see into the spirit realm. To commune with the dead.'

Did Leo Ballard really want to commune with the spirit of his dead daughter? wonders Tanya. She wonders if the students even knew of her existence.

'And did you?' she says. 'Commune with the spirit realm?'

Amber laughs, rather to Tanya's surprise. 'We didn't when we were in the mine shaft. I think Emad said something funny and we all got the giggles. Leo was rather cross. But, on the last night, we did see something. We were all sitting round the fire. We were singing. Tom was playing the guitar.' She gives her husband an affectionate look under her fringe.

'I don't play any more,' he says, as if musicality is a sign of weakness.

'And then, suddenly,' says Amber, 'this creature burst out of the woods. This creature in a mask. It danced around us and then it disappeared. It was terrifying.'

'It was carrying a stick,' says Tom. 'I'll never forget it. And it pointed the stick straight at Emily.'

'Or at me,' says Amber. 'I was sitting next to her.'

'Have you got any idea who this person was?' says Tanya. She's not going to have any truck with the word 'creature'.

'No,' says Tom. 'Mark and Cathbad followed it into the woods. But it had vanished.'

'Mark's dog wouldn't go with them,' says Amber. 'He stayed with Em and me.'

'Probably because you were feeding it crusts,' says Tom. 'That animal was always hungry.'

'We were all terrified,' says Amber, 'but eventually we went to bed.'

Tanya notices that Emily has become 'Em'. Amber even sounds different, her voice less clipped, her vowels flattened with what might be the remains of a northern accent.

'When was the last time you saw Emily?' Tanya asks Amber.

'She was asleep when I left the tent,' says Amber. 'I still get upset now. Wishing I'd said a proper goodbye to her.' And, to Tanya's surprise, there are actual tears in her eyes.

CHAPTER 17

'Congratulations, Dr Abioye.' Ruth stands up to shake hands with the successful PhD candidate who, having been calm and self-possessed for forty minutes, now wipes her forehead and says, 'Shit. That was scary.'

'You did very well,' says Ruth. 'I always find those Palaeolithic rock shelters so intriguing.'

'Congratulations, Chioma,' says David. 'What about celebrating with a drink in the pub? We haven't got any more vivas today.'

'I'll join you in a minute,' says Ruth. 'Could I have a quick word, Jeanne?'

David and Chioma leave, the former very reluctantly, and Jeanne turns to Ruth with a pleasantly quizzical expression on her face. She's American, which always reminds Ruth of Frank, and the two share an admirable ability to cut through academic jargon with a few simple, but deadly, questions. Ruth has heard that Jeanne runs marathons, but she still likes her.

'It's about Leo Ballard,' says Ruth. 'I wondered if you knew him.'

'I know him a little,' says Jeanne, looking at Ruth rather intently. 'Why?'

'I contacted him recently,' says Ruth. 'I've been ringing around asking for support. You know they want to close the department?'

'Yes,' says Jeanne. 'I'm so sorry. And, of course, if I can do anything to help . . .'

'It would be great if you could write a letter to the dean,' says Ruth. 'I think they've made their mind up but if we get lots of support from prominent academics, who knows?' She thinks she does know but doesn't want to sound defeatist.

'Of course I'll write,' says Jeanne. 'And don't give up yet. You've got a lot of fans in the archaeology world.'

Ruth doesn't know how to respond to this. Pop stars have fans; academics mostly have critics. She decides to get back to the investigation.

'I met Leo at Grime's Graves yesterday,' she says.

'Did you?' says Jeanne. 'I know that's his area of interest, though, of course, he's retired now.'

Ruth abandons subterfuge. The case will be all over the papers soon anyway.

'Have you heard about the Emily Pickering case?'

'The girl who disappeared? That was before my time but I've heard about it. They never found her, did they?'

'They've found her now,' says Ruth. 'It's confidential at the moment but I excavated what police think are Emily's remains. They're reopening the case. I know Leo was interviewed the first time. He was her tutor.'

'As I say,' Jeanne repeats, 'it was before my time but I've heard rumours about Leo.'

'What sort of rumours?'

'Affairs with his students. Sadly not uncommon twenty years ago. I like to think things are better now.'

'So do I,' says Ruth. She wouldn't bet on it, though. 'Is that why Leo left the college?' she asks.

'I think so. He had tenure but I think they leant on him to leave. You really need to ask someone from Jude's. You taught there, didn't you?'

'Yes, but I don't want to get too involved. The police will investigate. I just wanted to ask you . . . what you thought of him, I suppose.'

'I'll just say this,' says Jeanne, her accent sounding very clipped. 'When I heard the rumours, I believed them.'

'Thank you,' says Ruth. 'That's very interesting.'

'Shall we join the others in the pub?' says Jeanne. 'Is it the White Hart?'

'Yes,' says Ruth. 'Do you know the way? I'll join you in a minute.'

When the door shuts behind Jeanne, Ruth clicks on the email headed, 'Test results on Red Mount Street bones.'

She reads quickly. '. . . pathological lesions . . . anterior . . . posterior . . . arachnoid depression . . . preservation . . . radial head . . .' until she gets to the end, 'forensic analysis of the fabric fragments shows the presence of animal hair and a substantial amount of chalk dust.'

Ruth thinks of returning from Grime's Graves yesterday

and Prisha telling her, 'You've got white stuff on your trousers.'

Mark Oldbury has asked Bradley to meet him in the museum.

'It's near the university and there's an office I can use there.'

Bradley isn't a fan of museums although he remembers being taken to London as a child and seeing a dinosaur skeleton that had impressed him. He's pleased to see a Tyrannosaurus Rex suspended from the ceiling at Manchester Museum.

'It's a reproduction,' Mark tells him. 'We call him Stan after the man who discovered him. It was in America. South Dakota, I think.'

An American dinosaur, thinks Bradley. Even cooler. Mark has a slight accent but Bradley can't place it. He asks and Mark says he's 'an Aussie'. 'I went to Cambridge on a scholarship and never went back.'

Mark's 'office' is really just a cupboard next to the archaeology collection. There's no window and only enough room for a table and two chairs. Mark leaves the door slightly open, propped ajar by what looks like a mummified cat. Bradley doesn't raise any objection because he doesn't want to suffocate. Besides, the museum is almost deserted.

'As you know,' says Bradley. 'I wanted to talk to you about Emily Pickering. As I said on the phone, we've found what appear to be her remains.'

'Poor Emily,' says Mark. 'Poor little girl.' He's nearly fifty (Bradley checked the files) but still looks boyish, below average height and slim with light, almost colourless, hair. His eyes are very pale blue and he doesn't blink much. Bradley finds him slightly creepy and 'little girl' doesn't help.

'Can you tell us about the last time you saw Emily?' he says. 'We're asking everyone,' he adds, as Mark is looking rather panicky. There's sweat on his upper lip but, then, it is rather humid in the cupboard.

'It was at the end of the Grime's Graves dig,' says Mark. 'Such a magical time. On the last night we had a barbecue and sat round a camp fire. Cathbad had a thing about fires.'

'How was the mood in the camp?' asks Bradley.

'Happy. We'd had a few good days. You know these pampered kids; they're not used to roughing it. There are always complaints at first. The ground's too hard, there's no hot water and they have to pee behind a bush. They don't come prepared at all. One girl even brought her curling tongs. But, by the end of the weekend, they'd all settled down. There was a celebratory feeling that last night. One of the students played the guitar. We were all singing. There was one strange thing, though.'

'Yes?' prompts Bradley, as Mark seems to have gone off into a trance.

'While we were singing, this figure appeared. It just emerged out of the wood, wearing a mask. And, this sounds crazy I know, but it seemed to have horns.'

'Horns?' Oldbury is right: it does sound crazy.

'That could just have been my memory playing tricks on me. Anyway, I do remember that it danced around us waving a stick. We were all terrified. Cathbad and I chased after it, but it got away.'

'Who do you think it was?' says Bradley. He notes the use of 'it'.

'I've thought about it over the years and I've sometimes wondered if it was one of Leo's students. Leo was always going on about Grim, the masked one. Maybe someone thought it was funny to dress up as him.'

'Do you have anyone in mind?'

'Not really. Leo always got close to his tutees. I should know, I was one of them. There was a lot of jealousy. Maybe one of his ex-students decided to break up the party.'

Bradley taps a note into his phone, *Check other LB students.* 'Did anything else happen that night?' he asks.

He doesn't really expect anything – after all, one mysterious masked figure is enough for any camping trip – but Mark says, after only a slight hesitation, 'Yes.'

'Really? What?'

'I had to get up at night to let Odin, my dog, out for a pee. The fire was almost burnt out but I saw two people sitting beside it. They were kissing.'

'Who were they?'

'Leo and Emily,' says Mark.

Tanya interviews Emad Hussein in his office. Looking out over the London skyline, framed by floor-to-ceiling windows, she notes that Emad is another one who has done very well since leaving St Jude's. He's an accountant, a partner in his own company.

'How does an archaeologist become an accountant?' she asks.

'Anyone can become an accountant,' says Emad, with a grin. 'I applied for a graduate trainee scheme after university and got in. I remember being told that my excavation skills would be useful. They weren't wrong.'

Unlike Tom and Amber, Emad is still recognisable from his college photos. He's tall with dark hair that once flopped over his face but is now cut very short. His beaky nose and lopsided smile are the same, though. He says that it was 'tough' continuing to study with Leo after Emily's disappearance but he never thought the tutor had anything to do with it. 'He was devastated. We all were.'

Emad describes the camp fire and the masked figure emerging from the woods. 'I didn't chase after it,' he says. 'I was too scared. Failed the macho test. Not for the first time.'

'Did anything else happen that night?' says Tanya. 'You were sharing a tent with Thomas, weren't you?'

'Yes,' says Emad. 'Part of Leo's "stay pure so you can see the visions" strategy.' His voice is dry.

'Well, you did see visions,' says Tanya. 'Apparently.'

'Believe me,' says Emad. 'That was a distinctly human apparition. That's why I was so scared.'

This is interesting, after Tom and Amber's talk of a 'creature'.

'Did you have any idea who it was?' says Tanya.

'No,' says Emad. 'But I had a feeling that the figure was female.'

CHAPTER 18

Friday 18 June

'Female?' says Nelson, as if he has never heard the word before.

'Yes,' says Tanya, with what sounds like exaggerated patience. 'Emad Hussein thought the figure was female.'

'How could he tell? Wasn't it masked and wearing a cloak?'

'Women move in a different way,' says Tanya.

'Do they?' says Nelson. He is dimly aware that he is in dangerous territory. If only he hadn't left the course on 'how to avoid gender stereotyping' at lunchtime. 'This masked figure is very odd. It's not in any of the police reports.'

'Tom and Amber both said they mentioned it,' says Tanya. 'Maybe it wasn't thought to be important.'

'Cathbad said he mentioned it too. Of course, he thought it was old Grim Garden himself.'

'The god Grim,' says Tanya. 'I thought there was something odd about the way Leo talked about him. The hooded one, he called him.'

'There was something about Grimsby too,' says Bradley. 'I didn't follow it all but it was definitely weird. Mark Oldbury said the figure had horns too. No one else mentioned that detail.'

'Horns,' says Nelson. 'Jesus wept.'

'Oldbury thought it might have been one of Leo's ex-students,' says Bradley. 'I've asked the college for a list of all his personal tutees.'

'Good work,' says Nelson. 'By all accounts, Leo's got form for getting too involved with his students.'

'He kept going on about what a special relationship it was,' says Tanya.

'Mark was an ex-student too,' says Bradley. 'I thought he was a bit odd.'

'In what way?' says Tanya. Judy would have asked this too and Bradley colours, as if he knows he sounded unprofessional. But instincts are important, as Nelson could have told him if he hadn't wanted to avoid one of *those* looks from Tanya.

'He didn't blink much,' says Bradley. 'And he called Emily a "little girl". I mean, she was twenty.'

Bradley says this as if it's a great age but, then, he's only in his early thirties. To Nelson, twenty is still almost a child. Katie will be twenty in eight years. But Bradley's right, 'little girl' sounds distinctly creepy.

'Is Oldbury married?' asks Nelson.

'No,' says Bradley. 'And doesn't seem to be in a relationship. He said it was just him and his dog.'

Nelson is about to park this in his mental 'suspicious' file when he realises that it describes his own living arrangements exactly.

'Not the same dog that he had twenty years ago?' he says.

'No, this one's a rescue greyhound, apparently.'

'And what about Leo and Emily kissing that night?' says Nelson. 'Did anyone else mention that?'

'No,' says Tanya, 'and Amber shared a tent with Emily. You would have thought she'd have heard her leaving.'

'Did Oldbury mention it in his original statement?' says Nelson.

'I asked him,' says Bradley, 'and he said he didn't. Said he didn't want to upset Emily's parents. Maybe he didn't want to upset Ballard either. After all, he was his boss.'

'What about the last morning?' says Nelson. 'Do the accounts differ?'

'Not really,' says Tanya. 'Amber left early. Leo took her to the station and then came back for Emily.'

'Why not take them together?'

'He had a two-seater car, apparently.'

'Of course he did.'

'Amber had to catch an early train,' says Tanya. 'Tom said the rest of them packed up and Leo took Emily to the station at about eleven. Tom and Emad went back to Cambridge in Mark's van.'

'Mark said that he got up early to walk the dog,' says Bradley, 'and when he got back Amber had gone. He saw Emily in Leo's car but didn't say goodbye. Later he took the boys back to college.'

'How did Mark get on with the male students?' asks Nelson. 'Did he say anything about them?'

'He liked Emad,' says Bradley, 'but thought Tom was a bit stuck-up. Oldbury seems to have a thing about pampered students.'

'Shame he's a university lecturer then,' says Nelson. 'I've had something interesting from Ruth.' He still feels slightly self-conscious when he says her name. He opens a file on his computer and, with Leah's help, projects it onto the screen.

'The report on the Red Mount Street bones – Emily's bones – says that the fabric used to wrap the body contains traces of dog hair and chalk dust.'

'Dog hair?' says Bradley. 'Mark Oldbury's dog?'

'Possibly. I don't know if it's possible to disinter the animal and find out. Besides, there might be an innocent explanation.'

'That's true,' says Tanya. 'Amber said that Odin, the dog, sometimes slept in the tent with her and Emily.'

'The chalk dust is more interesting,' says Nelson. 'Ruth thinks it might have come from Grime's Graves. She's going to run some tests.'

'So Emily's body could have been kept at Grime's Graves?' says Tanya. 'In one of the mine shafts? Before it was walled up in the café?'

'It's possible,' says Nelson. 'Ruth says it would fit with the preservation of the bones.'

'That still points to Leo then,' says Bradley. 'He was the one who knew the site best.'

'Mark knew it too,' says Nelson. And so did Cathbad, he adds silently. 'We need to talk to Leo Ballard again,' he adds. 'And Emily's sister Sophie. Remember what Leo said about looking to the sister?'

'Wasn't he just playing games?' says Tanya.

'Possibly,' says Nelson. 'But we can't afford to leave any stone unturned.'

It's an unfortunate phrase, in the circumstances.

Tony had stretched the truth when talking to his parents. He doesn't live in a one-bedroom flat but in a one-*room* apartment. Most of the time this doesn't bother him. It's a pleasant enough space, with a kitchenette at one end and a sofa bed at the other. There's a tiny bathroom just big enough for a triangular shower and a loo. But there are two sash windows and, if you crane your neck, a nice view towards Cow Tower and the river.

Tony has always liked the bedsit but that was before he had to spend twenty-four hours a day in there. The first day wasn't too bad. He set up a workstation on the folding table by the window. Then he drew up a list – DCI Nelson style – of the principal characters in the case. He went through the original files, still in a pre-digital folder, and watched the CCTV footage of Emily in Ely on the day she disappeared. He printed out the picture of Emily, Tom, Cathbad and Freya and stuck it on the wall. By the end of the day he had the case running on a loop through his head.

Emily Pickering was a second-year archaeology student at St Jude's College, Cambridge.

Emily's parents, Gordon and Naomi, suspected her tutor, Leo Ballard.

Emily's remains were found behind a wall.

They said they'd come from an underground land.

Some of the stories are quite horrible . . .

He let them sit there for ages over one cup of coffee.

It's no wonder that he has some very strange dreams.

The next day it's far harder to get to work. Tony checks his emails and goes through the files again. He finds some pictures of the Green Child café in 2002. Then, remembering Freya and Folklore Fridays, he googles 'Fairy Cow'. He finds the legend on a fascinating site called Weird Norfolk. The cow was evidently a benevolent creature who appeared in a village called South Lopham when there was a drought and offered her milk to the villagers. When the drought ended, she stamped her hoof on a slab of sandstone, leaving a cloven print, which apparently survives to this day, and disappearing for ever. There is a less wholesome story, though, which involves a farmer mistreating the animal until she kicked the stone, leaving her mark. Pity she didn't kick the farmer, thinks Tony. He looks at his watch. Only an hour has passed.

Tony makes himself a coffee and allows himself ten minutes of online chatting with his WhatsApp group of uni friends 'Norfolk n' good.' Despite the name, most of them have moved away from the area and Tony misses them. After a brisk exchange of gifs, he goes back to his notes. He has the body-cam footage of Tanya and Bradley's interviews with Tom, Amber, Emad and Mark.

In his scrawling handwriting (really, he should have been the doctor) he writes:

Tom: in love with Emily. Married Amber. Gave up archaeology.

Amber: in love with Tom in 2002? Married him 10 yrs later. Jealous of Emily?

Emad: says he 'failed the macho test'. Says masked figure was female. Who?

Mark: resented 'pampered students'. Saw Leo and Emily kissing. Not corroborated. Why would he make this up?

Leo: inappropriate relationships with students. Wanted students to 'remain pure'. Last person to see Emily alive.

He thinks for a moment and then adds:

Freya: fascinated by Emily and friends but felt patronised by them. Sick of hearing about Ballard.

Peter: interested in legends and 'earth magic'. Built wall in café.

He stares at the list, forcing himself not to look up or check his phone. He's so deep in concentration that he jumps when the doorbell rings. Should he go downstairs to answer it? He's meant to be isolating after all. But the thirst for companionship is too strong. Tony goes to the window and looks down. He can see the top of a man's head. Grey hair in a ponytail.

Cathbad.

After Tanya and Bradley have left his office, Nelson opens his diary and sees the words, *Appraisal meeting with Jo 10.30.*

Leah has underlined it and written *Don't cancel again!* in the margin. Nelson looks at his watch. Ten fifteen. Time to call on Leo Ballard. He'll phone Leah from his hands-free on the way.

Nelson doesn't tell Ballard that he's coming. He wants to catch the man unawares. Even so, he's slightly shocked to find Ballard apparently wearing pyjamas at midday.

'They're lounging trousers,' says Ballard, when Nelson can't help mentioning the fact. Nelson mentally adds 'lounging trousers' to the list of things that he will one day make illegal. It joins wheelie suitcases, pumpkin-flavoured coffee and people who tell him to have a nice day.

Ballard leads him into a room that looks like it belongs to a mad librarian. Nelson is now used to Ruth's house, where books seem to appear on every surface, but this is something else. There are musty volumes everywhere and the smell makes Nelson want to sneeze. The floorboards are dusty and cobwebs sprout in every corner. Michelle would have a fit.

Ballard offers Nelson a cup of coffee which he refuses. He's not going to drink anything prepared in this house.

'Apologies for calling unexpectedly,' he says, 'but there are a few things I'd like to check with you.'

Ballard doesn't appear to be concerned by the visit. Like the Pickerings, he actually seems impressed by the presence of such a senior police officer.

'A DCI,' he says. 'I'm honoured.'

Nelson smiles thinly. 'We've been interviewing everyone who saw Emily on that last weekend,' he says. 'And a few anomalies have arisen.'

'Anomalies,' repeats Ballard as if it's a new one on him. But, if he's read half the books in the room, he must know every word ever invented.

'Anomalies.' Nelson ploughs on. 'All the students, and Mark Oldbury, talked about a mysterious masked figure appearing on the last night. I wondered why this didn't feature in your original statement and why you didn't mention it to DS Fuller.'

'It didn't seem relevant,' says Ballard. But he seems less relaxed now. His leg starts to jiggle and he stops it with an obvious effort.

'Why not?'

'It was obviously a prank. A student prank.'

'Do you have a particular student in mind?'

'No,' says Ballard. A lie detector would be exploding by now, thinks Nelson. He waits before asking, 'Why would a student play a prank like that?'

'Everyone knows about my interest in Grime's Graves. I've given lectures on Grim, the hooded one. I imagine that someone thought it was funny to dress up as him.'

'And was it funny?'

'Not really. Emotions were very high. We'd experienced great things that weekend, been on the edge of mystical discoveries. It didn't take much to tip those feelings into hysteria.'

'Who was hysterical?'

'Emily, for one. She was visibly shaking.'

'Is that why you comforted her in the middle of the night?'

The jiggling and fidgeting has stopped. Leo Ballard sits absolutely still. 'What do you mean?'

'One witness says that they saw you and Emily kissing that night, when everyone else was in bed.'

'Who told you that?'

'Just answer the question, please. Did you and Emily have an assignation that night?'

'Assignation. You do like these long words, DCI Nelson.'

Nelson can think of several words to describe Ballard, none of them long.

'Just answer the question.'

'No,' says Ballard. 'I went to bed and slept like the dead.'

The word seems to hang in the dusty air. Nelson lets it hover before saying, 'Did you ever meet Emily's sister, Sophie?'

To his surprise, Ballard laughs. 'So, you've been talking to Ruth Galloway. She's a fascinating woman, isn't she?'

'Answer the question, Professor Ballard.'

'I met her once, I think. Bright girl. Like Emily.'

'Did you kill Emily, Professor Ballard?'

'Now then, DCI Nelson.' Ballard sounds like a kindly teacher remonstrating with a pupil. 'You know I didn't.'

To make completely sure of missing Jo, Nelson drops in on Cambridge CID on his way home. He finds DI Dave Clough in his office, finishing what looks like a three-course McDonald's.

'What happened to the healthy eating?'

'I think there was a tomato in there somewhere.'

'How's things?' says Nelson, sitting in the visitors' chair and helping himself to a French fry.

'Not too bad,' says Clough. 'Are you watching the Euros tonight? England v Scotland?'

Nelson had almost forgotten that the European Football Championship is on, which shows how distracted he's been. The competition has been delayed for a year because of Covid and is still, confusingly, called Euro 2020.

'Probably,' he says. 'Just me and Bruno.'

'One man and his dog,' says Clough. He doesn't ask about Ruth and Nelson is grateful for this. He'd like to go round to Ruth's later but, in the light of their last conversation, doesn't want to push things. Also, she'd never agree to watching the football.

'I've just been to see Leo Ballard,' says Nelson. 'You know, the professor involved in the Emily Pickering case.'

'Oh yes. The last person to see her alive. Do you like him for it?'

'I don't like him at all. He's a creepy bastard. But is he a murderer? I'm not sure.'

'What are you doing interviewing suspects? Haven't you got a DS for that?'

'I had an appraisal with Jo.'

Clough laughs. 'Still winding Super Jo up, I see.' He sounds slightly disapproving. Clough always got on well with Jo but, then, he never reported to her directly.

'She keeps talking to me about retirement.'

Now Clough looks shocked. 'You can't retire, boss. I can't imagine the force without you.'

Nelson can't suppress a smile at the involuntary 'boss'. He says, 'I wasn't just avoiding Jo. We're seriously short-staffed on this case. I can't use Judy because of the Cathbad connection and Tony's isolating at home because of some bloody app.'

'That NHS app will be the death of me,' says Clough. 'I've got two officers cooling their heels at home as we speak.'

'That's a shame,' says Nelson, 'because I was going to ask you if you had anyone we could borrow.'

Clough uses his last chip to mop up tomato sauce. 'There is someone I can let you have,' he says. 'A very keen young DC. Lucy, her name is. She seems interested in the case and it would be good experience for her.'

Nelson had been hoping for an experienced detective, not someone still learning the ropes, but he knows he can't look a gift cop in the mouth. 'Send her over tomorrow,' he says. 'She can report to Tanya.'

'Heaven help her,' says Clough.

Back in his car, Nelson checks his messages. Several from Leah but, unexpectedly, three from Judy. He rings her back immediately.

'It's probably nothing,' says Judy. But she doesn't sound like it's nothing. Her voice is high and strained. 'But I'm worried about Cathbad. He didn't turn up to collect the children from school.'

CHAPTER 19

Nelson drives straight to Judy and Cathbad's house. As he parks the car, he sees Katie walking towards him. She looks so carefree, swinging her school bag, socks rolled down and jumper knotted round her waist, that Nelson spends a few minutes just watching her. He doesn't consider himself the sort of person who reminisces about schooldays but he suddenly remembers the smell of grass on the field, the siren call of the ice cream van, dawdling on the way home with his friends, hoping to see girls from the neighbouring grammar school. He doesn't want to disturb Katie's happy self-absorption with the news that her godfather is missing.

But Katie has recognised the car. She approaches the open window. 'Dad! What are you doing here?'

Nelson gets out and gives his daughter a kiss. 'Hallo, love. Just popped in to talk to Judy.'

'OK,' says Katie vaguely. Then, with more animation, 'I got ten out of ten in a maths test today.'

'That's my girl,' says Nelson. He'd been good at maths at

school and is still quicker than Ruth at mental arithmetic, something that never fails to give him quiet satisfaction.

Judy opens the front door. Thing is at her side, smiling his wide bull terrier grin. Nelson can hear Michael playing the piano. The boy sounds like a virtuoso to him and Judy recently confided that he'd passed his last grade with distinction. Cathbad doesn't approve of competitive music exams.

'Hi, Nelson. Hi, Kate. There are flapjacks in the kitchen if you want some. Miranda's in there.'

Katie disappears in search of nourishment and Judy's smile slides off her face.

'He's left his phone here,' she says.

'You know Cathbad,' says Nelson. 'He never has his phone. Thinks it sends out poisonous rays or some such crap.'

'He usually takes it when he collects the kids,' says Judy. 'And he's never late for them. Miranda was crying.'

'Did he say what he was doing today?'

'Just that he was going to take Thing for a walk and try to do some yoga. He wants to start his classes again.'

'And he didn't leave a note? Some ancient runes?'

Judy ignores this. 'I've checked,' she says, 'and there are no RTAs.'

Nelson feels chastened. If Judy is checking road traffic accidents, she must be seriously concerned.

'I'll put out a misper report,' he says. 'I'll classify it as high risk.'

This is a concession. Adult missing persons are not usually considered high risk at first. According to the files, Emily

Pickering's disappearance wasn't considered a priority until she had been missing for almost a week.

'Thank you. I'm really worried. Cathbad's still not back to his old self. After Covid and . . .'

She pauses. 'And?' prompts Nelson.

'And he's really upset about this Emily Pickering case,' says Judy, the words coming out in a rush. 'He hasn't said much but I can tell. He's been odd recently.'

Nelson is about to dismiss this – Cathbad has always been odd – but then he thinks of the walk on the beach, Cathbad saying that there wasn't much time left. 'In what way?' he asks.

'He made us go to mass last Sunday. Said he wanted to pray for Emily.'

Praying for the dead is something Nelson's mother would do. It doesn't sound wildly out of character for Cathbad, though. He says so.

'I don't know,' says Judy. 'Finding Emily's remains seems to have shaken Cathbad somehow. I think he was really fond of her and this has brought it all back.'

Nelson wonders how to put the next question. Cathbad said he was going to tell Judy that he had sex with Emily. Has he done so? Judy rescues him.

'Cathbad told me about Emily. About sleeping with her that time. He still feels bad about it. One-night stands are not really Cathbad's thing. He's a romantic.'

'Maybe they were Emily's thing?'

'Maybe but that seems such a misogynistic way of thinking. Blame the girl. Paint her as a femme fatale. She was only twenty. Cathbad was in his thirties. Ballard even older, if Ballard did have a relationship with her. And, you know, when I look at pictures of Emily, I don't see femme fatale. I see an innocent young girl with her whole life ahead of her.'

Nelson thinks of Cathbad saying: *I can see her now, walking towards me.* He says, 'When I saw her picture for the first time, I thought she looked like you.'

'Really?' says Judy. 'I can't see that at all.'

'I suppose you weren't much older than Emily when I first met you.'

'I feel a hundred now,' says Judy although, to Nelson, she looks the same. She's in her mid-forties, he thinks, but her face is still smooth and her hair untouched by grey. Nelson is mostly grey now and even Ruth has several streaks which, typically, she doesn't bother to dye.

'I think Cathbad was quite lost when he knew Emily,' says Judy. 'He'd split up with Delilah and was living in a commune and working as a postman. Emily and co must have seemed like a surrogate family.'

'Do you think his disappearance is linked to the case somehow? Could he be off on some crazy trail of his own?'

'That's exactly what I think,' says Judy.

Tanya leaves a message for Sophie Strachan, née Pickering, and the doctor calls her when she comes off shift. Tanya apologises for disturbing her.

'That's OK,' says Sophie. 'I thought you might get in contact. What with the case being reopened and everything.'

'The case' sounds rather cold. After all, they are talking about the death of Sophie's sister. The funeral is set for Tuesday next week.

'As I'm sure your parents have told you,' says Tanya, 'we're talking to everyone who was with Emily that last weekend.'

'Did you talk to Leo Ballard?'

'Yes,' says Tanya. She assumes that Sophie, like her parents, still suspects the lecturer.

But she's wrong.

'He didn't do it, you know,' says Sophie, her voice suddenly sounding much younger. 'Mum and Dad were obsessed. It was part of the reason why I had to get away. But Leo didn't do it. He loved Emily. And she loved him.'

So did you, thinks Tanya.

Ruth is surprised to find Cathbad's front door opened by Nelson. He explains, in his best police officer voice, that Cathbad is missing.

'He's left his phone here. We've checked and there are no accident reports. Let's hope he's just wandering around somewhere in some strange druid trance.'

'Oh my God! Judy must be so worried.'

'She is. I've been trying to tell her that he's probably just gone walkabout.'

Is this a racist term? Ruth suspects it might be. 'If he was going on a walk,' she says, 'he would have taken Thing.'

She can see the dog at the foot of the stairs. Is it her imagination, or does he look slightly worried?

'Let's all keep calm,' says Nelson.

He's obviously worried too.

Judy is in the kitchen, trying to keep up a jolly conversation with Miranda about sports day. Michael and Kate are watching her silently. Kate gives Ruth a hug, which is unusual in company.

'Stay for supper,' Judy says to Ruth.

'Do you want me to?' Judy's a reserved person but once before, on an occasion like this, she had seemed to welcome Ruth's company.

'Yes please.'

'I'll go back to the station,' says Nelson. 'Get this misper thing moving.'

'OK,' says Judy. 'Thanks, boss.'

When Nelson has left, Judy and Ruth look at each other. The children are in the garden with Thing and, suddenly, the house feels very empty.

'Cathbad will be OK,' says Ruth. 'He's like a cat with nine lives.'

As she says this, she thinks of Flint. He'll be desperate for his supper by now. Perhaps Zoe will feed him.

'He's used up a good few of them,' says Judy. She has taken some fresh pasta out of the fridge and is looking at it rather helplessly.

'He'll turn up soon,' says Ruth. 'He'll come in through that door talking about the summer solstice and spiritual energy.'

They both jump when the door is blown open by a sudden breeze. The wind chimes sing and the dog barks but Cathbad does not appear.

CHAPTER 20

Saturday 19 June

When Nelson arrives for work the next day, he sees a girl – a young woman, he corrects himself – waiting in the lobby.

'DCI Nelson?'

'Yes,' he says, rather warily. She looks harmless enough – dark hair in a ponytail, blue shirt and jeans – but she could easily be a reporter.

'I'm DC Lucy Vanstone. From Cambridge CID.'

'Oh yes.' Nelson tries to rearrange his face into a welcoming smile. 'Good to have you on board. Come upstairs and meet the team.' What's left of them, he thinks.

Tanya is already at her desk, frowning at her computer. Nelson introduces her to Lucy. 'You'll report to DS Fuller on this case. You can learn a lot from her.'

'I'm sure I will,' says Lucy earnestly. Tanya looks slightly friendlier.

'We'll have a briefing at nine,' says Nelson. 'There have been a few developments.'

He had fully expected to wake up to a message from Judy to say that Cathbad had turned up at midnight, fully refreshed from walking the pilgrims' way to Walsingham or some such nonsense. But, instead, his alarm call had been Bruno breathing meat fumes in his face. When Michelle was in residence, Bruno wasn't allowed in the bedrooms, but Nelson has let things slip. Nelson got up and checked his phone. Nothing from Judy. He took Bruno for a quick walk round the block and couldn't resist texting her. 'Nothing' is her answer to his question.

Tanya, Bradley and Lucy gather in Nelson's office for the briefing. Tony, thanks to Leah's IT skills, joins them via Zoom link.

'This is Tony,' Nelson says to Lucy. 'We keep him in a box.'

'Hi, Lucy.' Tony tries to project extreme friendliness from the confines of the screen.

Nelson tells the team about his interview with Leo Ballard. 'His manner is very odd but I'm still not sure he is our killer. He has an alibi for the day Emily disappeared, for one thing. We're still trying to trace the car he had in 2001. Forensics might be able to find something. Of course, we know Emily was in the car, so her DNA might well be there, but traces of blood, for example, would prove foul play.'

'I talked to Emily's sister, Sophie,' says Tanya. 'She seemed convinced that Ballard was innocent. It sounded like she once had feelings for him. Maybe she still does.'

'Could that be what Ballard meant by "look to the sister"?' says Nelson.

'Possibly,' says Tanya. 'At any rate, it caused a rift with her parents. Sophie says she hasn't spoken to them for years, although she's coming down to Lincoln for the funeral next week.'

'We need to have a presence there too,' says Nelson. 'Out of respect, if nothing else.'

'What about the café where Emily's bones were found?' says Lucy. 'Was her DNA found anywhere there?'

Nelson looks at the newcomer. It's a good question and shows that Lucy is up to date with the case. He wonders why he also feels a twinge of unease.

'We were able to extract DNA from the bones,' he says. 'Dr Ruth Galloway was the forensic archaeologist involved and she's a real expert.'

'I know she is,' says Lucy.

Nelson frowns slightly at the interruption. 'But we didn't get anything useful from the rest of the building. I think it's been altered and rebuilt so much that the site is hopelessly compromised. The man who owned the café in 2002 is dead now but he knew Emily and he must be a suspect for her murder. Tony's doing some research into the family.' There's a noise of agreement from the laptop.

Nelson takes a deep breath. 'I also need to tell you that Michael Malone, also known as Cathbad, was reported missing last night. Because of his connection to the case, this is now a priority.'

Tanya and Bradley both look shocked, but Lucy is staring at the computer screen. Nelson follows her gaze and sees that Tony is gesticulating but seems to have muted himself.

'Turn your mike on,' growls Nelson.

'Sorry.' Tony's excited voice fills the room. 'I saw him. I saw him yesterday. Cathbad.'

'When did you see him?' asks Nelson.

'About eleven in the morning. He just turned up at my flat.'

'What did he want?' says Nelson. This must be significant. Cathbad had said nothing to Judy about paying morning calls.

'He asked to see the CCTV footage of Emily in Ely. On the day she disappeared.'

'And did you show it to him?'

'Yes,' says Tony. 'I thought, because he knew her . . .' His voice dies away.

'Then what happened?' says Nelson.

'He thanked me and left. I thought he seemed a bit distracted.'

'And you didn't think it was worth reporting back?'

'I was going to tell you this morning. I didn't think it was urgent.'

'You were wrong,' says Nelson. 'We need to see this footage again.'

Like Nelson, Ruth hadn't been able to resist texting Judy first thing in the morning and had received the same response. *Nothing.* Nothing will come of nothing, as Ruth remembers Shona quoting once.

Ruth lies on her bed watching the clouds scudding across the sky. She had promised herself a Saturday lie-in but now can't get back to sleep. Flint pads noiselessly into the room and then gives a sudden unearthly yowl, a trick that never fails to galvanise his humans. Ruth gets up, puts on her dressing gown and goes down to feed him.

After making herself a coffee, Ruth sits at the table by the window. It's her favourite place. She never tires of watching the marshes, the grasses turning from grey to green in the morning light, the birds wheeling into the sky, the distant shimmer of the sea. Can she bear to leave it? She knows that the cottage isn't in the ideal location for Kate, especially as she gets older. Ruth can't spend her life taxiing teenage Kate into the bright lights of King's Lynn. But, when Kate and Ruth had briefly lived in the centre of Cambridge, they had both pined for the Saltmarsh.

If Ruth becomes dean, they could probably afford something bigger, a cottage in Wells perhaps. But does she want the job? She hasn't given Colin an answer but knows she will have to soon. It's a promotion, which is always agreeable, but Ruth suspects she'll be mostly dealing with admin and therefore further away from her real passion: teaching. She could leave UNN and get a job elsewhere. The word 'Blackpool' sounds in her head, like an instruction from a satnav. *Turn around where possible.* If Nelson took a civilian job in his home town, maybe she could work at Preston or Lancaster University. Or she could leave academia altogether and concentrate on writing. She dismisses this idea immediately. Writing would give her too much time alone with her thoughts and, besides, she'd need to quadruple her book sales to provide anything like a living wage. She has never really considered the possibility that, if they were living together, she and Nelson would share their money. For twelve years, her first priority has been to provide for herself and Kate. She's not going to stop now. She doesn't want to.

And then there's the smaller problem of the weekend. Tomorrow, Sunday, is Father's Day. Nelson's grown-up daughters, Laura and Rebecca, are taking him to lunch at the Fig Tree, a smart restaurant outside King's Lynn. Nelson had asked if Ruth and Kate wanted to come too. Ruth asked if he'd squared this with his daughters and Nelson admitted he hadn't. So, Ruth had declined. She doesn't think the time is right for such a show of togetherness. Will it ever be right? Besides, Ruth should really spend the day with her own father in London. But it's hard to think of anything when Cathbad is still missing. Ruth looks out over the glittering, cursed landscape. Cathbad knows all the secret paths, the crossing places. Has he gone somewhere where they can't follow him?

When Kate comes downstairs at ten, Ruth is still by the window, on her third cup, laptop open in front of her.

'What are we going to do today?' asks Kate, in her new world-weary voice.

'I thought we might go to see a church,' says Ruth.

Kate mimes total despair and boredom. Flint, who is as usual overflowing onto the keyboard, looks up with interest.

'St Mary's, Houghton-on-the-Hill,' says Ruth. 'I went there with Cathbad once. He was fascinated by the place.'

Kate cottons on immediately. Her spine, which had become liquid and forced her to collapse onto the sofa, straightens.

'Do you think Cathbad might be there?'

'It's worth a try.'

Nelson, Tanya, Bradley and Lucy gather round the laptop. Nelson notices that Lucy gets a black notebook out. Nelson sees Tanya noticing it too and producing her own, much grander, log book.

The screen fills with grainy CCTV footage. There is Emily's familiar bouncy hair, her St Jude's sweatshirt with the words 'Em Hockey' on the back. She walks away from Ely station with a determined stride. Seconds later a camera outside a church shows her crossing the road towards Jubilee Gardens. The last shot shows her looking in the window of Topping's bookshop.

'Pity there's so little footage,' says Nelson. 'There would be many more cameras now. What can Cathbad have seen to make him go rogue?'

'The bookshop?' Tony's face appears again. 'Topping's is great. It's like they've got every book in the world.'

'Bully for them,' says Nelson, thinking of Leo Ballard's study. 'Why would a bookshop make Cathbad go off like that? Did he suddenly remember that he'd forgotten to spend his Christmas book token?'

'Of course, we don't know that this CCTV has anything to do with Cathbad's disappearance,' says Tanya.

Nelson reins himself back from full sarcasm mode. 'That's true enough,' he says, 'but Cathbad obviously went to Tony's with the sole intention of viewing it. Judy must have told him Tony was isolating at home. And, after Cathbad watched the video, he left and hasn't been seen since.'

'I've put a description out to all units,' says Tanya. Nelson can just imagine how this would read: *Long hair, purple cloak, liable to talk about the Great Web.* Where the hell is the troublesome druid? After nearly killing them all with worry last year, he's at it again. When they find him, Nelson will roast him on his own personal sacrificial bonfire.

'Good work,' says Nelson. 'I'm going to ask Judy if she knows what all this Ely stuff means. Bradley, you carry on trying to trace Ballard's car. Tanya, start organising house-to-house. Lucy, you help her.'

'Yes, boss,' says Lucy. 'DCI Nelson, I mean.'

'Boss is fine. Do you call Cloughie boss?'

'Yes,' says Lucy. 'He says it reminds him of a mafia film.'

'He would. Now let's get on. I don't want anyone else disappearing.'

Tony can't help feeling rather responsible. He didn't immediately tell Nelson about Cathbad's visit, partly because he didn't think it was that important and partly because he knew that he should have been isolating. But, when he'd seen Cathbad at the door, he hadn't been able to resist the chance for a chat. Cathbad has been to China and usually loves the chance to talk to Tony about the country and its customs (to be honest, Cathbad knows rather more about these than Tony). But, yesterday, Cathbad had seemed rather subdued. Tony told him about the pinging so Cathbad kept his mask on but his eyes above it looked troubled. He'd watched the video footage carefully, thanked Tony and left. Tony hadn't asked him where he was going and he hadn't watched him leave. Some detective you are, he tells himself.

To make amends, Tony starts work early and doesn't take a social media break. His focus today is the Webster family. He writes their names down, having read somewhere that handwriting (as opposed to typing) stimulates brain and memory.

Peter Webster – died 2010.

Arabella Webster – in a home, dementia.

Freya Webster – lives in London, married, no children.

Gaia Webster – sister.

Tony looks at this last name for a few seconds and then goes to his first port of call, Facebook. There's no Gaia Webster but, after scrolling through a few names, he finds a Gaia Fernandez, who is about the right age. Tony looks at the picture of the striking woman with the Brunhilda hairstyle. Then he clicks on her 'about' info.

Studied at St Jude's College, Cambridge.

CHAPTER 21

It's very strange, sitting in Cathbad's kitchen without its resident druid, chef and house husband. Judy doesn't fill it in the same way. Both she and Thing keep looking towards the door as if they hope Cathbad will miraculously appear. Nelson tries to stop himself doing it too but it's hard.

Michael and Miranda are out at piano and ballet lessons. 'I thought we should try to carry on as normal,' says Judy. Thing looks at her sadly.

Nelson tells Judy about Cathbad's visit to Tony. 'Can you think of any reason why Cathbad would react to the CCTV footage? Has he got any special connection to Ely?'

'Only St Etheldreda's hand,' says Judy, with a slight smile.

'What?' says Nelson. Although he should be used to this sort of thing by now. Wherever Cathbad is, weirdness follows.

'The left hand of St Etheldreda,' says Judy. 'It's in a church in Ely. You press a button and the box lights up. Cathbad likes to visit it sometimes.'

'Cathbad likes to visit a disembodied hand?'

'Yes,' says Judy serenely. 'Ruth says the provenance is quite good. There's a good chance it really is her hand. During the Reformation it was hidden in a priest's hole in Sussex. Then it was presented to St Etheldreda's Church in Ely.'

There are many things Nelson could say but he contents himself with, 'Is there any chance that Cathbad could be at this church today? Shall I get Cloughie to send someone round?'

'It's worth a try,' says Judy. 'I thought I might drive to Walsingham too. Maybe he decided to go on a pilgrimage? The only thing is . . .' her face crumbles, 'why wouldn't he tell me?'

Nelson makes patting gestures without making contact. 'Steady on, Judy. We'll find him. We've got police from two counties looking for him. No accidents have been reported. I think maybe he could have lost his memory. That can happen with Long Covid.'

'Can it?' says Judy, brightening slightly.

'Yes,' says Nelson, though the information only appeared on a slightly dodgy website called 'Covid Conspiracies', discovered by Nelson in the early hours of last night.

'Cathbad likes Ely,' says Judy. 'The cathedral and the river. I just can't think why he'd go there without telling me.'

'What about the bookshop?' says Nelson. 'Top something? Tanya mentioned it. The video shows Emily looking through the window.'

'Topping's?' says Judy. 'Yes, Cathbad loves it there. It's his idea of heaven.'

'I'll get someone to call in there too,' says Nelson. 'You never know, they might remember Emily from nineteen years ago. People who work in those sorts of places live for ever.'

'Books are good for your body and your soul,' says Judy. 'That's what Cathbad always says.'

At that moment, Thing sits up, head on one side. He whines softly. Nelson and Judy look at each other. Then there's the sound of a key turning in a lock. They both spring to their feet.

'Judy?' calls a female voice.

'Maddie.' Judy sits back down. 'In here,' she says.

Maddie Henderson is Cathbad's adult daughter by a previous partner, Delilah. Maddie lived with Cathbad and Judy during lockdown but now shares a flat in Lynn with her boyfriend, Finn, a Cathbad-lookalike with long black hair and a wispy beard. His occupation, according to Cathbad, who said it approvingly, is 'travelling lute player'.

Maddie goes over to hug Judy. 'Any news?'

'No. I would have told you if there was.'

'I called Mum,' says Maddie. 'But she hasn't seen him.'

'Where's Delilah living now?' asks Nelson.

'Still in Blackburn,' says Maddie, with a flash of her startlingly green eyes. Delilah is a tricky subject for them. Maddie was only twelve when her little sister, Scarlet, went missing and was later found dead. She has always blamed the police for not saving her and for initially suspecting Delilah and her husband, Alan.

'And she hasn't heard from Cathbad?'

'No. Not since he sent her a card for the winter solstice.'

Only Cathbad would know where to buy a card like that.

'It's the summer solstice on Monday,' says Judy. 'I keep wondering if that's somehow significant.'

'It could be,' says Maddie. 'Maybe Cathbad's on his way to Stonehenge or somewhere like that.' She always calls her father by his name, or rather his alias. Alan is 'Dad'.

The trouble is, thinks Nelson, there are just too many places for a lunatic druid to hide.

'I'd better be off,' he says. 'Don't worry. We'll find him.'

'Thanks, Nelson,' says Judy.

Maddie is silent.

In the car, Nelson sees that he has a missed call from Tony. He presses 'hands free'.

'I think I've got something.' The DS's excited voice echoes round the car.

'Gaia Webster,' Nelson tells Tanya, Bradley and Lucy, 'studied archaeology at St Jude's College. Her tutor was Leo Ballard.'

'Look to the sister,' says Tanya. 'I wonder if that's what Ballard meant.'

'It's possible,' says Nelson. 'I want you to interview her, Tanya. She lives in Ely.'

This place name causes a murmur in the room and an excited noise from Tony on the screen.

'Tony,' says Nelson, 'tell the others about the photo.'

'I was looking again at the photo of Emily, Tom and Cathbad in the café,' says Tony, waving the photocopy in front of his face although it's too small for any of them to see. 'I wasn't sure who the figure in the background was. Freya said it was her but now I'm not so sure. Gaia still wears her hair like that, with plaits wound round her head. And Freya has a prominent mole on her cheek. I've zoomed in and can't see it on the woman in the picture.'

'Why would Freya say it was her?' says Tanya.

'I don't know,' says Tony. 'But she was evasive about Gaia. She said she'd left home but didn't say she went to university or who she studied with. In fact, Gaia had already graduated in 2002. She works in a museum now. I'm not sure I believe that Freya and Gaia lost touch either.'

'You need to talk to Freya again, Tony,' says Nelson. 'Ring her up. Do it at the same time Tanya talks to the sister, so they can't confer.'

'I've got some news too,' says Bradley, who has clearly been holding this announcement in. 'I've made a breakthrough on Ballard's car.'

'Good work,' says Nelson. 'Did you find it?'

Bradley looks at his phone. 'Ballard drove a Triumph Spitfire 1500. In April 2002 he put it into a classic car auction. It was bought by a man called Steve Elsing, who still has it. I spoke to him this morning. He's a collector but it doesn't sound like he drives his cars much. He's agreed to let us have it for forensic tests.'

'Better and better,' says Nelson. 'If it hasn't been driven much since 2002, we might be able to get some evidence from it.'

'A bit suspicious that Ballard got rid of his car a month after Emily vanished?' says Tanya.

'Very suspicious,' says Nelson. 'I'm surprised that the police didn't seize it at the time. It was a sloppy investigation, as far as I can see. Of course, they didn't realise it was a murder enquiry at first. It was never classified as such. Is there anything else?'

'We got something from the house-to-house,' says Tanya. She nods at Lucy to continue. The new DS hasn't spoken yet, although she has been taking copious notes in her black book.

Now Lucy clears her throat. 'We spoke to a Mrs Anne Bunting in Unthank Road, round the corner from Tony. She says that a man knocked on her door, about midday on Friday, and asked to use her phone. I showed her Michael Malone's – Cathbad's – picture and she made a positive identification.'

'Why did he want to use her phone?' says Bradley.

'He'd left his mobile at home,' says Nelson. 'Typical. Did this Mrs Bunting let him use her landline?'

'She did,' says Lucy. 'She said she thought he had an honest face.'

Nelson snorts but he knows what the woman means. Cathbad can radiate integrity when he wants to. It's very annoying.

He says, 'Did she hear any of the conversation?'

'At first she said she didn't,' says Lucy, 'but, when I pressed a bit, she said that she heard him say something about a gate.'

'A gate?'

'That's what she said. She said he sounded agitated and he said, 'it was by the gate'. Or something like that.'

'By the gate?' repeats Nelson. 'Why must that man always talk in riddles? But this is good. We know where he was at midday on Friday, at least. And we can check the caller ID records on this woman's phone. I'll get the tech boys onto it. You keep on with the house-to-house, Lucy. See if anyone else spotted a wandering druid.'

Every time Nelson calls Lucy by her first name, she blushes. He hopes she gets over this habit soon.

'What do you want me to do?' asks Bradley.

'I've got a disembodied hand for you to visit,' says Nelson.

CHAPTER 22

Ruth tries to make an adventure of it. She packs sandwiches and promises Kate a picnic. She parks the car by the verge and they walk up the rutted track to the church.

'Peddars Way, it's called,' she tells Kate. 'That means someone who travels around selling things. It's where we get the word peddler.'

'I've never heard that word,' says Kate. She's still inclined to be grumpy. Ruth hopes that the beauty of the day, the sky bright blue, the cow parsley foaming in the hedgerows, will work its magic. She's not holding her breath, though.

'It was probably a Roman road once,' she says, almost to herself. The path is quite steep now. Who says there are no hills in Norfolk?

The church appears through the trees. It looks solid and respectable, a typical parish church. Yet Ruth remembers Cathbad telling her that, when it was discovered in 1992 by a man called Bob Davey, the building was simply a mound covered in ivy, windowless and roofless. Even now, it's not a consecrated place of worship. The villagers that once

attended services are all dead and their cottages have disappeared, their bricks taken for farm buildings. St Mary's
was brought back to life by Bob and is sustained by a group
of volunteers. According to Cathbad, the Church of England
doesn't contribute.

Ruth doesn't expect that the door will be open, but the
handle turns easily and she and Kate are inside, blinking in
the sap-scented gloom.

'What's that on the walls?' says Kate. Her voice is full of
awe and Ruth is pleased that the church is having the same
effect on her daughter that it did on her.

'Paintings,' she says. 'They're over a thousand years old.
Can you see the angels?'

'The people with wings,' says Kate patiently. 'Yes, Mum.
And there's God and all the gang.' She went through a
brief religious phase at primary school, which had slightly
unsettled Ruth, but now refers to God as if he were a rather
boring uncle.

'The Holy Trinity,' says Ruth. The paintings, once brightly
coloured, have faded to a tasteful pink. Ruth would love to
do some carbon-14 tests on the pigment. 'It's unusual to see
Jesus without a beard,' she says. 'And that's the Last Judge-
ment. You can see the people going to heaven on the left
and the ones going to hell on the right.'

'That's a bit harsh,' says Kate.

You don't know the half of it, thinks Ruth. Her parents
had once believed utterly in the Saved and the Damned,
sheep and goats. Ruth, an unmarried mother, was firmly in
the latter category. It had been a shock to realise, after Ruth's

mother's death, that their stories weren't that dissimilar. Ruth's father has softened his stance since his marriage to Gloria. They are both still devout Christians, though.

'What's going on there?' says Kate, who is looking at the left-hand wall.

'That's the wheel of fortune,' says a voice from the doorway.

Mother and daughter wheel round and Ruth knows that they are both expecting Cathbad, even though the voice isn't like his. It's deeper with a trace of a Norfolk accent.

A small man with a beard is addressing them. 'Who controls the wheel of fate?' he says. 'One minute we are raised up, the next we are in the depths. "The wheel is come full circle, I am here."' His tone changes slightly. 'If that does show the wheel of fortune, it's the oldest depiction in Britain.'

Ruth can just make out what could be the outline of a wheel. A bearded man wearing what looks like a red beret appears to grasp the spokes.

'The red paint is interesting,' she says. 'It's very early to have vermilion.'

'It came all the way from China,' says the man. '*Before* Marco Polo went there.'

There's no way of challenging this statement. Ruth introduces herself and asks if the man knows Cathbad. Somehow, she thinks he will.

Sure enough. 'Of course,' says the man. 'Cathbad volunteers here sometimes. He's a good soul, even though he's a pagan. You know, we once had to defend this church from

Satanists? Cathbad's not one of their number. He's a godly man.'

'Have you seen him recently?' asks Ruth. The talk of Satan and godliness is reminding her unpleasantly of childhood services in the Nissen hut where her parents got to grips with their faith.

'Someone thought they saw him last night,' says the man. 'A cloaked figure. Maybe it's the ghost of the Carthusian monk who haunts this place.' He grins through his bushy beard.

Ruth has had enough. She gives the man her card. 'If you see him, can you call me? It's very important.'

'Dr Ruth Galloway,' the man reads her name aloud.

'Thank you. Now, if you'll excuse us, we're off to have a picnic.'

Judy is also on the Cathbad trail. She has parked at the Slipper Chapel and is preparing to walk to Walsingham. She is following the ancient route, when the pilgrims would leave their shoes at the chapel – hence the name – and walk the last mile, the so-called Holy Mile, to Walsingham. Judy doesn't know why but it suddenly seems very important to follow the pilgrimage path. It's what Cathbad would do and has done many times. She remembers him saying that he lit a candle at the Slipper Chapel to give thanks for his recovery from Covid. Is it possible that he made the journey here again?

Judy would have liked to have come on her own but, as soon as she mentioned going out, both children, not to mention Maddie and Thing, made it clear that they wanted to accompany her. So Judy's solitary expedition has become a family excursion. She might as well have brought sandwiches.

Judy has told the children that Cathbad has gone on 'a long walk', wishing that it didn't sound so much like a euphemism. But they both, especially Michael, know that something is wrong. Cathbad's non-appearance at the school gate, the visits from Uncle Nelson, the behaviour of their mother and their dog – they know that this isn't one of Cathbad's regular 'spiritual cleansing treks'. This is probably why they are now sticking so closely to their mother.

The Slipper Chapel is a strange building, somehow too grand for its size, like a miniature cathedral that has found itself by the side of a Norfolk lane. Judy knows that it's a fairly new restoration. The original chapel fell into disuse after the Reformation and was even used as a cowshed for a time. She remembers visiting the shrine with her school and finding it a slightly unsettling place, blazing with candles lit for supplicants' intentions. The prayer cards were pinned to the wall. 'For the souls of my grandparents'. 'For Susan, may she find peace'. 'Please God, help me pass my exams.' So much hope. So much faith.

They don't go inside the church this time. Michael and Miranda run ahead with Thing. Judy and Maddie follow more slowly.

'Do you think Cathbad believes in any of this stuff?' asks Maddie. 'Save our souls. Heaven and hell. Purgatory and limbo.'

'Well, he was brought up as a Catholic,' says Judy. 'I was too but all that stuff about limbo and purgatory was old-fashioned by then. It might have been different for Cathbad, growing up in Ireland.'

'What's the deal with purgatory again?'

They are walking between fields of yellowing wheat, the sky a bright hard blue above. The primary colours make Judy's head ache. It's like a child's painting.

'I can't remember exactly but I think, when you die, you go to purgatory to atone for your sins. People on earth can pray for you and get you time off your sentence. Then you go to heaven.'

'What about limbo?'

'It's a kind of in-between place, I think. People used to think babies went there if they died before being baptised.'

'I thought we all went to heaven when we died?'

'That's more or less what everyone believes now. I mean, how unfair to send a baby to a sort of waiting room.'

'I'm not baptised,' says Maddie. 'I sometimes wonder what my life would have been like if I'd been brought up by Cathbad instead of Delilah and Alan.'

'It might have had more sacred bonfires in it,' says Judy.

'Oh, Mum was keen on that sort of stuff too,' says Maddie. 'I suppose that's why they got together in the first place. But I'm glad they broke up. Otherwise Dad wouldn't have met you.'

Maybe it's the sweetness of the sentiment, or the fact that Maddie called Cathbad 'Dad', but Judy finds herself in tears.

She wipes them away and continues to walk between the yellow and the blue.

Tanya drives to Ely and drops Bradley outside St Etheldreda's Church.

'Have fun,' she says.

'Happy to lend a hand,' says Bradley. Tanya smiles but she hopes that Bradley isn't about to start making puns. It was one of Clough's more tedious habits.

'I'll pick you up after I've seen Gaia,' she says.

Gaia Fernandez, nee Webster, lives in a terraced house within sight of Ely Cathedral. Following Nelson's instructions, Tanya doesn't phone her until she is parked outside the front door. Luckily Gaia is in. She sounds surprised but says she'll be happy to talk. Tanya then texts Tony to give him the go-ahead to ring Freya.

Gaia is a tall woman with the kind of grey hair that fair-haired people describe as 'ash blonde'. It's coiled around her head in a style that Tanya considers unsuitable for a middle-aged woman. She's also wearing a floaty dress but, in spite of this, sounds quite rational.

'What's all this about, Detective Sergeant Fuller?'

She's got Tanya's name and rank right too.

'You're aware that human remains were found inside a building once owned by your family?'

'Yes,' says Gaia. 'Freya told me. How horrible.'

So, the sisters are in touch. Tanya is glad that they prevented Freya from warning Gaia about her visit. They are sitting in a small but immaculate sitting room: velvet sofa and carefully mismatched chairs, a bookcase that probably hides a TV, a few spotlit ornaments. No family photos on display and no sign of refreshments either.

'Are you also aware that they have been identified as being the last remains of Emily Pickering, who went missing in 2002?'

'Yes.' Gaia is sitting very still but there's nothing restful about her posture. Her clasped hands are white at the knuckles.

'You knew Emily, didn't you?'

'No. Not personally.'

Tanya gets out the photocopy of Freya's photograph. She offers it to Gaia.

'Is that you in the picture?'

'I'm not sure.'

'It looks like you.' And it's true that Gaia hasn't aged much, apart from the hair. She would have been twenty-four in the picture, according to the date of birth on her Facebook page.

'Maybe it is.'

'So you knew Emily well enough to pose for a picture with her.'

'I'm not posing. I was probably just working in the café. Dad always got me and Freya to help out. Cheaper than getting proper waiting staff. Mum was never interested.'

'You studied archaeology at Cambridge, didn't you?'

'Yes.'

'And Leo Ballard was your tutor?'

'I'm sure you already know the answer to these questions, Detective Sergeant.'

'For the tape,' says Tanya, pointing to her body cam. She has always wanted to say this.

'Yes. Leo was my personal tutor.'

'So you had that in common with Emily. And with Tom Westbourne?' She points at the photo where Tom is gazing admiringly at Emily. Or is he looking at Gaia?

'I didn't have anything in common with Emily,' says Gaia. 'She was like all the rest of Leo's students. A middle-class girl playing at being an archaeologist. I was working class, state educated. Neither of my parents went to university. My dad was an auto-didact.'

That sounds faintly perverted, but Tanya isn't going to interrupt the flow to ask what it means. It's interesting that Gaia obviously still feels resentful towards Emily and her fellow students. 'So, you had a special relationship with Leo Ballard?' suggests Tanya.

'Yes, I did,' says Gaia. 'Very special.'

'A sexual relationship?'

For a moment she thinks that Gaia is going to refuse to answer but, in the end, she simply says, 'Yes.'

'Even though he was married?' Tanya thinks of Alice Ballard, who is probably only a few hundred metres away, working at the Little Lives charity shop.

'It was a marriage only in name,' says Gaia. 'Alice was a bit strange, to tell you the truth. Leo was quite worried about her.'

I bet he was, thinks Tanya.

'Were you still seeing Leo in 2002?' she asks.

'Yes,' says Gaia. 'Our relationship continued until I moved to London in 2003. Then I met Gino.'

According to Facebook, Gaia married Gino Fernandez in 2005. They have one daughter, Inez.

'So you were seeing Leo when Emily disappeared?'

'Yes. He was very upset about it. Especially when the family accused him of all those awful things.'

Tanya assumes the police weren't aware of this relationship at the time, otherwise they would have interviewed Gaia. But, then again, the original investigating team didn't know about the link with the Green Child café.

'Was Emily also in a relationship with Leo?' she asks.

Gaia's eyes flash. This, combined with the hair, makes her look like a soprano about to let rip with an operatic aria.

'She had a crush on him. Amber too. They all did. But Leo wasn't interested in those posh girls playing at archaeology.'

Tanya isn't so sure about this. She decides to try another line of questioning.

'Was your father friendly with Emily?' she asks.

'Oh, come on now.' Gaia sounds really angry now. 'You can't try and pin it on Dad. Just because he can't defend himself.'

'I'm not trying to pin anything on anyone,' says Tanya. 'We're just trying to find out how Emily ended up buried behind a wall in your father's café.'

'Dad wouldn't hurt a fly,' says Gaia. 'He was a gentle soul. Pure. Almost childlike.'

Somehow it doesn't sound as innocent as Gaia intends.

'Hallo, Freya,' says Tony. 'How are you?'

'OK.' Freya sounds wary. Nelson might say that Tony

has built up a rapport with her but it's hard to do on the phone. He tells Freya about the pinging and the isolating. This seems to ease things. Covid is, of course, something everyone has in common.

'Oh no. That probably happened when you were in London. Our Covid numbers are still very high.'

'Probably,' says Tony. 'I shouldn't complain, though. I've got Netflix and a fridge full of food.'

'Sounds like heaven,' says Freya.

'I've been looking at the picture you gave me,' says Tony. 'The one of Emily and Tom in the café. The thing is, I don't think the girl in it is you.'

There's a pause.

'You've got a mole on your cheek,' says Tony. 'The girl in the picture doesn't.'

'Someone once told me that it was the mole of destiny,' says Freya.

'Was that someone Cathbad?' asks Tony, taking a risk.

'I think so.'

'It's not you in the photo, is it? Is it your sister? Gaia?'

Another pause.

'It could be. We look very alike.'

'Did Gaia know Emily well?'

'Not really. Gaia was older. She'd graduated from university when that picture was taken.'

'Gaia studied at St Jude's, didn't she?'

'Yes.'

'Why didn't you tell me?'

'I didn't think it was relevant. You were asking about me.'

Something in the way she says it makes Tony think that Freya is used to being overlooked in favour of Gaia.

'It's tough being the youngest,' he says. 'My parents are always going on about Mike, my brother. He's the clever one.'

He can almost hear Freya relaxing. 'Tell me about it. All my parents ever talked about what how clever Gaia was. How she got a scholarship to Cambridge. How her tutor thought she was *so* clever . . .' Her voice peters out.

'Was that tutor Leo Ballard?'

A longer pause. 'Yes.'

'No wonder you said you were sick of hearing his name.'

'Gaia never stopped talking about him,' says Freya. 'All his weird views on women and sacrifices and sacred rituals. He sounded like a nutter to me.'

'Did you ever meet him?'

'Once. At Gaia's graduation. I couldn't think what she saw in him. He looked like a scarecrow.'

'Did your dad know Leo Ballard?'

At the mention of her father, Freya's voice tightens again. 'I think he just met him that one time.'

'And your mum?'

'She didn't like him. She told me so.'

It's a pity, thinks Tony, that Mrs Webster is no longer able to tell anyone anything.

The priest, Father Tony, flicks a switch and a square in the wall is illuminated. Bradley goes closer. There's a glass box within the space, like a large test tube topped by a crown. Within it is a mummified hand.

'Is that it?' says Bradley.

'That's it,' says Father Tony. 'St Etheldreda was a Saxon queen and the founder of a monastery. Her shrine at the cathedral used to be a major pilgrimage site.'

'So why isn't the hand there now?'

'The Reformation,' says the priest. He doesn't offer any more information and Bradley doesn't like to ask. He dropped history for PE in Year 9. 'A good choice,' Tanya once told him.

'Her hand was found in a recusant house in 1811,' says Father Tony. 'People who continued to be Catholic when it was against the law,' he explains, seeing Bradley's blank face. 'Norfolk, and East Anglia generally, was very loyal to Catholicism.'

This is news to Bradley.

'Anyway, the hand was brought here. So there's a good chance that it really was hers.'

'Do many visitors come to see it?' asks Bradley. It seems an odd way to spend time but people are strange. Any police officer knows that.

'A few,' says Father Tony. 'But its existence is not that widely known.'

'What about this man?' Bradley produces a picture of Cathbad. 'Have you seen him?'

It's a fairly normal snap, no cloak or druid stuff. Not very recognisable really. But, to Bradley's surprise, the priest smiles. 'Cathbad? Yes. I know him well. He often pops in to say hallo to St Etheldreda.'

To bits of her, anyway.

'Have you seen him recently? In the last few days?'

'No. Sadly not. We've had barely any visitors since Covid.'

There's a joke here about hand sanitising but Bradley can't be bothered to make it.

Ruth and Kate have their picnic in the field opposite the church. Ruth finds some thin Roman bricks half-buried in the soil.

'I think there must have been a Roman building here once,' she says. 'I saw some of these bricks in the walls of St Mary's.'

'Mmm,' says Kate, not listening. She's lying on her stomach looking at her phone. A skylark sings, somewhere high above.

Ruth is suddenly aware of another, less tuneful, sound.

'Mum, your phone's buzzing.'

Ruth locates her mobile underneath her backpack. Nelson.

'Where are you?' asks Nelson. 'I called before but you didn't answer.'

'I'm fine, thanks,' says Ruth.

'Are you at home?'

'No, Kate and I are having a picnic.'

'A *picnic*?' says Nelson, as if this is an outlandish, and probably dangerous, custom.

'We went to see a church near Swaffham,' says Ruth. 'I visited it with Cathbad once.'

Like Kate, Nelson catches on quickly. 'And you thought he might be there?'

'I thought it was worth a try.'

'No sign of him, I take it?'

'A man we met, a custodian, said that a cloaked figure was seen last night. He thought it was probably just the ghost of a monk.'

'Jesus wept. Do you think it could have been Cathbad? Though, hang on, Judy said he wasn't wearing his cloak.'

'It's worth investigating, I suppose. Have you got any other leads?'

'Just one from the house-to-house. Cathbad went into a house to make a phone call and said something about a gate.'

'A gate?' Ruth looks at the sagging five-bar gate in front of her as if it can give her an answer.

'That's all we have. Oh, and Judy said something about a disembodied hand in Ely.'

Ruth laughs. 'St Etheldreda. I've been to visit her with Cathbad.'

'Figures,' says Nelson. 'I've sent young Brad round to the church, just in case. At this rate, we'll have coppers at every church in Norfolk and Cambridgeshire. And there are a lot of them.'

'One for every day of the year in Norfolk,' says Ruth, quoting an old saying.

'If you say so,' says Nelson. His voice changes slightly. 'Have you thought any more about tomorrow? Father's Day? About coming to the lunch? I shouldn't really take any time off but I can't disappoint the girls.'

Ruth notes, as she has before, that 'the girls' means Laura and Rebecca, not Kate.

'I don't think we should be there,' she says. 'It's too soon. Anyway, I'll probably drive to London to see my dad.'

'OK,' says Nelson. 'Maybe I can see you and Katie later?'

'Maybe,' says Ruth, deliberately noncommittal. After Nelson has rung off, she lies on her back in the long grass, looking up at the sky.

CHAPTER 23

Walsingham is surprisingly crowded. It's as if Covid and social distancing had never happened. There are people sitting outside the pubs and wandering up and down the high street, even though most of the shops only sell religious souvenirs or priests' vestments. Miranda wants an ice cream so Judy ventures into the Blue Lady Café where religious tomes jostle with cupcakes in the window. She buys them all cones and they walk to the gateway that leads to the abbey grounds.

Nothing much remains of the original building but Judy thinks that the giant archway, standing on its own, connecting earth and sky, is more impressive than any cathedral she's ever seen. The children and Thing run on ahead and Judy shouts after them to keep Thing on the lead. People tend to be odd around bull terriers.

Judy shows Maddie the small metal plaque in the ground that marks the place where the original Holy House once stood.

'I think it was built in the eleven hundreds. Ruth would

know. A woman called Richeldis had a vision telling her to build a church here.'

'I remember Cathbad telling me that he saw a vision here too.'

'Well, he thought he did. He was cat-sitting for a friend in a house by the church and he saw a woman in the grave-yard. She was wearing a blue cloak and he thought she was the Virgin Mary.'

'And was she?'

'Who knows? But I'm inclined to think she was a woman who got murdered that same night. The team investigated the case but I was on maternity leave with Miranda.'

Another body had been found almost exactly where they are standing, Judy remembers, but she decides not to say this.

'Do you think he might have come here?' says Maddie. 'Cathbad?'

Judy's glad she's no longer calling him 'Dad'. She doesn't think her emotions could stand it. That morning she had thought that Cathbad might be in Walsingham, following some trail of his own, perhaps hoping to see another vision. But now she knows that he's not here, amongst these day trippers, these coachloads from parish churches around England. But she has no idea where he can be. Cathbad says that they have a psychic connection, but it doesn't seem to be working very well at the moment.

'At least Thing's had a good walk,' says Maddie.

*

On the drive home from Houghton-on-the-Hill Kate gets a message from Isla inviting her to a sleepover that night. Ruth is reluctant. They have to set off early in the morning if they are going to London. Plus, she will have to drive all the way home for Kate's stuff and then back to Wells. But Kate wants to go, and Ruth can see that it would be more fun than sitting at home watching Ruth worrying about Cathbad. And she's always keen to foster Kate's school friendships. So they drive to the Saltmarsh, put together an overnight bag, and navigate the Saturday traffic back along the coast road.

Ruth's route home takes her past Cathbad's cottage and, on impulse, she stops and knocks on the door. No answer, not even Thing barking. Maybe this means that Cathbad has been found? But something about the silent house makes Ruth think that this isn't the case. She waves at a neighbour who is watching anxiously behind her net curtains and walks back to the car.

Back home, she feeds Flint and tries to get on with some marking. But it's hard to concentrate when the department might not even exist this time next week. Maybe she should update her CV, send it to a few recruitment sites. But the list of long-forgotten O- and A-levels makes her more depressed than ever. She adds her latest book and notes that the publication date was 2017. She should really write another book if she wants a professorship somewhere. The trouble is that she has used up King Arthur, the ghost fields and stone circles. She needs another iconic subject and about six months' uninterrupted writing time.

She's distracted by her phone buzzing its way across the table. Unknown caller. Normally Ruth wouldn't answer but she immediately thinks it's something to do with Kate. She doesn't have a number for Isla or her mother. Should she ask for Isla's number next time or would that be too weird?

'Hallo?'

'Hallo, Ruth. It's Jeanne. Jeanne Hanisko.'

'Oh. Hallo.' This is a surprise. Ruth and Jeanne are not really on telephone chatting terms, although they did have an interesting conversation about Anglo-Saxon burial sites in the White Hart after the PhD viva.

'I heard that Cathbad is missing,' says Jeanne. 'Is it true?'

'Yes. I'm afraid so. Do you know him then?'

'A little. I've met him on a couple of digs. He is rather memorable.'

'He is.' And not just because of the cloak.

'Well, it gave me a bit of a shock because the last time I saw Cathbad it was with Leo Ballard. And I remembered that you were asking about Leo.'

'Yes, I was. When did you see Cathbad with Leo?'

'A few years ago. It was a leaving do for one of my colleagues, Emma Thane. Cathbad was there. I think he knew Emma from Manchester, where he'd been one of her graduate students. Anyway, I was talking to Cathbad. He's really fascinating, isn't he? We had such a good talk about Morris dancing. Then Leo came over. I think he was a bit drunk. And he was saying that he and Cathbad were great friends, they went back such a long way. Et cetera, et cetera.'

'Really?' This wasn't the impression given to Ruth by either Cathbad or Leo.

'Cathbad seemed a bit uncomfortable. He kept trying to edge away from Leo. But then Leo said something a bit strange. That's why I'm calling you today. He said something like, "You can't escape me, Cathbad. After all, you know where the bodies are buried."'

'Where the bodies are buried?'

'I mean, it's just a turn of phrase, but thinking about what you said about Leo . . . and now Cathbad going missing . . . I thought I ought to tell you.'

'Thank you,' says Ruth. 'I'll tell DCI Nelson. He's the detective in charge of the case.'

'David said that you're involved with the local police.'

'Not really.' Ruth can just imagine the tone in which David said this. 'I've advised them on a few cases, that's all. Buried bones. That sort of thing.'

'I envy you forensic people,' says Jeanne. 'No one ever asks me about ancient manuscripts.'

But manuscripts are probably considerably safer, thinks Ruth.

'I wrote to your chancellor protesting about the closure of your department,' says Jeanne. 'Any news on that?'

'Not really. The emergency meeting was well attended and David's planning a rally next week. I can't help thinking that the board have already made their minds up. But thank you for writing. That's really good of you.'

'No problem,' says Jeanne. 'We archaeologists must stick together.'

After Ruth has said goodbye to Jeanne, she rings Nelson. He answers immediately.

'Ruth? What is it?'

This time Ruth doesn't bother with any niceties. She passes on the news given to her by Jeanne.

'Where the bodies are buried? What the hell does that mean?'

'Well, as Jeanne said, it could just be a turn of phrase.' Ruth thinks of Zoe talking about skeletons in closets. These clichés are starting to take on a sinister meaning.

'Or it could mean that Cathbad knew where Emily was buried,' says Nelson.

'I can't believe that. If Cathbad knew, he would have told someone. He wouldn't have left her family to suffer like that.'

'He fainted dead away when I first mentioned the café.'

'Cathbad's not well. Surely, that's what's happened now. He's wandered off and lost his memory or something.'

'I wish to hell I knew what was happening. You're visiting churches, Judy's gone to Walsingham, I've sent young Bradley to look at a disembodied hand. And we're no nearer to finding bloody Cathbad.'

'I know,' says Ruth. 'I just keep hoping I'll get a call from Judy saying he's turned up.'

'Me too,' says Nelson. Ruth hears his voice changing gears. 'Shall I come over? I'm going mad here, just turning things over in my mind.'

Ruth looks out of the window as if she can see Nelson's car drawing up outside. She imagines them talking, drinking wine, climbing the uneven stairs to her bedroom. And then what?

'Better not,' she says. 'I've got an early start in the morning.'

CHAPTER 24

Sunday 20 June

It seems that half the world is driving to see their parents on Father's Day. Ruth finds herself in two traffic jams before she has even left Norfolk. There are more hold-ups on the A10 and M11. Ruth's iPhone keeps gloomily readjusting their ETA and it's nearly one o'clock by the time they park in front of the terraced house in Eltham.

Ruth had been hoping for some time alone with her father to bring up the subject of Zoe. Arthur had been flabbergasted to learn, last year, that his late wife had a secret daughter, whom she had given up for adoption. 'It can't be true,' he kept saying. Ruth, prevented from hugging him by the social distancing rules at the time, had leant forward and touched his arm. 'It was before you met Mum. She was really young at the time. I really think you'd like Zoe if you met her.' But Arthur has stubbornly resisted doing so even though Simon, Ruth's older brother, has also tried to engineer a meeting. Simon seems delighted by his new sister. Almost insultingly so, in Ruth's opinion.

Simon and his wife Cathy are having lunch with her parents but have promised (threatened?) to pop in later. Ruth had hoped for a walk with her father, maybe to visit her mum's grave, a pilgrimage that Arthur makes, with Gloria's blessing, most days. But she knows that Gloria always makes Sunday lunch for one o'clock on the dot. They will have to find time afterwards.

Social distancing rules are relaxed now but Ruth still doesn't want to take any risks with her dad, who is eighty-three and rather frail. They don't hug but exchange warm smiles. Kate hands over her handmade card. It says 'Happy Father's Day, Grandad' in bubble writing above a rather good drawing of a bespectacled man sitting in an armchair. Ruth doesn't know if Kate has made a card for Nelson.

'That's terrific, Kate, love. It'll have pride of place on the mantelpiece.'

Ruth presents a shop-bought card and a plant that looked a lot healthier when it was in the garden centre. Gloria hurries away to give it water, like a nurse in A&E rushing a patient to the theatre. Arthur puts both cards on the shelf above the electric fire.

Gloria's plans to redecorate the house were somewhat stymied by lockdown but the sitting room is freshly painted in light green and there's a new chintz sofa and armchairs. The small dining room is a rather startling yellow but it's definitely cheerier than the old wallpaper. Ruth and Kate sit at the table which is laid with a flowery tablecloth and decorated with a vase of dog roses. Arthur passes the plates from the hatch. It's a cosy domestic scene and, not for the first time, Ruth thanks the fates, or the goddess, for Gloria, who has rescued Arthur from an old age of Co-op meals for one. She has always liked Gloria, who is nine years younger than Arthur but seems almost the same age as Ruth. Simon took a lot longer to come round to the marriage but, during lockdown, he came to appreciate Gloria's presence. Now he, unlike Ruth, actually refers to her as his stepmother.

As usual, Gloria has cooked a traditional Sunday roast, rather indigestible on a hot day but nonetheless delicious. At least the door to the garden is open, in the hope of blowing away Covid germs. Arthur keeps his cardigan on and shivers theatrically. Ruth thinks of Judy and the children. How will they be spending Father's Day? She texted Judy that morning and, again, received the one-word answer. *Nothing.*

After lunch, Gloria asks Kate if she'd like to call on a neighbour whose cat has just had kittens. Kate agrees eagerly and Ruth appreciates Gloria's tact. She and Arthur sit in the garden, Arthur now wearing his coat although the afternoon is still warm.

'This is lovely,' says Ruth. 'It's Midsummer Day tomorrow.'

'There's no real warmth in the sun, though,' says Arthur.

Should Ruth be worrying that her father is always cold? Maybe it's just the innate pessimism of his nature. Simon has inherited this trait. Has she?

'My garden's looking lovely at the moment,' she says. 'You and Gloria should come and visit.'

'It's a long way,' says Arthur.

'Only two and a half hours on the motorway,' says Ruth. Although today it had taken more like four. 'I'd come and pick you up.'

Arthur says nothing but he raises his face to the sun in a way that seems half acquiescence. Ruth says, 'It's Zoe who does all the gardening. I really think you'd like her, Dad. She's very like Mum in some ways.'

'I'm sure she's very nice,' says Arthur in a slightly quavery voice. 'But I don't feel ready to meet her. Thank you,' he adds after a pause.

'That's OK,' says Ruth. 'When you do feel ready, just let me know.'

They sit in silence for a few minutes until Kate bursts in asking if Flint would like a kitten friend.

Nelson has his doubts about the Fig Tree from the outset. First, he's asked to sign in with the NHS app. Nelson has always distrusted anything that tracks his whereabouts and, after Tony's experience, he doesn't want to receive a message, days later, saying that he's been near some stranger with Covid. So he shows his warrant card instead. Then, when he sits down at the large, round table he discovers that the restaurant serves 'Small Plates'. 'We recommend two or three dishes each' says the menu bossily. Nelson likes to order his own food and eat it all himself. With this sharing nonsense, he's bound to take too much or be forced to eat something revolting like octopus or beetroot. He sits gloomily at the table, the first one to arrive, taking in the décor with a jaundiced eye: whitewashed walls adorned with old farm instruments, straw on the floor, tiny trees on each table. He's willing to bet that the food will come on wooden boards instead of plates.

He wishes Ruth was with him. She'd give him one of her quizzical looks as soon as she saw the menu. Why did Ruth refuse to come today? She said she thought it was too soon to spend Father's Day with his daughters. And she'd wanted to see her own dad. Nelson can understand that. But he doesn't know why Ruth stopped him coming over last night. They have got into the habit of spending Saturday nights together and Nelson had been looking forward to it, as much for the company as anything else. As it was, he'd spent a depressing evening watching *The Sopranos* with Bruno.

'Dad!' Rebecca is walking towards him. Nelson is glad that she's on her own. He actually likes Asif, her boyfriend, but he feels that the lunch will be easier without him.

'Laura's just parking,' says Rebecca. 'She picked me up at the station. How are you, Dad?' She stoops and gives him a kiss. Rebecca, dark-haired like Nelson, has always been the more exuberant daughter. She seems in a particularly good mood today, almost glowing with energy.

'All the better for seeing you, love.'

Laura, appearing a few minutes later, also looks well. Nelson often worries about his oldest daughter, who has had issues with anxiety and sometimes looks too thin. But she seems well today, her blonde hair in a shorter style that suits her, her eyes bright.

'Shall we order some wine?' says Rebecca, after looking at the menu for a few seconds.

'What about Champagne?' says Laura.

'Steady on,' says Nelson. He's determined to pay and, in any case, is not a fan of Champagne. If he's going to drink something fizzy, he'd rather have lager.

'We have to celebrate Father's Day,' says Laura. She's smiling at him but, suddenly, Nelson sees her smile grow wider and realises that it's no longer directed at him. He turns around.

And sees his wife and son making their way through the tables.

CHAPTER 25

Miranda and Michael have made Cathbad a card and the sight of it on the breakfast table brings hot, painful tears to Judy's eyes. She's angry, she realises. She's angry with Cathbad for disappearing, after nearly killing them all with his near-death experience last year. Why the hell can't he stay at home and be a normal druid?

'What shall we do with the card?' says Michael, his voice wavering in a way that makes Judy want to howl or punch someone, preferably her life partner.

'Put it on the mantelpiece,' she says. 'Dad will see it when he gets back.'

'I want Daddy,' says Miranda, one eye on Judy.

Thing whines.

'You'll see him soon,' says Judy. 'Do you want to go to the beach today? We could ask Maddie to come too.'

Miranda is obviously torn between wanting to see her beloved half-sister again and wanting to create a scene. Judy pours herself a coffee and tries to think of a diversionary tactic. That's what she was taught in the hostage negotiating course, years ago. 'Defuse the tension, find a point of agreement.'

'Let's go and see if the hens have laid.' It's the best she can do. The rescue hens, Shirley, Darcy and Motsi, were a huge source of interest – and eggs – during lockdown. But they are all used to them now, except for Thing, who always hopes the birds will want to play with him.

The children follow Judy out into the sunshine. The coop takes up a good third of the small garden. It's locked at night, for fear of nocturnal foxes, and, at this point in the morning, the sisters are usually clamouring for their breakfast. But today the run is empty. Judy can see the broody shapes in the rafters of the hen house, but they don't respond to her chirrups and calls. She checks the nesting boxes. Empty.

Obviously, the hens are missing Cathbad too.

Bradley is feeling heroic. The boss has gone out for lunch, even Tanya is visiting her parents. It's just him and the new girl, Lucy, in the office, carrying on with their work. To be fair, Father's Day does not really feature in Bradley's calendar. He hasn't seen his male parent since he was sixteen and doesn't consider him a loss. He always sends his mother a card on Father's Day and, on Mother's Day, conspires with his brother and sister to spoil her rotten, although it's difficult to spoil someone who says, 'I've got everything I need' – this despite clear evidence to the contrary.

Bradley has had a satisfying morning. He has arranged for Ballard's old Triumph Spitfire to be towed to the forensics lab and has succeeded in expediting the results. He's been through the list of Ballard's ex-students and traced as many as possible. He's still a bit irritated that Tony got to Gaia Webster before him.

Lucy is still going through the house-to-house reports. Bradley can hear her computer mouse clicking but, at least, unlike Tony, she's not humming or whistling.

Bradley tries for some chit-chat. 'Looks like we're the only ones keeping the place going.'

Lucy looks up. She has very blue eyes and would be pretty with a bit of make-up, thinks Bradley. 'Well, it is Sunday,' she says. 'And Father's Day.'

'Not seeing your dad then?'

'He lives in Devon. I'll FaceTime him later.'

When he was five, Bradley's mother told him that their cat had gone to Devon when she meant heaven. He's distrusted the place ever since.

'Is that where you're from? Devon?'

'Not originally,' says Lucy. She smiles again, perhaps to make up for the lack of detail.

Bradley tries again. 'I'm Norfolk born and bred. Judy too. Not the boss, of course. He's from Blackpool. Always banging on about the place.'

'Norfolk's an interesting place,' says Lucy. 'Lots of secrets.'

'Lived here all my life,' says Bradley. 'Still live with the girl I met at school.' It sounds dull, put like that, but Bradley still can't get over his luck in finding a girl like Sienna. 'We're a boring lot here,' he says. 'Everyone's married, or as good as. Except Tony.'

Lucy smiles. 'I'm married too.'

'Are you? Blimey, how old are you?'

'I'm twenty-eight.'

Bradley is thirty. He'd thought Lucy was in her early twenties. Even so, twenty-eight is young to be married. Bradley and Sienna plan to tie the knot (as Bradley's mum calls it) one day but they're in no rush. Bradley hopes Lucy isn't a fundamentalist Christian. In his experience, they're the only ones who marry early these days. It's the only way they can have sex.

'Were you childhood sweethearts, then?' he asks. 'Like me and Sienna?'

Something seems to flicker over Lucy's face. 'Not childhood,' she says. 'Uni.'

'Oh,' says Bradley. He didn't go to university and has never regretted it. 'You'll have to bring him in one day,' he says. 'Your other half.' Where did that phrase come from? It sounds weird, like conjoined twins or something.

Lucy turns back to her screen. 'Maybe,' she says.

Afterwards, Bradley wonders what Lucy meant by 'secrets'.

It's lucky that George barrels over and jumps into Nelson's arms. It covers any awkwardness and, by the time Nelson sits down, Michelle has taken her seat between her daughters. Nelson had wondered why they had such a big table.

'Well, this is a surprise,' he manages. George is still on his lap.

'We thought you'd like to see George on Father's Day,' says Rebecca. There's a slight edge to her voice.

'It's grand,' says Nelson. He gives his son a squeeze. George is now five and goes to school in Blackpool. Nelson had forgotten the solid weight of him. He squeezes harder. George says 'Ow' and scrambles away.

Nelson is left looking at Michelle. Her hair is longer and caught up on top of her head with strands escaping around her face. Nelson knows, from experience, that this apparently casual style takes a long time to achieve. Has Michelle dressed up for him? Suddenly he can smell her perfume. It makes his eyes water.

'It was a good surprise, wasn't it?' says Rebecca. Her voice is softer now, possibly because she thinks he's in tears.

'Grand,' says Nelson again.

'I've brought my fire engine to show you,' says George. Is it Nelson's imagination or does George have a slight Lancastrian accent?

'It's nice to be in Norfolk again,' says Michelle. Her accent, too, has started to re-emerge. When Nelson first joined Norfolk CID, people imitated his voice all the time. 'Ee bah gum,' etc, etc. The words southern people think northerners use. This had made Nelson cussedly determined to keep his Blackpool vowels, but they have definitely faded over the years.

Nelson has so many questions. How long is Michelle staying? *Where* is she staying? He supposes in their marital home, which is still in both their names. Thank goodness Ruth and Katie didn't come to the lunch. But even as he thinks this, he feels guilty.

'The food's delicious here,' says Laura, with her eyes on her father.

'Two plates each sounds a lot, though,' says Michelle.

George produces his fire engine with a siren noise. Nelson's head starts to throb.

Ruth's brother Simon turns up at three, accompanied by his wife Cathy and their youngest son, Jack, who is home from university. Cathy is carrying a bunch of sunflowers, tastefully tied together with string. They were Ruth's mother's favourite flowers and Arthur often puts them on her grave. Does Cathy know this? Does Gloria? Nothing in her face suggests she does. She arranges them in a vase and puts it on the mantelpiece between Simon and Cathy's wedding portrait and Ruth's graduation picture.

They sit in the garden, still being Covid-safe, although Arthur now has a blanket over his knees. Kate tells Jack about the kittens and he asks his mother if they could have one.

'No, thank you,' says Cathy, 'I've never liked pets.'

'Anyway, you're at university,' says Simon to Jack. 'George too. We're the ones who'd have to look after it.'

'I'd love one,' says Gloria. 'But Kezzie, Ambrose's youngest, has asthma.'

Gloria has three granddaughters and two grandsons, but she also seems genuinely fond of George, Jack and Kate. She even tells Jack he's looking handsome, which only a grandmother would do.

Cathy, surprisingly, asks Ruth about work so Ruth tells her about the proposed closure of her department. She didn't expect anyone to be interested. Her family have always professed to find her job baffling although her mother was impressed when she got a book published. But there is general consternation.

'How can they do that to you?' says Simon. 'You're famous.'

'Tell the TV people,' says Gloria. 'They'll interview you about it.' Gloria, rather to Ruth's embarrassment, has watched every episode of *Women Who Kill*.

'I did do an interview for local TV,' says Ruth. 'But I don't think it'll do any good. We are fighting, though. We're having a rally next week.'

'You need to put stuff on social media,' says Jack.

'I have,' says Ruth. 'Or rather one of my colleagues has. SaveUNNArch was trending last week.'

Jack is the only person to be impressed with this, although he joins the SaveUNNArch Twitter account and seems disappointed that they only have five thousand followers.

'Five thousand and one now,' Ruth tells him. She's touched by her family's concern.

Only Arthur has been quiet. Suddenly he says, 'If your department closes, you could come back to London. Get a job at UCL. It would be nice to have you closer.'

'Kate could go to my old school,' says Jack. 'If she likes drug dealing, that is.'

'Jack!' Cathy waves a shushing hand.

'We have drugs in King's Lynn too,' says Kate, sounding rather offended. Ruth must talk to her about the school's drug policies.

'What do you think, love?' Arthur turns to Ruth, his eyes suddenly shiny. 'Would you like to come back home?'

*

Lunch seems to go on for ever. Nelson orders things almost at random but, when they arrive, they are unrecognisable, swimming in green sauce or arranged in a tower with berries on top. The girls say it's delicious. So does Michelle although Nelson notes that she doesn't eat much. George demands chips but the nearest thing the restaurant can provide are thin wafery things that, according to George, taste of poo. Nelson tries one and agrees with his son. He can't be entirely sure that they're not beetroot.

They do end up ordering Champagne. Rebecca drinks rather a lot and so, unusually, does Michelle. Laura and Nelson are driving and let the bubbles go flat in their glasses.

George is bored before the tiny puddings arrive, glistening evilly in old-fashioned teacups. Laura takes him outside to see the ducks on a nearby pond. Nelson hopes that this isn't a way of avoiding eating. Eventually, Nelson is paying the (eye-wateringly expensive) bill. His daughters had wanted to pay but he insisted. He's getting more like Tony Soprano by the second.

It seems that Michelle and George stayed in London last night. Laura met them at the station when she collected Rebecca, who travelled up from Brighton. But Laura's Yaris is small, so it makes more sense for Nelson to drive his wife and son back to the house. Back home. It's clear that this is where they're staying.

'I can't wait to see Bruno,' says Michelle. She does love the German shepherd, who once saved her life. And it's clear that the animal hasn't forgotten. He goes mad when he sees Michelle, running around the house trying to find her presents. George runs after him. Nelson is pleased. It covers any possible awkwardness attached to Michelle's return. Also, he's glad that George hasn't become scared of the large dog.

Laura and Rebecca arrive a few minutes later, both of them in high spirits. Laura arranges the Father's Day cards on the mantelpiece. Nelson examines them in a rare moment's peace. Laura's is an old-fashioned photograph of footballers. 'Was it like this when you played for Bispham Juniors?' she has written inside. Rebecca's has a joke about being northern. The one supposedly from George has a cartoon elephant on the front. 'Happy Father's Day, Daddy,' Michelle has written inside, 'with love from Georgie'. Her writing hasn't changed since Nelson first met her. George has added his own string of Gs. Nelson wonders, with a sudden lurch of his heart, whether he'll get a card from Katie.

Laura makes tea and a sandwich for George, who says he's hungry. 'You'll have to get Daddy to make you fish finger sandwiches,' says Michelle. 'They're his favourites.'

'Food of the gods,' says Nelson, but he's finding it hard to concentrate on the conversation. It's just so *odd* to see Michelle sitting in her usual chair, with Bruno leaning against her legs. Rebecca is lying on the floor looking at an old photo album. 'Is that me?' George asks about every picture. 'No,' says Rebecca, 'they're all me and Laura.' Nelson and Michelle must have taken hundreds of photos of George but they're all on their phones, or on the laptop, not squashed between the pages of a velvet-bound album.

George is soon bored again so his sisters take him into

the garden where his climbing frame is still fixed between the trees. Nelson looks across at Michelle and sees that she's asleep. She's obviously tired after the travelling. Or the Champagne. Or is she just avoiding talking to him? Nelson gets out his phone. Could he text Ruth? But she'll probably be driving. He wonders what sort of day she's had. Her father always sounds a bit of an odd stick, although he has managed to find himself a new, younger, wife. Ruth's parents have proved full of surprises. Ruth's mother with her secret daughter, her father with his autumn romance. Even Nelson's mother, as fixed as the sun in his universe, once said something that shook him to the core. Not far from here, in Sandringham Woods, she tacitly gave her blessing to Nelson leaving Michelle for Ruth. But it was Michelle who made the first move towards this. Why, then, has she come back?

From the garden come the sounds of George's shouts and Bruno's barks. Nelson feels his head drooping.

Judy is looking through Cathbad's papers. It's not snooping, she tells herself, I'm investigating. There's a small desk in their bedroom, the old-fashioned kind with a sloping lid. Judy used it as a workstation during Covid. Inside she finds the usual jumble of old Christmas cards and flyers from local restaurants but there is also a file tied together with string. A piece of lavender is threaded through the knot. This is a document that is waiting to be found.

Judy's hands shake as she unties the knot. The children have taken Thing for a walk. She's told them not to go far so she only has a few minutes.

The Last Will and Testament of Michael Malone, also known as Cathbad.

The words seem so strange, so theatrical, that Judy can't quite take them in. It seems odd seeing Cathbad's real name like that. Judy never uses it. Michael is her son's name.

'I leave all my worldly goods to my life partner, Judith Mary Johnson . . .'

Judy's eyes swim. 'Life partner' is what Cathbad always calls her. They are not legally married although a pagan friend of Cathbad's performed a surprisingly moving ceremony on the beach one evening. Her own legal name evokes a rush of feelings. She's always disliked Judith and Mary seems almost obligatory for a Catholic female. She thinks of the Virgin Mary appearing to Richeldis in Walsingham. It's a more powerful name than people think.

Cathbad makes several other bequests including his books to Ruth and his cloak to Nelson. What would the boss make of that? Judy wonders. Funnily enough, she can almost imagine him wearing it. There are no witness signatures but, at the end of the will, there is a date. 17 June 2021.

The day before he disappeared.

There are several other papers in the file. One details a 'woodland burial': no embalming, a wicker casket, pan pipes to play. The last few pages are written in Cathbad's characteristic flowing hand.

My earliest memories involve my grandmother Fionnuala. They aren't the usual sepia tinted shades of knitting and shawls, of scones baking in the oven and tea in a twice-brewed pot. No, my first image is of a woman walking up from the sea, fit and muscular in a black one-piece, flicking water from her short hair. Fionnuala swam every day and, afterwards, she sat on the pebbles and smoked a cigarette. It was the only time I ever saw her do this. The Irish Sea is cold and unforgiving, but I never remember Fionnuala shivering or even wrapping her towel round her shoulders. She is laughing, white teeth in a tanned face, little lines around the eyes, ready to face whatever life had to throw at her ...

Judy carries on reading until she hears the children at the front door.

It's seven o'clock by the time Ruth reaches the A148. Her head is aching and her foot is hurting from pressing down on the clutch. Maybe she should invest in an automatic. But her Renault is only eight years old, which is practically new in Ruth's eyes. She just wants to get home and have a glass of wine with Flint.

At the South Street turning, Kate says, 'This is near Dad's house.'

'So it is,' says Ruth, edging forward in the queue.

'I've made Dad a card,' says Kate. 'Like the one I made Granddad but better.'

Ruth tries not to imagine the card. Kate, tongue protruding, carefully writing 'Happy Father's Day Dad' in bubble letters. She tries to think of Flint and the Saltmarsh in the evening, of the white wine she is sure lurks somewhere in the fridge. She feels like she has been driving all day.

'I drew a cat on it,' says Kate.

Ruth sighs. 'Do you want to take it round to him?'

Kate sits up straighter. 'Yes, please.'

Ruth misses the turning to the cul-de-sac and has to do what feels like a thirty-three-point turn. Why is she feeling so nervous? They'll just deliver the card and drive away. Nelson might even have gone back to the station. But his car is in the drive, next to a Toyota Yaris Ruth recognises as belonging to Laura. Presumably Laura and Rebecca have come back to the house after lunch in the restaurant. This complicates things but both daughters know about Ruth's relationship with their father and Kate adores her sisters. Ruth parks two doors down and smiles at Kate.

'Got the card?'

'Look!' Kate points.

The front door opens, and a German shepherd appears, grinning with what looks like inane happiness. A small boy is holding his lead. 'Steady, Georgie,' comes Nelson's voice. Then a woman says something and Nelson laughs. Both sounds put Ruth on alert. Even so, she isn't prepared for the lurch in her heart when the door opens wider to show Nelson and Michelle, Nelson's hand resting protectively on his wife's arm.

CHAPTER 26

Monday 21 June

Nelson drives into work on Monday feeling twitchy. It had been strange sharing the house with Michelle again. Strange because it felt so natural. When they got back to the house after that excruciating lunch, Nelson and Michelle had both fallen asleep in their chairs. They were woken by George and Bruno clamouring for a walk. 'You looked like Darby and Joan sitting there,' said Rebecca. Nelson doesn't know who these people are but he had got the message. They looked like a long-married couple. Which they are, of course.

The whole family set out for walk in the Sandringham woods. Bruno, who has become quite grown-up with Nelson, reverted to puppyhood and spent his time running around in circles, retrieving sticks and laying them at Michelle's feet. She seemed delighted with these attentions although she wouldn't touch the sticks because they were covered in slobber.

Returning to the house, Nelson had had the strangest

feeling that he was being watched. Specifically, that he was being watched by Ruth. But, although he scanned up and down the road, something he'd been too preoccupied to do when they set out, he couldn't see her battered Renault anywhere. After Laura and Rebecca had gone home, he and Michelle had settled into a replica of a thousand other domestic evenings. Michelle had given George his bath and put him to bed. Afterwards Nelson and Michelle watched a crime drama on TV (like no police investigation Nelson has ever seen) with the dog snoozing beside them. Then Michelle had retired to bed in the spare room and Nelson was left sleepless in the master bedroom. He had managed to text Ruth when George was in the bath but, though the message was read, received no answer. He tried again, 'See you tomorrow?' but still the two blue ticks and nothing else.

When Michelle had returned from being locked down in Blackpool to say that she wanted a separation, Nelson had been, in turn, shocked, saddened, admiring and relieved. He knew that something had to change. He'd spent most of lockdown with Ruth and Katie and could finally see a future for them as a family. But there was sadness too. When Michelle said that she wanted to return to Blackpool with Georgie, Nelson had seen one door opening and another slamming shut. He wanted to be with Ruth, but he also wanted to watch his son growing up. Katie had been brought up by a single parent – very well, he has to admit – and now the pattern was going to be repeated. But Nelson had agreed to a separation. What else could he do? And now, over a year later, he is living on his own and Ruth seems no closer to making a commitment to him. Then, suddenly, his wife is back and his house feels like a home again. Sitting in front of the TV last night, Nelson had been surprised how content he had felt. He's nearly fifty-four now. Maybe he's too old to begin again?

When Nelson finally asked about her plans, Michelle said that she wanted to stay for a week. 'It won't hurt George to miss school at his age. And I've missed Norfolk.'

'I never thought I'd hear you say that,' said Nelson.

'I'm the one who's always liked it here, remember?' said Michelle. 'You were the one pining for Bloomfield Road.'

Edging through the one-way system around the city walls, Nelson wonders if he'd miss King's Lynn. On balance, he thinks not. But he would miss Ruth and Katie. Unless he can persuade them to accompany him back up north. There are too many variables, he thinks.

But there are not enough variables at work. Cathbad is still missing. They put out a Twitter alert on Saturday and received the usual unhinged responses. The next step is the local news. Nelson will need to consult Jo about that. He knows that his boss will remind him that they are no nearer to finding out who killed Emily Pickering. Suspicion still centres on Peter Webster but there's no evidence that he knew Emily well or even saw her outside the café. Emily's parents don't remember ever hearing his name. They still point the finger at Leo Ballard but, although Nelson is pretty sure that Emily had an unhealthily close relationship with her tutor, there's nothing that ties him to her murder. One moment Emily was happily wandering around

Ely, walking through the cathedral grounds and looking in the bookshop, the next she is dead. They don't even know how she died, only that her bones turned up nineteen years later hidden behind a brick wall. That wall was built around Christmas 2002. Where was Emily before then? Alive or buried in a Neolithic flint mine?

Nelson holds a briefing meeting in his office. Tony is, once again, contained within the laptop. Bradley has done well with Ballard's car and with tracing his former students. Nelson has been impressed with his work on the case. Bradley could even be the new Cloughie if only he'd lighten up a bit. Lucy has been methodical with the house-to-house but there are no real leads.

Tanya reports on her meeting with Gaia Webster. 'She admitted that she'd had an affair with Ballard. She said that Emily had a crush on him too. Gaia was very dismissive about Emily and her friends.'

'What did the sister say?' Nelson asks Tony. 'What was her name? Freya? Why did she say that it was her in the picture?'

'She claimed to be genuinely confused,' says Tony, from the screen, 'but I don't buy that. The two sisters don't even seem very alike.'

'They're hiding something,' says Nelson. 'Could it be about their dad?'

'Maybe,' says Tanya. 'Gaia seemed very defensive when I asked about him.'

'Freya too,' says Tony. 'She says that she met Leo Ballard with her parents at Gaia's graduation. But there could well have been some other contact. She said that her mum didn't like him.'

'I think we should try to talk to Mrs Webster,' says Nelson. 'We might get something. People with dementia often have lucid moments.'

'It won't stand up in court,' says Tanya.

'We have to try,' says Nelson. 'We need answers for Emily's parents' sake. Tanya, can you go to see Mrs Webster? Do you know if the nursing home is local?'

'Freya said it was near Downham Market,' volunteers Tony.

'That's only ten minutes away,' says Nelson.

'Twenty,' says Tanya.

'See if you can get an appointment,' says Nelson. 'We have to find out what happened to Emily between getting off the train at Ely and being found dead in King's Lynn.'

'What about the chalk dust on the bones?' asks Tony. 'Does that give us a link with Grime's Graves?'

'I'll check with Ruth,' says Nelson. 'She was going to do some soil analysis.'

It's an excuse, at any rate.

Somehow Ruth gets through the morning. She drives Kate to school and promises to pick her up at three thirty. Judy has said that Kate can still go back to their place but Ruth doesn't want to bother her. She knows there has been no news of Cathbad.

Last night in Nelson's cul-de-sac, Ruth had put her hand on Kate's arm.

'Let's give him the card another time.'

'I want to give it to him now,' said Kate. Nelson did not glance in their direction. He and Michelle followed George and the dog along the pavement. Nelson was no longer touching Michelle but they were walking so closely together that no daylight was visible between them. Laura and Rebecca followed, Rebecca checking her phone, Laura calling ahead to her parents. 'Wait for us!' 'Walk faster then,' shouted Nelson. Laughter. Bruno barking.

Kate was looking at Ruth. 'Let's go home, Mum.'

Kate was uncharacteristically silent for the rest of the journey home. What did she make of what she had seen? Ruth suspects that Kate is concerned for her. After all, seeing Nelson with his wife is nothing new for Kate. It seems wrong for a daughter to worry about her mother but, last night, Ruth couldn't find the words to reassure her. Ruth made supper and they watched a Marvel film. Later, Ruth found the wine and drank it all. Now, as she drives the short distance from the school to the university, she still feels slightly hungover and cushioned from reality. Nelson had texted her last night: 'Michelle and George here. Will explain.' Well, maybe he would explain but he couldn't eradicate what Ruth had seen with her own eyes. A happy, united family going for a walk with their dog. Later Nelson had texted, 'See you tomorrow?' Ruth hadn't answered.

Ruth parks her car in its usual space under the lime tree. She takes out her briefcase and walks towards the Natural Sciences building. The banner still hangs from the windows.

Save UNN Arch. Dr Ruth rocks. At least, thinks Ruth, feeling slightly cheered, this is somewhere I will always belong. Until her department is closed, of course.

It's nearly the end of term and the campus is quiet. Lots of students have already left and there's a melancholy feeling to the empty lecture theatres and the notices offering text-books for sale. 'Never used,' boasts one. Ruth has a marking meeting in the morning and she knows that David wants a 'council of war' about their campaign. She's also planning to avoid Colin until she has made up her mind about the dean's job.

She's further soothed by her office and a cup of strong coffee. So much so that she actually answers a call from Nelson on her phone.

'I'm ringing about the soil samples from Grime's Graves,' says Nelson. 'About matching them to the dust on Emily's remains.'

So, this is how he's going to play it, thinks Ruth. Work first, reunion with his wife later.

'I'll ring Jamie Stirland at the site today,' she says coolly. 'Perhaps I can go over after work.'

'Won't you have Katie with you? I don't suppose she can go back to Cathbad's house . . .'

'*Kate*,' says Ruth, emphasising the name, as she has done hundreds – thousands – of times before. 'Kate will find it very interesting.'

Nelson is silent for a minute and then says, 'Why didn't you answer my texts yesterday?'

Ruth sighs. 'What was there to say?'

'Michelle and George turned up unexpectedly. Laura and Rebecca planned it. As a surprise. For Father's Day.'

'How nice.'

'Well, it was nice to see Georgie,' says Nelson, sounding goaded.

'I bet it was. Kate and I drove to London to see my dad. That wasn't so much fun.'

'I bet your dad was pleased to see Katie, though.'

'He was,' says Ruth, relenting slightly. 'Kate's made you a card.'

'That's nice. Shall I pop round tonight? After you've been to Grime's Graves?'

It's the word 'pop' that does it. Nelson is allotting them a brief portion of time before rushing back to his wife. Again. 'How long is Michelle staying?' asks Ruth.

'A week,' says Nelson.

'Then I'll see you in a week,' says Ruth. 'Bye now.'

Nelson wishes he could slam the phone back down on its cradle. But that's impossible with a mobile. He contents himself with throwing the device across the room. Really, he thinks, getting more aggrieved by the moment, it's not his fault that Michelle and George turned up out of the blue. And Ruth was the one who didn't want to come to the lunch, for God's sake. He tries not to remember how relieved he had felt about this decision.

The door opens while someone is still knocking on it. Only one person does that.

'Can I have a word?' says Jo. 'Is that your phone? What's it doing on the floor?'

'Dropped it,' mutters Nelson.

Jo places the phone on Nelson's desk and settles herself in the visitors' chair. She's wearing tight black trousers and a top that Nelson would describe – possibly wrongly – as leopard-print. The general effect is of a tiger coming to tea. A tiger in high-heeled ankle boots.

Nelson expects Jo to mention the missed appraisal but her first words are surprising. And rather alarming.

'It's about Cathbad,' says Jo.

'I've got all units looking for him,' says Nelson.

'This disappearance,' says Jo. 'Does it strike you as *suspicious*?'

Nelson is aware of his senses snapping to attention. Suddenly he's on high alert. Waiting for the pounce.

'Unusual, certainly,' he says. 'Even worrying. Not suspicious, exactly.'

Jo recrosses her legs. 'Cathbad knew the missing girl. He may even have had a sexual relationship with her.'

'He did,' says Nelson. 'He told me last week. Not in a formal interview. Just a chat.'

'That's my point,' says Jo. 'It should have been a formal interview. I know Cathbad's your friend. I know he's in a relationship with one of our officers. But we have to treat him as a suspect.'

'All the evidence so far points to Peter Webster,' says Nelson. 'The owner of the Green Child café.'

'But he's not the one who's gone on the run,' says Jo.

'Webster's dead,' says Nelson. He is taken aback by the phrase 'gone on the run'. But, Jo's right, in other cases that's just how he'd view the disappearance of a key witness.

'Cathbad's not well,' he says. 'Judy thinks he might be heading for some kind of breakdown.' She hadn't said that exactly but all the churchgoing and suchlike could point in that direction.

'Guilt can do funny things to you,' says Jo. 'I just hope he turns up soon.'

So do I, thinks Nelson. He can't bring himself to think that Cathbad had anything to do with Emily's death but there had certainly been something strange in his manner during that last walk. All that talk about putting his affairs in order. When they had parted, Cathbad had kissed Nelson on both cheeks, much to the latter's discomfiture. It had certainly felt like a farewell.

After Jo prowls away, Nelson sits at his desk, deep in thought. A knock on his door makes him jump. Too hesitant to be Jo, thanks be to God.

'Come in!' barks Nelson.

Lucy Vanstone approaches rather warily. 'I think I've got something from the house-to-house,' she says.

'Oh yes?' He gestures for her to sit down and Lucy does so. She's rather old-fashioned in her manner, sitting up very straight with her hands in her lap. You couldn't imagine her lounging or yelling in the way that Nelson's daughters do. Yet despite this – or perhaps because of it – she makes Nelson feel rather nervous.

'I spoke to a man who runs a café on Unthank Road,' she

says. 'He saw someone answering Michael Malone's description getting into a car on Friday lunchtime.'

'Really?' This is a breakthrough.

'He says the car pulled up and Malone got inside. Like he was waiting to be collected.'

'What sort of car was it?'

'He said he thought it was one of the new electric ones. It was silent, he said.'

Like Leo Ballard's Kia EV6.

CHAPTER 27

Judy and Thing are walking along the beach. At least, today, they are on their own. Michael and Miranda are at school, Maddie at work. It's just Judy and the dog on the Cathbad trail. They're not on 'their' beach at Wells but Ruth's beach by the Saltmarsh. This is where, twenty-four years earlier, a timber circle had emerged from the sea, a great archaeological discovery, certainly, but also an event that, in Cathbad's opinion, created a disturbance in the ether, a cosmic jolt that is still causing repercussions in the lives of the people involved. 'Things are still slightly out of balance,' he said recently. 'Ruth and Nelson. That only happened because of the energies from the dig.'

'What about you and me?' asked Judy. Because she sometimes still can't believe that she, rational police officer Judy, is in a relationship with someone who thinks they can talk to cats.

'We were always ordained to be together,' said Cathbad.

Is that why she's here today? Because of cosmic repercussions? Judy doesn't know but she has learnt enough from Cathbad, over the years, to follow her instincts. She read more of his memoirs last night, growing up under the guardianship of kind, tough Fionnuala and ethereal Bridget, whose magic powers Cathbad never seems to doubt. Judy reached Cathbad's fifteenth birthday and his first kiss, with a girl called Niamh. She was reluctant to read further, not just because she knew that Bridget died when Cathbad was sixteen. But she woke up that morning with the Saltmarsh in her head, her path pulsating like an electronic map, the blue dot moving ever closer to its destination. It must be a message, surely? Does she really think Cathbad will be here? It seems ridiculous but is it any stranger than the fact that they once found a girl here, kept captive in a hide for ten years?

The hide is in front of them now. Judy has Thing on the lead because bird watchers get very worked up about dogs frightening the wildfowl. But the wooden building is deserted. It was taken apart by forensics teams thirteen years ago but rebuilt by the RSPB. It's just a hut really, raised up over the flat ground, but Judy remembers that it was originally built over an old Second World War air-raid shelter. The marshes are full of reminders of this, more recent, human conflict: pillboxes, anti-tank defences, even a target range. All human life is here, thinks Judy. She was once part of a team that found Second World War skeletons buried on a Norfolk beach.

The hide smells of sheds. There's a chart showing the most commonly spotted birds and a bench running the length of one wall, with viewing holes at eye level. Judy scans the hut for signs of human activity. She finds them quite easily. There are muddy footprints all over the rubber floor and, in the very centre of the room, a bunch of flowers next to a stone with a hole through the middle.

Cathbad has always thought that Judy and Clough share a psychic connection so perhaps he wouldn't be too surprised to see that Clough, too, is journeying into the past. Clough surprises himself, though. With all the work of a busy DI on his plate, not to mention the Emily Pickering investigation, why is he knocking on the door of 'Madame Rita, Psychic Investigator'?

Clough first came across Rita when Michael, Judy's son, was abducted. She'd given him a clue which, although maddeningly cryptic at the time, turned out to be accurate, when looked at in the right way. Impressed, despite himself, Clough had consulted the psychic when another child went missing. Again, she had been helpful, even if only in retrospect. Clough is not sure why he thinks that Madame Rita will lead him to Cathbad this time. Maybe because neither of them ever explains quite what they mean but, perhaps for this very reason, it's hard to prove them wrong.

A quick google search has revealed that Rita now lives in Girton, on the north-west fringes of Cambridge. It's one of those leafy villages that always make Clough think of horror films. There's the church where the vicar will be horribly murdered, there's the pub where every head will turn at the entrance of a stranger, there's the cottage where a face will appear in an upper window, mouth open in a silent scream.

All that appears in Madame Rita's window is the psychic herself, wearing a prosaic NHS face mask.

'Come in,' she shouts down. 'The door's open.'

Clough finds himself in a small sitting room. There's a crystal ball on a side table but, otherwise, it could be a room belonging to any elderly person, lots of doilies and ornaments, framed grandchildren on the walls.

'DS Clough.' Rita has made a soundless entrance. 'Good to see you again.'

'It's DI now,' Clough can't help adding.

Rita laughs. 'You can't expect me to know everything. You don't mind if I keep the mask on, do you? Compromised immune system.'

Clough mutters something about it being better to be careful. He's already regretting the visit.

'Did you bring something belonging to the missing person? Like I said on the phone?'

Clough produces three stones threaded together. It had been a wedding gift from Cathbad (along with a rather more useful John Lewis voucher from Judy). 'Hag stones have powerful magic,' he'd said at the time. 'They guard against witches and some say that, if you look through the central hole, you can see the fairy realm.' Cassandra usually keeps the stones hanging in the porch.

Now Rita takes them in both hands and shuts her eyes. Clough doesn't know where to look and fixes his gaze on the church tower, visible through the latticed window. The blue face of the clock says ten past eleven. What would Nelson say if he knew Clough was wasting his time in this way?

Clough looks back at Madame Rita. Her eyes above the mask are compassionate.

'He is no longer walking on the surface of this earth.'

Tanya feels as if she, too, is in the underworld. Five Oaks Nursing Home looks pleasant enough on the outside – green lawns, yellowing in the heat, flower beds, strategically placed benches – but, inside, there's a pervasive smell of urine and despair. The staff seem friendly, though. The woman on reception knows who she is and says that she'll send for the manager. She also asks Tanya to put on an NHS issue mask. Tanya wants to complain because her own mask is the top-rated KN95 version. But she does what she's told, adjusting the elastic to fit her face.

The reception area tries its best, with flowers and magazines on a coffee table, but the smell is still there. As Tanya waits, a nurse in blue scrubs passes, pushing a man in a wheelchair and talking with a kind of determined cheerfulness that Tanya could never achieve. Her own parents are healthy sixty-somethings. She can't imagine them ever needing a place like Five Oaks but, if that day ever comes, Tanya knows that she will go to pieces and leave everything to her brother and sister. Joe would be great at the helm of a wheelchair.

'Detective Sergeant Fuller? I'm Adele Masters. The manager.'

Tanya is surprised to find herself liking Adele, who has short hair and a no-nonsense manner. She's also wearing a KN95 mask. They don't shake hands, because of Covid, but Tanya is sure that Adele's handshake would be a firm one.

'Arabella's in the visiting room. I'll take you there. You'll have to talk to her behind a screen, I'm afraid.'

Arabella is a young person's name, thinks Tanya, as she follows Adele along green-painted corridors. She can hear a television blaring somewhere and occasionally blue-uniformed figures scurry past, but she doesn't see any of the inmates. Arabella is a heroine's name, or one belonging to an artist with flowers in her hair. She's pretty sure that's not who she's going to meet.

'Does . . . er . . . Arabella have many visitors?'

'Well, of course, for much of last year we couldn't allow any visitors,' says Adele. 'It was heart-breaking. Early on in the pandemic, hospitals routinely sent patients back to us with Covid. We had several deaths and we couldn't let relatives be with their loved ones, even in their last hours. Our staff were fantastic, though. Many of them voluntarily locked down with us. We lost two staff members to Covid.'

'That's terrible.' Tanya is beginning to see the blue figures in a new light.

'We were able to relax restrictions in May,' says Adele. 'Although we've had to limit the number of visitors and we can't allow any physical contact. Even so, it's amazing to see the effects on the patients. Social distancing was very hard for people with Alzheimer's. We couldn't explain what was going on.'

'Does Arabella have Alzheimer's?'

'Yes, I understand it was early onset. Very sad. She's been with us ten years. I've only been here for five.'

Peter Webster died in 2010, Tanya remembers. His wife must have entered the care home two years later. She wonders which of the sisters made the decision. She asks again about visitors.

'Gaia comes quite often,' says Adele. 'About once a week now that restrictions have been lifted. I understand that she lives near by. The other sister comes occasionally.' She pauses. 'In fact, Arabella will probably think that you're one of her daughters. Don't let that upset you.'

'I won't,' says Tanya.

The visiting room is large with French windows opening onto the lawn. 'Ventilation,' explains Adele. 'Don't forget to use hand sanitiser.' Tanya squirts the gel liberally and finds her eyes watering. This stuff must be neat alcohol.

There's a plastic screen across one corner of the room and a woman sits behind it, slumped awkwardly in an armchair. She's wearing a Perspex face shield and her eyes seem to be closed.

'Visitor for you, Arabella,' says Adele, in a loud, cheerful voice.

Tanya approaches as the woman's eyes open.

'Emily,' she says.

Nelson has planned another surprise visit to Leo Ballard but is, in his turn, rather taken aback to see two cars parked outside the lecturer's house, the electric Kia and a large

BMW, which is almost certainly diesel powered. Before he can hammer on the door, it opens and a couple appear, clearly the BMW's owners because they match the car so well: a tall man in well-cut chinos and a glossy woman in a green dress. They both stop when they see Nelson glowering on the doormat.

'Ah, DCI Nelson!' Leo is hovering in the background. Nelson can just see his untidy hair. 'What a pleasant surprise.'

Nelson is about to disabuse him of this idea when Leo says, 'Have you met my former students Tom and Amber Westbourne?'

Nelson looks at the BMW couple with new interest. They look so much older than the girl in the photo on the incident room board but, had she lived, Emily Pickering might also be a well-groomed forty-year-old in a posh car. Nelson assumes that Tom and Amber are in the area for Emily's funeral, which is scheduled for tomorrow. He thinks it's interesting that they have taken time to call in on their old tutor.

'I think my sergeant paid you a visit the other week,' he says, unsmiling.

'Yes,' says Amber, chin lifting. 'DS Fuller. She was very nice.'

If so, thinks Nelson, Tanya is losing her touch. He wonders whether her caring side is emerging in the nursing home.

'We wanted to call in on Leo before the funeral tomorrow,' says Tom. 'Just for support.'

Who is supporting whom? wonders Nelson. But it's

interesting that Tom has offered this explanation. Especially when Nelson didn't ask for one.

'I'll see you at the funeral,' he says. 'Now I'd like a word with Professor Ballard.'

He stands in the hallway while Amber kisses Leo on the cheek and Tom shakes him by the hand. Then the car roars away over the gravel.

'What's all this about, DCI Nelson?' Leo sounds slightly less affable as he leads the way into the fire hazard of a study.

'Do you know who this is?' Nelson proffers a recent photograph of Cathbad. Supplied by Judy, it shows the druid on the beach with his dog at his side.

'That's Cathbad,' says Leo. 'He hasn't changed much. Clean living, I suppose.'

'When did you see Cathbad last?'

'Years ago,' says Leo. 'It must have been when he was working at UNN. I think we met at an archaeology dig.'

'One of your colleagues says that she saw you and Cathbad together at a party a few years ago,' says Nelson.

'Who said that?' says Leo. 'I can't remember any party.'

Nelson is not about to give him the name. 'This colleague said that you made a remark about Cathbad knowing where the bodies were buried,' says Nelson. 'What did you mean by that?'

'I can't remember ever making any such remark,' says Leo. All the swagger has gone now and he looks wary, one leg jiggling convulsively.

'On Friday lunchtime,' says Nelson, 'a man answering

to Cathbad's description was seen getting into your car.' This is stretching things a bit but Nelson wants to see Leo's reaction.

'Impossible!' says Leo. It sounds genuine enough, but Nelson thinks that there's something theatrical about the tone. Leo has also turned away so Nelson can't see his face.

'Is it?'

'Yes. I was here all day on Friday. Ask my cleaning lady.'

'I will.'

'Why are you asking me about Cathbad anyway? He's not in trouble, is he?'

'Possibly,' says Nelson. 'He's gone missing.'

'Missing? He's probably just gone off for a long walk somewhere. Cathbad was a great walker, as I remember.'

'We're treating his disappearance as suspicious,' says Nelson. He adds, 'Just as Emily's was.'

'You can't think . . .' Leo stops.

'What can't I think?'

'That anything's . . . happened to him.'

'Tell me, Professor Ballard,' says Nelson, 'do you own any other properties in the area?'

It's just because I have similar colour hair, thinks Tanya. Also, a lot of her face is covered by the mask. Still, she mustn't waste this opportunity. For some reason, Emily Pickering is in the forefront of Arabella's mind.

'Hi, Arabella,' she says, facing her through the screen. 'I wanted to talk about Emily actually.'

'Emily,' says Arabella, but more vaguely this time.

Tanya gets a photo out of her bag. It's an enlarged image of Emily, Tom, Cathbad and Gaia at the Green Child café.

'Do you remember Emily?' says Tanya. 'She was a friend of Freya's and Gaia's.'

'Gaia's getting married,' says Arabella. 'I'm pleased. I didn't like the one before. He was bad for her.'

'Leo Ballard?' says Tanya hopefully. 'Why didn't you like Leo?'

'Gaia never visits any more,' says Arabella.

Adele had said that Gaia visited often but Tanya supposes that 'often' has a different meaning when you have dementia.

'What do you remember about Emily?' she says. 'Were Gaia and Emily friends? Or was she Freya's friend?'

'Tom was Emily's friend,' says Arabella. Her voice sounds different. Younger, more certain. 'That's Tom there.' She points at the photograph.

'What about Peter?' says Tanya. 'Your husband. Did he like Emily? Were they friends?'

'Peter liked to take photographs,' says Arabella.

'Did he take photographs of Emily?'

'He put his photos in a special book.'

'What sort of photos? Was Emily naked in them?'

Has she gone too far? Arabella's chin sinks onto her chest and she looks as if she's about to go to sleep. Tanya holds the picture up against the screen.

'Arabella, what happened to Emily?'

'They put her behind the wall,' says Arabella. And closes her eyes again.

CHAPTER 28

The marking meeting goes on and on. The sun beats in through the open window as they talk about grade boundaries. Ruth tries not to think about Cathbad, or about Nelson and Michelle. She tries to concentrate on her students, who have had a rough deal over the last few years. Their grades will show some leniency to reflect this but, at the same, the board must be careful not to let standards slip. By the end of the meeting, Ruth's head is pounding. She tries to slide two ibuprofen out of her desk drawer whilst listening to David, who has stayed behind to talk about 'the campaign'.

'We've had so many messages of support,' he is saying. 'From Mary Beard and Tony Robinson. From the British Archaeological Society. From lots of academics including Leif Anderssen from Uppsala and Leo Ballard from Cambridge.'

Ruth has some misgivings about both these names. Leif is the archaeologist son of Ruth's old university tutor, Erik. Like his father, Leif is brilliant, charismatic and, in Ruth's opinion, slightly dangerous. Still, he's another high-powered backer. It's also interesting that Leo is still willing to offer his support.

'That's great,' Ruth says, swallowing the pills with some cold coffee. 'What's our next move?'

'We've got a rally planned for Thursday,' says David. 'I'm hoping for some national press coverage.'

Ruth is not sure that the media is interested in universities or archaeology – unless they can get Tony or Mary to attend the rally. Or borrow the dinosaur skeleton from the Natural History Museum.

'Are you OK, Ruth?' says David. 'You look a bit pale.'

'I'm fine. Just a headache.'

'Do you want to go for a walk around the lake? Clear your head?'

'OK,' says Ruth. As she leaves the room with David, she reflects that she never thought she would be grateful for his company. But she is.

Nelson's next visit is to Leo Ballard's cleaning lady, Jenna Hopkins. Jenna lives about a mile away, in a cluster of cottages near the entrance of a place called Madingley Hall. The hall itself is at the end of a long driveway and its many windows glitter in the sunlight. Nelson has no idea if it's a private home or a Cambridge college but there's something sinister about its solitary grandeur. A lake gleams in the middle distance and there's a timbered house at the gates that calls itself The Lodge.

Jenna's cottage is one of three that probably once belonged to servants at the hall but Jenna herself is a reassuringly modern presence, with dyed pink hair and multiple pier-cings.

'I've known Leo and Alice a few years,' she says. 'They're not bad employers. By Cambridge standards anyway. I like Alice a lot.'

'What about Leo?'

'He's not so bad when you get to know him.'

Hardly a ringing endorsement, thinks Nelson. He asks how often Jenna cleans for the Ballards.

'Three times a week. Mondays, Wednesdays and Fridays.'

Why do an elderly couple whose children have left home need a cleaner so often? wonders Nelson. He once tried to persuade Michelle to get domestic help, when the girls were small, and she said she'd feel guilty letting someone else do her cleaning. Nelson's mother would have said the same.

'Were you there last Friday?'

'Yes,' says Jenna, looking at Nelson curiously. 'Why?'

'It's all part of an ongoing investigation,' says Nelson. 'Did you see Leo or Alice last Friday?'

'Friday is one of Alice's days at Little Lives,' says Jenna. 'Leo was there. He made me a coffee. He's got a thing about using the machine. It's a bit bitter for me but I'd never say.'

'What time was that?'

'About eleven thirty, I think. I start at eleven. I've got another job from eight thirty to ten thirty.'

'What did Leo do then?'

'Went into his study. He spends hours in there. I'm not allowed in to clean it.'

'What time did you leave?'

'About one. It normally takes me two hours.'

'Was Leo's car there when you left?'

'I think so. I cycle so I don't always notice cars.'

Nelson shows Jenna the picture of Cathbad.

'Have you ever seen this man?'

'Yes,' says Jenna. But, before Nelson can get too excited, she adds, 'I think there was something about him on Twitter.'

'He's gone missing,' says Nelson. 'Have you ever seen Leo Ballard with this man?'

'No,' says Jenna. 'I think I'd remember.'

As Nelson leaves, he asks Jenna if Leo has ever mentioned Emily Pickering. 'I don't think so. He normally talks about gods and goddesses. He's a strange man but there's no harm in him.'

That, thinks Nelson, is very much a matter of opinion.

Ruth and David don't talk much as they skirt the lake. With exams over, a few of the students are trying kayaking and windsurfing. There's not really enough space for water sports but it gives the campus a holiday feel. It's another beautiful day with just enough breeze to flutter the surfers' sails but not enough to propel them across the water. Ruth feels her headache lifting.

'It's such a shame,' she says.

She doesn't have to say more. David knows what she means. 'I'd be sorry to leave too. I went to school in Nor-folk – as you know – and I never thought I'd come back here. But I've been happy here.'

Ruth knows that David's schooldays were not happy. Now

he lives in a cottage in Stiffkey and seems reconciled to the county. For herself, she has loved the flat landscape ever since she saw it on the henge dig, more than twenty years ago.

'It's a good department,' says David. 'It deserves to survive. Those things you said in the TV interview, about archaeology being the study of ordinary people, that's why it's so important. That's why this government hates it, of course. They'd prefer history to be an endless study of kings and queens and battles that were won by the English.'

'Our Island Story,' says Ruth. 'But, all that stuff about being an island race, undefeated in battle, invictus, it's just rubbish. This country is the result of recurrent waves of invasion.'

'You don't have to tell me,' says David. 'I'm writing a paper on the Bell Beaker Culture at the moment.' The Beaker Folk, who spread across Europe during the Bronze Age, are particular favourites of David's. Ruth wonders if he's writing the paper in the hope of getting another job.

'What will you do?' asks David. 'If they do shut us down.'

Ruth tells David about the job offer from Colin Bland. She's surprised at his reaction.

'You can't become dean! It'll be endless admin. You love teaching. You should get a job somewhere else. Any university would be proud to have you.'

'Except there aren't that many archaeology departments left,' says Ruth.

'Ruth . . .' David puts his hand on her arm. Ruth's senses are all suddenly on high alert. Her headache returns and she feels as if her skull is actually pulsating. She doesn't know when she's been so relieved to hear Shona's voice, hailing them from the other side of the lake. 'Yoo-hoo!'

Shona is with Phil but even this doesn't discourage Ruth. The two couples walk towards each other and meet at the jetty where another group of students are feeding the ducks.

Phil, who had a heart attack a few years ago, now looks tanned and well. He greets Ruth with a kiss on both cheeks and exchanges hearty handshakes with David.

'Is this a council of war?' he asks.

'Yes,' says Ruth. Although that wasn't what it had felt like.

'It's a bad business,' says Phil. 'But I'm not really surprised. Archaeology was always under fire, even in my day. That was why I was always so keen on raising our profile.'

Ruth remembers mocking Phil for his obsession with 'relatable archaeology', projects that would attract the attention of the press, especially TV. She now feels that she misjudged him.

'Ruth is one of the highest profile archaeologists in the country,' says David, sounding rather belligerent.

'*Women who Kill*,' says Shona. Ruth remembers that she had been fascinated by the programme, even at the time.

'And other things,' says David.

'I must say,' says Phil, 'I'm glad I retired when I did. Things are going to get nasty.'

'Well, all we can do is fight,' says Ruth. She looks across the water to the cluster of buildings, the ugly modern bricks mellow in the sunshine. She has a feeling that, like Boudica at Watling Street, she is about to be defeated.

*

Nelson leaves Madingley feeling frustrated. He's sure that Leo Ballard is hiding something. But what? Jenna Hopkins would certainly have noticed if he was keeping Cathbad imprisoned somewhere in the house. But it would have been possible – just about – for Leo to have sneaked out on Friday, glided away in his soundless electric car, and abducted Cathbad. He might even have been back by the time Jenna left at one. But she hadn't been certain that the car was there. In Nelson's opinion, cyclists never notice cars. Leo's alibi is certainly not watertight.

Leo told Nelson that he owned a 'holiday cottage' in Old Hunstanton. 'Somewhere we can get away from it all. Right by the sea. Very peaceful but convenient for the village and the shops.' Nelson can't see what a retired lecturer has to get away *from*. Presumably he's got all the time in the world to sit in his book cave and think dark thoughts. But he asked Jenna if she cleaned the cottage and she said no. It might be worth a look on his way back to the station. Old Hunstanton isn't far from King's Lynn.

The address is hard to find, due to the Norfolk habit of refusing to have street signs, but eventually Nelson draws up outside a row of cottages. The Ballards' holiday home is number five. It doesn't look very special and is certainly not as grand as the Madingley house. Nelson knocks loudly on the door but is not surprised when there's no answer. He knocks on number three and number seven and, at the latter, is met by an elderly man wearing horn-rimmed glasses. Good, Nelson needs someone with good eyesight. He asks the man, who gives his name formally as Mr Lowe, if he knows Leo Ballard.

'Yes. He often comes here with his wife. Nice lady.'

Nelson notes that Ballard is not described as 'nice'.

'When did you see them last?'

'A few weeks ago, I think. Yes, it was when there was all that rain and the road flooded.'

The rainstorm was at least a month ago. Nelson asks if anyone has been to the house in the last few days.

'No,' says Mr Lowe, 'and I see most things that happen around here.'

Nelson believes him. He goes back to number five and, for the first time, notices a statue in the front garden. At first it looks like a weathered stone but, when Nelson gets closer, he sees that it's actually a head with two faces, one gazing towards the road, the other back at the house. Janus, thinks Nelson. The two-faced god. He encountered the old boy on a previous case and the sight of him now isn't exactly cheering.

Nelson walks to the end of the street which peters out into a sandy track. The houses back onto the beach and the sea, which must be why the Ballards bought the place. Across the bay there's a white house standing on its own. Nelson doesn't know why but he treks across the sand to get a closer look. The house is very square and solid, white stucco with a slate roof, overlooking the sea. There's a garden, full of windswept trees and out-of-control roses, a garage and what looks like an outhouse. At first sight it looks isolated, but Nelson sees that it's actually connected to the road that leads to the high street. The village can only be five minutes' walk away.

Nelson can't see any sign of habitation. There's a 'Remain' poster on one of the upstairs windows but the EU referendum was in 2016, almost ancient history now. As Nelson stands by the gate, a boat with red sails skims across the bay and seagulls call high above. It occurs to him that he's finally found a place in Norfolk that he likes.

CHAPTER 29

Nelson arrives back at the station to find Bradley obviously bursting with news. Tanya nobly lets him take centre stage.

'We've had the forensics back on Ballard's car. The Triumph Spitfire.'

'That was quick. Anything interesting?'

'Yes.' Bradley pauses and looks round the room. Tanya nods impatiently. Lucy looks genuinely enthralled.

'Emily's DNA isn't anywhere in the car.'

'What do you mean?'

'Ballard's DNA is there. And the current owner's. He gave a sample. There are at least five other people who left trace DNA but not Emily. Not a scrap.'

'Does that mean she never went in the car?'

'I asked the lab that question and they said they couldn't be a hundred per cent certain – they always say things like that – but it was very unlikely that she'd been in the car.'

'Why would Ballard lie about that?' says Tanya. 'I mean, it was all the police had on him. That he gave her a lift that day, that he was the last one to see her alive. Tom saw her in the car too.'

'Maybe she wasn't in the car for long,' says Bradley. 'We know she was in Ely,we just don't know how she got there. Maybe Mark Oldbury took her?'

'Why would *he* lie?' says Nelson. 'I don't suppose he's still got the car he had nineteen years ago.'

'It was a van,' says Bradley. 'And I could check.'

'Do that. It might be worth talking to him again. In fact, he may well be back in the area for Emily's funeral tomorrow. How did you get on with Arabella Webster, Tanya?'

'She's pretty far gone, poor thing,' says Tanya. 'She thought I was Emily at first.'

Not another one of his officers resembling Emily Pickering, thinks Nelson. In Tanya's case, he can't see the likeness.

'She said her husband liked to take photographs,' says Tanya.

'Well, that's not necessarily a crime,' says Nelson.

'I know,' says Tanya. 'It was just something about the way she said it. I asked if he took naked photos of Emily but she didn't answer.'

Trust Tanya to go there, thinks Nelson. He asks if Arabella said anything about Emily.

'Yes,' says Tanya. And Nelson can tell that this is what she has been waiting for. 'I showed her the photo, the one taken in the café, and she said, "They put her behind the wall."'

Nelson feels his skin prickling.

'They put her behind the wall,' repeats Bradley. 'That

must mean that Peter Webster killed her. And his wife knew all about it. We'll never get a conviction now.' He sounds deflated.

'Not necessarily,' says Nelson. 'Arabella used the word "they". I still think Leo Ballard might have been involved. I went to see him this morning and guess who was there, paying a cosy morning visit? Tom and Amber Westbourne.'

'I suppose they're here for the funeral,' says Tanya. 'But why go to see Ballard?'

'My thoughts exactly,' says Nelson. 'Tom said it was "for support" but he didn't say who was doing the supporting. I still think Ballard is hiding something.'

'He could have killed Emily with Gaia Webster,' says Tanya. 'They could have been the "they" that Arabella mentioned. She said something about not liking Gaia's previous boyfriend, said he was bad for her. I asked if she meant Leo Ballard but she didn't answer. It was very frustrating.'

'Did Ballard say anything about Michael Malone?' asks Lucy. Nelson is pleased that the new recruit hasn't forgotten their other case but he can't help hearing Jo's words. *This disappearance, does it strike you as suspicious?* They need to find Cathbad, for more reasons than one.

'Ballard claimed not to have seen Cathbad for years,' says Nelson. 'I told him that a colleague of Ruth's saw them together at a party only a few years ago. Apparently, Ballard said something about Cathbad knowing where the bodies were buried. Could have been nothing but, then again, it could have been something. I asked Ballard where he was on Friday lunchtime. He said he was at home. I went to see his cleaning lady, Jenna Hopkins, and she said the same. She said Ballard made her a coffee and then went into his study. But I think it would have been possible for him to sneak out.'

'When Brad and I interviewed him,' says Tanya, 'Leo Ballard said that he never let the cleaner in his study. Remember, Brad?'

'That's right. He wouldn't let his wife in either.'

'Jenna said the same to me. Ballard's wife was out that day. I think he could have driven off, abducted Cathbad, and driven back again.'

'Is that what you think happened?' says Tanya, frowning.

'It's hard to imagine why he'd do it,' says Nelson. 'But something's happened to Cathbad. I went to Ballard's holiday cottage in Old Hunstanton. It looked deserted but I think we need to get some search warrants. I'm starting to get worried.'

He looks at the clock. Three p.m. And he hears Cathbad's voice. *There's not much time left.*

Ruth enjoys collecting Kate from school. In the morning, the pupils approach the gates in ones and twos, heads down, seemingly weighed down by books and the pressure of study. But, at three thirty, they stream down the hill in a glorious blue tide, bags flying out behind them. An opportunistic ice cream van is parked nearby and Ruth watches the teenagers become children again as they jostle for 99s. When Kate appears with Isla and another girl, they are all holding ice cream cones.

'Can we give Isla a lift home, Mum?' says Kate. 'And Megan too? She's on the way.'

'Oh, I'm sorry,' says Ruth. 'I've got to go somewhere for work first.'

'Are you digging up bones?' asks Isla, who is more interested in Ruth's work than Kate is.

'I'm afraid not,' says Ruth. 'Probably just looking at soil.'

'Still cool, though,' says Isla, before waving to Kate and slouching away. Megan waves too and performs a little dance which makes Kate giggle.

'Megan seems nice,' says Ruth, as Kate gets in the car.

'Mmm,' says Kate, who is already on her phone. The ice cream is dripping but Ruth doesn't mention this. She puts the car into gear and they set out towards Grime's Graves.

Jamie Stirland had seemed pleased to hear from Ruth. 'Of course, come any time. I'm here until six.'

'I won't stay long,' said Ruth. 'And I'll have my daughter with me.'

'That's fine,' said Jamie. 'We've got lots of interactive activities for her to play with.'

Now, glancing at Kate immersed in her phone, Ruth can't imagine some 'What would Neolithic people have had for breakfast?' display keeping her entertained for long. But Kate looks up after a while and they have a good conversation about school and the SaveUNNArch campaign.

'Megan's really good at art,' says Kate. 'She could make you a poster.'

Ruth hopes that Megan isn't supplanting Isla as Kate's best friend. Isla has been a real support in Kate's first year but, like Ruth and unlike Kate, Isla is slightly shy and socially awkward. Megan didn't look like she is either of those things. Ruth hopes that Kate isn't becoming dazzled by her new acquaintance. But, then again, Ruth was part of a friendship triangle at school. Ruth, Ali and Fatima. The three amigas, they called themselves. So maybe it could work. Ruth knows better than to say any of this, though. After all, Kate might only be on walking-to-the-bus-stop terms with Megan. Ruth tries to think of some neutral remark that nevertheless boosts Kate's self-worth.

'You're good at art too. I loved the cards that you made for Dad and Granddad.' Nelson still hasn't seen his, she realises.

'Not as good as Megan,' says Kate impatiently.

Ruth decides to abandon art appreciation and launches into a description of Grime's Graves. Kate is fascinated by the mention of Grim, the hooded one.

'It's one of the names of the Norse God Odin,' says Ruth.

'Sounds a bit like the devil,' says Kate.

'The devil isn't real,' says Ruth. She's usually circumspect when talking about God, but she's not prepared to pay Old Nick any such respect.

'Nor is Odin,' counters Kate.

'I suppose that's where the word "grim" comes from,' says Ruth. 'As in Grim Reaper.'

'Or the Grim in Harry Potter,' says Kate.

Ruth can't remember the Grim in the endless volumes about the boy wizard. Is he an owl? A winged horse? Kate explains that he's a dog, or rather he's Harry's godfather disguised as an animagus. Or something like that.

'I read somewhere about church grims,' says Ruth. 'They're spirits that guard a particular church. Sometimes they take the form of a black dog.'

'Maybe that man we saw was one of those,' says Kate. 'The man in the church with the paintings.'

Ruth thinks of the bearded man at St Mary's Houghton-on-the-Hill. *Who controls the wheel of fate? One minute we are raised up, the next we are in the depths.* Didn't he also talk about protecting the building from Satanists?

'He was probably just the church warden or something,' she says. 'Great, we're here. At last.'

'Where is it?' says Kate. They are driving along the tree-lined road.

'Just wait,' says Ruth. 'Here it is.' Once again, the sky opens up and the green and yellow fields are all around them.

'Where are the graves?' asks Kate.

'Under the earth,' says Ruth. She parks by the visitors' centre. There's only one other car there. Is it Jamie's? Ruth and Kate walk over the grass, Ruth pointing out the undulations that betray the presence of the mine shafts.

'Can we go down the mines?' asks Kate, as Ruth knew she would.

'Maybe,' says Ruth. 'Just the one that's open to visitors.' She remembers the electric light and the solid metal staircase. It wouldn't be so bad to go down again and it would mean she could get some proper samples at the right depth.

There's no sign of Jamie but, on the horizon, Ruth sees a man walking by the edge of the woods, near the mound known at Grimshoe. The trees look dark and sullen in the airless afternoon. Thetford Forest is manmade, planted after the First World War, but, nevertheless, Cathbad has some sinister stories about the place. Ruth also remembers Nelson mentioning a hooded man emerging from the woods during that fateful dig nineteen years ago. So, when the figure detaches itself from the shrubbery and moves towards her, she's hard put not to scream.

'Sorry, Ruth,' says Leo Ballard. 'Did I scare you?'

'Of course not,' says Ruth, moving closer to Kate.

'You know,' says Leo, as if he's carrying on a conversation that has already started, 'Cathbad and I also thought there were bodies buried here, in the mound. I tried to get funding for a dig but without success. Jamie thinks it was just a meeting place but I'm not so sure.'

Is this what Leo meant about Cathbad knowing where the bodies are buried? An innocuous explanation, if so. Why doesn't Ruth feel reassured?

'Where's Jamie?' she says.

'He's had to leave. His wife's just gone into labour. He was in a bit of a panic. I said I'd wait for you.'

'I remember him saying his wife was pregnant,' says Ruth. 'I hope everything's OK.'

'I'm sure it will be,' says Leo. 'Childbirth is a natural process, after all.'

Ruth distrusts anyone, especially a man, who says this. She remembers talking to Leo's wife about childcare, all those years ago, but Leo has never mentioned any offspring.

'I just want to take some samples,' says Ruth. 'Where's the best place? Can we get into the shaft we saw before?'

'I'm afraid it's all locked up. There's another shaft near here, though.'

'Is it the deep one? The one with just a ladder?'

'Oh no,' says Leo. 'This one's quite shallow. It's just here.'

He points and Ruth sees what looks like an open manhole cover, a few metres away. She can see a metal ladder protruding from the lip. Ruth gets her sample bag and trowel out of her bag.

'You wait here, Kate.'

'Oh no,' says Kate. 'I want to see in the mine.'

Ruth is torn. She doesn't want Kate to go into the mine shaft but then she doesn't much want to leave her above ground with Leo. He might well start to talk about initiation rites.

'Just a quick look,' she says.

'I've brought some hard hats,' says Leo. They are lying on the grass. Ruth is encouraged by this evidence of responsible behaviour. She and Kate don their headgear. Kate's is too big and comes down over her nose.

'Is there light down there?' says Ruth.

'There are torches at the bottom of the shaft. Jamie and I went down earlier.'

This is even better. Ruth approaches the ladder and turns to make the descent. Going backwards in time.

'You go after me, Kate.'

'I'll keep watch here,' says Leo.

Ruth starts her downwards climb, feeling for each step. She can feel the darkness around her as if it's a tangible thing. Above her she can see Kate's school shoes descending.

They'll be covered in chalk soon. Ruth will have to wash her uniform tonight.

'Be careful, Kate,' she says.

'I will. Are you nearly at the bottom?'

'I think I must be.'

As she says this, there's a sickening clang and mother and daughter are left in the darkness. In the womb of the earth.

CHAPTER 30

Nelson arrives home to the sound of Bruno barking. This is unusual. These days, Nelson picks Bruno up from Maura, the dog walker, on his way back from the station. But that morning Michelle asked if the dog could stay with her. 'It will be nice for George to spend some time with him. He's really missed his dog.' It would take a colder heart than Nelson's to deny George and Bruno, both of whom were staring at him out of big brown eyes. Even though Nelson thinks of Bruno as *his* dog.

But it's not just the canine welcome that stops Nelson on the doormat. It's the smell. Nelson is suddenly catapulted back through the years, a feeling that is both pleasurable and slightly dizzying. He's a teenager coming home from football practice, he's a DS in Blackpool and he can hear his children's voices in the garden, he's older but not much wiser, returning from a crime scene in King's Lynn. All these memories are linked to the fact that someone inside the house is cooking shepherd's pie.

Bruno stops barking as soon as Nelson comes through

the door. The dog rushes upstairs in a frenzy of delight, trying to find Nelson a present. George appears from the sitting room, wanting his father to view his Lego tower. By the time that Nelson has done this and accepted Bruno's gift of a sock, Michelle has materialised. She's in jeans and a T-shirt, with her hair pulled back in a ponytail. She's also carrying a can of beer and a glass.

'I've made shepherd's pie,' she says. 'Not the right thing for summer but I know you like it.'

'I do,' says Nelson, pouring beer. Has he gone back, not just to his younger years, but to the 1950s?

'I like beer,' says George.

'Beer's for grown-ups,' says Michelle.

'Adrian lets me have beer,' says George.

Nelson's detective senses are on alert. Who is this Adrian who is giving his son prohibited substances? Is it possible to have him arrested immediately?

'Let's sit in the garden,' says Michelle, slightly too smoothly. 'You and Bruno can play in the sprinkler, George.'

'Bruno gets overexcited near water,' says Nelson. But he follows his wife and son into the sunshine.

The shock makes Ruth lose her footing. She panics and lets go of the ladder, falling several feet onto the hard earth.

'What's happening?' comes Kate's voice. 'Why's it gone dark?'

'Don't worry,' says Ruth. 'Just keep hold of the ladder and come down. I'll try to find the torches.'

Ruth gets to her knees and then her feet. Her ribs hurt

but that's not important. All that matters is getting out of this hell hole. It's pitch black but she feels as if she's in an open space, just like the one at the bottom of the previous shaft. She feels along the ground, brushing against dagger-sharp flints and soft chalk. But she knows in her heart that the torches were just an invention. Leo has trapped them in the darkness.

'Mum?' Kate is beside her. Ruth hugs her close.

'It's all right, Kate,' says Ruth. Though, of course, it isn't.

'He tricked us,' says Kate. 'That man.'

'Yes, he did,' says Ruth. She thinks they are about ten feet down. Looking up, she can see a faint line of light outlining the place where the trapdoor must have been slammed behind them.

'I'm going to see if I can push the door open from this side,' says Ruth, with more confidence than she feels.

'Did you find the torches?' says Kate.

'I don't think they're here,' says Ruth. 'And it's not so dark.' It's true that, in the few minutes that she's been underground, she's starting to make out shapes, glimmers of white stone. She thinks of Jamie saying that the miners might have used chalk as a light in the darkness. Well, it's not much but it might have to do.

'Have you got your phone?' says Kate.

Oh, thank you, Kate. Her phone. Her miraculous mobile phone. She prays to the earth goddess that she didn't leave it in the car. She remembers now that Kate left hers recharging but, when Ruth feels in her pocket, there's the comforting rubber case. She prays again that the screen hasn't been broken by the fall. But, when Ruth presses the side button, a welcome green light glimmers. She can call for help. Nelson will rescue them; he'll arrest Leo and they'll be safe again. It's only then that she realises that she doesn't have a signal.

'Is it working?' says Kate.

'Yes,' says Ruth. 'But no signal. Yet,' she adds optimistically. But at least they have light. She clicks on the torch app. They are in a circular space, roughly hewn from the rock. Ruth sweeps the light along the floor and sees a pile of tiny bones, probably the remains of a rabbit that fell into the shaft. She raises the phone slightly and sees that, all around them, there are dark openings in the chalk.

'What are they?' says Kate, moving closer to Ruth.

'Galleries,' says Ruth. 'Tunnels the miners used to quarry flint.' The nearer one is propped up by what looks like an antler. There are no metal grilles here.

'I don't want to go in there,' says Kate.

'Don't worry,' says Ruth. 'We won't.'

She gives Kate the torch to hold and climbs the ladder again. Her entire body hurts but she manages to swing herself upwards. When she reaches the trapdoor, she pushes with all her might. It gives way slightly, just enough to let Ruth see that it's bolted in two places. She bangs her fist against the metal. 'Help! Let us out!' Her voice echoes impotently.

'Let me try,' says Kate.

'Bring the phone,' says Ruth. 'See if you can get a signal at the top of the ladder.'

This leaves Ruth in the darkness as Kate climbs. She sees the blue tartan skirt ascending, the white lines suddenly seeming almost luminous. Kate climbs quickly. She's good at gym and, besides, she's forty years younger than Ruth, who had been what the hospitals call 'an elderly prima-gravida'. Kate manages to get her hand in the gap between the door and the opening but she's unable to reach the bolt.

'Can you get a signal?'

Kate holds the phone to the gap. 'No,' she says. 'Nothing.' Ruth remembers that she hadn't been able to get a signal at Grime's Graves when she'd visited before. Leo had blamed ley lines.

Kate bangs on the trapdoor. 'Help!' She's sobbing now.

'Come down, Kate,' says Ruth. 'Don't cry. Someone will rescue us. At the very worst, Jamie will be back tomorrow.'

Or will he, she thinks, if his wife has just given birth? Or was that another of Leo's lies? She doesn't voice either of these thoughts to Kate. Instead, she hugs her until she stops crying. Despite everything, she thinks how lovely it is to hold her almost-teenage daughter in her arms. It's only when Kate's sobs have turned to sniffs that Ruth hears another sound.

A groan coming from the very centre of the earth.

Zoe is gardening. This is now her daily routine. As soon as she gets in from work, she feeds Derek, then she takes off her scrubs (everyone at the practice wears them now), puts them in the washing machine, has a shower, dresses in old clothes and goes into the garden. There's something so soothing about earth and air, about seedlings pushing up out of the ground, about mulch and compost, even about the bindweed that always insinuates its way across from Ruth's garden. There's now no barrier between the plots, to allow Zoe ease of access, and she crosses the lawn to water Ruth's hanging baskets. Somehow these never do as well as the ones by Zoe's own front door. 'I'm death to plants,' Ruth said apologetically. 'Maybe it's being an archaeologist. I can only dig things up, not grow them.' Zoe watches the water drip down and wonders where Ruth is. She sent a message earlier, saying that she'd be home late and asking Zoe to feed Flint. Zoe has left food out but there's been no sign of Ruth's beloved cat. She'd like Flint to turn up now, meowing and looking hard-done-by. Ruth would never forgive Zoe if something happened to Flint on her watch.

The sound of a car makes Zoe turn, welcoming smile ready. But the car is an unfamiliar one, dark and boxy-looking. The figure who emerges isn't entirely unknown, though. It's the girl who's been to the house twice before, asking for Ruth.

Zoe straightens up. She doesn't know why but she moves to stand in front of Ruth's door, barring the way.

'Hi,' says the girl. 'Me again. I'm looking for Ruth.'

'She's not here,' says Zoe.

'Do you know where she is? It's just, I keep missing her . . .'

'She's working late.'

'At the university?'

'No, something to do with the police case, I think.' Zoe

regrets these words as soon as they are out of her mouth. Something about the stranger's demeanour, or maybe the 'well-spoken' voice, has lulled her into indiscretion.

'Is Kate with her?'

How does this woman know Kate's name? Zoe clamps her mouth shut, determined not to say any more.

'When she comes back, can you give her my number? Can you tell her it's an old friend?' The woman hands over a post-it note. There's no name on it, Zoe notices.

Zoe watches as the car drives away. She looks at her watch. Eight o'clock. She hadn't realised it was so late. The sky is still bright, but it feels rather artificial, like stage lighting. Isn't today the twenty-first, the longest day? The summer solstice. The date suddenly seems rather sinister. Images rush into Zoe's mind: stone circles, the Wicker Man, a druid with his arms upraised, a locked room. She is aware of how isolated they are, the three little cottages in the middle of the Saltmarsh. When Flint jumps heavily from the roof and lands in the hollyhocks, Zoe can't stop herself emitting a tiny scream of fear.

'What was that?' asks Kate. Her voice is trembling. She grabs hold of Ruth's hand and, again, despite everything, Ruth enjoys the contact. It's been so long since they've held hands.

'Maybe it was something above ground,' says Ruth. 'A car. Someone coming to rescue us.' If she says it enough times, it might come true.

But, seconds later, the sound comes again. The cry of a

human in pain. Or an animal. Ruth remembers Jamie saying that a dog's skeleton was found in one of the shafts. She thinks of the little pile of bones she saw at the foot of the ladder. Is this an animal that has somehow fallen into the mine? If so, they need to help it.

Ruth approaches the nearest opening and gets down on her hands and knees. She projects her phone torch into the void and sees a neatly hewn tunnel that takes several turns, propped up here and there with wooden stakes or antlers. The sound comes again, from deeper into the earth, echoing against the miles of rock.

'I'm going to see what it is,' she says. 'You stay by the ladder.'

'No,' says Kate. 'I'm coming with you.'

Ruth and Kate crawl into the tunnel. Ruth tries to keep one hand on her phone but she's afraid of dropping it. Eventually she puts it in her mouth, biting down on the rubber case. This makes the light shaky and uneven. Soon she will have to turn it off in order to save the battery. They inch slowly forward, following the sound. Then Ruth turns into a wider space.

And sees a headless torso.

CHAPTER 31

The shepherd's pie is excellent. Even George eats some, in between leaping up to check on Bruno or his Lego. Michelle was strict with Laura and Rebecca about their behaviour at the table, but she seems to have given up with George. Nelson doesn't know how Ruth was with Katie in the early days but now the two of them chat like conference delegates. 'What did you do today, Mum?' 'Well, I had a meeting about Iron Age relics . . .'

'He's excited to be home,' says Michelle, apologetically. Nelson realises that he must be looking disapproving, something that often happens when he's thinking deeply. It's a few seconds before he thinks of the implications of 'home'.

'Of course he is,' he says. 'It's good to have him here.'

'Shall we have our coffee outside?' says Michelle. Nelson is rather surprised she hasn't made a treacle pudding to round off the nostalgic meal.

Nelson had got out the patio furniture before supper. It would never occur to him to sit in the garden on his own and the steamer chairs were covered in cobwebs. Even now,

Michelle dusts hers carefully with the sleeve of her cardigan. Nelson and Michelle drink their coffee while George and Bruno run laps of the lawn. It's still very light. Nelson thinks of Judy reminding him that today is the summer solstice. Hordes of nutters will be descending on Stonehenge. He prays that Cathbad is amongst them, that this whole disappearance is one crazy druidical pilgrimage.

'Are you all right, Harry? You're looking very grim.' He must be doing the face again.

'Fine,' says Nelson. 'Who's Adrian?'

Michelle sighs. Now we're coming to it, thinks Nelson.

'Mum's boyfriend,' says Michelle. 'It seems strange to say boyfriend when they're both in their seventies but that's what she calls him. They're like a couple of teenagers. It's a bit much, actually.'

'A bit much', Nelson knows, is one of Michelle's strongest terms of disapprobation, used for football hooligans, litter louts and people who don't pick up their dogs' poo. Presumably his affair with Ruth was 'a bit much'.

'A boyfriend?' says Nelson, filled with a relief that he doesn't like to analyse. 'Good for Louise.' Michelle's mother, unlike his own, is a youthful-looking pensioner who drives a pink Fiat 500 and enjoys Pilates. Nelson is not surprised that she has an admirer.

'I suppose so,' says Michelle. 'And he's not a bad sort. He's very nice with George. And Mum obviously adores him. It's just, it makes it rather awkward being in the house with them. Like when the girls brought boyfriends home. But worse.'

Nelson can quite believe this. He never allowed the girls to share bedrooms with their boyfriends when they were younger, but he can't really object now that Rebecca is living with Asif. For this reason, he's never invited the couple to stay overnight, although Rebecca is always welcome to occupy her old room. On her own.

'I want to come back,' says Michelle.

Ruth opens her mouth to scream and drops the phone. Kate cannons into the back of her legs. Ruth scrabbles for the phone and, thank God, finds the soft rubber. The light is still on. With a shaking hand Ruth illuminates the white shape, grotesquely misshapen, missing a head, arms and legs.

'It's a rock,' says Kate. And Ruth sees that she is right. It's a piece of stone in the rough shape and size of a human torso. Was that why the miners left it down here, a petrified sacrifice, an offering to the gods? Or maybe it was just too heavy to carry. Ruth edges past. It's wider here and easier to move but it's impossible to stand upright. The air smells of damp chalk. She tries not to think of the weight of rock above them. There's no sound now but their own breathing.

'What's that?' says Kate. 'That thing in the corner?'

A crumble of white, a shoe picked out in the beam of the torch.

'Is it real?' says Kate.

Ruth crawls closer. The body lies slumped against the wall. It's definitely a flesh and blood human. It's only when she gets closer and sees the long grey hair that she recognises Cathbad.

By ten o'clock it's still not quite dark but Zoe is definitely worried. She keeps returning to the window, willing Ruth's car to appear. But the road is empty, still spotlit by that strange, theatrical glow. Flint crosses the garden on a nocturnal mission. Derek, a more indoor creature, is lying on the chaise longue. The television flickers in the background, sound down.

Maybe Ruth is meeting friends? Maybe she's with Judy? Maybe Cathbad has come home and they're celebrating? Maybe Ruth is with Nelson? Zoe could ring Nelson. She has his number but something makes her hesitate. Although Zoe would never say so to Ruth, she distrusts Nelson. He's Kate's father but, as far as Zoe can see, only sees her when it's convenient to him. For years, he stayed with his wife and allowed Ruth only measured fragments of his time. During lockdown, he broke the rules to visit. Zoe had been comforted by his presence – it was a frightening time in her life – whilst strongly disapproving of his actions.

Zoe sits at her window and waits.

The longest day.

CHAPTER 32

At first Ruth thinks that Cathbad is dead. He's lying in such an awkward position, half slumped against the chalk wall. His chin is on his chest and his long grey mane is tangled across his face, like a corpse whose hair has continued to grow after death. But, when Ruth lowers her head, she can hear him breathing.

'He's all right,' she says to Kate although, again, this is very far from the case.

'Cathbad!' Ruth touches his shoulder. 'It's Ruth.'

Cathbad's eyes flicker open. 'Hecate?' he says.

This is Cathbad's name for Kate but it's also the name of the goddess of witchcraft. Ruth would rather not think about her just now. She's aware of the dark caverns around them. *It's always a good thing to appease the gods.*

'It's Ruth,' she says again. 'Ruth and Kate.'

'Leo,' says Cathbad. 'Leo Ballard.'

'Yes,' says Ruth. 'Leo did this.' Cathbad's lips are dry and chapped. Ruth looks round for something to moisten them. Surely, everyone carries water these days? But her UNN bottle and Kate's school-issued receptacle are still in the car. Has Cathbad been here for three days with no water? He'd be dead, wouldn't he?

'Mum.' Kate is holding out a plastic container, half full of water. 'There's a sandwich wrapper here too.'

So someone – presumably Leo – has been feeding Cathbad. Ruth holds the water to his lips. She doesn't want to waste any. She looks at her phone. Still no signal. She should turn it off and save the battery but she dreads being left in the darkness.

'What's going to happen to us?' says Kate. She crawls even closer to Ruth and Ruth can feel her trembling.

'Someone will find us,' says Ruth. She draws on all her years of mothering, all those times she's said, 'It'll be all right,' not knowing whether it would be, all those times she has smiled when she wanted to cry, all those cheery meals and comforting stories. Ruth is Kate's mother and, while she's around, Kate will never be really afraid. That's the power of the mother goddess.

'Don't worry, Kate,' she says. 'It's darkest before dawn.'

'Hecate,' whispers Cathbad.

Michelle is also fairly lax about George's bedtime. Nelson always used to be the one initiating noisy games in the evenings or persuading Michelle to let the girls stay up to watch a film. But today he finds himself longing for some peace and quiet, for some time to himself. But, eventually, after several more games with Bruno and on his Nintendo Switch (isn't he too young for such a device?), George consents to go upstairs for a bath and a story marathon.

'I'll come up to say goodnight,' says Nelson. But he stays in the garden. What does Michelle mean by coming back? George had interrupted after she said the words and Nelson hadn't wanted to raise the subject again. It's as if his life is spooling backwards. One moment he was with Ruth and their adolescent daughter, thinking about retirement. Now he's back at home, eating shepherd's pie with his wife while their almost-toddler rampages around them. Even Bruno is exhausted. He lies at Nelson's feet, sighing occasionally.

Nelson is thinking so deeply that he doesn't hear the patio door open.

'Harry?'

'Is George ready to say goodnight?'

'He's asleep,' says Michelle. 'He went out like a light.'

She sits in the chair next to Nelson and shakes out her hair. The gesture still has the power to stir him.

'I think I'm ready for bed too,' she says.

Ruth is trying to ration her phone. A quick look every ten minutes or so. She has thirty per cent battery left but who knows how long that will have to last? She and Kate sit in the darkness with Cathbad lying beside them. He's still breathing, a rattling and distressing sound, echoing against the stone walls, but seems to have lapsed into unconsciousness.

Ruth and Kate have both crawled past the headless torso to the ladder and climbed to the top, hoping to get a signal. But there were no comforting bars in the corner of the phone screen. Ruth hadn't liked leaving Kate underground while she climbed and she hadn't liked seeing Kate's school shoes, now completely covered in chalk, disappearing through the tunnel when it was her turn. She'd really like them both to wait at the bottom of the shaft. At least they can stand upright there and can see that thin square of light, their link to the outside world. But she doesn't want to leave Cathbad. What if he died here in this awful cave? At least if she sits next to him, Ruth can will him back to life. And Ruth wants Kate next to her.

'Shall we sing?' says Kate.

They try 'Thunder Road'. Ruth taught Kate the lyrics when she was still a baby. The song had been playing in the car when Ruth first met Frank. When she crashed into him, in fact. Ruth hopes that someone will hear the voices under the earth declaring singing about the screen door and there being magic in the night, but, of course, Grime's Graves is deserted. Only the sinister trees will hear them. Perhaps they are even now moving closer, turning the field into a forest. Burnham Wood coming to Dunsinane.

After 'Thunder Road' they sing 'Born to Run' and a medley from Disney.

'My throat's dry,' says Kate.

Ruth gives her some water. There's less than half a bottle left. 'We shouldn't sing any more.'

'Shall I try the ladder?'

'OK.'

Ruth gets out her phone. A brief glance at the comforting home screen with its picture of Flint. It's ten past ten. Everyone will be safely in their own homes by now. Zoe

with Derek. Judy with her children. Nelson and Michelle . . .
Don't think about that, she tells herself, but it's too late,
the mental screenshots come flooding in: candlelit meals,
his and hers chairs, who's going to walk the dog, time to
turn in, up the wooden hill to Bedfordshire, bedside lights
switched off, bodies turning towards each other . . .

Ruth passes the phone to Kate who tucks it in the belt
of her skirt and crawls away. Her poor knees must be in
agony. Ruth is in trousers and hers feel as if the skin has
been scraped away. It's true that, even without any light, the
shapes of the caverns are starting to emerge. Ruth dismissed
Leo's 'womb' comment at the time, but it occurs to her now
that the grey shapes with their dark openings look like her
first scan when she was expecting Kate. She'd gone on her
own. Nelson hadn't even known that she was pregnant at
the time. She remembers the cold gel on her stomach and
the sight of the pulsating screen, the four circles that would
form Kate's heart, that indomitable organ.

Kate is back. Her face is very pale as it emerges from
the dark O of the cave, but she still looks determined. She
hasn't given up yet and neither will Ruth. Kate takes up
her position next to Ruth. There are hollows in the rock
that almost seem to fit their bodies. Perhaps the miners
slept here sometimes? Perhaps their spirits are around
them now.

'Mum?' says Kate. 'Can you tell me a story?'

Ruth's mind is blank, but she knows the comfort of the
spoken word. She dredges her memory for books that she
has read to Kate. Perhaps it's no surprise that she lights on

one with a famous, though rather unfortunate, opening line.

'In a hole in the ground,' says Ruth, 'there lived a Hobbit . . .'

Judy is also lost in Middle Earth. When Cathbad was ill, the children found the *Lord of the Rings* films a great comfort. Now they are working their way through them again. Maddie is here too, just as she was in lockdown. In fact, the whole situation seems like a nightmarish case of déjà vu. Judy has to remind herself that Cathbad is not in hospital. He is missing and no one knows where he is.

Judy loved the Tolkien books as a child, but she finds the films rather too heavy on battle sequences. There are, after all, only so many ways that you can kill an orc. As far as she recalls from *The Hobbit*, Bilbo spends the whole of the climactic Battle of the Five Armies unconscious. In the three films (three!) that cover that book, there's a great deal of extraneous slashing, cleaving and writhing. But Judy is grateful for carnage as a babysitter. Leaving all three of Cathbad's children, and his dog, occupied, she escapes to the kitchen.

Judy pours herself a glass of wine. If Cathbad were here, he'd want them to go out into the garden, lie on the grass and look up at the sky as it eventually darkened and the stars appeared. 'I believe in God,' he once told her, 'except that I now call Him Mother Nature.' But now Cathbad has left her alone on the summer solstice, to live through this endless day on her own.

Judy has Cathbad's file with her, the lavender now crushed between the pages of his Last Will and Testament. But she finds that she doesn't want to read more about Cathbad's childhood in rural Ireland with Fionnuala and Bridget. Just at this moment, she's too angry with him. What she needs is work.

Judy opens her trusty notebook. She hasn't been involved in the Emily Pickering investigation, but she has created a timeline of events, based on Cathbad's memories and her own deductions. Tucked into the pages is a picture Cathbad found showing three women sitting round a café table. Emily with Peter Webster's daughters Freya and Gaia. 'I can't believe Peter could have killed Emily,' Cathbad said. 'He was a peaceful presence, not a talker, interested in history and folklore.' But how many murderers have been described in similar terms? Quiet. Loner. Introverted. Was Peter Webster a domestic tyrant? Judy scans the girls' faces for signs of trauma, but they stare blandly back at her. They aren't that alike, Gaia is taller and more striking, her hair in two buns on the top of her head. Freya's hair is loose. Judy turns to her timeline.

Friday 22nd March 2002	Emily, Tom, Emad and Amber arrive at Grime's Graves, Thetford for weekend camping/archaeology trip. Also present: Leo Ballard and Mark Oldbury.
Sunday 24th March 2002	During a final meal around the campfire, a mysterious figure

	appears from the woods. Cathbad says it was 'neither male nor female'. Also that it was horned.
Monday 25th March 2002	*Camp breaks up. Amber driven to station by Leo Ballard at approximately 7 a.m. Leo later (11 a.m. approx.) drives Emily to Thetford station. She says she is catching train to Lincoln, a journey which takes approximately 1 hour 30 minutes with one change. Tom and Emad driven back to Cambridge by Mark O.*
12.05 p.m.	*Emily seen at Ely station (25 mins by train from Thetford)*
12.07	*Emily seen crossing Jubilee Gardens*
12.20	*Emily seen outside Toppings bookshop*
Friday 11th June 2021	*Emily's remains found behind a wall in a King's Lynn house, formerly the Green Child café.*

Angry though she is with her life partner, Judy follows Cathbad's meditation techniques. She empties her mind and allows the receptive space to fill up with words and images.

What did Emily want? I was never sure.

A horned figure.

A cathedral.

A green child.

Cathbad told her about the Green Children of Woolpit some years ago but Judy fears that she went into listening mode and missed the finer details. She searches for the story in one of Cathbad's folklore anthologies which are interspersed with his cookery books.

The children were bright green, spoke an unknown language and would only eat broad beans [they remind Judy of Miranda and her various food fads]. *The boy was sickly and died but the girl slowly adjusted to her new life* . . .

Two children, thinks Judy. There were two of them.

An hour later and Ruth has only just got to the encounter with the trolls. Kate keeps remembering details she has forgotten (like Thorin not helping with the washing up) so progress is slow. But Ruth blesses JRR Tolkien and story-telling in general. Nothing else could have filled this ghastly time. Ruth feels as if her back has become moulded into the rock and her ribs hurt when she speaks. Cathbad has groaned a few times but now he's ominously silent. Ruth tried to moisten his lips but she didn't want to waste water. What if he's dead? But, like the ebb and flow of the tide, she can hear his stertorous breathing. Keep breathing, Cathbad, Ruth tells him, as she is sure she did once before. When Ruth last looked at her phone it was eleven o'clock, but the battery was down to fifteen per cent and she hasn't dared look again.

But, luckily, the story is in her head and not dependent on light or batteries.

'The trolls started to build their bonfire to cook and eat Bilbo and his friends. But, before they could light the fire, a mysterious voice said, "What about some tomato ketchup?"'

Kate is chewing the ends of her hair. Ruth can't see her, but she knows she's doing it. Now she says, 'They didn't have tomato ketchup then.'

'Humans have always had tomato ketchup. Anyway, the mysterious voice spoke again . . .'

At that moment, Ruth is aware of another sound. If she didn't know better, she'd think it was an actual mysterious voice. One calling her name.

'Did you hear that?' whispers Kate.

'I think so.' Ruth starts to crawl forward. She knows that Kate is right behind her. When she reaches the space with the ladder, her legs shake when she tries to stand up. She croaks, 'Hallo?' But it's Kate who shouts, at the top of her youthful lungs, 'We're down here! Help!'

There's a grinding sound and a square of light appears above them. Ruth shields her eyes. It must be night-time now, but the glare of the outside world is still dazzling. A face appears, as if in a halo.

'Ruth? Is that you?'

And Ruth has the strangest sensation, as if time has rewound itself and, in the process, become distorted, inverted. She has a vision of herself peering into an underground prison, a girl's face looking up at her.

'Lucy?' she says. 'You're Lucy, aren't you?'

CHAPTER 33

'Are you hurt?' shouts the woman. Lucy.

'We're not,' Ruth's voice is hoarse from storytelling, 'but there's an injured man down here.'

'I'm calling an ambulance,' says Lucy. 'The police too. Can you climb the ladder?'

'Yes,' says Ruth, 'but I think we should stay with Cathbad until the ambulance comes.' She doesn't explain who Cathbad is, but Lucy seems to understand. Ruth wants, more than anything, to escape the pit but she can't leave Cathbad on his own and she doesn't want Kate to go above ground without her. The appearance of Lucy is so odd, so dreamlike, that Ruth can't imagine what else they will find in the real world. The god Grim? All the victims Ruth has excavated over the years, wandering through the forest in a zombie-like state?

A few minutes later, Lucy calls down. 'I'm throwing down a bottle of water. Help is on its way.'

The plastic bottle ricochets down the rungs of the ladder. Ruth takes it and crawls back, through the tunnel, past the headless torso, to Cathbad. Once again, Kate is close behind her. She holds the water to Cathbad's lips.

'We've been rescued,' she says. 'It's going to be OK.'

But Cathbad seems to have sunk back into unconsciousness. Please, Ruth prays to whatever being guards the underworld, please don't let it be too late. Cathbad looks peaceful now, almost as if he is sleeping. Ruth remembers when Kate was a baby and refused to go to sleep. Cathbad had stayed at their house, taken hallucinogenic drugs and contacted the afterlife. After that, Kate slept like an angel.

'Michael and Miranda are waiting for you,' Kate tells Cathbad.

Ruth blesses her daughter for thinking of invoking the magical names. She joins in: Judy, Maddie, Michael, Miranda (Cathbad obviously has a thing for the letter M), Thing, Kate, Hecate, Ruth, Nelson, Michelle, Laura, Rebecca, George. The litany of their shared past.

After what feels like ages but is probably fifteen minutes there's a loud clanging sound. 'Paramedics coming down,' shouts a male voice, sounding wonderfully breezy and confident.

'We're here,' shouts Ruth. 'In the tunnel.' She switches on her phone, now on its last five per cent.

After a few minutes, a large moustachioed face appears in the entrance to the cave.

'He's here,' says Ruth. 'He's called Cathbad.'

The man crawls forward, with difficulty because he's bigger than Ruth or Kate. 'Hi there, Cathbad, let's look at you.' He takes Cathbad's pulse and listens to his chest. 'Vital signs not too bad. I'll get a colleague down here and we'll wrap him up and pull him out. You two should go now. You've looked after him really well, but we need the space in here.'

'OK,' says Ruth. She touches Cathbad's hand. 'See you soon,' she says. Then she edges past the paramedic and crawls back along the underground passage.

Kate is up the ladder in a trice. Ruth finds it much more difficult. Her arms seem to have lost all their strength and her ribs hurt. But, finally, she feels the blessed cold air on her face. The night seems full of lights and people. Someone puts a silver blanket over Ruth's shoulders and guides her to a patch of grass where Kate is sitting next to a young woman with dark hair pulled back from a pale face. As Ruth looks at her, she knows.

'Am I dreaming?' she says. 'Are you Lucy Downey?'

'It's Vanstone now,' says Lucy. 'DC Lucy Vanstone. But yes. Yes I am.'

'DC? Are you with the police?'

'Yes. I'm working with DCI Nelson.'

'Does he know? Who you are, I mean?'

'No,' says Lucy. 'It's hard to find the words somehow. Anyway, I wanted to tell you first. I keep going to your house but you're always out. I think your next-door neighbour is getting suspicious.'

'Is that how you found us?' says Ruth. 'Did Zoe tell you where I was?'

'She said it was something to do with the case,' says Lucy, 'so I drove around all the locations connected with it. When

I arrived here, I saw your car, so I knew I was in the right place.'

'Who are you?' says Kate. After being so brave in the mine, her voice now sounds as if she's on the verge of tears.

'Your mum saved my life when I wasn't much older than you,' says Lucy.

'And now you've saved ours,' says Ruth, getting tearful in her turn. Silhouetted against the arc lights, she can see figures approaching the entrance to the shaft.

'Cathbad will be OK, won't he?' she says.

But Lucy has stood up to greet a new arrival.

'OK,' says Tanya to the group at large. 'I'm in charge now.'

Thirteen years ago, Ruth found a fifteen-year-old girl imprisoned in an old air-raid bunker. She had held the girl in her arms and whispered platitudes remembered from her own mother. Tomorrow's another day. All's well that ends well. It's darkest before dawn. They had been chased by a madman, but they had escaped. Nelson and Cathbad crossed the marshes at night to rescue them but, in the end, they had rescued themselves. They had rescued each other. The girl, who had been abducted ten years earlier, was reunited with her parents. Her name was Lucy Downey.

At first, Ruth tried to keep in touch with Lucy and her parents. But they moved from Norfolk and Ruth thought this meant that they wanted a fresh start. Ruth was a reminder of the worst time in their lives. So, she stopped sending letters. But she never stopped loving Lucy.

Now Ruth sits on the grass with Lucy on one side of her

and Kate on the other. Tanya squats in front of them asking questions and Ruth has real trouble answering succinctly, like the professional woman she is, and not babbling about Hobbits and goddesses and being Born to Run. A stretcher has been lowered into the mine for Cathbad and Tanya says Ruth and Kate have to go to hospital too, 'just to get you checked over.'

'I'm OK,' Ruth begins before realising that her whole body feels like one big bruise. She supposes that she should check that nothing is broken. In any case, no one is arguing with Tanya.

'Have you told Judy?' she asks. 'About Cathbad?' When Ruth checked her phone, she had one per cent of battery left. After a few seconds' thought she messaged Zoe. Then the screen went blank.

'I rang Judy,' says Tanya, standing up and wiping chalk off her jeans. 'She's meeting us at the hospital. DC Vanstone will drive you.'

It's a few seconds before Ruth realises that she means Lucy.

It was past midnight when Nelson got the call, but he was still in the garden. Bruno was sitting loyally at his side, ears on alert to the night-time sounds, foxes and owls and the intermittent yelp of a neighbour's car alarm.

'Boss?' When he heard Tanya's voice, Nelson was on alert too. He could almost imagine that he had German shepherd ears, as sharp as mountain peaks.

'We've found Cathbad.'

'Thank God. Where was he?'

'Grime's Graves. Down one of the mine shafts. Ruth and Kate were with him.'

'Ruth and Katie?' Nelson was already in the hallway, gathering up his car keys. Bruno watched despondently. He knew this trip wasn't going to involve him.

'It's a long story. Apparently, Leo Ballard trapped them there.'

'Ballard.' Nelson heard himself growling the word. Bruno whined softly. 'Arrest him.'

'Bradley and a couple of uniforms have gone round to his house. They're bringing him in.'

'Good. I'm on my way.' Nelson pressed the buzzer to open the garage door.

'Meet us at the hospital. The Queen Elizabeth.'

Tanya should have called him earlier, thinks Nelson, as he speeds through the dark streets. But he understands that events must have moved quickly. The important thing is that Cathbad has been found and that Ruth and Katie are safe. Tanya said that Cathbad was unconscious. 'We won't know more until the doctors see him.' 'And Ruth and Katie?' 'Fine. Very chipper considering the circumstances.' Chipper. It's an odd word. Very Tanya somehow.

The hospital is blazing with light, like a spaceship that has landed by a Norfolk roundabout. Nelson parks on the yellow lines and runs into the building. The first person he sees is Lucy Vanstone. She is standing as if she is on parade duty, hands behind her back.

Nelson screeches to a halt beside her. 'Where's Ruth?'

'The doctor is checking her and Kate now. But they seem fine,' says Lucy, perhaps noticing the wild look in Nelson's eye. 'They were amazingly brave. It was quite an ordeal.'

'What happened? How long were they trapped down there?'

'I'll tell you all about it,' says Lucy. 'Do you want a coffee? I think it will be a while before they're discharged.'

Judy just misses Lucy and Nelson. She runs through A and E, swerving to avoid the beds that line the corridors. It's like a war zone, she thinks, and this is just a normal Monday night. At the door of the triage zone, she runs into a doctor she knows. 'Harpreet! Have you seen Cathbad? He's just been brought in.'

Harpreet shakes her head. She looks tired, a small but doughty figure in her scrubs. There's blood on them, Judy notes.

'I've just been with an RTA,' she says. 'But I'll check.'

She's back in a second. 'He's been taken up to the Edith Cavell ward. That means they don't think he's seriously injured.'

'Thank you.' Judy is pelting along the corridors, wondering for the hundredth time why hospitals are so confusing. She takes several wrong turns before arriving at the – locked – doors. 'Police!' she barks into the entry phone.

Cathbad is in the bed nearest to the nurses' station. He's sitting up and drinking a cup of tea.

'Hallo, Judy,' he says. 'It seems I've had quite an adventure.'
Judy bursts into tears.

Nelson has trouble taking in Lucy's story. They are sitting
in the 'Friends' café which is, to all extents and purposes,
closed. There's a grille over the counter and the chairs
are stacked on the tables. But Lucy persuades someone to
open the door and even takes time to collect coffees from a
machine. Nelson drinks his without noticing the taste.

Underground, rescue, tunnels, escape.

'Leo Ballard is in custody,' says Lucy. 'Apparently he's not
making much sense.'

'Do I know you from somewhere?' says Nelson. 'Somewhere before this.'

Lucy smiles and her face changes completely.

'My maiden name was Downey.'

Lucy Downey. The worst, and best, experience of Nelson's career. A girl who went missing aged five and turned
up again, aged fifteen, alive but having suffered a terrible
ordeal. The parents never blamed him although he blamed
himself. He should have found her earlier and he might
never have found her if it hadn't been for Ruth. He still
remembers the reunion, Lucy huddled in a police jacket,
the sound she'd made when she'd seen her mother again. It
brings tears to his eyes, even now.

'We moved away,' says Lucy. 'To Devon, where my mum
was from. I needed a lot of help at first. I couldn't go to
school. Couldn't socialise. My parents were great, though,
and I saw a fantastic therapist. Eventually I went to college

and did my A levels, a few years late, went to uni and became a police officer. It was all I ever wanted to do.'

'Why?' says Nelson. He can't imagine what it would be like to be kept a prisoner for ten years but he's not sure it would have given him a taste for a career in law enforcement.

'You saved me,' says Lucy with another of her sudden smiles. 'You and Ruth. You saved me. I wanted to save people.'

'You said Downey was your maiden name,' says Nelson. 'Are you married then?' He doesn't know how old she is, but she looks younger than his daughters.

'I married my university boyfriend,' says Lucy. 'It was a mistake. We're separated.'

'I'm sorry.'

'Don't be.' Another dazzling smile. 'It was an experience. I want as many experiences as I can get.'

'You're in the right job then,' says Nelson.

'Don't cry,' says Cathbad. 'I'm going to be all right. The doctors think all of it – the fainting, the flashbacks, the memory lapses – are all part of an inner ear thing linked to Long Covid. They're going to do an MRI scan to make sure but they think antibiotics will sort it out.'

'I thought you were dead,' says Judy. 'I thought you'd gone off somewhere to die.'

'I did think I was going to die,' says Cathbad. 'I thought I had a brain tumour. I'd looked up all the symptoms. Always a mistake.'

'Is that why you made us go to mass that day?' says Judy.

'Yes,' says Cathbad. 'Old habits and all that. I thought I should have a blessing. I didn't realise that blessings were all around me.'

'I went to Walsingham to look for you,' says Judy. 'I was on the wrong track. I kept thinking it was some sort of pilgrimage. Ruth went to St Mary's Houghton-on-the-Hill. Even Nelson sent someone to St Etheldreda's.'

'Well, time spent on pilgrimage is never wasted,' says Cathbad, with a grin. He looks so much like his old self, despite the bandage round his head, that Judy almost cries again but laughs instead. A nurse, obviously sensing imminent hysterics, offers her a cup of tea.

'I'd love one,' says Judy. She can feel her professional self re-emerging. 'What happened with Leo Ballard?' she asks Cathbad.

'The frustrating thing is that I still don't remember all of it,' says Cathbad. 'I know I went to Tony's for a reason, but I can't remember what it was.' He looks troubled again.

'It'll come back,' says Judy. 'Do you remember anything else?'

'I remember being in Leo's car then in a dark place, voices all round me. I saw Ruth and Hecate.'

'You mean Kate.'

'I know what I saw.'

When Nelson arrives back at the waiting area, still reeling from his journey into the past, Ruth's sister Zoe is there. Nelson approaches her cautiously. There has always been a constraint, almost a mutual distrust, between them.

'Have you heard how they are?'

'A nurse has gone to check.' Zoe doesn't meet his eyes. People say she looks like Ruth but Nelson can never see it.

'I'll wait with you.'

'There's no need.'

But Nelson sits down next to Zoe. He takes out his phone and texts Michelle. He forgot to do so earlier but he doesn't think Michelle will be worried if she wakes up in the night to find that he's gone. She's been married to a policeman for nearly thirty years.

He wonders how many times he's been in this situation, in a hospital waiting for news. There was the time when Ruth was in a car crash. That was Cathbad's fault too, come to think of it. There was the time when Nelson was shot. Ruth and Michelle had both waited for him on that occasion. When he'd heard that, Nelson was glad that he'd been unconscious. Except that a tiny part of him wished he'd been there, to hear what they'd talked about, what they'd said about him.

'Are you here for Ruth Galloway?'

A nurse is smiling at them. She looks more fresh-faced than Nelson would be at this time of night. It's nearly two a.m.

'Yes,' say Nelson and Zoe.

'There's a possibility of a broken rib so the doctor has sent her for X-rays. Nothing to worry about, though. Kate is fine. No ill effects at all. Children bounce, don't they? Does one of you want to go and wait with her?'

Nelson and Zoe both say that they will.

'I can only let one of you go up. Who's next of kin?'

'I am,' says Zoe. 'I'm Ruth's sister.' And she follows the nurse through the swing doors without a backward glance.

CHAPTER 34

Tuesday 22 June

'Seems to me that we're no further along.'

Nelson is in a bad mood. He knows it and the whole team knows it. Leah gives him a sidelong glance when she places his morning cup of coffee in front of him. Even Jo seems to choose her words carefully when she demands an update on last night's events. Nelson tries to fight it. He praises Lucy and Tanya for their work last night. Lucy had received a round of applause when she entered the incident room. She blushed but looked pleased, flashing that sudden smile. Nelson still thinks Tanya should have called him earlier, as soon as she knew Ruth and Katie were involved, but there is no doubt that she handled the occasion efficiently. Ballard is in custody and Cathbad is safe. Tanya says this now, sounding rather aggrieved.

'But we're still no closer to solving Emily's murder.'

Ballard has been charged with false imprisonment. Tanya and Bradley have interviewed him, with Nelson watching via video link. Ballard admitted locking Cathbad in the mine three days ago and trapping Ruth and Kate there. When asked why he did these things, he replied 'no comment'. His solicitor had nodded approvingly.

'Ballard must be guilty, surely?' says Tanya. 'Otherwise why did he want Cathbad out of the way?'

According to Judy, Cathbad can't remember anything between visiting Tony and finding himself underground. The doctors say that it's all to do with his condition – something to do with Long Covid – but it's still very annoying. But Nelson thinks Tanya is right. Cathbad must have telephoned Ballard after watching the CCTV footage at Tony's flat. Ballard picked him up in his electric car, took him to Grime's Graves and somehow tricked him, or coerced him, into entering the abandoned mine. Why? What had Cathbad seen that made him contact his old friend? Why had Ballard behaved in the way he did?

'We should keep an eye on the others today,' says Nelson. 'Tom, Amber, Emad and Mark. They'll all be at the funeral.'

Emily's funeral is at eleven o'clock in Lincoln. Tanya and Bradley are both attending. In their black suits they look out of place amongst the casually dressed civilian staff, like undertakers on a beach. Nelson is planning to go too but he's in his shirtsleeves, his black jacket on the back of a chair.

'Are you coming, boss?' says Tanya, as she prepares to leave.

'You go on ahead,' says Nelson. 'There's something I want to do first.'

*

Ruth wakes up ribs first. There's a stabbing pain every time she breathes but apparently nothing is broken. 'Just bruising,' the doctor said cheerfully. 'Take ibuprofen and try to rest.' Last night, Ruth had been so tired that she had fallen asleep as soon as she lay on her bed. Kate, who had slept in Zoe's car on the way home from the hospital, woke up as soon as they entered the house and had been full of questions. Why had that man trapped them? Would Dad arrest him? Would he go to prison? Could she miss school tomorrow, she means today?

'Let's talk about it tomorrow,' Ruth had said, sleepwalking up the stairs. 'You don't have to go to school.'

It's nine o'clock so Ruth clicks on her phone and rings the school's 'absence hotline'. It'll be the first day's absence Kate has had. An unearthly yowl from downstairs reminds Ruth that her other child needs attention. Ruth sneaks a look in Kate's room as she goes past. Her daughter is sound asleep, cheek pillowed on her favourite toy monkey. Ruth envies her.

Ruth feeds Flint and makes herself tea and toast. She swallows down two painkillers and tries to eat. She feels slightly sick but maybe that's just tiredness. She feels better after a shower. Kate is still sleeping so Ruth dresses in her loosest clothes, goes back downstairs and checks her phone. Three missed calls from Nelson. Zoe said that he'd been at the hospital last night. Ruth can't help feeling pleased to hear this but she's relieved that Zoe saved her from another bedside conversation with him. What is there to say that hasn't been said before? Perhaps Michelle will keep coming back to Nelson until all three of them are old and grey and past caring. Is it up to Ruth to break the impasse? If only she didn't feel so tired and achy and generally terrible.

The doorbell makes her jump. Visitors are rare and the postman usually just leaves parcels on her doorstep. She hadn't heard a car draw up but, looking out of the window, she sees a jeep-like vehicle. Who could it be? Zoe is at work and the weekenders are away again. Ruth thinks of her sleeping daughter. Should she ring Nelson? But then she tells herself not to be ridiculous. It's broad daylight. Probably just someone to read the meter. Does she even have a meter?

The bubble of glass at the top of the door shows some-one's head. A tall visitor then. Feeling frightened all over again, Ruth opens the door an inch.

'Hallo, Ruth. Just thought I'd drop by.'

It's David Brown.

'Come on, Lucy,' says Nelson, 'let's talk to Leo Ballard.'

Lucy looks quizzical but stands up immediately. Nelson knows that he's taking a risk. He's going against their agreed interview strategy which is led by Tanya with Bradley as her deputy. The last thing Nelson wants is to jeopardise their case against Ballard. This is why he asked Lucy to sit in, to show that he's following procedure. Except that he isn't. No harm in a few extra questions, he tells himself, as he signs them into the interview suite.

'Do I need my lawyer?' That's the first thing Ballard says. His hair is untidier than ever, but he looks remarkably bright for someone who has spent the night in the cells. Chipper, as Tanya might say.

'You're entitled to legal representation, of course,' says Nelson, 'but this isn't a formal interview. Just a few questions.'

'All right then,' says Ballard. 'Always happy to help the police.'

Like hell you are, thinks Nelson.

'I want to talk to you about Emily Pickering,' he says. 'About that weekend at Grime's Graves in 2002.'

'Why do you want to talk about Emily?' Ballard's composure slips a bit. He runs his hands through the haystack of grey curls. Nelson tries a smile. Lucy sits as still as a statue beside him. Did she learn this discipline when she was a captive? Nelson pushes the thought away.

'There are a few questions that remain unanswered about the weekend,' says Nelson. 'The masked figure that appeared from the woods, for example.'

To his surprise, Ballard laughs. 'Oh, that was Gaia.'

'Gaia?'

'Gaia Webster, Peter's daughter. She had been one of my students and we remained . . . close.'

'Close? Were you having an affair?'

'If you want to reduce it to the carnal level. Yes.'

'Why did Gaia do it? Why did she turn up that night?'

Ballard sighs, as if Nelson is a student who hasn't quite grasped the nuances of an intellectual argument. 'Gaia always resented my students. Emily and co in particular. She thought they were spoilt middle-class kids. Gaia did it the hard way, working class family, comprehensive school. She thought that most Cambridge students had it too easy. I think she just wanted to give everyone a fright.'

'Why didn't you tell them that it was Gaia? You could have stopped them being scared.'

'I didn't want to give her away. Besides, it's good for young people to be scared.' He smiles. A gap-toothed grin that is, in Nelson's opinion, enough to give anyone nightmares.

'If we'd interviewed Gaia earlier,' says Nelson, 'it might have given us the link to the café. We would have found Emily's body. Saved her parents a lot of heartache.' Ballard says nothing but, to be fair, it isn't a question.

'Why did Cathbad contact you on Friday?' says Nelson. 'What had he seen on the video?'

'Janus,' says Ballard. 'Our old friend, Janus. I'm not saying anything more without my solicitor.'

'Come in,' says Ruth. She suddenly wishes that she wasn't wearing tracksuit trousers and an old 'Eat the patriarchy' T-shirt.

David has to duck to enter the threshold. Ruth suddenly thinks of Janus, the god of entrances and exits. The Romans used to bury animals, and sometimes children, under doorways as offerings to the two-faced god. Ruth once discovered a child's bones under the doorway of a house in Norwich.

'Coffee?' says Ruth.

'That would be great. Thanks.' He moves away to examine her bookshelves. Ruth would do the same in a strange house, but she rather wishes that there weren't so many pony books and Georgette Heyers scattered between the academic tomes.

When Ruth comes back with the drinks, David is immersed in *Jill's Gymkhana*.

'This is great,' he says. 'Maja would love it.'

David's daughter, Maja, is the same age as Kate. They once spent a day together and are now, apparently, Facebook friends.

'Does Maja like horses?'

'Mad about them.'

'I've never been on a horse,' says Ruth, 'but I love pony books for some reason.'

'It's a soothing world,' says David. 'Like Georgette Heyer.'

'Georgette Heyer was an excellent historian,' says Ruth. 'They use *An Infamous Army* to teach military history at Sandhurst.' She thinks of Zoe's adoptive mother, starting with Georgette Heyer and ending with Lady Nicola de la Haye.

David smiles in an irritatingly understanding way. 'That's what I came to talk to you about.'

'You came to talk to me about Georgette Heyer?'

'No, about Maja. About Sweden.' David's ex-wife is Swedish, Ruth knows. That doesn't explain this visit, though.

'If the department closes,' says David, 'and I hope it won't, I'm going back to Sweden to teach at Uppsala. I spoke to my head of department yesterday and he said that he'd like to offer you a post too.'

'At Uppsala?' Ruth knows it's a prestigious university, but she doesn't think she could find the place on a map.

'Uppsala is beautiful,' says David. 'The library in the Carolina Rediviva building is just incredible. And the town is so historic. You know St Erik is buried there?'

Ruth thinks of her old university lecturer, Erik Anderssen. He's been dead now for thirteen years, but Ruth wouldn't put it past him to be meddling in her life.

'There are these standing stones all over the town,' says David. 'Viking stones decorated with runic animals. Then there's Old Uppsala where they've found Bronze Age and Iron Age settlements. You'd love it there.'

'I don't want to move to Sweden,' says Ruth.

'Think about it,' says David. 'It's a great university and Sweden is a wonderful place to live. Besides, it would make me very happy.'

'Why?' says Ruth. The conversation seems to be getting stranger by the minute.

'Because I'm in love with you,' says David. 'I thought you knew.'

CHAPTER 35

When Nelson gets back upstairs, Judy is waiting in his office. Nelson gives her a quick hug.

'How's Cathbad?'

'Pretty good. All things considering. The doctor thinks that the fainting and dizzy spells are caused by Long Covid. It's an umbrella term really. Doctors still don't understand all the implications because the symptoms are different for every patient. But they can include an inner ear condition that's similar to vertigo.'

'Vertigo? Isn't that fear of heights?' Nelson remembers that Cathbad once scaled the highest roller coaster in Europe trying to save Katie (who was actually safely on the ground at the time). Cathbad isn't a person who is scared of heights. He's also extremely brave and he loves Nelson's daughter.

'It's similar but the feeling usually doesn't last.'

'Poor old Cathbad. Covid really took it out of him.'

'It did but I think he's relieved it isn't worse. He'd convinced himself that he had a brain tumour.'

'He was going on to me about wanting a woodland burial or some such lunacy. Was that why?'

'Yes,' says Judy. 'He wrote all the instructions down. I found them when I was going through his things. I found his will too. He's leaving you his cloak.'

'Jesus wept.'

'I found some writing too. About his childhood.'

'Memoirs of a mad druid? A sure-fire bestseller.'

'I don't think they're for publication. Just his thoughts and memories. All about his mother and grandmother. It made me realise how little I really know about him.'

'Well, you've got plenty of time to find out now.'

Judy smiles. 'I have.'

Nelson clears his throat. Time to get back to business.

'Cathbad still can't remember what happened when he visited young Tony?'

'No,' says Judy. 'He says he's trying but he can only remember arriving at the flat and, some time after, finding himself underground.'

'We think Ballard took Cathbad to Grime's Graves and persuaded him to go into the mine somehow,' says Nelson.

'He wouldn't have needed much persuading,' says Judy. 'Ballard just needed a good story about a horned god or a fertility goddess.'

'Ruth would have been the same,' says Nelson. 'Bloody archaeologists. Did you hear that young Lucy saved them? Do you know who she is?'

'What do you mean?' says Judy.

'She's Lucy Downey.'

He doesn't need to say more. Judy was involved in that case too. She was with Lucy's parents when they saw their daughter for the first time in ten years. A few days earlier, she'd had to tell another set of parents that their child was dead.

'Lucy Downey? I can't believe it!'

'All grown up and a policewoman,' says Nelson, nodding towards the incident room where Lucy is diligently writing notes.

'Police officer,' corrects Judy automatically.

'Makes you think, doesn't it?' says Nelson.

'Cathbad would say it was all part of the great web.'

'He certainly would. But he's not here. There's no need for you to start saying stuff like that too.'

'Sorry,' says Judy. 'What about this case then? Are we any nearer to finding out what happened to Emily?'

'It's very frustrating,' says Nelson. 'We've got Ballard in custody, but we still can't get him for Emily's murder.'

'Are you sure that he killed her then?'

'I'm not sure of anything but what other explanation is there? Ballard is clearly a desperate man. He kidnapped three people to stop them from speaking out but, the problem is, we don't know what he thought they were going to say.'

'What did he say in the arrest interview?'

'Mostly no comment. But just now he told me that Gaia Webster was the figure who came out of the woods and scared them all, back in 2002.'

'The horned figure,' says Judy. 'I've seen a picture of Gaia with her hair in two buns on top of her head. Space buns, they're called. Miranda sometimes asks me to do her hair like that. They could look like horns.'

'Ballard wouldn't say anything else, though,' says Nelson. 'Just babbled on about Janus.'

'Janus. He's the one with two faces, isn't he?'

'I think so. Ballard had a statue of him in his garden. Creepy-looking thing.'

'I was looking at my notes yesterday,' says Judy. 'I don't have the official files, of course, just what I've pieced together. But I kept thinking: two people. There were two green children. Two sisters. Gaia and Freya.'

'And Emily and her sister Sophie.'

'Yes,' says Judy.

They look at each other. Nelson's mind is struggling, like a carriage creaking its way to the top of a roller coaster. Sooner or later will come the plunge, the vertigo.

Look to the sister.

Our old friend Janus.

I'm Ruth's sister.

Nelson goes to his computer and opens the case file. He scrolls through the interviews until he finds Mark Oldbury.

'Listen to this,' he says to Judy. Oldbury's voice, with its slight Antipodean twang, fills the room.

'We'd had a few good days. You know these pampered kids; they're not used to roughing it. There are always complaints at first. The ground's too hard, there's no hot water and they have to pee behind a bush. They don't come prepared at all. One girl even brought her curling tongs. But, by the end of the weekend, they'd all

settled down. There was a celebratory feeling that last night. One of the students played the guitar. We were all singing . . .'

'Very interesting,' says Judy. 'But why is it relevant?'

'When Cathbad watched the video of Emily in Ely he went to a total stranger's house and asked if he could use their phone.'

'That sounds like Cathbad.'

'It does. Anyway, the woman thought she heard him say something about a gate.'

'A gate?'

'Yes. But what if it was *gait*? The way someone walks?'

'Do you mean Emily?'

'Yes.' Nelson grabs his black jacket. 'Come on. We're going to a funeral.'

'What do you mean?' says Ruth. But she knows what he means, only too well. She's just trying to stall things. Preferably for ever. She wishes she was anywhere else in the world. She almost wishes she was still buried in the underground mine shaft.

'I'm in love with you,' says David. He says it in the same irritable way that he puts the case for the arrival of the Beaker People in 2000 BC. 'I assumed you knew.'

'I certainly didn't,' says Ruth. 'We seem to argue most of the time.'

'That's always a sign, don't you think?'

Is it? When Ruth first met Nelson they had clashed, disagreeing on almost everything. Ruth was an atheist, Nelson a lapsed Catholic. Ruth was an academic, Nelson a hard-nosed police officer. Nelson was a family man, Ruth happy living alone with her cat. And yet . . . there was definitely something, a connection between them, something that transcended all the differences. Cosmic balance, Cathbad said once, yin and yang. Is it the same with David?

'I'm sorry, David,' says Ruth. 'My life is . . . complicated at the moment. I can't really think about relationships.'

'Oh, I know about Nelson,' says David. 'But he's never going to leave his wife.'

'She's left him,' says Ruth. Her voice sounds small and unconvincing.

'She'll be back,' says David. 'That marriage will last for ever. You deserve someone who loves you wholeheartedly. Someone who admires you as a person and an archaeologist.'

It sounds like the beginning of a speech but, nevertheless, the words are good to hear. Has Nelson ever said that he admires her as an archaeologist? David leans towards her.

Ruth has no idea what would have happened if, at the very same moment, Flint hadn't emitted one of his spine-chilling screams and Kate called from the top of the stairs that the Wi-Fi wasn't working.

The funeral is over and the mourners are walking towards the graveyard. Nelson and Judy watch from a discreet distance. It's unusual these days to have a burial in a country churchyard. Usually there's a grim trip to the crematorium or an out-of-town cemetery, the suburbs of the dead. Nelson's father had been cremated; Tim, Nelson's officer killed in the line of duty, had been interred following a private ceremony. Maybe Emily's parents chose this plot years ago, when she first went missing. Nelson forces himself to stop this depressing train of remembrance.

Emily's parents are following the coffin. Gordon is staring straight ahead; Naomi's eyes are hidden by sunglasses. Is this giving them any peace, thinks Nelson, any of the much-vaunted closure? Behind them is a woman so like Emily that she must be her sister, Sophie. She is holding on to her husband's arm and looks ready to collapse. Not much closure there.

Nelson scans the crowd, all of whom are now making their way between the tombstones. There are Tom and Amber, looking like models from a feature entitled Mourning à la Mode. With them is a tall man Nelson doesn't recognise. Emad Hussein? He spots Mark Oldbury only because he's brought his dog with him, a sleek greyhound who is the most elegant being present.

Tanya and Bradley bring up the rear. Nelson is not surprised to see Cloughie with them. It's his patch, after all. Clough is wearing dark glasses too and no doubt imagines himself to be acting out one of the more lugubrious scenes from *The Godfather*. Still, Cloughie's presence might prove useful later.

There's no dissembling with a burial, no tactful drawing of the curtain. The undertaker's men lower the coffin into the ground. The wreaths and flowers lie on the grass, cellophane rustling in the breeze. Seagulls call high above. Nelson watches as Gordon and Naomi throw soil into the grave. Nelson imagines, rather than hears, the rattle on the coffin lid. Sophie shakes her head, obviously too distressed. The vicar speaks, his robes flying out behind him, creating an unexpectedly heroic silhouette.

The words, too, are blown by the wind.

'I am the resurrection and the life, saith the Lord. He that believes in me, though he were dead, yet shall he live . . .'

It's a nice thought, thinks Nelson, but you wouldn't bet on it. Even so, he knows that he wants these verses spoken at his own funeral. A wordless woodland burial is not for him.

The dreadful ritual is over and the mourners are walking to their cars. There's a general sense of relief, of hats taken off and cigarettes lit. Amber shakes out her tawny hair and laughs at something Tom says. Mark's dog is running free through the stone crosses and weeping angels.

Nelson and Judy approach.

'Amber Westbourne, I'm arresting you on suspicion of the murder of Emily Pickering. You do not have to say anything but it may harm your defence if you do not mention when questioned something you later rely on in court . . .'

Nelson does not finish the caution. Amber falls to the ground and lies motionless amongst the gravestones.

CHAPTER 36

'I killed her,' says Amber. 'She was kissing Leo and I just saw red.'

When Amber fainted at his feet, Nelson had been afraid that this would mean a trip to the hospital and another delay to the much-delayed justice. But Amber soon sat up and rubbed her eyes.

'I'll come with you,' she said to Nelson.

'So will I,' said Tom.

Amber's husband had been bemused at first but now sounded grimly determined. Nelson had been afraid of this. He didn't think that Amber would confess with Tom present. Besides, he's a lawyer. They both are. To be on the safe side, he arrested Thomas Westbourne too. With Clough's help, the team escorted the couple into separate police cars. The mourners stood watching. Oldbury's dog barked and was quieted by its owner. Nelson heard someone crying. He thought it might be Sophie, Emily's sister.

At the station, Amber waived her right to a solicitor. Interviewed by Tanya and Bradley, she looks pale but composed.

Nelson, Judy and Clough watch on the screen. Just like old times, Nelson can't help thinking. 'You're too nostalgic,' Michelle used to tell him when he got sentimental about the girls' old toys. Except that Michelle is now feeling the pull of the past.

'When did this happen?' asks Tanya.

'Sunday night,' says Amber. 'I woke up and Emily wasn't in the tent. I was worried about her. Or maybe I was suspicious. I can't be sure now. Sometimes I go over the events in my head and I'm the hero, saving Emily from some random attacker. Or from the horned figure in the woods. But that's not what happened.'

'What did happen?' says Tanya. She's playing it by the book, but Nelson can hear the slight impatience in her voice. Take it slowly, he tells her silently. PEACE. Planning, engagement, account, clarification, evaluation.

'I got up to look for her,' says Amber. 'I didn't have to go far. Emily and Leo were by the campfire. It was low by then but still glowing. They were kissing. I just . . . it's a blank really . . . but I was so angry. I picked up a rock, a flint, and hit Emily on the head with it.'

'What happened then?' asks Tanya.

'She went down so quickly.' Amber shudders. 'I never expected that. It was just one blow. Honestly.'

Tanya stays silent. Well done, thinks Nelson.

'Leo said she was dead,' says Amber. 'He knew what to do. I was in such a state. I wanted to call an ambulance, but Leo said no. He said that Emily was dead and there was nothing we could do about it. "She's a sacrifice," he said. "A sacrifice to the ancestors."'

Nelson hates the word sacrifice. He makes a silent vow to include enough charges to keep Leo in prison for the rest of his life.

'Leo put Emily's body in one of the mine shafts,' says Amber. 'He said that he'd say he took me to the station early, while Mark was walking Odin and everyone else was sleeping. Then I would pretend to be Emily. It was quite easy. We had similar hair colour in those days. I sneaked into Mark's van and used my curling tongs to make my hair more like hers.'

Bingo, thinks Nelson.

'Then I put on Emily's hoodie and waited in Leo's car. Emily could be standoffish. No one thought it was odd that she didn't say goodbye. Even Tom and he was meant to be *so* in love with her. I remember waving at him and he waved back, never noticed a thing.'

There is acid in her voice now.

'Leo said that there should be a sighting of Emily in some other place, to put people off the scent. A red herring. So he took me to Ely. I walked around a bit, then I got the train – several trains – back to Durham.'

'What happened to Emily's body?' asks Tanya.

Good work, thinks Nelson. With luck they'll be able to charge Ballard with preventing the lawful burial of a body.

'It stayed in the mine,' says Amber. *It*, thinks Nelson. 'Later on, Leo told me that he'd moved it to the café. They were building a wall and he thought it could be hidden there. He said that Emily could be in a place she loved. I expect Gaia gave him the keys to the café. She was always hanging around Leo.'

By his own admission, Leo was having an affair with Gaia at the time. Was he also having one with Amber? But when Tanya asks, Amber is surprisingly coy.

'We never . . . you know . . . did it. But we were in love. Leo said I was special, but he didn't want to spoil it by anything . . . carnal. We had to remain pure. So that was why, when I saw him kissing Emily – that was carnal, all right – it seemed such a betrayal.'

'Carnal', Nelson recalls, was one of Leo's words. *If you want to reduce it to the carnal level,* he'd said, only that morning. Well, the carnal level was where many crimes happened. Leo wanted his students to remain 'pure', presumably so that he could seduce them one by one. Nelson thinks that Emily's parents were right to blame her tutor for her death. One thing is for sure: it certainly wouldn't have happened without him.

Nelson gets his own round of applause when he enters the incident room.

'It was all Tanya,' he says. 'She and Bradley did all the legwork.'

Tanya, who hadn't joined in with the ovation, looks mollified. 'How did you guess about Amber?' she asks. 'Has some of Cathbad's sixth sense rubbed off on you?'

Maybe it has, thinks Nelson. He remembers the feeling of being on a roller coaster, the sudden fall. If that's what sixth sense feels like, it's no wonder Cathbad has vertigo.

'We kept thinking in doubles,' he says. 'Emily and Amber. Emily and Sophie. Freya and Gaia. Then I thought: maybe it was just one girl. One girl who left the camp alive that day. Cathbad must have seen something on the video that told him the girl in Ely wasn't Emily. He said something about gait. Maybe he'd spotted something odd about her walk.'

'Emily broke her ankle playing hockey,' says Tanya. 'Her mother told me. She stopped playing after it. That could have affected the way she walked.'

'That could be it,' says Clough. 'I remember hearing a forensic podiatrist give evidence in court once. He said that a person's gait is entirely individual to them.'

'I thought about what Cathbad said the last time I saw him,' says Nelson. 'We were talking about Emily and he said, "I can see her now, walking towards me." Cathbad must have remembered Emily's particular way of walking. He went to Tony's to see if it really was her on the CCTV footage.'

'Cathbad always notices things like that,' says Judy. 'But if only he'd come to you rather than confronting Leo Ballard.'

'I suppose Ballard had been his friend,' says Nelson. 'Cathbad probably wanted to give him the chance to explain. He might not even have suspected Ballard of Emily's murder. He just knew that the girl in Ely wasn't Emily.'

'All those hints and clues,' says Tanya. '"Look to the sister" and all that. It was as if Ballard wanted to be caught.'

'Maybe he did,' says Nelson. 'Or maybe he was just showing off. He cared enough about his reputation to sue Emily's parents. He must have felt secure to do that. Of course, he had an alibi for the day Emily supposedly disappeared, the Monday, because she'd actually been killed the night before.'

'That explains why Emily's DNA wasn't in Ballard's car,' says Bradley, the motoring correspondent. 'She was never in it.'

'I'm sure we'll find Amber's there, though,' says Nelson. 'But we might not need it. We have a full confession. And we have Amber and Ballard in custody. Tom Westbourne too but we'll have to let him go. We don't have anything to charge him with.'

'Do you think he knew?' asks Clough. 'What Amber did?'

'I don't think so,' says Tanya. 'Tom left Cambridge after Emily disappeared and only met up with Amber at law school. It was as if she'd reinvented herself. You should see their house. Everything perfect. Perfect couple. Perfect children.'

'Not that perfect,' says Nelson. 'This was always there in the background. Nothing in the world is hidden for ever.'

Where did *that* come from?

'Arabella Webster knew,' says Tanya. 'She said, "they put her behind the wall". I think she and her husband both knew. Perhaps Peter even helped.'

'Why would he do that?' asks Bradley. 'I thought he adored Emily.'

'Maybe Ballard had something on him,' says Nelson. 'Maybe Webster's photography habit wasn't so innocent after all. Maybe he had some indecent images. Didn't his wife say something like that?'

'She said "he put his photos in a special book",' says Tanya. 'I thought it was creepy at the time.'

'Well, we can't get at either of the Websters now,' says Nelson. 'We need to question Gaia. She gave him the key. Did she know what it was for?'

'I don't think she will have asked,' says Tanya. 'She seemed completely under his spell. God knows why.'

Nelson doesn't understand either, but he remembers Cathbad saying that Leo found out what you wanted and then offered it to you. Maybe that's what he did with Gaia?

'We'll just have to make sure that the charges stick with Ballard and Amber,' he says. 'Make sure they pay for what they did.'

'When are you going to tell Emily's parents?' says Clough. 'They saw the arrests. They must guess something's up.'

'I'll drive over there now,' says Nelson. 'Want to come for the ride, Cloughie?'

Nelson knows that Emily's parents had planned a wake in the church hall. He hopes that, in the light of the disturbance after the funeral, this will be a short-lived affair. Sure enough, when Nelson and Clough park outside the Victorian house in Lincoln, Naomi is in the garden with the chocolate Labrador panting beside her. She has changed out of her black dress and is back in her gardening dungarees. She stands stock-still when she sees the two men approaching, soil cascading from her trowel.

'What is it?' she says.

'Let's go inside,' says Nelson.

In the sitting room they find, not just Gordon Pickering, but Sophie and her husband Steve too. A large baby is sitting on the carpet, banging plastic bricks together. The child hadn't been at the church earlier.

As succinctly as possible, Nelson tells the Pickerings that Amber Westbourne, née Fletcher-Ellis, has confessed to Emily's murder.

'Amber was always jealous of Emily,' says Sophie. 'She was another of Leo's girls.'

Were you one too? wonders Nelson. But now is not the time for that question.

'Was Ballard involved?' asks Gordon hoarsely.

'Yes, he was,' says Nelson. 'You were right about him. We're charging him with being an accessory to murder. Also with false imprisonment and preventing the lawful burial of a body. I'm hoping he goes to prison for a long time.'

'I hope he dies there,' says Gordon. Both parents, Nelson notes, are still fixated on Ballard. Amber hardly registers with anyone except Sophie.

'Amber married Tom too,' says Sophie. 'She wanted everything of Emily's. She even said that she wished I was her sister.'

Look to the sister, thinks Nelson. Did Ballard know about this conversation?

'At least we know now,' says Steve. He's a quiet man but he's a calming presence. Nelson thinks that he would be a comforting doctor.

'Yes,' says Naomi, who is stroking the dog's head with muddy hands. 'We've laid her to rest and now we know.'

She looks as if she's about to cry but Steve scoops up the baby and puts it in her lap. Naomi buries her head in the sparse curls.

And Nelson remembers that the child's name is Emily.

CHAPTER 37

After Kate and Flint's various demands succeed in driving David away, Ruth wants nothing more than to go back to bed. But she's got to get through the day somehow. She makes lunch for herself and Kate and then the two of them sit on the sofa and watch the first Harry Potter film. How young the actors look, thinks Ruth. She remembers going to see this film with Shona, before either of them had children. She'd been rather embarrassed by this, had briefly considered kidnapping a nephew for the day. But they hadn't been the only child-free adults in the cinema. Ruth had been captivated by the film, as she had by the books. The effects, which seemed wonderful then, now seem charmingly old-fashioned. But Ruth lets it flow over her, occasionally checking her phone. No more missed calls from Nelson.

When a car draws up outside, Kate says, 'Is that Dad?' Because Nelson was around a lot during lockdown, Kate is no longer quite so excited by his visits. Or maybe she's just reached the age when neither of her parents can compete with a screen. Ruth goes to the window and sees Judy getting out of her Fiat. Ruth opens the front door.

'Hi, Judy. How's Cathbad?'

'Much better. They've given him antibiotics, which has helped a lot. His memory's still very patchy, though.'

On the TV Harry is being confronted by a three-headed dog. It reminds Ruth of Black Shuck, a spectral hound said to haunt parts of Norfolk and Suffolk. Kate looks up when she sees Judy. 'Is Uncle Cathbad OK?'

The 'uncle' brings unexpected tears to Ruth's eyes. It's because I'm tired, she tells herself. Judy gives Kate a hug. 'He's going to be fine. He said you were very brave in the mine.'

'Mum was too,' says Kate, in the tones of one determined to be fair.

'She's always brave,' says Judy.

Leaving Kate in the company of the boy wizard, Judy and Ruth take their mugs of tea into the garden. Flint emerges from the long grass like a tiger.

'How do you feel?' asks Judy. 'That must have been quite an ordeal.'

'OK,' says Ruth. 'I'm quite bruised from the fall but mostly just relieved to be here. Did you hear that Lucy saved me? Do you know who she is?'

'The boss told me. I couldn't believe it.'

'When I saw her face looking down at me,' says Ruth, 'it brought everything back. The thunderstorm. Running across the marshes. Finding the hidden room under the hide.'

'I was there a few days ago,' says Judy. 'Someone had left flowers.'

'That was probably Lucy. She said that she'd been back to the Saltmarsh. Do you think the flowers were for Scarlet?'

'I suppose so.' They are both silent for a moment, thinking of the girl who didn't leave the marshes alive.

'Anyway,' says Judy. 'I came to tell you that we've made an arrest for Emily's murder. Amber Westbourne, one of her university friends.'

'Oh my God!' says Ruth. 'How did you find out?'

'Nelson had a brainwave,' says Judy. 'It was quite weird actually. He listened to a taped interview about some curling tongs and suddenly you could see the cogs whirring. Cathbad would say that he was acting on his instincts at last.'

Nelson is quite capable of acting on his instincts, thinks Ruth. But at least this explains why he hasn't been to see her.

'Amber has confessed,' says Judy. 'Apparently she killed Emily because she saw her kissing Leo Ballard.'

'Bloody hell,' says Ruth. She thinks of the emaciated figure with his dandelion hair. Why would anyone kill over him? But human motives are often unaccountable. That's something she's learnt over the last few years.

'Nelson and Clough have gone to tell Emily's parents,' continues Judy. 'Trust Cloughie to get in on the action.'

'Tanya wanted me to give a proper statement,' says Ruth. 'I suppose that isn't so important now.'

'We'll still want a statement,' says Judy. 'The boss wants to charge Ballard with as many things as possible. He helped cover up the murder. He put Emily's body in one of the mines and then moved it to the café. Cathbad cried when I told him. I really think he was in love with Emily. He told me that they slept together once.'

Ruth doesn't admit that she already knows this.

'Do you know what happened with Cathbad?' she says. 'Why did Ballard kidnap him? Me and Kate too?'

'When Cathbad saw the video of the girl in Ely,' says Judy, 'he knew it wasn't Emily. Something to do with the way she walked. He told Ballard who panicked and trapped Cathbad in the mine. Nelson thinks he did the same to you because you were looking at soil samples. You might have worked out what happened to Emily's body.'

'It was hardly a foolproof plan, though,' says Ruth. 'Locking us in a mine shaft.'

'Like I say,' says Judy, 'Ballard panicked. I only hope he doesn't put in a plea of diminished responsibility. Apparently, he's been behaving oddly for years.'

'I've heard that too,' says Ruth.

'Guilt,' says Judy. 'It gets them all in the end.'

And they sit in the garden thinking about crime and guilt and the unknowability of the human race. Flint watches them from the apple tree.

It's late by the time that Nelson leaves the station. But the case is closed and the charges have been made. Emily is at rest and her parents have some answers. 'Thank you, DCI Nelson and DI Clough,' says Gordon, when he showed them to the door. 'I knew it was a good sign when the big guns got involved.' The big guns. Nelson could see that Clough loved this description.

But Clough can still surprise him. Before driving back to Cambridge, he admitted to Nelson that he'd consulted a medium about Cathbad.

'Madame Rita. You remember her from when Michael went missing?'

'I remember lots of odd things about that case, Cloughie.' Including his sergeant babbling on about red hearts and white ladies.

'She said that Cathbad was no longer walking on the surface of the earth. And he wasn't, was he? He was underground.'

'These people always say things that can be interpreted a million different ways. You twisted it to make sense because you wanted to believe it.'

Clough hadn't answered but he didn't look convinced. Nelson hopes that Cloughie isn't about to start wearing a cloak. For himself, he feels quietly pleased that justice has been done. One thing in his life, at least, is settled.

Nelson sits in his car for a few moments wondering what to do next. It's second nature to drive home but what will be waiting for him there? More shepherd's pie and faux marital bliss? Nelson thinks of Ruth's cottage. He's always disliked the remote location but now it seems to him to be a haven, a place of open views and peaceful air. He says 'Ruth' into his phone. There's no answer.

Nelson types, 'R u there?' But the message remains unopened. Nelson sighs and starts for home.

*

Ruth sees the message. What's the point? she thinks. Nelson would probably come over, full of concern and paternal anguish, berating her for putting Kate at risk. They'd argue and, later, they'd have fantastic sex. But, the next day, Nelson would go back to Michelle. She thinks of David saying, 'That marriage will last for ever.' Of course, in the light of David's surprising declaration, his opinion might not be unbiased. But Ruth is sure that's what everyone says. Her friends, her colleagues, her family. 'He's never going to leave his wife. Poor old Ruth, when's she going to wise up?'

Maybe now's the time to wise up, in all senses. She could take the dean's job and devote herself to an academic career. Or she could go to Uppsala, with or without David. Sweden. The word conjures up clean lines, raw fish, tight four-part harmonies. Is Ruth ready for such a tidy country? She could go back to London, as her dad suggested, and maybe get a job at her alma mater. She could be near Arthur and Gloria and, despite Jack's comments about drug dealers, there would be good schools for Kate. But Kate loves her current school and her friends. And Ruth loves Norfolk.

At six, Zoe comes home from work and appears at the door with a bottle of wine and a box of chocolates. For almost the first time in her adult life, Ruth doesn't feel like either of those things.

'How are you feeling?' asks Zoe. 'How are the bruises?'

'A bit sore,' says Ruth. 'But I'm OK. Judy came round earlier. They've caught the person who killed Emily, the student that went missing all those years ago.'

'Has Nelson been round?' asks Zoe.

'No,' says Ruth. She tells Zoe about Lucy Downey. 'She was the girl that came here looking for me.' But even this news doesn't make much of an impact. Zoe tells her to rest and goes back to her side of the wall. Kate rifles through the chocolates and says they all have funny flavours. Ruth suppresses the ignoble thought that they were an unwanted gift from one of Zoe's patients.

Ruth and Kate watch another Harry Potter film, eat supper in front of the TV and are both in bed by nine. Flint comes upstairs with Ruth and settles on her duvet, starting one of his all-over washing routines that shakes the whole bed. Ruth can hear Kate chatting in her room, presumably FaceTiming with Isla, but she has left her own phone downstairs. She looks out of the window. It's not yet dark on this day after midsummer but there are flickering lights on the horizon. Are they the lantern men, malevolent sprites luring unwitting travellers to their deaths?

'Tomorrow is the first day of the rest of my life,' says Ruth aloud.

But the words do not have the motivational glow usually associated with this statement.

CHAPTER 38

Wednesday 23 June

Kate is adamant that she wants to go to school the next day, so Ruth drops her off on the way to UNN. She thinks that Kate is looking forward to regaling Isla and Megan with her adventures. For Ruth's part, she plans to avoid her colleagues as much as possible.

But her luck is out. The first person she sees, as she walks across the car park, is David Brown. He's supervising the erection of a structure which, to Ruth's still slightly bleary eyes, looks very much like a scaffold.

'It's a stage,' he says. 'For the rally tomorrow. You haven't forgotten, have you?'

'Of course not,' says Ruth. She had but, then, she's had quite a lot on her mind.

'I've even got a megaphone,' he says, brandishing it.

'Jolly good,' says Ruth. His voice, even without amplification, is making her head hurt. As long as he doesn't mention the L word.

'There's been quite a lot of media interest,' he says. 'I gave a quote to *Lynn News* this morning. I'm hoping that Tony will put in an appearance.'

For a moment, Ruth thinks he means Tony Blair. Isn't he off earning millions as an after-dinner speaker somewhere? Then she realises that he means Tony Robinson, the ex-*Time Team* presenter.

'Do you think he reads *Lynn News*?' she asks.

But David is off. He seems to think that tomorrow's news will be dominated by the possible closure of a small department in a little-known university. Ruth rather thinks that there will be more coverage of the arrests in the Emily Pickering case. Will Nelson do a press conference? That might be the only time she sees him, these days. On TV flanked by a glamorous Super Jo and a smug Tanya.

'I've got to go,' she says, heading towards her staircase.

'I meant what I said yesterday,' David shouts after her.

Nelson decides to visit Cathbad on his way to work. It's a way of avoiding Jo's inevitable press conference. But, also, he wants to check that the crazy druid is recovering. Cathbad claims to have saved Nelson's life once, by dint of voyaging through the dream world in a stone boat. Climbing a few stairs at the Queen Elizabeth hospital is the least Nelson can do.

He parks in the multistorey and checks his phone before getting out of the car. Three messages from Jo. Nothing from Ruth. Then a news item catches his eye. Or rather three words do. Dr Ruth Galloway.

'If the department closes,' says senior lecturer David Brown, 'this country will lose one of its foremost academics. Dr Ruth Galloway is planning to take up a post at Uppsala University in Sweden. That would be a great loss to British archaeology. And to Norfolk.'

Bugger Norfolk. What about him, Nelson? Is Ruth really planning to relocate without telling him? Is this why she's been keeping him at arm's length? And what about Katie? Ruth is going to take *his* daughter out of the country. To bloody *Sweden* of all places. Nelson punches the steering wheel so hard that the alarm goes off.

He's still fuming when he reaches Edith Cavell ward. Cathbad, who has a rather rakish bandage round his head, is lying back on his pillows, reading what looks like an antique tome. The title is something about ancient runes. Cathbad puts the book down when Nelson approaches.

'What's the matter?'

'Shouldn't I be asking you that?'

'I'm not blind yet, Nelson. There's a cloud of negative energy around you.'

'Bollocks,' says Nelson. But his heart's not in it. He sits on the visitors' chair and tries to control his breathing.

'You've heard we made an arrest,' he says.

'Yes,' says Cathbad. 'Judy told me. Poor Amber. She was always in Emily's shadow.'

Nelson does not think Amber deserves any sympathy. She put Emily in the shadow of death and did not even seem very contrite about it.

'I kept thinking about Emily,' says Cathbad. 'I didn't

want to die with her murder unsolved. Something about her going to Ely didn't seem right to me. Emily had been at school there and didn't like the place. When Judy said that Tony was at home looking through the CCTV footage, I thought I'd go round to have a look. When I saw the video, I knew it wasn't Emily. She had a certain way of walking, favouring one foot, very slightly. Amber had a very bouncy, athletic stride. I knew that it was her. My first thought was that I had to tell Leo.'

'Pity your first thought wasn't to tell your partner. Or the police,' says Nelson. 'Can you remember anything else?'

'It's still behind the veil,' says Cathbad. 'Like being in the dream world. Remember?'

'How can I remember something that has only ever existed in your overheated imagination?'

'The first thing I remember is waking up in the hospital,' says Cathbad. 'But I heard voices. Ruth. Hecate. Judy. Lucy Downey. I always thought Lucy would come back, you know. I always thought she'd have a part to play before the end.'

The end of what? thinks Nelson. He thinks of Clough, hard-headed Clough, consulting Madame Rita. Of Cathbad, lost in the dream world. Who knows any more what's real and what isn't?

'So, what's happened to upset you today?' Cathbad asks Nelson. The unexpected tenderness in his voice, or perhaps the childish word 'upset', almost brings treacherous tears to Nelson eyes. He clears his throat and says, in his gruffest voice, 'Ruth's going to live in Sweden.'

'Is she?' says Cathbad. 'Who told you that?'

'I read it. Or I saw it on some online news thing.'

'And you believed it? Have you asked Ruth?'

'No.'

Cathbad struggles to sit up. 'Ask her, Nelson. Or rather, tell her. Have you ever told Ruth what you think about her? What she means to you?'

'I must have.'

'That means you haven't. Ruth's life is changing. She's having to make decisions. How can she make them if you don't tell her what you feel?'

'She knows.'

'For someone who doesn't believe in clairvoyance you're expecting a lot of mind-reading from Ruth. She's an academic. She needs evidence. Go and tell her that you love her.'

A nurse comes over and tells Cathbad not to overexcite himself. She looks reproachfully at Nelson.

'Just tell my friend,' says Cathbad, lying back on his pillows, 'to shout out what's in his heart.'

'Shout it out,' says the nurse. 'But don't do it here, if you don't mind.'

It seems to Ruth that, all day, she has had one unwelcome visitor after another. First Colin Bland, asking if she's decided about the dean's job. Then Shona in a cloud of perfume and curiosity, followed by various members of her department asking for references because they're applying for other jobs. Finally, David appears with a brochure for Uppsala.

'I'm just going out for some air,' says Ruth. Her head is pounding.

'I'll come with you,' says David.

They walk round the lake. The windsurfers are there again but the air is still and they keep capsizing, with shouts of laughter. Across the water a group of volunteers are hammering in a huge sign above the stage. It reads, 'Save UNNArch'.

'Do you think we will?' asks Ruth. 'Save it, I mean?'

'I doubt it,' says David. 'They'll close us down and this whole university will crumble.'

Ruth looks at the square modern buildings, softened by ivy and by multicoloured posters for concerts and protests. Someone has crowned the statue of Elizabeth Fry with a flower wreath. Ruth thinks of the sukebind in *Cold Comfort Farm*. Over the past few years Ruth has seen many nasty things in many different woodsheds. Perhaps it's time to leave? But, then, one of the windsurfers finally gets her balance and she skims across the water, red sail taut, body braced in an impossible arc. Ruth realises that she loves this place. She doesn't want to go anywhere.

David, who has been looking over towards the stage, says, in a tone of great annoyance, 'What's *he* doing here?'

Ruth looks and sees a familiar dark shape moving across the car park. There's impatience in every line and sinew. Nelson approaches the volunteers. Ruth can't hear what he says but, suddenly, she sees Nelson raise the megaphone to his lips.

'RUTH,' he shouts, his voice echoing around the campus. 'I LOVE YOU. DON'T LEAVE ME.'

'Oh my God,' says Ruth.

'He's trespassing,' says David. 'I'll get the security guards.'

But Ruth is already running away from him. Following the path around the lake. Towards Nelson.

CHAPTER 39

It's August. The marshes are pink with sea lavender and Ruth is packing up to leave the cottage. She's alone, apart from Flint, who is watching her from the top of one of the kitchen cabinets. Kate has gone out with Isla for the day and Ruth is glad she isn't around to see the empty rooms, the rolled-up carpets, the marks on the walls where their pictures used to hang. The sitting room is full of boxes. Most of them seem to say 'Books'. 'Why don't you recycle some of them?' Nelson said yesterday. 'I'd rather recycle you,' said Ruth, only half-joking.

Ruth and Nelson are moving to Old Hunstanton. Ruth thought Nelson was joking when he announced that he'd found a place in Norfolk that he actually liked but, when she saw the square, white house, she had understood. She thought that she, Nelson, Kate and Flint could be happy there. It was nothing like the cottage or the cul-de-sac and that was its saving grace. It was itself, self-sufficient, facing the sea, sheltered by old trees. But the school bus stopped only a few hundred metres away and Ruth could be at the university in thirty minutes. That day, standing in the wind-swept garden, looking out towards the sea and the sand, Ruth had felt a frisson of excitement. Her life was changing and change was good.

But, today, she feels very different. How can she leave her cottage, the home she bought when she was still with Peter? The place where she first brought her kittens, Flint and dear departed Sparky. The threshold she stepped over, holding her new-born baby in her arms, wondering how on earth she was going to manage on her own. Cathbad had been with her that day, she remembers, just as he had been an unconventional but reassuring birthing partner. On Kate's bedroom door, Ruth has recorded her height over the years. The last line shows that she is now almost as tall as her mother. Will future archaeologists puzzle over these marks, wondering if they represent some sort of twenty-first-century religious ritual? The cottage is the only home Kate has ever known, apart from the Cambridge years. How can Ruth tear them both away?

But Kate is keen on the new house. Her bedroom will be bigger and she will be nearer her friends. There will be a spare room for George when he comes to stay. Nelson is talking about getting a kayak.

It turns out that Michelle didn't want to come back to Nelson; she wanted to come back to Norfolk. She missed her house and her friends. She wanted to be nearer her daughters and to take up her old managerial role at the hairdressing salon. So now Michelle and George are back living in the cul-de-sac. Nelson and Michelle are sharing custody of Bruno and his living arrangements are far more complicated than any concerning the children.

UNNArch has been saved. The rally was an unexpected success, partly because both Tony Robinson and Mary Beard turned up, and the board decided that they didn't want the bad publicity of closing such a popular department. Ruth's profile was further raised by giving evidence in the Emily Pickering inquest. No one wants to cross Dr Ruth Galloway, now Dean of Humanities. David Brown was offered the post of head of department but has decided to return to Sweden.

Ruth will miss teaching but she's excited about the possibilities of her new job. She'll be able to travel, write more books, shape policy at UNN. One thing she has learnt, over the last few months, is how much she loves the ramshackle, plate-glass university. She will turn it into a centre of excellence.

Flint meows loudly from on high and Ruth sees Zoe approaching. Her heart sinks. Leaving the cottage means leaving the sister she has only just found. Zoe has been understanding, she has even said that she's glad Ruth and Nelson 'have finally sorted things out'. But Ruth prepares herself for emotional scenes as she opens the back door.

'Is Flint stuck?' says Zoe, looking at the cat wedged between ceiling and cabinet.

'No, he's sulking,' says Ruth. 'But I think he'll like the new place. Nelson says it's probably full of mice. Nobody's lived there for years.'

'Are you all packed then?' says Zoe.

'Pretty much,' says Ruth. 'The moving van comes tomorrow.'

'I wonder when the new people will move in?' says Zoe. 'Have you heard anything?'

'Not yet.'

Ruth is going to rent the cottage unfurnished. It seems less final than selling. Ruth hopes that Zoe will have congenial neighbours.

The sisters move into the sitting room and sit on two of the packing cases.

'I can hardly believe I'm leaving,' says Ruth. 'I've been here twenty-three years.'

'But I'm still here,' says Zoe. 'You can always visit.'

It won't be the same, Ruth wants to say, but isn't that the point of all this? She hadn't wanted her life to stay the same but now she feels as if she's taking a dizzying leap into the unknown. But what is unknown about it really? She and Nelson have known each other for fourteen years, she is moving less than ten miles away, she'll be working at the same university. Only this will be different, she thinks, looking out at the flat landscape, water shimmering through the long grasses, but she will still see the sea, the same sea, from her new windows.

'I'll still be here,' says Zoe again. 'You know, you have a home wherever you have family.'

Ruth thinks of her father in Eltham, her brother in Shooter's Hill, even of Michelle in King's Lynn. It's true, she thinks, it's the people who matter.

'Everything changes,' she says, 'but nothing is destroyed. I read that on an archway once.'

'I know you're feeling all right when you say things I don't understand,' says Zoe.

They sit in companionable silence as the swallows swoop low over the marshes, getting ready to fly south for the winter.

EPILOGUE

17 August 2021

'May your marriage always bring glory to God, joy to one another and blessings to your family for many generations to come. May love and laughter fill your hearts and your home for all of the days of your lives . . .'

As Father Hennessy pronounces these words, a flock of seagulls flies overhead, cawing loudly, and the guests collapse into laughter. Miranda, thoroughly overexcited, throws her flower petals into the air and they are caught by the breeze and whirl, with the gulls, over the sea.

The bride, who is barefoot on the sand, wearing a long white dress, leans forward to kiss her husband as the priest raises his hands in a final blessing. The groom, also in white, but with a purple cloak over his shoulders, gathers his wife into his arms. Ruth blames the sand for the sudden grittiness in her eyes.

'So, she finally did it,' says Nelson. 'Never thought I'd see my best detective marry a mad druid.'

'Well, you were the best man,' says Ruth. 'So you must have had some idea.'

The legal part of Cathbad and Judy's wedding took place that morning at King's Lynn register office, celebrated by a charming registrar called Shirley. Michael was the ring bearer and Maddie and Miranda were bridesmaids, accompanied by Kate and Clough's daughter Amélie. But Father Hennessy, who knows the couple well, agreed to perform a Catholic blessing in the decidedly pre-Christian environment of the Saltmarsh.

'We've already had a pagan hand-fasting ceremony,' Cathbad explained to Ruth. 'We wanted all spiritual bases covered.'

'What did Father Hennessey say?' asked Ruth. She knows that Judy is divorced and so, presumably, any future marriage cannot be sanctioned by the Catholic Church.

Cathbad laughed. He is having experimental oxygen therapy and seems to be back to his old, pre-Covid, self. 'He said, "It's not exactly according to canon law but I'm sure God will have no objections."'

Father Hennessey, Ruth remembers, has always taken a rather relaxed approach to the Church's rules and regulations.

The wedding guests are now walking towards the ceremonial bonfire. Michael, Miranda and Kate run across the beach scattering petals. Thing, who is wearing a bow tie, chases after them, barking joyfully. Judy hitches up her skirt and walks in the shallow water. Cathbad joins her, not seeming to worry about his cloak becoming waterlogged.

Some of the guests follow suit, including Shona and Phil. Seeing Shona in this setting, burnished hair flying around her face, reminds Ruth of the henge dig, twenty-five years ago now, when they first became friends.

'I wish I hadn't worn heels,' says Tanya, who is close behind them. Ruth hopes she didn't hear Nelson call Judy his best detective.

'Take them off then,' says Tanya's wife, Petra, who is in trainers.

'I will,' says Tanya. And she takes Petra's hand as the two of them run towards the sea. They're so fit they overtake most of the other guests. Ruth and Nelson are left walking with Super Jo, who is having no trouble with her vertiginous sandals.

'What a lovely service,' she says. 'Makes me want to tie the knot one day.'

Does Jo have a boyfriend or a girlfriend? Nobody knows. But she seems in a mellow mood.

'I'm glad we're not losing you to Blackpool,' she says to Nelson.

'Are you?' Nelson can't hide his surprise.

'Of course. Who would I spar with if you left?'

'You'd find someone,' says Nelson.

'This is a lovely spot,' says Jo, putting on her designer sunglasses as she scans the beach, white sand and sparkling sea. 'Will you be sorry to leave, Ruth?'

'Well, we won't be far away in Old Hunstanton,' says Ruth. 'And it's much more convenient for Kate and school.'

'You're a real Norfolk person now, Nelson,' says Jo.

'Jesus wept,' says Nelson.

Amber Westbourne has been charged with Emily's murder and a trial date has been set for early 2022. Leo Ballard has been charged with conspiracy to murder, obstructing a police investigation and preventing the lawful burial of a body. His wife is divorcing him and both the Madingley house and the holiday cottage are up for sale. Super Jo might not have to spar with Nelson for long. He's been offered a job heading up a cold-case team in Norfolk. He hopes that, if he does leave the Serious Crimes Unit, Judy will become the new DCI.

A group called the Dancing Druids are playing a strange mix of Celtic rock and heavy metal. Tanya and Petra are dancing. Ruth watches Tony Zhang approach Lucy Downey who laughs but takes his hand and joins the impromptu quadrille. Bradley and Sienna are already there. Maddie is dancing with her boyfriend, Finn, his long black hair flying.

'What a racket,' says Clough, who is elegant in a sand-coloured suit. Amélie is holding his hand. She is wearing a pink fairy dress with wings. Miranda chose the bridesmaids' outfits. Clough's son, Spencer, now six, is running in the waves with the other children.

'Want to paddle, Amélie?' asks Clough's wife Cassandra. Amélie shakes her head but, when Kate comes over, she takes her hand and joins the other children. Cassandra follows, a dryad turned naiad in her long flowery dress.

'She's a little star, your Katie,' says Clough to Ruth.

'Kate,' murmurs Ruth. Some battles are still worth fighting.

But Kate *is* a star, glowing brightly today in her pink dress, a more age-appropriate version of fairy-chic. Isla and Megan are here too, and Ruth loves to see the three of them together, a perfect triangle. A strong shape. A female friendship made to last, like hers with Alison and Fatima.

'Want to dance, Dave?' says Jo. 'I like a good boogie.'

Clough protests but they all know it's in vain. Soon Super Jo and Clough join the figures cavorting in the liminal zone, between land and sea, the thin strand between life and death.

Later, after food and speeches and cake, the fire is burning low. The druid band is still playing and Cathbad and Judy sway together under the moon. Father Hennessy is discussing classical poetry with Shona. Zoe is sharing a bottle of wine with Tanya and Petra. The children, ranging from Amélie to Maddie, are telling stories in an enthralled circle on the beach. The tide is out now, the sea a whispering presence in the darkness. Ruth thinks of all the other times she has heard its voice: gathering samphire with Peter, rescuing Lucy during the storm, celebrating Imbolc with Cathbad, running away from a man with death in his heart, taking long lockdown walks with Kate. She hears Erik too, no longer a malevolent presence, more a comforting echo of her past, 'the landscape itself is important . . . a crossing place over sacred ground.'

She thinks of the church grim and the wheel of fortune.

'Who controls the wheel of fate? One minute we are raised up, the next we are in the depths. The wheel is come full circle, I am here.' This last, Shona informs her, was a quote from *King Lear*, declaimed by the evil Edmund as he dies. But now, these words too seem to have a gentler meaning. 'I am here,' she repeats. Nelson looks quizzically at her but doesn't ask what she means.

Ruth and Nelson sit on a patch of seagrass with a sleepy George beside them. Michelle has joined the party and Ruth can see her talking animatedly to Jo. She'd give a lot to know what they are discussing.

'It's been a grand day,' says Nelson.

'It really has,' says Ruth.

'Fancy doing it one day?' says Nelson. 'The wedding thing?'

'Marriage is an outdated patriarchal concept,' says Ruth.

'Is that a yes then?'

'Maybe,' says Ruth.

ACKNOWLEDGEMENTS

The Last Remains features a variety of real-life places in magical Norfolk. The Exorcist's House in King's Lynn is real, although the Green Child Café is definitely fictional. St Mary's Houghton-on-the-Hill is also real and I'm very grateful to Alan Brinsdon for showing me round and telling me the fascinating history of the church and its restoration. You can visit the Neolithic flint mines at Grime's Graves and they are, in my opinion, one of the archaeological wonders of the world. Huge thanks to Tim Lynch and Maria Nicholson for giving Andy and me a special tour of the mines. We even descended into one of the shafts and saw the stone shaped like a human torso. The actual site is very well curated and the events of this book could never occur in reality. Thanks to Michael Rosen for allowing me to quote from his beautiful poem, 'Charms for Grime's Graves'.

Thanks to Lars Burman and his team for showing me round Uppsala University. It's a really special place and I can see why David loves it so much. Cathbad would adore the rune stones.

Thanks to Jeanne Hanisko who made the winning bid in an auction to be a named character in this book. The character is fictional although she does share some of Jeanne's many interests. All the money raised goes to the charity Young Lives Vs Cancer (previously Clic Sargent). Thanks also to Colin Bland, who won a similar auction to raise money for St Martins, a charity that helps homeless people in Norfolk. Once again, the fictional character does not represent the real Colin, who is the Chair of St Martins.

Thanks as always to my wonderful agent, Rebecca Carter, and all at Janklow and Nesbit. Thanks to the fantastic team at Quercus who have worked on this book and all the others. Special thanks to Joe Christie, Florence Hare, David Murphy, Ellie Nightingale, Ella Patel, Hannah Robinson and Hannah Winter. It's definitely a team effort. Thanks to Liz Hatherell for her matchless copy-editing and to Chris Shamwana for the beautiful cover. Biggest thanks of all to Jane Wood, who has edited all my Elly Griffiths books. I can't thank you enough, Jane, for everything that you've done for me. It's only right that this book ends on our joint birthday.

Thanks, as ever, to Graham Bartlett, for his help on policing questions and Linzi Harvey for her advice on bones, putrefaction and much else. Thanks to Mary Williams – also now a dean – for information on the academic life.

Thanks to all my crime-writing pals for their friendship and support, especially Lesley Thomson, William Shaw and Colin Scott. Thanks also to Lynne Spahl, whose late mother Shirley makes an appearance in the Epilogue.

Finally, thanks to my husband Andrew and, now grown-up,

children Alex and Juliet. This book is for you but so are all the others really. Final word is in memory of our beloved cat, Gus, who died while I was writing *The Last Remains*. I have preserved his last editorial comment, which reads, rather enigmatically,

'loooooooooooooooooooooo'.

EG February 2023

WHO'S WHO
IN THE DR RUTH GALLOWAY MYSTERIES

Dr Ruth Galloway

Profession: forensic archaeologist

Likes: cats, Bruce Springsteen, bones, books

Dislikes: gyms, organised religion, shopping

Ruth Galloway was born in south London. Growing up she had a difficult relationship with her parents, who were Born Again Christians, but excelled at school and went on to study archaeology at University College London. As a postgraduate student at Southampton University, she met Professor Erik Anderssen who became her mentor and friend. In 1997 she participated in Professor Anderssen's dig on the north Norfolk coast which resulted in the excavation of a Bronze Age henge. Ruth subsequently moved to the area to take up a post at the University of North Norfolk. She's now head of the archaeology department. In 2007, she met DCI Harry Nelson and her life got a whole lot more complicated. As well as involving her in several murder cases, Nelson is the father of Ruth's beloved daughter Kate.

Pets: a ginger cat called Flint

Surprising fact about Ruth: she collects pony books and would love to own a horse.

Harry Nelson

Profession: Detective Chief Inspector

Likes: driving cars, solving crimes, his family

Dislikes: Norfolk, the countryside, management speak, retirement

Harry Nelson was born in Blackpool. He came to Norfolk in his thirties to lead the Serious Crimes Unit, bringing with him his wife, Michelle, and their daughters, Laura and Rebecca. Nelson has a loyal team; they have been through a lot together and are a close unit, despite Clough's recent defection. Nelson thinks of himself as an old-fashioned policeman and so often clashes with his boss, Superintendent Jo Archer, who is trying to drag the force into the twenty-first century. Nelson is fiercely protective of his family, which now includes his son George and the daughter he insists on calling Katie. He knows that whatever decision he makes in the future will result in hurting someone he loves.

Pets: a German shepherd dog called Bruno

Surprising fact about Nelson: he's a huge Frank Sinatra fan.

Michelle Nelson

Profession: hairdresser

Likes: her family, exercising, socialising with friends

Dislikes: dowdiness, confrontation, talking about murder

Michelle married Nelson when she was twenty-four and he was twenty-six. She was happy with her life in Blackpool – two children, part-time work, her mother nearby – but encouraged Nelson to move to Norfolk for the sake of promotion. When her daughters were old enough, she took a job managing a hair salon. The last few years have been challenging for Michelle: Nelson's affair with Ruth; her own tragic relationship with Tim Heathfield, a detective on Nelson's team; an unexpected pregnancy in her mid-forties. She loves her son, George, but sometimes feels that her life is travelling very fast in the wrong direction.

Surprising fact about Michelle: she once played hockey for Blackpool Girls.

Michael Malone (aka Cathbad)

Profession: druid, teacher, house-husband

Likes: nature, mythology, walking, following his instincts

Dislikes: rules, injustice, conventions

Cathbad was born in Ireland. He was brought up as a Catholic but now thinks of himself as a druid and shaman. Cathbad came to England to study first chemistry then archaeology. At university he came under the influence of Erik Anderssen, though they found themselves on opposite sides during the henge dig. Cathbad's friendship with Ruth came later and he's a devoted godfather to Kate (whom he calls Hecate). Cathbad has a grown-up daughter, Maddie, from a previous relationship and two children with Judy, his life partner. He's happy looking after the children and teaching meditation classes, but sometimes still hankers after the nomadic life.

Pets: a bull terrier called Thing

Surprising fact about Cathbad: he can play the accordion.

Shona Maclean

Profession: lecturer in English Literature

Likes: books, wine, parties

Dislikes: being ignored

Shona is a lecturer at the University of North Norfolk and one of Ruth's closest friends. They met when they both participated in the henge dig in 1997 and their friendship has survived Shona's marriage to Phil, once Ruth's head of department. Shona and Phil have a son, Louis, who is the apple of their eye and one of Kate's least-favourite people.

Pets: none

Surprising fact about Shona: as a child she won several Irish dancing competitions.

David Clough

Profession: Detective Inspector

Likes: food, football, his family, his job

Dislikes: political correctness, graduate police officers

David Clough ('Cloughie' to Nelson) was born in Norfolk and joined the force at eighteen. He was a loyal member of Nelson's team until he was promoted to detective inspector and moved to Cambridge. Clough's star seems to be in the ascendent: he has a new job, a beautiful wife, Cassandra, and two adored children. He has also, in Nelson's opinion, started dressing like a teenager. Clough still misses Nelson, though.

Pets: a bulldog called Dexter

Surprising fact about Clough: he can quote the 'you come to me on my daughter's wedding day' scene from *The Godfather* off by heart.

Judy Johnson

Profession: Detective Sergeant

Likes: horses, driving, her job

Dislikes: girls' nights out, sexism, being patronised

Judy Johnson was born in Norfolk to Irish Catholic parents. For a while, Judy's life proceeded along cautious, conventional lines: she joined the police at eighteen and married her childhood boyfriend. But then she met Cathbad and discovered an unexpectedly wild and passionate side to her nature. Judy now lives with Cathbad and their two children. Judy is an excellent police officer and has passed her inspector's exam but she knows that, if she wants to progress in her career, she will have to leave Norfolk.

Pets: half-share in Thing. Judy also once inherited two hamsters called Sonny and Fredo.

Surprising fact about Judy: she's a keen card player and once won an inter-force poker competition.

Tanya Fuller

Profession: Detective Sergeant

Likes: sport, succeeding, being called 'ma'am'

Dislikes: history, being overlooked

Tanya studied Sports Science at Loughborough University. She joined the police as a graduate trainee and moved to Norfolk shortly afterwards. Tanya is fiercely ambitious and often clashes with Judy, although a grudging respect exists between them. Tanya recently married her girlfriend Petra, a secondary-school teacher.

Pets: none

Surprising fact about Tanya: she enjoys knitting and once made Petra an Inca-inspired alpaca cardigan.

Tony Zhang

Profession: Detective Constable

Likes: chatting, socialising, art

Dislikes: family expectations, silence

Tony Zhang was born in London to first-generation Chinese immigrants. As a child, Tony lived through tragedy when his sister, Lily, died of meningitis. Tony studied economics at the University of East Anglia and joined the police force as a graduate trainee. He's a good officer, keen, hard-working and sensitive. He has to learn to stop whistling, though.

Pets: none

Surprising fact about Tony: he has a Blue Peter badge.